Elizabeth Harris was born in Cambridge and brought up in west Kent, where she now lives. After reading English and Psychology at Keele University, she worked briefly in the Civil Service before setting out to fulfil an early ambition, to go round the world. She spent three years in Hong Kong before completing the journey, returning to England via America. She has also travelled widely throughout Europe, often in the pursuit of research.

She is a past chairman of her local writers' circle, and has lectured at the Arvon Foundation and Southampton University Writers' Weekends.

Elizabeth has two teenage sons, whom she supports vigorously from the rugby touch-line. Her interests range from meditation and aromatherapy to cycling and distance walking, the latter designed to remove the kinks in her back put in by too many hours at the word processor.

A GOOD MAN'S LOVE

Hal Dillon and Ben MacAllister had been deeply affected by the appalling death of their university friend Laurie. Hal journeyed to Mexico to continue his anthropological studies, and there found distraction in his passionate affair with Magdalena. But was he inviting even more heartache? Ben became a wanderer. While working in Cyprus he had met English girl Jo Daniel, and, after a nomadic summer together, they travelled to England to embark on what promised to be a lifetime of marital bliss. But Jo discovers that promises don't always come true.

Books by Elizabeth Harris
Published by The House of Ulverscroft:

THE EGYPTIAN YEARS

ELIZABETH HARRIS

A GOOD MAN'S LOVE

Complete and Unabridged

ULVERSCROFT
Leicester

First published in Great Britain in 1996 by
Severn House Publishers Limited
Surrey

First Large Print Edition
published 1999
by arrangement with
Severn House Publishers Limited
Surrey

British Library CIP Data

Harris, Elizabeth
    A good man's love.—Large print ed.—
Ulverscroft large print series: romance
1. Large type books
I. Title
823.9′14 [F]

ISBN 0–7089–4072–2

Published by
F. A. Thorpe (Publishing) Ltd.
Anstey, Leicestershire
Set by Words & Graphics Ltd.
Anstey, Leicestershire
Printed and bound in Great Britain by
T. J. International Ltd., Padstow, Cornwall

This book is printed on acid-free paper

For Joan and Geoffrey Harris,
who were there at the beginning,
with much love

PART ONE

Hal

Spring 1968 – Summer 1971

1

Mexico City, Spring 1968

Hal Dillon drained the last inch of beer in his glass. In the two hours he'd been sitting at the café table, the morning sun had moved round so that it now shone full on him. He'd managed to add three pages to the letter to Ben that he'd begun last night, and had come to the end of what he intended to say. Not all that he wanted to say. How could that be, when Magdalena filled his thoughts and he longed to pour out the tale of loving her to Ben's sympathetic ear? But Magdalena wasn't for sharing, even with Ben. Hal had got used to the habit of secrecy where she was concerned.

He put on his glasses and read through the letter. He wouldn't have considered his life sufficiently interesting to have filled five pages without mentioning Magdalena; in the few months since he'd met her, she'd become everything. And there would have been no point in telling Ben MacAllister about his work; students together, they'd been different sides of the arts/science divide. No way would Ben have bothered with page after page on Hal's studies of the ancient peoples of Mexico.

He put the letter in the airmail envelope, thinking of Ben receiving it. It would be cool in San Francisco now, a lot cooler than this dusty pavement at the corner of a square where the traffic screeched and revved impatiently, and the fumes from overworked engines lay on the air like heavy exhausted sighs.

He wrote Ben's name and address in his quick handwriting, then stood up. Throwing some money on to the saucer holding the pencil-scrawled bill, he pushed his way between tables and walked briskly away. The waiter glanced up as he passed.

'Crazy, that one,' he remarked to the customers in general. He watched Hal's tall departing figure. Yes, crazy, sitting in the sun so long and staring at nothing. Why wasn't he like all the other Americans, rushing here and there, seeing everything, stopping only long enough to order a drink and finishing it even before the frosting on the glass turned to water?

'Crazy,' he repeated. Then turned back to wiping his tables.

* * *

Hal was different; he would have agreed with the waiter about that. He was different even from the man he'd been when he arrived in Mexico City the previous autumn. He had quit San Francisco still the detached cynic he had always been, despite three years among the Flower People. Despite the friendship with Ben, which had intensified into something deeper because of the horrific death they'd been involved in.

It was Mexico that had changed him.

He moved impatiently through the lunchtime

4

crowds, head and shoulders above the thronging Mexican humanity. Savoury smells snaked invitingly from innumerable bars and restaurants. A Saturday mood was in the air; people were talking, laughing, eating together in cheerful groups that grew merrier as the drink went down.

It seemed to Hal that he was the only person on his own. He knew he should eat, but he could summon no enthusiasm. He posted Ben's letter then, for the sake of something to do, bought a days-old copy of the *New York Times* and found a bench in the shade where he sat and read it.

He was putting off returning to his apartment. It would be hot, for one thing; the midday heat could be stifling in those two cheaply-furnished little rooms. But — a more powerful deterrent — long afternoons of lying on his bed trying to read were irrevocably associated with waiting for Magdalena, and with what always happened when — if — she came.

She was coming later this afternoon. But she wouldn't be coming any more.

He swore under his breath. The *New York Times's* reporting of events that had happened nearly a week ago wasn't sufficiently distracting, and he reached in his pocket and took out the letter from Ben. He realized, with an uncomfortable sense of guilt, that he hadn't dealt with it in the depth he knew Ben wanted.

With a sigh, he turned to the relevant page, knowing as he began to reread Ben's generous writing that this would be almost as painful as thinking about Magdalena. But at least these events were in the past, and had happened thousands of miles away. Nothing Hal or any of them thought or did could alter anything.

'I saw Laurie's sister last week,' Ben had said. 'I asked her how were her folks, and she said they were on vacation. She looked sad, like she didn't sleep well. I still dream about it. Do you, or does being away alter things? Maybe I'll go away too.'

Hal thought of his scant reply to that appeal. 'Sure I dream of Laurie,' he'd said dismissively, 'once in a while. Something like that ain't going to leave us in a hurry.' Then he'd gone on to talk about something else.

But what could I have said? he thought, frowning. Isn't it better for Ben — for all of us who knew Laurie — to put it behind us? Get on with our own lives?

Hal had made the discovery at a relatively young age that life was a tough business, that the only way to stop the knocks from flooring you was to build up a carapace strong enough to prevent the aftershocks getting too close to your heart. Yes, Laurie's death had been frightful, the most gruesome thing Hal ever wanted to see. And yes, he'd probably walked around for a while looking as sick and ashen as Ben. But he'd recovered, pulled himself together and gotten out. Only now, sensing the emotion behind Ben's words, did he begin to feel that maybe Ben's reaction was the more noble.

It was no use. The stout door in his mind which he'd slammed shut on Laurie's death stood wide open. In that alien place, his mind muzzy with too much beer and too little food, every sense was assaulted with memory. The sharp-sweet, herby smell of cannabis seemed to float in the heat, and he could hear the whining nasal voices singing 'Hey Mr Tambourine Man'. Goddam it, he thought, I never even *liked* that music. He shut his eyes and instantly he could see Laurie's face, thin and perpetually pale, dark-brown eyes intense behind round Grandpappy spectacles, long dark hair bound with a plaited leather thong around the forehead.

Laurie. Hal smiled bitterly. If you'd scoured the West Coast in 1967 for the archetypal student, the hippie who out-hipped the rest, you'd have picked Laurie. And he was such a nice kid. To Hal, who'd come from the East, older, more world-wise, they'd all been kids. Laurie was gentle, and the light of conviction had shone bright in his eyes when he'd gone on about the Peace Movement, telling them where the next demos were to be, convinced they all felt as fervently as he did.

But they didn't. Some of them might have done, but Hal could recall all too clearly the exact words he'd used to express his opinion of the things Laurie held so sacred.

'There's going to be a blood-doning session on campus!' Laurie had cried as he burst into Hal's room, his thin face luminous with joy.

'Great,' Hal replied.

Laurie came closer, frowning in concern. 'You don't understand! It's a bleed-in, it's for the North Vietmanese!'

Maybe I was sick of it all, Hal thought, he

7

caught me on a bad day. He remembered what he'd replied.

Laurie, who didn't swear much and who got upset by blasphemy and gross obscenities, looked at him for a long moment, eyes like a child's whose mother has just bitten him. Then he walked out, quietly closing the door behind him.

It was all so intense, Hal thought, that was what bugged me. Being out of step with the majority didn't bother him; other people's opinions were their own business. But the clinging tentacles of the Peace and Love kids had a way of pervading everything. In his last few months at college, he'd turned his back with relief on most of what went on around him and concentrated on his studies. Outside work, there were only two people to whom he spoke more than a handful of words in the spring and early summer of his graduation year: Laurie, and Ben.

Ben was the antithesis to Hal in almost every way. On the rare occasions he questioned his closeness to Ben, he concluded it must have come about because Ben was a sort of light relief. The six years' difference in their ages was irrelevant; although younger, Ben was as set in the mould of his character as Hal was in his. Nothing that happened ever eroded Ben's basic philosophy that life was for enjoying, that most people were pretty much okay and, if one or two weren't, they could be abandoned in favour of the vast majority who were. Hal watched with amusement Ben's charmed progress through his college days, forever almost coming unstuck, always being saved at the last moment by some unexpected stroke of luck.

Hal himself had been the saviour, the first time they'd met. He'd given Ben a lift to a football game Ben had forgotten about.

'Cutting it fine, aren't you?' Hal said, finding himself trying to speed through thick traffic so that Ben didn't miss the kick-off.

Ben shrugged. 'Maybe.' Then he smiled. 'I guess they won't start without me.'

To Hal, who had stayed to watch the game, the irritating thing was that they hadn't.

He and Ben had recognized early on the strength of each other's personality. They disagreed over many things, but both saw the futility of trying to win the other over. It was impossible to row with Ben; he was far too easy-going and, if Hal became over-forceful on some point, would remark amicably that it wasn't worth arguing over. Hal would suppress his irritation at Ben's supremacy in the art of fence-sitting; Ben's generosity and warmth were too valuable to risk losing them by giving in to a momentary anger.

So the friendship continued and deepened. Neither of them minded when Laurie, attracted perhaps by their stability, took to hanging around with them; Hal was too indifferent, and Ben too kind-hearted, to get rid of him. And anyway, Laurie was a nice kid. When he could be distracted from his holy crusade to bring about single-handedly American withdrawal from Vietnam, an intelligent, humorous boy emerged from behind the dirty-footed protester.

Hal and Ben were witnesses to Laurie's progressive disintegration. With increasing frequency, they had to get him home when he was drunk out of his skull. Sit with him while he raved and sobbed on the steep descent of LSD; it was indicative of his state of mind that now he only had bad trips. Persuade him against losing yet another weekend to a two-day high on pot. Weeks had passed since he'd made any sustained effort to work; he was heading for trouble on that score, too.

Hal was for the direct remedy. 'Get him to a doctor,' he snapped when Ben anxiously asked what they ought to do. 'Get him to his head of faculty, home to his family even.'

But Ben disagreed. 'No,' he said. Then, as if Hal's suggestion breached student solidarity in the face of authority, 'It's down to us. We'll look after him.'

Hal shrugged. 'Okay,' he said. 'Then in your own immortal words, admittedly in a different context, let him be.'

Towards the end Laurie seemed to be improving. Although he still got drunk, he gave up drugs. With hindsight, Hal thought it was probably because he was running out of money. He talked less about the things that troubled him so deeply and, as the last traces of drugs left his system, no longer saw the visions of destruction and carnage that tormented him.

★ ★ ★

On the last evening of Laurie's life he called on Ben, and the two of them went to drag Hal out for some beers. Hal, deep in his work, told them to go away, but when he finished his sentence and looked up, he saw with annoyance that they were still there.

'Go away!' he said again.

Ben grinned winningly. 'There's going to be a beautiful sunset,' he pointed out.

'Wouldn't it be great, man, sitting by the ocean and watching it?' Laurie added.

Hal sighed. Then he closed up his books with a bang.

'You guys are only asking me because I'm the one with the car,' he grumbled, putting on his shoes.

Ben and Laurie looked at each other. Then they said simultaneously, 'Why else?'

They stopped at a drugstore to buy beers, then Hal drove south along the coast highway for some miles, stopping on a deserted piece of shore.

The evening started happily, and the mood deepened as the hours went by. Ben built a fire of driftwood, and the three of them lay around it working their way through the beers, getting gently drunk. Hal thought hazily, this is the first time in ages I've heard Laurie laughing.

It was after midnight when they roused themselves to go home. Laurie, gazing into the embers of the fire, had a faraway look. 'I wish I could stay,' he said quietly.

Hal watched him. He seemed strange, somehow, but Hal had had too many beers to puzzle it out.

'Don't we all?' Ben said. Then he added prosaically, 'But you can't, you have a tutorial in the morning.'

★ ★ ★

Hal dropped them off, then went back to his room. He had intended to go to bed, but the books still laid out on his desk called to him. With a mind full of sea air and starlight, he got down to an exhilarating spell of work.

He heard running footsteps in the corridor outside. The door burst open and Ben stood there wearing nothing but his jeans, his feet bare and a toe running with new red blood.

'Jesus, Hal,' he gasped, 'it's Laurie. *Come on!*'

He turned and pounded back the way he had come.

His extreme panic got to Hal like a shot in the arm. Overturning his chair, he leapt after him, catching up with him on the gravelled path outside; the sharpness of the stones under Ben's bare feet had slowed him down. They ran on together, speeding up as they got onto grass.

They didn't have to run far. 'I know where he's headed,' Ben panted; as he led the way, soon Hal knew too.

There was a stone war memorial on campus, a small monolith that stood in a quiet marble square surrounded by cypress trees. Recently, it had become the focus for peaceful demonstrations.

Now Laurie was there.

A reek of petrol filled the air. As Hal and Ben

raced up, Laurie was emptying the last of a jerrycan over himself. A big pile of petrol-soaked wood was arranged neatly at the foot of the memorial's plinth. He stepped onto the pile, a box of matches in his hand.

Hal roared, '*No!*'

Ben threw himself forwards, but with incredible speed Laurie swooped down, picked up a batten of wood and swung it at Ben's head.

'Ben, I'm sorry, I'm sorry!' he wailed, tears rolling down his cheeks, as Ben sank to the ground.

'Put the matches down, Laurie,' Hal panted, trying to control his breathing, trying to make his voice sound reasonable and calm in the midst of nightmare.

'No.' Laurie's voice had all the calmness Hal could have wished for. 'No, Hal. I can't live with it any more.'

Hal thought, I've got seconds, at most.

'I know, Laurie,' he said gently. 'But it won't last for ever.'

Laurie looked at him, his eyes deep wells of all the misery in the world.

'Babies, Hal, burning babies,' he said. 'No food, because the land's dead and poisoned. People in despair.'

Then abruptly the words stopped and became a scream. In a great whoosh of flame that leapt as high as the stone monolith, Laurie set light to himself.

The ignition of the petrol-soaked wood threw out a blast that knocked Hal backwards. The sound of

Laurie's agony filled his head, and he covered his eyes and ears from the joint assault of the intense heat and the sound of Laurie dying.

It was all so quick. In a few seconds, Laurie had collapsed into the depths of his pyre. Hal's hands blistered as he made two approaches, but self-preservation stopped him from the futility of any more.

Suddenly he remembered Ben. He ran round to the left of the fire to where Ben had fallen.

Sparks and cinders were dropping out of the sky all over Ben's still body. Stooping low, Hal got his shoulder into Ben's stomach and hoisted him up into a fireman's lift. Then he stumbled with him away from the hellish sight in front of the plinth and out through the circling cypress trees, to fall onto the cool dewy grass beyond.

Physically, Ben and Hal recovered quickly. The deep cut in Ben's head required fifteen stitches, and he was confined to bed with concussion. The burns on Hal's hands and arms weren't too severe. He had already completed most of his final exams, and the college offered to waive the remainder, under the circumstances; his professor already had a pretty accurate assessment of Hal's intellectual capability.

But Hal said, 'No. I'll do it.'

Sitting in the vast examination hall, writing slowly and painfully, he made his mind detach from Laurie and concentrate on the Mediterranean of the fifteenth century. If I can do this, he reasoned, then it's going to be okay.

The last paper was the best that he did.

Ben's dreams began on the first night he tried going to bed without the sedation the doctor had prescribed. They were to continue on and off for the rest of his life. It seemed, though, that this was to be his mind's outlet for the horror of it all; nightmares apart, Ben soon returned to what, for want of any other description, had to be called an ordinary life.

A lot of people were affected by Laurie's death. But, other than the grieving, bemused parents, it cut into Hal and Ben most deeply. They had been there, they had felt the despair as Laurie prepared to kill himself. And Hal had witnessed his death. In the round of ritual and inquiry that followed, Hal and Ben would often catch one another's eye and move wordlessly to stand side by side, in an unspoken desire to be united against the rest.

Guilt attacked them, although nobody held them to blame; when they appeared still lurid with wounds at the inquiry, they were commended for their heroic efforts in trying to save Laurie. Too damned late, Hal thought bitterly. And Ben hung his head and walked away.

★ ★ ★

They spent a long night talking it out. When Ben said for the tenth time that they should have seen it coming, that he especially, who'd born the brunt of Laurie's dependence while Hal was doing his finals, should have watched more closely, Hal suddenly found he'd had enough.

'Ben, we were his buddies,' he said. 'But that's

15

the bottom line. We weren't responsible for him, and if he couldn't handle life then choosing death was his option.'

'We could have stopped it!' Ben shouted.

'How?'

'By listening to him, helping him . . . ' Ben's voice trailed off.

'No we couldn't. Goddam it, I put up with his Peace shit till I was sick of it. But you couldn't turn the guy off the path he'd chosen.'

'So you reckon if someone has decided to kill himself, then you just let them go ahead?'

Hal was silent for some moments. Then he looked up, straight into Ben's eyes.

'Yeah. That's what I reckon.'

'Then why did you try to save him?'

'Pure instinct. Maybe I'm a nice guy, underneath.'

Time helped. The two of them spent a lazy vacation, and it seemed to Hal that Ben returned to college in the fall with a lighter heart. Observing him as the long days of summer came to an end, Hal thought that his naturally optimistic outlook was reasserting itself. He decided Ben'd make out okay back at college.

Hal wasn't staying around; he was off down to Mexico to do a postgraduate year studying the Mayan civilization. He was eager to go, not only to put the events of the recent past behind him but also to take up the challenge of what he was going to do next.

But Mexico had brought him more than he had planned. Going to Mexico ushered Magdalena into his life.

16

2

Hal looked at his watch. Two-thirty. He got to his feet, stretching. I'll work, he thought. I'll shut everything else out of my mind, and I'll finish my article. He threw the *New York Times* into a trash can and set off.

His time in Mexico was coming to an end. The academic year was almost over, but he knew he wouldn't be able to stay after Magdalena was gone. The people, the habits, the very streets and buildings of her city spoke to him of her, and female voices overhead would stab at him with familiarity, speaking with her accent and using her phrases.

Not that Magdalena was the sort of girl to stand gossiping in the street. She belonged to one of the old families, to a wealthy dynasty with centuries of tradition and links with Spanish nobility. It was an odd quirk of fate that led her to fall in love with an American postgraduate making out on a small income in crummy rooms on the other side of town.

He had succeeded in getting an article published in an American review, and he was eventually commissioned to write a regular monthly column. The articles were of local interest, they were circulated to the very faculty where he was studying, and one had caught the eye of a learned doctor who showed it to a friend. So it was that the foreigner, the outsider Hal Dillon, was invited to dinner by

Juan Alfonso Alvarez, one of the wealthiest men in the city; he turned up one winter night at the gracious Alvarez mansion, in a worn suit that he had spent the afternoon getting pressed.

Alvarez greeted him. 'Come in, Señor Dillon, come and talk!' He crossed the echoing hall, arms open in welcome.

He showed Hal into a high-ceilinged room lined with bookshelves and smelling of leather. Over several drinks they discussed Hal's article and what he was doing in Mexico. They talked for a good two hours and, once he was over his awe at the surroundings and the celebrity of his host, Hal relaxed and began to enjoy himself.

Suddenly Alvarez shot up out of his chair. He looked at Hal from deep-set dark eyes, comically remorseful.

'Dinner!' he exclaimed. 'My family will be weak with hunger.'

The family were waiting patiently. Alvarez presented Hal to his wife, then introduced his four young sons. The Señora had a pleasant smile, but apparently spoke no English; Hal tried a couple of polite remarks, to which she responded graciously. The sons all looked alike, four olive-skinned boys in their teens.

'And this,' Alvarez said, 'is my daughter. Magdalena, this is Señor Hal Dillon.'

She was slight, and not very tall. She had long black hair, which was held off her heart-shaped face by a velvet ribbon. She had the biggest brown eyes Hal had ever seen.

She said, in a quiet voice with a trace of

18

huskiness, '*Buenos tardes*, Señor Dillon. Welcome to our home.'

Then she smiled at him.

The Señora said something in Spanish which sounded gently reproving. Hal started guiltily.

'Yes!' Alvarez said. 'Let us eat — as my wife says, you must be wondering whether indeed there *is* any dinner!'

They all went through into the dining-room. Alvarez and his wife sat at each end of the long table, and Hal was invited to sit on Alvarez's right hand.

'And Magdalena shall sit opposite you,' Alvarez said, 'since out of all my children,' and he paused to glare at the sons, 'she is the only one whose English is intelligible.'

Piece of luck, Hal thought. He raised his eyes and found that Magdalena was watching him. There was another hint of her dazzling smile, then she bent her head as her father prepared to say grace.

Conversation over the five-course dinner was carried out largely in Spanish. It was reasonably comprehensible to Hal, and as the excellent wines helped him relax, he joined in. The family encouraged him kindly, and they didn't laugh too much when he made mistakes. Once or twice Magdalena perceived what he was trying to say, and provided him with the words. He found it slightly uncanny that she should know with such accuracy what was in his mind.

In a gap in the conversation, Alvarez said, 'Soon there will be another member of the family.

19

Magdalena has become engaged to be married in the spring.'

Hal wondered why he should suddenly feel leaden. He cast around for a suitable response.

'He's a very lucky man,' he said quietly, staring straight into Magdalena's eyes.

She didn't answer.

'Indeed,' Alvarez said. 'He is the son of my oldest friend. Our families are related by marriage many times over. There is a stability in such arrangements, is there not?'

'Right.' Hal wondered if Alvarez had noticed the exchange of glances between himself and Magdalena, if he was saying subtly, my daughter is promised to a man who is worthy of her, and of her family. 'I wish you both every happiness.'

To his relief they had reached the end of a course, and maids were coming in to clear the dishes. When the conversation was resumed, Alvarez began to talk about Mexican art treasures.

Hal thought afterwards that he should have seen it coming. He mentioned the riches he'd seen in the churches, and the Señora made some remark about how wonderful it was to see those beautiful, valuable things, residing in God's House to the greater glory of Our Lord and Our Lady.

Hal said, 'Maybe. But I reckon God might be a deal more pleased if some of that wealth went to feed the poor. A few minutes' walk from any church, and there they are, starving, begging, filthy dirty and breeding like flies.'

He heard the echo of his words die away in the

total silence that followed. He thought of the great house in which he was a guest, of the enormous wealth this family possessed, evident in every item on the table, every stick of furniture, every painting on the walls.

The air hummed with disapproval. Then Alvarez said, 'That is politics. Our Lord cannot be referred to in political terms.'

Hal was about to make a quiet apology. He'd earned that reproof; whatever his own views, this wasn't the time or the place for such a comment.

But before he could speak, Magdalena quoted softly, ' 'Give to the poor, and thou shalt have treasure in heaven. Take up the cross and follow me.' '

Her father gave her a look of icy reproach. But she held her head high. 'I think Hal is quite right. I — '

'Enough.' The one word, in a quiet tone of absolute command, was sufficient. Magdalena's head dropped.

Hal watched her, feeling enormous gratitude. She looked up briefly, her eyes catching his.

'The women and children will leave us.' Alvarez's voice cut across his thoughts. 'We shall drink a liqueur, and then join them for coffee.'

★ ★ ★

Hal and Alvarez sat with balloons of brandy, and Alvarez smoked a large cigar. He was talking about New York City, which he had visited several times, but Hal, suffering from the joint blows of his

21

discomfiture and the explosion that Magdalena had set off inside his head, could only respond with trivia.

She stood up for me, he thought. She took my side against her father. She's incredible. And she's so goddam beautiful. He pictured her smile. He felt as if he were in a dream.

Eventually they followed the family through to the drawing-room. The Señora sat behind a large silver coffee pot, pouring cups for her husband and for Hal. Magdalena came to sit beside him. She glanced across at her parents, who were deep in discussion with one of the sons.

'Do you like Mexico? Apart from the churches?' she asked him.

He saw that she was smiling. 'I can handle the churches,' he said. 'I love Mexico.'

She bowed her head in acknowledgement. 'I am glad.'

She asked him which places he'd seen, which he liked especially. Even if her words had been audible to her mother or father, they would have appeared quite innocent.

Then she said, 'There is a little park that I like very much.' She described where it was. 'Sometimes I go there in the afternoon. It is pleasant to sit in the shade.'

He stared at her, meeting her huge eyes questioningly then looking hurriedly away. Was that intentional? he wondered, following Magdalena with his eyes as she took his cup back to her mother for a refill. Or was she just making conversation? Hell, there are a million things she could have said apart from hinting where she goes on weekday afternoons.

There wasn't a chance to find out. Magdalena was waylaid by her mother to do some errand, and by the time she returned, Alvarez had come to sit beside him.

But, in his heart, he knew.

★ ★ ★

He spent three afternoons sitting in Magdalena's little park. On the fourth day, she came.

She looked extremely nervous. She didn't stop to sit down, hardly glanced his way. She quickly circled the park, then turned to go.

He leapt to his feet and ran after her.

'May I carry your parcels?' he said.

She spun round. She went white, and then blushed a delicate pink.

'How nice to see you,' she said politely. Then the careful surprise was elbowed off her face by a radiantly happy smile.

He couldn't think what to say. But she's engaged, she's going to marry someone else. I can't make any moves, I don't know what she wants.

Magdalena said, 'It is a long walk.'

'D'you want to take a cab?'

'No!' The reply shot out of her. 'No,' she said more quietly, 'I was thinking of you, carrying my parcels.'

'They're not heavy.' He'd have carried ten times as much. 'What's in them? Something nice?'

A smile dimpled her cheek. 'Nice, no. An old

23

pair of shoes and four bags of flour.'

He opened his mouth to ask her why she was carting bags of flour around the city when she laughed, and he realized she was teasing him.

After that it was easy.

★ ★ ★

'I'll leave you here,' he said as they came to the alley that led to her garden gate. 'If anyone saw us, you can tell them I was helping you home with your shopping.'

She raised her eyes to look solemnly at him. 'That is what you did do.'

He paused. Then he said, 'Would you like me to have done more?'

Slowly she nodded.

His mouth felt dry. 'Tomorrow?'

'Not tomorrow. But the next day, yes.'

'Same place?'

'Yes.'

Then she hurried off up the alley.

★ ★ ★

Two days later, at precisely the time she'd arrived before, she walked in through the park gates.

They sat on a seat concealed by thick foliage. He took her hand, and it was cold and sweaty with nervousness. She talked about where she had been and what she had been doing, gabbling quickly in inaccurate English.

Suddenly she stopped. Unexpectedly, she began

to tell him about her fiancé, what he did, what he looked like, when they were to be married, where they were going to live. He waited till she paused for breath. Knowing exactly why she was loading him with all this information he didn't want, he said simply, 'It's okay. I understand.'

Then he leaned forward and kissed her.

They went back to his room, and he made love to her. She was trembling, but so eager and responsive that he couldn't stop himself. He knew he must be hurting her, but she made no protest, just clung to him, her mouth against his flesh to stifle the sounds he could feel trying to burst out of her. When it was over she went on clinging, whispering over and over that she loved him.

He couldn't believe it. He had thought of her as being way out of his league, a beautiful, thoroughbred, high-born woman who belonged to a proud society whose women conformed to a rigid pattern of behaviour.

No way was what she'd just done with him included in the rules.

★ ★ ★

They saw each other whenever she could get away. He knew how the lying and the deceit hurt her. She was a devout Catholic, and making love with him was a mortal sin. All the time they were lovers, she couldn't receive Holy Communion; he felt the edges of her deep-rooted terror at what that meant to her. And he hadn't the power in him to make the strong decision and tell her to go away. It would have been like cutting out a piece of himself.

He loved her more than he'd thought he could love anyone. It was crazy, when she was going to marry somebody else. She was beautiful, elegant, fine-boned. She made him laugh, and her mind was lively and quick, and she was a deep thinker. Often she'd anticipate what he was going to say, almost before he'd thought it. And making love to her was like . . . He didn't have the words. It wasn't like anything he'd ever known before, but maybe that was because he'd never loved anyone like he loved Magdalena.

Irrational it might be — it was — but he couldn't keep away.

★ ★ ★

A few weeks ago a dam had broken in her; flood-tide of emotion poured from her that she couldn't stop. Amongst the tangle of hopes, fears, dreams and torn loyalties emerged two irreconcilable facts: she loved Hal, but she was going to marry the man her family had chosen.

He asked her to marry him instead. She broke into sobs, her head on his chest and her soft black hair covering him like a blanket.

'That is what I want, with all my heart.' He felt her tears on his bare flesh. 'But I must marry my fiancé.' It was only afterwards that Hal realized he had never known the other man's name. 'My family, his family, suffer great shame if I do not,' she went on. 'If I go away with you, what will they do?' What indeed, Hal wondered cynically.

Elopement with an American wouldn't be Alvarez's idea of happily ever after for his daughter. And what an American, not even a Catholic, not even rich, but an impoverished rag-bag agnostic with a good bit of Jew in him.

'They have done me no harm,' Magdalena said touchingly, 'they love me, they think they do the best for me. I cannot hurt them all so badly. It is honour.'

Honour, Hal thought bitterly. What can stand up against honour?

★ ★ ★

The closest she came to giving in to him was when she told him about the babies. Tears had become synonymous with her being with him, but now she was deeply disturbed. Eventually she said hysterically she was no good for him, no good for anyone, shouldn't be marrying at all.

'Why ever not?' He was mystified.

'Because of babies. I am so scared, so frightened!'

He held her tightly, not sure how to respond. 'Sure you are,' he said eventually. 'Most girls are, probably. But they all seem to manage okay.' He turned her face so he could look at her, trying to raise a smile.

But she was beyond smiling. 'No!' she cried. 'No, you do not understand! My mother, she has four more babies after me, and I see, I hear . . . ' Her face twisted with distress. 'Hal, I could not live through it, I know I could not!'

He stroked her hair, soothing her, and gradually

the storm subsided. God, she's so young, he thought. She's just twenty. Sometimes I feel old enough to be her grandfather.

And she was so sheltered. It was not necessary for good Catholic girls to know about contraception, and when he had taken care of it that first time, as every other time, he guessed she'd thought that was what always happened. So he explained the ways two people could avoid having any babies, and he told her about the operation a man could have that would ensure his wife never got pregnant by him.

'Now will you marry me?' he begged. 'I'll do that. You'll never have to have babies. If you want kids, we'll adopt them.'

He told himself he could feel her wavering. The combination of Hal plus no babies, guaranteed, was tempting.

She detached herself from his arms and stood up, crossing to the basin to wash her face. He watched her in the mirror. Her eyes looked mournfully out at him.

She said quietly, 'I cannot.'

★ ★ ★

Now it was under a week till Magdalena's wedding day. He knew she was desperately unhappy, and had suggested they shouldn't go on meeting. But she said she must see him, just once more.

He'd managed to finish his article. He'd taken a shower, and now lay on his bed in jeans and a shirt, hands linked behind his head, gazing out of the window.

28

Magdalena came in, locking the door behind her. Even now, amid such unhappiness, the sight of her made him smile.

'Hi,' he said, opening his arms to her.

The late sun slanted across the room, and in the streets outside there was activity and laughter as the city shook itself out of the torpor of the long afternoon. And here we lie, he thought, nothing left to say, knowing that from here on in we have to begin life without each other.

'Hal?'

'Yeah?'

She began to cry. 'I'm so sorry, Hal.'

He shut his eyes tight against the pain. After a moment he said, 'Don't give it a thought, sweetheart. I wouldn't have missed you, not for the world.'

'I don't want . . . You know that I love you, that . . . ' Her words trailed off.

'It's okay, Magdalena.' He held her tightly. 'Don't say any more.'

★ ★ ★

Eventually Hal sat up. 'Come on,' he said, 'it's getting late.'

She sat up too, swinging her feet onto the floor and reaching up to tidy her hair.

'I shall wear it like this, now,' she said, twisting it up on top of her head and turning to show him. 'Do you like it?'

He found it hard to speak. 'Sure I like it.' He forced a smile. 'Makes you look like your mother.'

29

Then she was in his arms, both of them clinging so tightly that no force from outside could have broken them apart. When at last he pushed her gently away it felt like the action of someone else.

'Do you want me to come down with you?'

She straightened her back and held her head high. 'No.' She didn't sound like Magdalena. 'Goodbye, Hal.'

'Goodbye, sweetheart.'

He listened to her light steps going down the stairs. He stood for a long time, his mind in neutral. There was no more to think; everything had come to an end.

★ ★ ★

He saw her once more. Some small part of him went on believing that still she might change her mind. To end the uncertainty, he went and stood outside the large church where the marriage was being solemnized.

The ceremony went on for hours. At last the tall doors opened, and figures began to emerge from the church. Men with cameras. Boys, running up and down the steps, hectic with long-pent up energy. Then Magdalena and her husband. The distance was too great for Hal to focus on her face, but every feature was etched so deep in his mind that his memory filled in what his eyes couldn't see.

White, so much white. A fierce stab of loss seared through him as he thought, only she and I in this whole city know how inappropriate that is.

He went back to his rooms, packed in ten

minutes and walked out, leaving the key in the door. His rent had been paid in advance; there was no settling-up to be done. He took a cab to the airport, and after consulting the departures board bought a ticket to Lima.

He ordered a large brandy as soon as he could after take-off, and followed it with another one in lieu of dinner. But his mind quixotically refused to be distracted or numbed. Shutting his eyes wearily, he wondered how long it was going to last.

3

He stayed in South America for almost a year. Hanging around Lima, doing little more than staying alive, he realized just how badly he'd prepared himself for life after Magdalena.

Gradually his eyes and his mind opened up. At the very edge of his mind, like a small flame beginning to singe paper, intellectual curiosity began to reawaken. He went to a museum and, standing absorbed in a display of Inca artefacts — shards of pottery, tools, mummies — he heard a guide's voice.

'The Inca was one person, and he was descended from the sun. His sister-queen was the daughter of the moon.'

Hal was flooded with the thought that here was a civilization he knew nothing about.

For a month he soaked in the Incas. Work was a well-remembered habit, and he went back to it with relief. Information was abundant, and after a year in Mexico his command of the Spanish language was adequate.

He rediscovered the pleasure of planning. Consulting maps and travel agents, he worked out a route down south along the Andes. Before he left Lima, he decided on a drastic reorganization of his baggage. Two thick notebooks packed with notes on the Incas had to be fitted in, and a fat guidebook. He exchanged his suitcase for a rucksack; after packing the reading and writing materials he had room only for a change of clothes, a pair of shoes and a rudimentary washing kit. Well, I always wondered what I'd look like with a beard, he thought philosophically, giving up on trying to squeeze in his electric razor. What he couldn't pack he left on his bed.

The morning he left Lima it poured with rain. On the way to catch his flight to Cuzco, he bought a rainproof poncho and a wide-brimmed hat. He caught a glimpse of himself in a shop window and smiled. In his unaccustomed clothes, with a couple of days' growth of beard, he looked like someone else. Maybe I'll get some spurs and take up smoking cheroots, he thought. His passport still said he was H. S. Dillon; he didn't feel so sure.

★ ★ ★

Cuzco appealed to him even before he arrived: there was something irresistibly charming in the concept of a city built in the shape of a puma. It was the Incas' Holy City, the heart of their empire; they had built a great stone culvert through it fed by cold, fast mountain water to keep it clean.

He engaged a taxi driver called Luis to drive him around. Luis smoked incessantly and spat loudly and frequently out of the car window. Hal got used to his sentences being punctuated by voluble rattles in the throat.

'Ten-dollar tip if you don't spit all morning,' Hal said.

Luis grinned uncomprehendingly. 'Is the

Acllahuasi,' he said, pointing out of the window at a long façade, 'the House of the Chosen Women. Virgins of the Sun,' he added, 'women who look after the Inca, bear him sons.' He spat through a gap in the traffic. Hal reckoned his money was safe.

He wandered amongst the remains of huge stone walls, thinking about the pride of man, the perpetual over-confidence that builds to last for ever and is always disappointed. He went to the fortress of Sacsayhuaman ('you say it 'sexy woman',' Luis told him with a leer. Christ, Hal thought, just what I need to think about), a powerfully impressive structure that had taken 20,000 men fifty years to build. Now it was nothing more than Cuzco's stone quarry.

But his thoughts were not typically pessimistic. There was a vitality about Cuzco, something rooted in the town and its people, exacerbated by the exhilaration of violently blue skies and distant white-topped mountains. The clear air made the bright colours of the Indians' clothing shine like jewels, and without really knowing why he felt his spirits lift.

There came a day when he wanted to make contact with home. He bought a pad of airmail paper to take with him off into the countryside, and when he returned he had written two long letters, one to Ben and the other to his father, settling down to the prospect of another Chicago winter.

He saved his trip up to Machu Picchu until the end of his time in Cuzco. He got up for the early train, and, sitting in his corner seat half-asleep, was suddenly surprised to find the train was going backwards.

'Back to Cuzco so soon?' he said in Spanish to the man opposite.

The man shrugged. '*No sé*,' he replied morosely.

Then it dawned on Hal that this was the only way the train could get up the steep gradient out of the town. Bends in the track would have had to be impossibly tight, and instead the train pulled forwards on the first leg of each zig-zag and reversed on the next.

When the train would take them no further the passengers went on by bus, upwards around incredible hairpins, spectacular drops falling sheer below them. Steep granite cliffs rose almost vertically from the valley floor; perched on top of one of them was Machu Picchu.

He tried to stop himself thinking and analysing; he concentrated on recording it all. Narrow grassy terraces where llamas grazed indifferent to the sheer drop, inches from their forefeet, down to the Urubamba river impossibly far below. Strange trapezoidal doorways and windows, a recurrent shape that gave the architecture so alien a look that it was unlike anything else surviving from the world of long ago. Did they build like that from instinct or out of knowledge born of experience? he wondered. Inca walls, Inca buildings, withstood earthquakes with a greater resilience than anything devised since.

He sat deep in thought before the Hitching Post of the Sun, remembering the Polynesian legend of Maui, who threw a net around the sun and tied it to the earth to slow its progress through the sky and make the day longer. Ideas were flowing through his head, and he wished after all that he had brought pen and paper with him.

He wandered on. The location was superb, a perfect natural fortress. Where the road entered there had been a gate built into the city wall; because this civilization did not have the wheel, nor the horse nor anything it might pull, the main entrance had been made pedestrian-sized. And the incongruity of that, he thought, really took you aback.

★ ★ ★

That night he had an early dinner and retired to his room. His mind was so full that at first the hectic jumble of impressions and thoughts threw out no obvious starting point. Then he thought again of the gateway, seeing in his mind the narrow opening in the walls. Words began to pour out of his brain faster than his hand could write; he worked on right through the night.

His series of articles on Cuzco and Machu Picchu remained for many years his proudest achievement. Apart from earning him a great deal more money that he'd expected, they proved to him that he was capable of working as well as before he had lost Magdalena. If not better.

He woke late the morning after he'd finished the Machu Picchu piece. After packing it up, with a covering note asking his editor to forward his next cheque *poste restante* to La Paz, he set off to post it, then went to buy himself a large celebratory lunch.

★ ★ ★

The next stage of his wanderings took him on south through Peru and towards Bolivia. It was October now, spring in the Andes, and the sunny weather of winter was changing. Now it was less settled, and the Lima poncho was proving useful. He wished he'd bought more wax for his boots. A helpful shopkeeper in Cuzco had provided him with a jar of grease of some animal origin, which was an effective waterproofer, once Hal had accustomed himself to the smell.

He left Cuzco on a train heading for Puno. Around Cuzco, the countryside looked like a tapestry, a patchwork of fields embroidered with clusters of farms. But the scenery changed as the surrounding hills got steeper; terraces staggered up the slopes wherever a flat space could be made, and everywhere people seemed to be struggling with effort.

As the train gasped its way upwards, the strange succulent greenery of the valley was left behind and the land became more arid. Tiny villages rolled by, mere collections of houses with mud tracks, few vehicles and little of anything except children. Sometimes the train stopped at stations in the middle of nowhere, and people would be waiting on the platform to sell food, drink, hats, T-shirts and stuffed llamas to the passengers. Hal noticed that the carriage doors were locked; transactions were carried out through the open windows. Supposing I wanted to get off here? he mused, waving away a brown hand that was pushing a fur hat insistently at him. Not that it was very likely; there didn't seem to be a great deal to do in that vast empty land so high up under the sky.

The last stretch of the journey followed the shore of Lake Titicaca. By then he was dozing, his thoughts far away. It was a relief to get off at Puno, if only to stand up and stretch his legs and his back. It was even more of a relief later, once he had checked into a hotel, to sit in the unbelievable luxury of a deep porcelain bath decorated with entwined red roses and full of piping hot water.

Later he went out to eat. He returned to the hotel's little bar and was enjoying his second *Pisca Saur*, braving the kick of the Peruvian brandy, when he heard the cultivated tones of a very English voice speaking in reception.

'There is no hot water, and this morning you guaranteed that there would be.'

The receptionist made non-comprehending noises. Hal thought guiltily of the hot water that had lapped up to his chin. It seemed that he had robbed the Englishwoman of her share.

'No thank you,' she was saying, 'I have no desire to trot along to your cousin's hotel clad only in my housecoat. Yes, I know, *mañana*, always *mañana*.'

Hal got up and walked through to reception. A tall, broad-shouldered woman stood at the desk. She had short grey hair that curled around her face, and she was wearing a silk blouse and a pleated tweed skirt, a long grey cardigan on top. Her legs were well-muscled and strong, and on her feet she wore stout leather lace-ups.

He walked up to her. 'Excuse me, ma'am, but it was me used all the hot water,' he said.

She turned, and he caught a twinkle in her blue eyes. 'I see.'

'Sorry if I had yours too. Only I was very dirty.'

'Please don't do it again.'

'I won't.' He hesitated. 'May I buy you a drink?'

'You may.'

They walked together back to Hal's table in the bar. 'What'll it be?' He beckoned the waiter.

'Gin and tonic.'

'One gin and tonic,' he said to the waiter, 'and — '

'A large one,' the Englishwoman interrupted. 'I really did want that bath.'

'A large one,' Hal echoed, 'and another *Pisca Saur*, please.'

The waiter disappeared. Hal studied his companion, and noticed she was doing the same. He held out his hand, half rising. 'I'm Hal Dillon.'

She put her hand in his. 'Helen Arnold. How do you do?'

The drinks arrived, and Helen poured a small amount of tonic into her gin. She took a large sip, then tipped in the rest of the tonic. He watched with interest.

'Ah, lovely,' she exclaimed.

'I hope it makes up for the bath.'

'It does. Actually, although it seems ungrateful to say so, I prefer a pink gin. But I doubt if they have angostura here. They should have, of course, since it comes from Venezuela, which is far closer to Peru than to, say, Hong Kong. And they all drink pink gin there.'

He felt slightly at sea. He said, 'I've never been to Hong Kong.'

'Really? A fascinating place.'

'I've never been to England, either.'

'And I have never been to the United States.'

It was a long time since he'd conversed at any length in his own language. It felt weird, sitting in a small hotel in Peru and talking to an elderly Englishwoman who seemed totally at home. He wondered what she was doing here.

'What are you doing here?'

'I came on the steamer from La Paz,' she said. 'It was a delightful trip, but one way was enough. I shall return to La Paz tomorrow, but I shall go on the bus.'

'Me too.'

Helen looked up and smiled. 'Shall we travel together?'

'Sure. I'd like that.'

'And what are *you* doing here?'

He told her how he'd stood in Lima and felt the pull of the Incas. Once he began he didn't want to stop. Neither did she, and he realized she knew far more than he did, about the Incas, Cuzco, Peru, about South America in general. He ordered more drinks, then Helen ordered a round. Every time she stopped speaking he was ready with something else to ask her.

'Pardon me, Helen, but how come you know so much?' he asked eventually.

She smiled. 'I used to teach history. What the syllabus referred to as the long, varied tale of European colonization was one of my favourite themes, and I was repeatedly struck by the horror of what the Spanish did in the Americas. So when I retired, I came to see for myself the places I thought I knew all about.'

Gutsy old dame, he thought. 'You taught in England?'

'Yes. At a girls' boarding school in Suffolk. A lovely county, you know. Rather flat, but rich in history.'

'And you travel widely?'

'Yes, I suppose I do. I have family all over the place — cousins, aunts, that sort of thing. One likes to visit. The ones who live somewhere interesting, at any rate,' she added disarmingly. Suddenly she laughed, and Hal, who was beginning to feel drunk, found he was laughing with her.

'Why are we laughing?' he asked.

'Does it matter?' she replied.

And for the life of him he couldn't think that it did.

'Let's have another drink,' he suggested.

She sat up abruptly, straightening her face although her eyes were still full of merriment. 'I think not, thank you.' She stood up, and he did too. She was a lot more firm on her feet than he was.

'I think I shall go to bed,' she said. 'Until tomorrow, on the La Paz bus.'

'Okay. Goodnight, Helen, sweet dreams.'

★ ★ ★

He was paying his bill in the morning when he heard Helen coming up behind him. He knew it was Helen because she was humming the opening bars of the Sibelius violin concerto, very accurately, and he reckoned it was unlikely anyone else in Puno was that familiar with it.

'Good morning.' He turned to smile at her. She travelled light: she was wearing the same outfit as last night, except that she had added a hat with a brim that turned up at the front. Like Yosemite Sam, he thought, without the whiskers. Her only luggage was a large canvas holdall.

'Good morning, Hal,' she returned. 'Have you had breakfast?'

'Yeah,' he said shortly. He was feeling considerably better now than when he had woken up. Some food and several cups of coffee had dispersed the after-effects of the Peruvian brandy.

While Helen ate her breakfast, Hal carried their luggage out to the bus's departure point. Soon she joined him, and when the bus arrived he muscled in with the scrummage of locals and acquired for them a double seat at the front.

'Oh, well done!' Helen said. 'We shall have a superb view.'

'Well I sure hope it makes up for us sitting in the suicide seat.'

42

He heard her chuckle.

For two hours the road ran along beside Lake Titicaca. Helen pointed out floating islands of reed. 'The Uru build them. They're the natives of the lake. They build boats of reed, too.'

The lake shore gave on to a wide, fertile plain, crowded with people and livestock, rich with cultivation. Small settlements of a few thatched buildings appeared now and again. He gazed out of the window, wondering what life would be like there.

'Hal, how long have you had your beard?' Helen's voice interrupted his thoughts.

'Month or so. Why?'

'I don't wish to be personal, but you keep fingering it, and it occurred to me that you weren't used to it.'

'No, I ain't.' Aren't you observant, he thought. Bet you gave those schoolgirls one hell of a time.

'I keep trying to imagine you without it,' Helen said. Obligingly he got out his passport and showed her his clean-shaven face in the photograph. 'That's much nicer. Whatever possessed you to grow it?'

He explained about packing his rucksack in Lima, and about how the fat book on the Incas had had to be accommodated at the expense of his shaving kit.

She sniffed disapprovingly. 'Forgive me, but that sounds to me like a flimsy excuse.'

He grinned. 'Sounds to me like one, too.'

★ ★ ★

They changed buses at the Peru-Bolivia border, and had time to look at the cathedral in Copacabana. It was a place of pilgrimage, which Helen said put her in mind of the Canterbury Pilgrims. During the next stage of the trip she entertained Hal with a sparkling account of the medieval Englishmen and women who travelled on that journey.

'And look,' she said, waving a hand towards the fields, where an endless march of people worked and walked, 'we've even got Piers Plowman's Fair Field Full of Folk.'

He'd never heard of Piers Plowman, but he liked the alliteration. It was apt, too. People and livestock were everywhere, children leading llamas on long ropes, old women following flocks of sheep, spinning wool as they walked, men digging, straining. Cattle, donkeys and pigs grazed and foraged around them. Whenever the bus stopped, barefoot children ran up to shout and stare.

Helen intoned, ' 'I cried because I had no shoes, until I met a man with no feet.' '

Hal said cynically, 'Hope he gave you his shoes.'

★ ★ ★

The bus descended to the lakeside to cross the Straits of Tiquina, and shortly afterwards they left the lake behind. It was getting late, but the long journey was almost over. They came down off the Altiplano and arrived at last in La Paz.

Helen had said she'd be flying home to England the next day. Sorry to be losing her company, Hal had proposed they have dinner together. They walked out into the bustle of the city, the streets full of peasants selling everything from bubble gum to telephones. Helen stopped to watch a woman sitting on the pavement, spinning llama wool, surrounded by what appeared to be the beginnings of a compost heap.

'I think they're herbs,' Helen said. 'Do I smell coriander?'

He sniffed. 'I can smell a whole lot of things,' he observed. 'Coriander doesn't seem to feature.'

The city teemed in its scooped-out bowl, the snow-topped Andes circling it protectively. The activity seemed to increase as evening grew into night. They found a restaurant, then adjourned to a bar close to the hotel.

Tonight they drank beer. He watched as she half-drained her glass at the first onslaught. She caught his eyes on her, and patted her lips with a linen handkerchief.

'I have a swallow like a navvy,' she said apologetically.

He'd given up trying to understand all that she said. Sometimes she seemed to be talking a different language, and it made him feel gauche to keep asking her to explain. One day I'll go to England, he thought.

They talked over the events of their day. He loved her dry wit: he had caught a little of it on and off, but now as she relaxed over the beers he began to appreciate her more.

'You laugh like a girl,' he told her.

She turned to smile at him. 'It must be the result of all those years in a girls' school.'

'And you have a dimple, just there.' He leaned across and kissed her cheek. It was soft, like a peach, and smelled sweet.

'I'm seventy-two, and you're twenty-six,' she said, her smile deepening. 'Nobody male and under sixty has kissed me since 1945, and that, I suspect, was merely the exhilaration of VE Day.' She laughed happily. 'Can you imagine what a picture we make?'

He grinned back. 'What the hell.'

★ ★ ★

They walked slowly back towards the hotel.

'Where will you go now?' Helen asked.

'On south. Chile, maybe.'

'Were I staying, I should have gone to Pótosi. The Spanish built a town there, when they found silver in the middle of the sixteenth century. They say that by 1600, it had the largest concentration of Europeans anywhere in the American continent.'

'Maybe I'll give it a try.'

'Yes, do. Write and tell me about it.'

They went into the lobby. Helen stopped. 'I shall be leaving early tomorrow,' she said. 'I'll say goodbye now.'

'Goodbye, Helen.'

She put out her hand and took his arm. 'Whatever it is, I do hope you get over it.'

'I didn't realise it showed.'

She looked at him, her head on one side, her eyes full of compassion. 'It doesn't, really. But as I've come to know you better, I see how well your

46

face is adapted to laughter. And you don't laugh as often as you should.'

He couldn't answer.

She was a tall woman, and when he put his arms around her, her head was not a great deal lower than his.

'I like hugging,' he muttered, feeling the need for an explanation.

She hugged him warmly in return, then broke away and took a step back. She held out her hand, and he grasped it.

'Good luck, Hal.'

'And to you, Helen. Happy landings.'

4

Throughout the long Andean summer Hal travelled on steadily south. He went to Pótosi, where he stayed for some time writing a vivid article on its Indians, still looking and living largely as they had done for hundreds of years in their time-frozen city of narrow cobbled streets. He sent a copy to Helen, together with a long letter. She sent him a thick, appreciative reply.

'I am preparing for Christmas,' she told him. 'When I return from church on Christmas morning I shall drink a private toast to absent friends, and amongst others I shall think of you.'

He hadn't thought much about Christmas. Helen's words made him feel rootless and lonely.

He put through a telephone call to his father. There was a great satisfaction in actually getting through to Chicago, after a morning of mistakes and inexplicable delays, and he felt unfeignedly happy when he and Sam finally got to speak to each other.

'Hi, Dad,' he said.

'Hal! Where are you, son?'

There was a long crackle, then the line became much clearer. 'Bolivia. How are you?'

'I'm fine. I'm going up to Thomas and Eleanor for the vacation, you only just caught me.'

'Give them my best.'

There was a pause. Hal thought in sudden

irritation that the gulf between what you wanted to say and what you could say over a long-distance phone call was impossibly vast.

'Dad, I just wanted to wish you well and tell you I'm okay,' he said hurriedly.

'Sure, son, I understand. You take care, now.'

'I will. Bye, Dad.'

'So long, Hal.'

Putting the receiver back, he couldn't think of a time he'd felt more lonely.

★ ★ ★

Christmas was a well-remembered low spot in his year away. Suddenly all he'd achieved, all the progress he thought he'd made, seemed to slip away. He thought constantly of Magdalena, and he felt more desolate than when he had first quit Mexico. The low hit him at a bad time; as January began, the wettest months were ushered in. Travelling laboriously down the Andes into Chile, sometimes he couldn't think of one good reason for being there. Wet, dirty, and with a stinking cold, he arrived at the end of January in a small town on the coast near Valparaiso. That's it, he decided, I ain't going any further.

He had reached the southernmost point of his travels. He shut his mind to what was around him and began to work. He bought a second-hand typewriter, and typed out his great volume of notes and drafts into a long work that followed the Inca civilization from its mystical beginnings to the point when the Spanish stamped it out.

After four months he had written himself out.

He sold the typewriter, posted all his papers and books by surface mail to himself care of Ben in San Francisco, then bought an air ticket to Mexico City.

* * *

Part of him had known all along he'd go back. He told himself it was just to hear news of Magdalena, to make sure she was all right. But he was too honest to deceive himself; as the aircraft sped northwards he sat in self-loathing, well aware he'd have no hesitation in taking her away from her husband if she were willing to come.

He checked into a hotel. He felt affluent, after almost a year of earning good money and spending very little.

He decided to get a haircut and have his beard shaved off. Back in Mexico City the tension was mounting, and he'd been finding it hard to relax. The warm, soothing ministrations of the barber were pleasant, and he closed his eyes drowsily.

'Señor, is done,' a voice said gently. Hal opened his eyes.

'Good grief!' He stared at himself in the mirror. He couldn't remember his face being as thin as this. But the barber had made a good job; Hal looked once more neat and northern, and the itinerant bearded stranger was gone.

He had a hankering for some new clothes.

'Can you recommend a good tailor?' he asked the

barber as he paid him, rubbing his palm across his denuded chin.

'*Sí, sí.*' The barber hurried to the door, pointing down the street, giving directions.

'*Gracias.*' Hal grinned at him.

The tailor's shop was imposing, large and air-conditioned with a few customers being looked after by a lot of staff. Seeing a man he thought he recognized, he approached him.

The man turned. 'Señor Dillon! Good morning! I thought you had left Mexico?'

'I did. I've had a year in South America.'

'Ah, very interesting. The Incas, no?'

He had been right — he did know the man, although until that moment he hadn't remembered where from. It was this Dr Garcia who had spotted his article in the magazine and shown it to Alvarez.

Dr Garcia was a direct link to the Alvarez family; Magdalena was suddenly within reach. He felt nervous sweat breaking out on his body.

A tailor was standing patiently at Garcia's side, holding open a book of cloth samples. Garcia turned back to him, pointing. A second assistant approached Hal.

'Señor wishes something?' he asked politely.

'Er — yeah, maybe.' His mind was racing.

Garcia said, smiling, 'You have written many fine articles, no, while you have been travelling?'

'Some. It's a nice part of the world.' *Nice*! he thought, trying to get his brain to work. God, what a word to use.

Garcia smiled encouragingly. 'So, you finish with

51

the Mayans and the Toltecs and the Aztecs, and now you know all about the Incas too!'

'I wouldn't say all,' Hal said, attempting to smile with a face gone stiff. 'Too much to learn, to say you know it all.'

Garcia was being invited to go with the tailor to be measured. He began to take off his jacket. Then he clapped a hand to his head and came back, his face perturbed.

'You knew Alvarez, didn't you?'

Hal could feel his heartbeat thumping like echoing feet. He swallowed. 'Yeah.'

Garcia's brown eyes looked mournful. His voice sank to a murmur. 'Wasn't it a sad thing, about his daughter?'

He had known it was coming. From the moment Garcia had turned back to him, he had felt part of himself begin to slip away.

He croaked, 'What?'

'You didn't hear?' Garcia clicked his tongue sympathetically. 'Poor Magdalena — she died, you see.'

He felt a desperate need to sit down before his legs gave way. He ground his teeth and leaned against the counter.

He said hoarsely, 'How did she die?'

He had to know, even if his question made him out to be a ghoul; he couldn't remain in ignorance. But Garcia, wrapped up in the sorrow of his good friend and his family, was hardly aware of Hal. He leaned to whisper in Hal's ear, and his breath smelt of garlic.

'She was trying to have a baby. Imagine, only

52

ten months of marriage! So sad, no?'

Hal raised his eyes to meet Garcia's. He had to get out. He pushed himself away from the counter, trying to force his limbs to stop shaking.

'Yeah, that's sad. I sure am sorry. Excuse me — I just remembered something.'

'Señor?'

'Señor Dillon!'

He heard the surprised voices, could imagine the interested chatter. Another rude American, they'd say, no respect, couldn't even wait to utter the required civilities. Ah, Magdalena, Magdalena, he was crying in his head. Just her name. Nothing more would come.

★ ★ ★

He found he'd made his way to Magdalena's little park. He sat down heavily on a bench. His mind was reeling, quite unable to come to terms with his loss. Like a very deep cut with a finely-honed blade, the pain took a while to bite. But as he sat there, in the place where he had first held Magdalena's hand, first kissed her, it came.

This was Mexico; people were more emotional here. Perhaps it wasn't unusual for a man to sit alone with his eyes shut and tears on his cheeks. Nobody bothered him, and eventually he got up and walked away.

He found a travel agent.

'I want to go to San Francisco,' he said.

'Si, Señor. When would you like to travel?'

'As soon as possible.'

53

The woman thumbed through her timetables, tapping a fingernail against her gold hoop earring. 'Señor wishes which airline?'

'Señor doesn't give a damn.'

She looked up, affronted.

'I'm sorry,' Hal said, 'I'm in a hurry.'

She went back to her thumbing and tapping, slightly mollified. She offered him a Pan-Am flight, leaving early the following morning.

'There's nothing sooner?'

'No, Señor.'

'Okay.'

He paid for the ticket, and the woman said he could collect it at the Pan-Am check-in desk in the morning. He wandered out through the door, forgetting to close it behind him. The woman got up, irritated. Hadn't he noticed the office was air-conditioned?

He went back to his room and methodically packed his rucksack. Then he sat down until he could think of something else to do.

He went down to reception.

'Can I send a wire?' he asked.

'Sí, Señor.'

He wrote out Ben's name and address, and the clerk, watching him, nodded. For a moment he couldn't recall his flight's arrival time. Then he remembered he had put the piece of paper the woman had given him in the back of his passport.

'Arriving San Francisco twelve-thirty Wednesday Pan-Am from Mexico City STOP,' he wrote. 'Please meet STOP Hal.'

He pushed the pad across the desk.

'Okay, Señor,' the clerk said.

★ ★ ★

Then he went out into the night. The city was full of life, and the people all seemed to be laughing. Amongst them he moved like a ghost, his face white and stiff.

Churches did not close their doors in Mexico City. He went to the one where Magdalena's wedding had been; he had no way of knowing where she was buried. He sat in an ornately-carved wooden pew, his eyes resting on the endless tormented effigies of Christ in agony. Then his gaze moved to a statue of the Virgin, in a flower-decked niche above the sanctuary lamp. She had black hair, too, and her hands lovingly cradled a baby.

Magdalena hadn't even wanted babies. Vividly into his mind came a picture of her face, twisted with distress as she poured out to him her terror. What was it like for you, sweetheart, the waiting? he asked her silently. Did you know all along? Was it a premonition?

And what was it like, suffering, dying?

As his intolerable thoughts overcame him he slipped to his knees. Folding his arms on the back of the pew in front, he dropped his head. To anyone passing, it looked as if he were simply praying: possibly he was.

★ ★ ★

San Francisco. Home again. Hal emerged from the International Arrivals Hall into the meeting area, and spotted Ben lounging against a pillar.

He called, 'Ben!'

Ben turned, a broad welcoming smile on his face. But it withered as he caught sight of Hal. Sorry, Ben, Hal thought; he knew only too well what he looked like, having just washed his face and seen himself in the mirror over the basin. He was thin, sallow and looked as if he hadn't slept for days, and he wasn't in the least surprised Ben hardly recognized him.

'Jesus, Hal, you look terrible,' Ben said bluntly. He stood uncertain. Then: 'D'you want to go get a drink?'

They left the airport. Ben drove them in silence to a bar. He got them both a beer, and as an afterthought a measure of brandy for Hal. Then he sat down.

'Shoot,' he said.

So Hal told him. Ben didn't say a word, but when Hal, face grey with sorrow, came to the end, he silently got up and bought two more brandies.

After some time Ben said, 'C'mon. You got to eat.'

Have I? Hal thought. The idea nauseated him slightly; he had no desire for food. But then he had no desire for anything. He got to his feet and followed Ben out to the car.

They went to Ben's parents' house. Nobody was home, and Ben clattered about the kitchen putting a haphazard meal together while Hal sat like stone at the breakfast bar.

'Eat,' Ben ordered, putting plates of food down. 'We're not having any more to drink, not till we've eaten.'

Hal ate mechanically, and when he had finished Ben made them coffee. The house was very quiet.

'What are you going to do?' Ben asked.

He lifted his head. His hand resting against his coffee was shaking, so that the spoon rattled in the saucer. He noticed, and moved his hand away.

'I don't know. Get away from here.'

Ben watched him. 'We could go on a trip together,' he suggested tentatively.

'Where?'

'Anywhere. Wyoming, maybe, up in the Grand Tetons?'

There was the sound of a car outside. Hal started sharply, and an almost furtive look came into his face.

'It's okay, it's my mother,' Ben said. He got up and went to the door.

Hal heard him say, 'Hi, Mom. Hal's back, I just met him from the airport. I fixed us some lunch.'

His mother said something in reply. God, Hal thought, I have to be normal. With an effort he stood up. Ben's mother came into the kitchen, a warm smile on her face. In an exact copy of her son's reaction a couple of hours earlier, Hal watched her expression fall from happiness to concern.

But she was less forthright than Ben.

'Hi, Hal. You look bushed,' she said kindly.

'Hi, Mrs MacAllister,' Hal said. 'Yeah, it's been a long day.'

She offered more coffee, eyeing Hal with an anxious expression. But he wanted to get away. He didn't think he could handle the sort of loving sympathy she'd be likely to offer him. He caught Ben's eye. Ben nodded slightly.

'Mom, Hal and I are thinking of taking a trip,' he said.

'Sure, why not? When'll you go?'

Hal was beginning to feel odd. The nausea was coming back, and the room seemed to swim slightly. As if from a distance, he heard Ben say, 'As soon as we can. Tomorrow.'

Always the great improvisor, Ben, Hal thought. Despite everything, he felt a moment's admiration.

'Okay,' Mary MacAllister said. 'You're through with college, and I guess it won't take either of you long to pack.' She put out her hand to take Hal's. 'Back home, and off again so soon,' she said, smiling at him.

He tried to smile in reply, but his face seemed to have forgotten how. 'I have to go,' he said quietly to Ben. 'I have to sort out some things, if we're leaving tomorrow.'

'Sure, Hal.' Ben reached for the car keys.

'Bye, Mrs MacAllister.'

'Bye, Hal. See you real soon.'

He caught sight of her as he got into the car. She was standing in the doorway, so deeply concerned that she looked as if she were about to cry.

5

They left San Francisco and headed across the Sierra Nevada and then north-east through Nevada State towards the Rockies. Ben still had the eating and sleeping requirements of an ordinary man, but Hal was possessed, desperate to get away into the wilds of the north lands far from the dead heart he had left in the south. His despair forced him on, and Ben understood; he made no comment but curled up in the back of the car with a Coke and a Hershey bar while Hal drove on hour after hour through the long night.

'Ben, I have to stop for gas,' Hal said. There was no answer. As he slowed down and pulled into an all-night service station, Ben's deep regular breathing became audible over the diminishing noise of the engine. Hal glanced at him; he was lying relaxed with his head on a sleeping-bag.

The forecourt attendant was chatty. 'Ain't seen a soul in hours,' he remarked as the big car endlessly gulped in petrol. 'Shame, it's a nice night to be driving.'

'Yeah,' Hal agreed. He wasn't sure where they were: somewhere in the vast desert of Nevada. He walked away from the chatter of the attendant and the tick, tick of the petrol pump and stood for a while on the edge of the arid waste that stretched far away in all directions. The air smelt tired and dry, and there wasn't a sound. He looked up into the enormity of black space above him. Only the lowest of hills disturbed the flat land; the star-dotted sky arching above was unimaginably vast. He walked quickly back to the car.

'Why's your buddy got his fingers crossed?' The attendant was grinning. Hal peered into the back of the car. In the lights of the service station, he could see that Ben had his arms folded over his chest. Although he was fast asleep, his fingers were tightly crossed.

He smiled slightly. 'I guess I was driving too fast. Check the oil, will you?'

★ ★ ★

Dawn came, the sun jabbing its long rays into the car. Ben woke up and said he was hungry.

'Okay,' Hal said. 'Next place I see.'

After breakfast they alternated shifts, two hours on, two hours off. As the route began to climb into the Rockies, Hal found that lack of sleep was affecting his performance. But forcing himself to concentrate stopped him thinking; he didn't pause to consider the effect on Ben's nerves. He knew he was bad company, but there was nothing he could do about it.

Whenever he was driving, he would play on the car's cassette music that echoed his desolation; symphonies and string concertos in minor keys, disturbingly reluctant to be resolved. Closing his eyes during one of Ben's shifts at the wheel, he heard Mahler stealthily replaced with the trite jollity of the Beach Boys.

He shot out his hand to punch the *eject* button. 'I'm not asleep,' he said sharply. 'And I can't stand that crap.'

Ben said nothing. But a little later he started humming 'California Girls'. Hal frowned at him angrily. Ben glanced at him, and the expression on his face struck even Hal as comical.

'Okay, I'm sorry,' he said. He felt a guilty twinge of sympathy for Ben, and pushed the tape back in again. 'Have your crappy Beach Boys.'

Ben said, a laugh in his voice, 'Thanks, Hal.'

★ ★ ★

They crossed into Wyoming and turned northwards into the Grand Tetons. Without consulting Ben, taking his agreement for granted, Hal took them ever further up, searching for the pure, empty wilderness he craved. Then they abandoned the car, left the well-trodden roads behind them and set off along hiking trails, through deep canyons and up into alpine meadows where the wildlife was abundant and unafraid.

The days were warm and they would walk for miles, with a spirit of companionship that didn't need words. Late in the day they would make camp and get a fire going; the nights could be bitingly cold. In the mornings they would sometimes steel themselves to swim, plunging into icy, clear lakes or hurrying streams.

Ben just let him be. He seemed to know instinctively that there was nothing he could say that would help, and he wasted no time trying. With a willingness for which Hal was eternally grateful, he quietly took on the role of undemanding, unquestioning companion.

The beauty and the peace all around him affected Ben like a blessing, and even Hal's silent misery didn't get him down. He had known Hal a long time; with a tolerance typical of him, he was happy to accept that Hal would come out of it when he was good and ready. It was not, Hal thought, in Ben's nature to bang his head against brick walls.

A morning came when Hal slept on late. Since he had flown home his sleep had been uneasy, disturbed by recurrent dreams of worrying violence that shot him into wakefulness. But at last his mind seemed to have given in to his exhaustion; when he finally stirred he found he'd slept for ten hours. He stretched, feeling refreshed.

It was mid-morning, and he could hear singing. He looked down the mountain path leading from the high, flat meadow where they were camped.

Ben had obviously been swimming. He hadn't dried himself very well, and his jeans were dark with water. He was vigorously towelling his hair, sometimes pausing to shake his head so that drops flew off and sparkled in the sunshine. As Hal watched, he began waving the towel above his head, dancing elaborate steps, jumping and weaving among the tall grasses and the flowers, accompanying himself with some unrecognizable song. Oblivious to Hal's presence, he was wholly wrapped up in a boyish happiness.

A tiny finger of his euphoria reached out and

touched Hal. The load of his sadness shifted, very slightly, and he found he was smiling.

★ ★ ★

After that things got better. They began to talk about everything, anything, no longer only about where they would go that day and what they would eat for supper. Hal had forgotten the pleasure of conversation, after so long on his own. And it was a novelty, to want to talk.

'Hell, you sure are making up for lost time,' Ben grumbled when Hal finished relating an endless saga on how the Mayans cut and transported stone for their temples. 'Think I preferred it when you didn't say a word.'

And gradually, Hal came to think that talking about Magdalena might take some of the pain out of him. Hesitantly, he started mentioning her name, remarking almost in passing, Magdalena used to say this, or, sometimes she and I used to do that. He found the night was the best time, when the great concealing darkness could almost make him feel he was talking into the void. Ben was easy; he accepted Hal's stumbling remarks without any particular comment. He would say something light in response, then, when he judged that Hal was through, go off on some new topic.

They would lie in their sleeping-bags either side of the fire. Looking upwards at the brilliant sky, Hal would fancy the distant stars were coming closer to get a better look at the earth in all her beauty. When there wasn't much moonlight they let the fire die down so as to enjoy the stars better, and Ben taught Hal the names of all the northern constellations. They went over a new piece of sky each night, and Ben would test him till he got them all right. Never afterwards could Hal look at the night sky without thinking of Ben, hearing his voice out of the darkness saying, 'No, dummy, Cassiopeia's up by the Pole Star!'

Gradually it became easier for Hal to come to terms with what had happened. But, in the way of someone struggling to overcome grief, he would think he was doing well and then be annihilated by some little association that brought the devastation right back. He would be smiling, laughing with Ben, and then a blackness would descend and he'd think, Magdalena's dead. What's there to laugh at?

Then a recklessness would overtake him. The first time it happened, he was aware of Ben watching with alarm as he resolutely drank himself unconscious. Nothing would have stopped him, short of physical restraint; sensibly, Ben baulked at that since Hal was bigger than him. When it looked as if it would happen again, Ben apparently decided that, as he couldn't prevent it and it upset him too much to watch, he'd better get drunk as well. So Hal boozed himself senseless, and Ben went right down with him.

When he realized that Ben was intent on matching him shot for shot, Hal was too far gone to be as grateful as he later felt he should have been. That was friendship, he thought afterwards, blearily watching Ben wince ashen-faced at the morning light and surreptitiously massage his temples. A guy that gives himself an almighty hangover just to keep his buddy company is worth having.

But Hal discovered that even staggering amounts of drink didn't help. When reality blurred into irrelevance, Magdalena was the only image that remained clear and inviolate.

Very drunk one night he said, 'Sometimes I think I'm glad she died, because that way she was always mine, she didn't stop loving me and start with someone new.' He focussed with difficulty on Ben. His eyes felt sore and puffy with drink, and smarted in the smoke from the fire. 'Now what sort of a bastard does that make me?'

Ben had long gone beyond diplomacy. 'A human bastard, I guess.'

'But you oughta want people you love to be happy, for Christ's sake.'

'Nobody's that mag . . . nam . . . ' Ben couldn't control the wayward syllables of ' 'magnanimous' '. 'No one's that nice. You love someone, you want them. It's just high-flown shit to say you'll be happy s' long as they are, even if it's with someone else.'

Hal pushed the almost-empty bottle at him. 'I still feel a bastard.'

'Sure you do.' Ben hiccoughed. 'We all do. I'm a bastard, you're a bastard, he, she or it's a bastard.'

Hal reached out and took back the bottle. It was now quite empty. He cuddled it to his chest, then rolled over and closed his eyes.

★ ★ ★

They took risks, egging each other on in a foolhardiness that had always been in Ben's character but that Hal recognized came to him as a by-product of grieving. One day they climbed with rash persistence right up a fast mountain stream so steep and so flooded that when Hal slipped, it tumbled him down fifty feet before he could stop.

'Terrific,' Ben said, having leapt down the bank in frantic pursuit and looking greatly relieved to find Hal still alive. 'It's gonna have to be steak tonight, your eye's swelling like a red toad.'

Then they decided to get to the top of a peak because they wanted to roll in the snow, and came close to dying of exposure when Ben dropped the compass on the way down.

'I am never doing this with you again,' Hal said, shivering violently as they crouched in the shelter of a rock trying to avoid the icy wind, waiting for the clouds to clear so that Ben could take their bearings from the stars.

'I can live with that!' Ben said, stung.

* * *

Hal wrote to his father, a brief account of what had happened between him and Magdalena. He forced himself to describe how the affair had ended, and how Magdalena had died. It's better, this time, he thought with faint surprise, it doesn't hurt as much as it did when I told Ben.

But that was a dishonourable thought; he hated himself for allowing the violence of his feelings to abate.

66

He read through what he'd written. In a way he would have liked his father's company, although he realized that Sam Dillon couldn't have helped him. They understood one another too well, and were too close; Hal felt he would only have dragged Sam down into sorrow along with him.

But it was different with Ben. Hal came to realize how right he had been to listen to the instinct that had said, get to Ben. He knew just how much he owed him; nobody, no matter how full of sadness, could think the world all bad in his company. In a moment of uncharacteristic lyricism Hal thought, he's one in a million, he's one of the people that puts the warmth in the world. Then he heard a clatter as Ben dropped a bag of tent-pegs on his foot, smiling briefly at the incongruous juxtaposition of the practical present with his idealistic thoughts as Ben shouted, 'Oh, *shit!*'

★ ★ ★

The summer was coming to an end, and Ben said he had to get back. He was going to Florida to start a postgraduate course in marine biology.

Hal decided he'd go to Europe.

They met for a few beers the night before Ben left for the East. Hal was flying to Chicago the following week, to stay with his father before going on to Europe. He had decided on Italy first, largely because of Helen Arnold's enthusiastic descriptions of Florence and Venice. He was intending to continue making his living by his writing.

67

'That's one way Magdalena will always stay with me,' he said quietly to Ben. 'Because of her, I discovered I could write.'

'That's the only sentimental thing I ever heard you say,' Ben remarked. 'Reckon you would have found you could write anyway.' He looked wryly at Hal. I'll let that one pass, Hal thought; Ben had earned the right, after all, to make any goddam comment he wanted to.

He shrugged. 'Maybe.'

'It won't be a bad way of life,' Ben went on cheerfully, 'will it? Bumming up and down Italy, sending the odd thousand words back to the States now and again?'

'You try it,' Hal said crushingly.

'No, I'll stick to the sea and what's in it.' He smiled in sudden eagerness. 'Did I tell you I'm going to learn scuba-diving?'

'I thought you could do it already.'

'No. I only go under the water when I jump in.'

★ ★ ★

They left the bar late, standing outside on the sidewalk for a moment before going their separate ways home.

'Enjoy Italy,' Ben said.

'Sure. You enjoy your bivalves and barnacles.'

It was to be two years before they saw each other again.

68

Interlude

Greece, Summer 1971

It was through a man Ben met in Florida that he came to go to Cyprus. At the end of two years in the East he returned home to San Francisco, spending a desultory summer enjoying his family's company and looking up West Coast friends.

One day the Florida acquaintance telephoned. 'They're making up a team to take to Famagusta,' he told Ben. 'They've located an old wreck, and they need experienced divers to work on it.'

Ben didn't know where Famagusta was.

'Cyprus,' said the friend.

Ben thought that was in the Mediterranean. Or it could be the Aegean. 'Great,' he said. 'Count me in.'

Telephone calls and letters were exchanged, and Ben was taken on. He was sent a lot of information about trade in the Mediterranean in the fourteenth century, most of which went straight over his head. More importantly, he was told that a reservation had been made for him on a flight out to Cyprus at the beginning of October.

It was now the end of August. Hal was in Athens; Ben knew that because Hal had sent him a postcard. It seemed crazy to be going so close — he still hadn't looked at a map — and not call by. So he telephoned the team leader and asked if he could exchange his reservation for one a month earlier and going via Athens.

'Certainly,' the man said, 'provided you make up the cash balance.'

'Oh, I will,' Ben agreed.

In fact nobody ever asked him for it, so he didn't bother.

* * *

Hal looked very different from the last time Ben had seen him. He was very brown, and he was no longer thin. Not that he was fat either, Ben thought; just bigger, and stronger-looking. He was also a great deal more self-contained. Ben listened to him order something in Greek at a café on Syntagma Square; it turned out to be ouzo and little snacks of cheese, smoked meat and olives on pieces of bread, all of which Ben took to as if he'd been consuming them all his life. He thought Hal seemed relaxed, confident and pretty unapproachable.

It took a couple of days to rediscover the easy friendship of before, for which Hal apologized in a roundabout way.

'I ain't used to people,' he said. 'Sure I talk to lots of folks, but I don't stay any place long enough to make good friends. I've gotten too used to my own company.'

But he was still Hal. In a way Ben was glad to see him like this. He was a lot nearer now to the detached and self-sufficient person Ben had first known at college. The pale, skinny man who had come back from Mexico with deep-sunk, haunted

70

eyes had gone for good. Neither of them mentioned Magdalena. Ben would have liked to, but there was something about Hal now that put you off asking him questions you weren't sure he'd welcome.

Ben said he'd be in Greece for a month, and Hal immediately took it into his head that they'd do a trip round the classical sites.

'We'll do Delphi,' he said enthusiastically, 'I've been there already, but it's beautiful; I'd welcome going again. Then down to Argos, Epidauros, Tirens . . . '

'Hold up,' Ben said. 'If you really want to do that, I'll come with you. But I don't go a lot on a heap of ruins.' Hal glared at him. 'Are any of them near the sea?' Ben went on. 'You could tramp round your old sites, and I could swim.'

'God, Ben, I'd forgotten what a philistine you are. Okay, we'll skip the ruins.' Hal laid emphasis on the word, but the mild sarcasm was lost on Ben.

* * *

They had a wonderful month. September was reliably hot in the Peloponnese, the *meltemi* having blown itself out at the end of August. Hal found that being with Ben, spending endless days in the sea, lounging about on beaches and nosing around little harbours, opened up a whole new facet of Greece, quite different from the intellectually-inclined avenues he usually explored. Occasionally he would cast longing eyes at signs that said 'Sparta' or 'Mycenae', but then he'd think, I have plenty of time, and abandon himself once more to Ben's happy hedonism. Ben was pleased to see Hal enjoy it all, although after he'd almost drowned him trying to teach him how to water-ski, he decided maybe he shouldn't impose his way of doing things on to Hal quite so single-mindedly.

Ben adapted to Greece instantly. There wasn't a great deal of adapting to do, for his easy, relaxed manner and friendly interest in people were very close to the Greek philosophy of life. His dark-blond hair and blue eyes were not the usual Greek colouring of nowadays, but he was brown after the Californian summer, and could have made a passable ancient Greek. As he and Hal made their way down into the Peloponnese, the local people began to take him for one of themselves.

'*Yasu*,' a young man said as Ben stood back to let him pass on some steps. He added a sentence in Greek.

'Hey, Dimitrios, you've cracked it,' Hal said, amused. 'That guy thought you were a local, he just asked you if the bus has gone yet.'

Ben shrugged modestly. 'He was fooled by my worry beads.' He'd bought himself some that morning and hadn't stopped practising since. 'I nearly had his eye out.'

★ ★ ★

They went right down to the tips of the Mani, exploring the three promentories of land pointing south-eastwards into the Aegean. They found quiet fishing villages with few tourists, and the best olive oil in Greece. They were met with courtesy and a friendly welcome everywhere.

Hal told Ben some of the ancient myths, of gods coming down from Olympus in disguise to test out mortal hospitality. Ben especially liked Zeus threatening to destroy all of humanity because nobody would give him and Hermes any supper.

'That's some overreaction,' he said admiringly. 'We could try it. You'd better be Zeus, you're taller than me and you speak Greek.'

'Okay,' Hal said. 'But nobody hasn't given us any supper.'

Ben was silent a minute, working out Hal's remark. Then he said darkly, 'So far. It'll pay us to be ready when they do. Don't.'

'Ever the optimist,' Hal said.

'Sure. I don't like to have unreasonable expectations. How did Zeus rub them out?'

'With a flood. But he didn't destroy them all. The last house they tried belonged to Philemon and Baucis, and although they were the poorest people in the village, they were nicer than the others and were willing to share the little they had. Zeus gave them a feast of Olympian standards in thanks, and gold plates to eat it off.'

'Nice reward.'

'That wasn't all. He asked them what was their dearest wish, and they said, 'to die together, because we've been married so long we'd be sad without each other'. So Zeus fixed that too, and when their time was up they died in the same

73

instant and were turned into intertwining trees.'

Ben smiled happily. 'Knew I'd like Greece.'

* * *

Back in Athens, Hal told Ben he had to see the Acropolis. He refused to let him leave until he had done so.

'But my flight goes at eleven tomorrow,' Ben protested. 'There won't be time.'

'Yes there will.'

He made Ben get up at six o'clock, and marched him up empty streets through the sleeping Plaka and the Agora to the Acropolis, only to find that they couldn't get in till eight on a Sunday. They found a stall selling refreshments, and bought coffee.

'That has to be the worst coffee in Greece,' Ben complained. 'Don't they know they have to heat the water?'

They watched as a uniformed police band and a coachload of Ephzones disappeared up the stony slope to the Acropolis. Faint sounds of brass came to them on the still morning air, and shortly afterwards the police and soldiers all clattered down again.

Ben laughed. 'What was all that about?'

'Maybe they were raising the flag,' Hal suggested.

'Or greeting the dawn.' Ben still hadn't got over being woken up at six o'clock. 'They wouldn't have to do a whole lot of fighting,' he added, lowering his voice and nodding towards the Ephzones in their distinctive ceremonial dress, 'looking like that, they could just march around the battlefield and the enemy would laugh themselves to death.'

Hal grinned. 'I'll miss you, Ben,' he said. 'I'll miss your reverent attitude and your endless intellectual curiosity.'

'Nuts,' Ben said. 'Come on. Let's look at your old ruins, then we can go get a drink.'

Ben

Autumn 1971 – Autumn 1973

6

The Famagusta operation was on a more luxurious scale than Ben had imagined. He was met at Nicosia airport by a uniformed chauffeur holding up a board saying, 'MR MACALSITTER.' Close, Ben thought. A gleaming Mercedes waited outside for them, and Ben was driven to a large villa on the coast north of Famagusta.

A rotund maid in a navy uniform came upstairs to his room and offered to unpack for him.

'Sure, thanks.' He watched her carefully hanging his shirts and jeans in an enormous wardrobe. He wondered if she spoke English. 'Room to spare,' he observed, pointing to the empty space all around his few belongings.

She giggled, making her face even more apple-like. He remembered remarking to Hal in the Peloponnese that he hadn't yet seen a Greek woman to make him sit up and take notice. Hal had gone 'Mmm,' non-committally. Ben thought he probably hadn't had much to do with women since Magdalena. Wouldn't surprise me, he thought, if this little one's typical.

'I can do something else?' The maid was smiling shyly.

He felt sorry for thinking unchivalrous thoughts about her. 'No, that's fine. Thanks,' he said, and gave her a couple of hundred-drachma notes. She beamed widely, and disappeared.

A gong summoned the household to dinner. He took a look at himself in the great mirror on the landing. If they're all dressed up, he thought, then I'll find a dark corner. He straightened his tie, glad that he'd listened to his mother and packed it.

Conversation was stilled over the meal. Nobody seemed to know anyone else, and Ben reckoned that most of his companions were equally awed by the sumptuous surroundings.

They were ushered into a hall, where seats were set out facing a raised dais. Twenty of us, Ben counted. Four more men walked up onto the dais.

'Jeez, I hope it's a big wreck,' he remarked to the man sitting next to him. 'We'll be falling all over each other.'

'They're not all divers. Those guys are the crew,' he nodded to a swarthy group talking in Greek, 'and the pale-looking ones are the smart-asses.'

'Huh?'

'The archaeologists. Historians. Whatever.'

'Ah.' Guiltily Ben recalled the wodge of academic-looking papers he'd chucked in the trash. 'So how many of us underwater guys are there?'

The man grinned. 'Well, there's you and me.'

Over the next hour Ben listened as the details of the operation were outlined. The villa and the boat they'd be using belonged to a wealthy Athenian who made a habit of financing such projects. Probably, Ben thought, so he can make sure exhibits end up in museums with his name on them.

A professor from Thessalonika got up and talked endlessly about artefacts. He showed slides of pieces of pottery, which all looked exactly the same to Ben. He wondered that all this time and energy should be spent on bits of old pots. Then he thought, who am I to query it? and frowned in a belated attempt at concentration.

The rich Athenian asked for questions — there weren't any — and wound up the meeting. As Ben and his neighbour got up, a man sitting at the back of the room beckoned to them. He was short, thick-set, and had a reddish, leathery face under a thatch of auburn hair.

'That's William,' Ben's companion said, 'the team leader. He's English, he comes from Ireland.'

'Then he's probably Irish,' Ben said pedantically. A month with Hal had temporarily cured him of sloppy inaccuracies.

William greeted them, and Ben recognized the voice he'd talked to on the telephone. At first he thought William was angry about something, but soon he realized that it was just his way.

'They want us down on the fuckin' wreck tomorrow,' William said, scowling at Ben, 'but I said, we won't go near the bugger till we've had a couple of days learning to work together as a team.'

Ben wanted to laugh, but controlled it. He heard a mutter from behind him, where the remaining three members of the diving team had gathered.

'Well?' William barked.

'Sounds fine to me,' Ben said. Nobody else seemed about to disagree.

'Right. Nine o'clock in the morning, on the quay.'

Ben found the next two days a challenge as he tried not to let his concentration be distracted by William's unique handling of the English tongue. William knew what he was talking about, and he knew exactly what he wanted from his team. Ben was willing to follow his drilled-in instructions to the letter; William was good, there was no doubt. With a different part of his mind he was trying to record the wonderful motley of curses that William used. Ben had never heard anyone swear so much without repetition.

At the end of the two days, what William referred to as their 'sea trials' were finished. The affection Ben had developed for William increased on the first morning, when, sitting on the boat's rail as excited as a child on his birthday, William shouted, 'Last one in's a sissy!'

Ben loved the work, from the moment when he kicked down into the deep navy-blue sea beside William and they first caught sight of the remains of the wreck, lying on her side in a sheltered stretch of clear water. He didn't care whether or not they found anything. Had the ship been carrying gold or precious jewels, it might have been different. But in that case, he reckoned, it'd have been unlikely to stay there undisturbed till the twentieth century. The shards of pottery they brought up from the sea-bed didn't look like anything to get excited about, although the professor from Thessalonika clearly thought otherwise.

At the end of the first day he went to sit in the

evening sun, his feet up on the ship's rail, a beer at his side. Gazing out at the flat-calm water, feeling pleasantly tired, well-fed and totally contented, he thought happily, they're *paying* me to do this.

★ ★ ★

November came, and the water got cooler. The team were issued with wet suits and went on working, except on days when the wind got up, creating currents that stirred the seabed into dirty dishwater. Then the team had a free day.

William announced one windy morning that he was going off for 'a bit of fun.' He asked Ben if he wanted to go along and Ben agreed, pleased at the prospect of a day doing something different. And that, he thought as the hours went by, was some understatement.

The outing was a revelation. For a man who disciplined himself and his team so tightly, the fury with which William went about abusing his system on his day off had to be seen to be believed. He started with a large intake of whiskey at a bar, then took Ben for a gargantuan, gut-stretching meal with an endless variety of dishes, most of them extremely rich and swimming in oil.

Ben had to stop after three courses. William frowned at him. 'You drawin' stumps, me boy?'

'Right,' Ben said apologetically. 'Sorry William, I only have on my ten-pounder stomach.'

His defection didn't seem to bother William, who ploughed on for another three quarters of an hour before finally pushing himself away from the table with a resounding belch.

'Nine out of ten,' Ben remarked.

William roared with laughter. 'Ah, they all do that here!' he said, unembarrassed. 'You live here long enough, you'll be doin' it too.'

'Great, I like to have something to look forward to.'

They left the restaurant and emerged onto the street. 'Let's hit the women!' William said.

Ben followed as he led the way with tell-tale familiarity through the maze of streets behind the port. As he pushed boldly into the bar of his choice a chorus of female voices greeted him; he sat down with a girl snuggling up either side of him, and another brought bottles of beer.

A pretty girl with dark curly hair sat herself on Ben's knee. She whispered in his ear. He smiled, and shook his head.

'Okay,' she said indifferently. 'I sit here, then I go.'

'Fine,' Ben said. 'Don't let me keep you from your work.'

William was studying him intently. 'You queer, boy?' he demanded.

Ben prided himself on the fastidiousness which, while providing a fair amount of variety, had got him through his college years without catching anything worse that a cold. He considered several answers to the question. Then he said, 'No, William. I'm saving myself for marriage.'

'They're a fine bunch of women,' William said wistfully.

'I'm sure they are. You go right ahead.'

With an impatient gesture, William waved the women away. 'Ah, no. Another time, me darlin'.' He pulled the nearest girl to him and kissed her proffered lips. 'You've put me right off!' he said accusingly to Ben.

'Stop sulking. I'll buy you another beer instead.'

William grunted, then shrugged. 'All right, boy. It'll probably do me a lot more good. You can buy me two, then I won't feel so bad.'

Ben was afraid that, as the evening wore on, William would want to eat dinner. But lunch and nineteen beers seemed to be his swansong: 'No,' he said regretfully in the last bar, 'I can't make the round twenty. Must be gettin' old.'

They strolled out along the waterfront and found a seat. William launched into a rambling tale of the unlikely adventures that had led him to this spot. Ben, who had the measure of him by now, believed about a quarter of it. But it had been an entertaining day.

★ ★ ★

By spring of the following year, the old vessel had been emptied of her cargo, and a party was thrown to celebrate the end of the operation. A TV news crew came from Nicosia, and Ben watched the wealthy Athenian enjoying his moment of glory. He felt sorry it was coming to an end.

After the drinks, the speeches and a lavish buffet supper, William appeared by Ben's side. 'What'll you do now, boy? Back to America?'

'No, I'm staying on,' Ben said. He'd bought

a third-hand Chevrolet from one of the divers who'd left earlier in the year, and was keen to start exploring. 'What about you?'

A smile spread over William's face. 'I'm goin' home,' he said happily. 'Back to Dublin, then to the south-west, and I shall sit by a wide, wild shore and watch the Atlantic rollin' up the sands.' His eyes fixed on Ben's. 'I've taught you all I know,' he said. 'You've learned well — you'll do all right. If you need work, remember you've valuable knowledge and skills that others will pay you to acquire.'

They parted company in the morning. William shook Ben's hand, then gave him a bear-hug that made Ben's ribs creak.

William's words of the previous evening stayed in Ben's mind. Gradually, he evolved a plan for what to do next.

★ ★ ★

He made his way up the east coast of Cyprus, then cut across north-westwards to the northern shore, arriving in Kyrenia. Sitting at a pavement café looking out at the harbour and at the impressive golden bulk of the castle up to his right, he thought, I'll stay. For a while.

He rented a room and made some enquiries, and the idea sparked off by William's suggestion began to seem workable; it appeared there was a market for teaching the skills he now possessed. A week's hard work resulted in advertising cards in several hotels, a handful of contacts who would hire out boats, and, most important, a list of potential pupils.

'You've cracked it, Dimitrios,' he said triumphantly out loud, standing on the small balcony of his new quarters. He felt sufficiently confident to lay out a fair amount of money on two full sets of scuba-diving equipment, consoling himself with the thought that he could always sell them again. When the time came to move on.

★ ★ ★

He worked hard through the remainder of the summer and into the autumn. As well as holidaymakers, he taught foreigners working in Kyrenia. He discovered with pleasure that he was earning a good reputation; people would approach him with some variation on the words, 'my friends told me to see you, they say you're good'.

He liked most of them. The exception was a good-looking, dark-haired Englishman called George Fleming, who was, in Ben's opinion, a lot too pleased with himself. George was an eager pupil but over-confident, which was, Ben pointed out to him, not a good idea when you were a novice under water. Ben had to admit — grudgingly — that George had taken the reprimand in good part. But there were other reasons for Ben's antipathy: George constantly talked about his girlfriends. And the sort of biological descriptions he went in for were not, Ben considered, the sort of thing the girls would like shouted out to a bar full of half-drunk men.

Ben would have liked to tell George to get lost.

Unfortunately, George put more work Ben's way than the rest of his students put together.

★ ★ ★

One day in early autumn Ben was sitting on a beach sorting through some stones he'd found on the seabed. They were pretty; they looked as if silver had been sprayed into them. Becoming aware that somebody was standing behind him, he turned to see a spare, grey-haired man.

'*Kalimera*,' the man said.

'Good morning.'

'Ah, you are English.'

'American.'

'Excuse me. My name is Michael Stanissoupolos.'

Ben got to his feet to shake the Cypriot's hand. 'Ben MacAllister.'

'I am a jeweller. Will you sell me your stones?'

Ben smiled. 'You can have them. They didn't cost me anything.'

'Ah, but if I — er — reimburse you for your trouble, I may feel free to ask you to obtain more.'

'I will anyway.'

The man bent to examine the stones. Then he stood up. He took a card out of his pocket. 'Come to my workshop.' He gave the card to Ben. 'I will show you my work.' He picked up Ben's rocks. 'May I take these?'

'Sure.' Ben was studying the card. 'Okay, I'll call by sometime.'

The man said, 'I hope you will.'

* ★ *

A month later, after quite a long search, he found Michael's card. He hadn't forgotten the invitation, but had been preoccupied with an intense but short-lived affair with a German girl on holiday with her parents. He'd liked the way she looked, especially the long corn-coloured hair that came almost to her waist.

But he was less keen on the way she tried to organize him. By the time she'd started to talk about exchanging addresses and going home, he'd cooled off, despite the corn-coloured hair and the superb suntanned body.

'I will write to you, Ben, and you will write back,' she ordered when he dropped her at her hotel on the last night of her holiday.

'I don't know how to write,' he replied, straight-faced. 'I'm a beach bum, I'm illiterate.'

Her pale blue eyes clouded. 'You cannot write? But you are an American, no, not one of these natives?'

'No, I'm a Greek, my real name's Dimitrios. I sound American because of all the sailors.'

Now she was frowning. 'Sailors?'

'My mother's friends.' Mom, I'm sorry — he was trying not to laugh — but this is an emergency.

She turned towards the stairs. 'Goodbye, Ben,' she said stiffly.

'*Auf wiedersehen*. Please write, I'll get someone to read it to me.'

He got into his car and burst out laughing. I'm a bastard, he thought, a real bastard.

★ ★ ★

He found Michael's house, and a dumpy Greek housekeeper showed him through to the workshop. Michael turned and saw him, but did not get up.

'I am glad you have come,' he said. 'A minute, please.'

Ben moved closer and saw that he was polishing a huge sapphire in a gold setting shaped like an eye. 'To avert evil,' Michael said. 'A modern version of an old charm.'

He wrapped it in tissue paper and laid it in a box. Then he got up and opened a safe. On its shelves were several pieces of rock similar to the ones Ben had found — possibly even the same ones — but they had been shaped, and polished. They had been put in chunky silver settings.

'You see?' Michael said. 'The silver sheen in the stones matches the metal. Can you can find me some more?'

'I'll try,' Ben said. 'I'll dive a few more times before the winter, and I'll get what I can.'

'There is no hurry,' Michael said. 'This year, next year, it does not matter.'

'Okay.'

'But I have to pay you.'

Ben smiled. 'No, you don't.'

Michael shook his hand in farewell. 'We shall see.'

★ ★ ★

90

Ben delivered a consignment of stones soon afterwards, and received an invitation to dinner for the following week. It was a formal affair, and he found that not only was he the only foreigner but also the only person under fifty. Somewhat to his surprise, he had a good time: the food was excellent, and the novelty of a sophisticated evening appealed to him. He thought how Hal would have enjoyed it. I'm not such a philistine now, Hal.

Christmas came, and Ben was invited to join a house party up in the Troodos mountains. The holiday went with a swing until the fourth day, when Ben quietly slipped away.

He enjoyed the peace of Cyprus in the winter, and by April was ready to start teaching again. He was full of enthusiasm and good intentions, and was surprised when, after only a fortnight, it was becoming heavy going.

Why? he wondered. What the hell's wrong? He'd liked it well enough last season, and had planned to spend at least another summer here. The last thing I want, he thought dejectedly, is to start feeling sick of it all. Because if it doesn't get better — and it doesn't look like it's going to — I'll have to do something about it. And God knows what sort of efforts that's going to mean.

He finished work one evening, dropping off his pupils and mechanically seeing to the equipment. He was thinking hard. Then he went home and had a long bath.

He listed the things that were getting him down. Topmost was that he was going to a dressy party and he didn't want to. He'd done hardly any

91

socializing since Christmas; he couldn't shake off the feeling that he was always the outsider, on the edge of a group that knew each other intimately and did everything together. Not that he wanted to be that close to them — they were nice people, but casual acquaintance was enough.

I was spoiled for good friends in the past, he thought. I took them for granted. Now I'm away from them, I'm realizing I'd rather have my own company than be with people I'm not in sympathy with. But sometimes — like when I see people happy together — I get lonely.

Why am I going to the goddam party? Because there's nothing else to do. He picked up the sponge and threw it angrily at the tiled wall. He'd have to put on a jacket and tie and make conversation with a load of people he didn't know. He retrieved the sponge and threw it again. And the room'll be hot, crowded, noisy and smoky. Shouldn't have said you'd go, should you, dummy?

It's a birthday party, he recalled. I'll have to go. If I go off on my own somewhere or just stay in, I'll feel bad about it.

He got out of the bath, dried himself and got dressed. He scowled at himself in the mirror as he tied his tie.

'Your trouble, buddy,' he said aloud to his reflection, 'is that you want to move on and you have nowhere to go.'

7

The party was everything Ben had thought it would be. The May night was clear and still with the moon almost full. How wasteful, he thought, to be standing in this packed room, crammed into a house with too many people.

He got himself a beer, opened it and said quietly, 'Cheers, Ben.' He stood back to let a couple of new arrivals get to the drinks, and inadvertently pushed open a door into the corridor.

He went through it. Immediately opposite were French windows, standing slightly ajar. He went outside, emerging onto a balcony. He walked over to stand by a wide stone parapet, breathing in the warm night air.

The view was wonderful. A lawn sloped away to the garden's end, marked by tall cypress trees standing black against the sky. Beyond was a distant white beach. The moon traced a gleaming pathway over the water. He thought it was a great improvement on inside; he moved into the shadows and leaned against the wall to enjoy the solitude.

The doors opened, making him jump. 'Damn,' he muttered. He didn't want company. He watched the figure leaning against the parapet, standing exactly where he had stood. It was a girl, and in the moonlight she looked all shades of silver, white and black; light hair, lighter skin, dark dress, its thin straps bars across bare shoulders.

He thought she knew he was there. But then she said angrily, 'Oh, *bugger* it!' and he decided probably she didn't.

He moved forward and she started, turning to face him. He smiled at her. 'Sorry I made you jump.'

'I thought you were George.' She sounded English.

'I'm not.'

She smiled back. She seemed pleased he wasn't George. 'Isn't it awful in there?' she said surprisingly.

'Sure is.'

There was something about her, he thought. She went on smiling at him, and he didn't want her to go away. 'It's a wonderful view,' he said. Great conversation, he thought.

'It is.' She nodded earnestly. 'It looks magical, but it's probably just the moonlight.'

He watched her mouth as she spoke. He wanted very much to kiss her. He couldn't remember ever having felt such instant physical attraction. He felt drunk. Enchanted.

He moved closer, putting his beer down on the parapet. She didn't back away, but went on staring at him. Her eyes were light, the pupils wide.

'I don't think you're real,' he said softly. He was amazed at himself. At her. What am I doing? he wondered wildly. Her face turned up to his was irresistible. 'I think I'm going to kiss you.'

She didn't protest, so he kissed her very lightly on the lips.

She said softly, 'Again.' Or he thought that was

what she said. He didn't wait to check, but gently closed his lips to hers once more.

He put his hands on the warm, smooth skin of her shoulders. She leaned towards him, and he put his arms round her and pulled her close. She was affecting him strongly; he very much wanted to make love to her.

Crazy, a still-sensible part of him protested. You don't know who she is, only just met her!

But she was laying her face against his chest, wrapping her arms around his waist. She murmured, 'Nice.'

'I don't believe this,' he said. She muttered something into his neck. 'How's that?'

'I said, neither do I. I feel as if I must have miscounted my drinks. Or wandered into a Fellini film.'

He'd never seen a Fellini film, but decided not to say so. 'Right.'

'And we haven't even been introduced. Haven't even met, till now.' She leaned away slightly and stared up at him as if it was a lapse in etiquette.

'Why, I wonder?' He didn't care in the least, but couldn't think of anything better to say.

'I only got here yesterday.'

He kissed the top of her head. 'Let's go.'

'That could be a problem.'

'Why?'

'I came here with someone. I don't think I can just leave.'

'Who did you come with?'

'George Fleming.'

Christ. I should have realized, he thought, when

she said I thought you were George. But there are dozens of Georges in Cyprus, the Greeks like the name for some reason. 'Oh,' he said. 'Hell.'

'Friend of yours, obviously,' she observed ironically.

He was repelled at the thought of her being a girlfriend of George, yet already making excuses. She can't know him well. Hasn't come across his less attractive traits. 'I taught him scuba-diving last summer,' he said neutrally.

'And you don't like him. I can tell from the way you've gone tense.'

Perceptive as well as beautiful, he thought. He stared at her. Deciding the only way was to be honest, he said, 'I don't. He's full of shit.'

She didn't respond at first. Then she began to smile. 'Full of shit,' she repeated. 'I think you're absolutely right.' He started to speak, but she interrupted. 'Yes, I know. In that case, what am I doing out here with him? Good question. If you've got an hour or two, I'll tell you.'

He said, 'I have an hour or two.'

She understood: they both did.

'When?' he asked.

'I'm staying in Kyrenia — that little hotel by the fishermen's quay just outside the town. Do you know it?'

'I do.'

'Tomorrow morning?'

'Yes.'

She broke away from him, but he pulled her back. 'I have to kiss you goodnight.' He did so.

'Goodnight.' She turned and went towards the French windows.

He whistled softly, and she stopped. 'Aren't you going to tell me your name?'

'Oh. It's Jo, Joanna Daniel.'

'I'm Ben MacAllister.'

He heard the doors close behind her.

He rested his elbows on the parapet. He could still smell her perfume, and he still wanted to make love to her.

★ ★ ★

He went home to bed and lay thinking about her. He was awake again at dawn, still thinking about her, and after a couple more hours' restless dozing gave in and got up.

He had a shower and made some coffee. Still only 7.30am, he noticed in disgust, you can't go visit a woman that early. Hell, but I can't stay here. He ran down to his car and drove out to the fishermen's quay.

It was a perfect morning. The sky was cloudless, and at this early hour still a deep blue. The calm sea lapped gently against the shore, making soft plopping noises as tiny waves expired onto the sand. He took off his sneakers and rolled up his jeans, walking in the water away from the hotel, then turning round and walking very slowly back again.

He saw the glass door of one of the hotel's bedrooms slide open. A towel-wrapped figure emerged onto a balcony, rubbing its head in a second towel.

He watched as she pushed towel and hair out of her eyes and slowly scanned the beach. Hi, he said to her silently, and she looked right at him. Then she waved, and disappeared back inside her room.

He sat down on the sand. Ten minutes? Make it twenty — she'll have to dry her hair. He checked the time, then made himself sit and stare out to sea without turning round.

A voice called, 'Ben?'

He looked at his watch: eight and a half minutes. He stood up and faced her, beginning to smile as she ran down the beach towards him. He folded her in a hug.

'Come on in, the water's fine,' he said as she splashed about beside him. 'You've got your sandals wet.'

'It doesn't matter, they're only flip-flops.' She was slightly breathless, and her hair was damp.

He said gently, 'And how are we this morning?'

She smiled radiantly at him. 'I'm marvellous. I had this fantastic dream about meeting someone very nice at a party, and the next morning there he was in the sea, waiting for me.'

'How unlikely. That'll teach you to stay up late drinking too much.'

'I didn't!'

'I know. What do you want to do? I have my car, we can go for a drive. Did you have breakfast yet?'

'No. I'm not sure if I'm hungry.'

'You look hungry to me. We'll have rolls, honey, oranges and figs.'

He wasn't sure he was hungry either, but they had to do something. He was feeling decidedly odd, finding it hard to believe this was really happening.

They went across to a small provisions shop, calling itself *Supermarket* with grandiose inaccuracy. She looked impressed when he was able to buy exactly the things he'd suggested for breakfast. But then, he thought, she doesn't know how long I've lived here.

The rolls were warm from the oven and smelled delicious. He reached in his pocket for his keys.

'I bet he never got far off the ground,' she said suddenly.

'Who?'

'This bee.' She was studying a fat and vividly-striped bee on the lid of the honey pot. Ben came to a halt in the middle of the road and gave the matter his full attention.

'I reckon it's a bumble bee, not a honey bee,' he said eventually. 'One of nature's miracles, the bumble bee — its wings are so small in relation to its body weight that it shouldn't be able to fly.'

She laughed, a warm sound filled with happiness.

'What are you laughing at?'

She looked at him, and the expression in her eyes made his heart thump. 'God knows.'

He opened the car, leaning in and lifting a couple of air-tanks from the passenger seat and swinging them into the back.

'Do you always carry this much around with you?' she asked, picking up a face-mask and three flippers from the floor in front of her seat.

'Have to. The car's bigger than my room.'

'Will you take me diving?'

'If you like.' Baby, he thought, I'll take you anywhere.

He started the car and drove out westwards from the town, following the line of the coast. He tried to see the landscape through her newly-arrived eyes. It was still early in the season, and the land retained some of its springtime green; the island was looking beautiful.

He turned his thoughts to more urgent matters.

'Did you come out here to see George?' he asked.

'Oh! Yes, I did.'

He was silent. Then he said simply, 'Why?'

'Don't ask.' She frowned. 'Bloody big mistake. I realized that ten minutes after he'd met me off the plane. But I've known him for ages — we were almost engaged, two years ago.'

'Christ.'

'Ah, but I was very young then.' He heard the amusement in her voice. 'He wrote to me out of the blue a few weeks ago inviting me out here. I accepted, because I wanted a holiday, and I'd never been here. And he said there would be a big group of us. *Bastard.*'

'There isn't a big group?'

'No. Thank God I'd made it quite clear I wasn't going to stay with him, even if there had been a big group. I'm safe, in my nice little hotel.'

Safe, he thought. Strange choice of words. 'Why was it a mistake?'

'Because as soon as I saw him I remembered all

100

the reasons I hadn't got engaged to him.'

'Okay.' He felt as if he'd been running hard. 'What'll you do now?'

'I don't know. Tell him politely it's no good, I suppose. I feel sort of . . . responsible. I came out at his invitation, after all.'

He said nothing. This was something she had to sort out for herself: he couldn't interfere. Instead he asked her where she lived, and she said London. 'What do you do?'

'I'm a commercial artist. I do book illustrations. Or I did.'

He reached out and took her hand. 'Out of a job, huh?'

She laughed ruefully. 'I just might be. Anyway, I don't care. I don't enjoy it any more, and I'm thinking of chucking it in. I want to write my own stories, and illustrate them,' she added in a burst of confidence.

'What's stopping you?'

'I don't think anything is, really.' She was thoughtful for a moment. Then she said, 'It's your turn. How long have you been in Cyprus?'

'Eighteen months.' He claimed his hand back as they slowed down to pass a couple of donkeys in the care of a little boy. He told her about Famagusta, and how he'd come to Kyrenia to start the diving courses.

'What will you do now?'

He glanced at her. On impulse, he said, 'I'll probably run away with you.'

He came to the turning he was looking for and steered the Chevrolet down a rough track that led to the sea. He drove slowly through quiet olive groves, making black floppy-eared goats start away in surprise. The track emerged onto a wide sandy beach.

He accelerated suddenly, wanting to distract her from her surprised reaction to his last remark. He raced along the firm ground, swinging into a tight turn, wheels sliding, to come to a halt some ten yards from the belt of olives at the end of the beach.

He looked at her. She was laughing, pushing her hair out of her eyes and wiping dust off her lips. She didn't look like someone about to ball him out for being pushy; she looked alive, joyful. He reached out for her and she moved across the bench seat towards him.

Putting his arms round her, he felt her mouth eagerly meet his. She relaxed against him, and with a thrill he felt the tip of her tongue slide against his. His pulse stepped up, and a quiver like faint static ran through him. He pulled away slightly to look into her eyes as they blinked open, then kissed her again.

Lovely woman, he was thinking, why do you have this effect on me? I want you so much. Their lips parted, and he heard her sigh as she leaned against him.

He wondered if she knew they were going to be lovers.

He did.

★ ★ ★

They swam for a long time, then ate breakfast in the shade of a pine tree, the shadows steadily shortening as the sun climbed towards midday.

Suddenly she said, 'I'm afraid I'm having lunch with George.'

Shit. 'Hell.'

'He wants me to go off into the mountains with him.'

He watched her face. 'And will you?'

'Of course not!' She sounded irritated. 'I don't even want to have lunch with him. But it's difficult. Do you see?' She turned to look at him. 'It's because of him I'm here at all,' she added inconsequentially.

He was developing a facility for filling in the gaps her leaping thoughts left out.

'Okay. Shall I come and see you when he's gone? If . . . ' He stopped. He was straying onto dangerous ground. Possibly she liked having two men at a time and wanted to spend the evening with George. The night.

'If what?'

'If you don't want to be with him.'

She muttered 'Shit!', and he thought, if it's okay for her, it's okay for me. 'Ben, this is awkward.' She pushed the hair off her forehead, staring him straight in the eyes. 'I want to be frank with you, but not knowing how you feel is holding me back. In case you don't feel the same. It's the old who-makes-the-first-move thing. If I say I want to be with you and you don't want it too, I'm going to look an idiot. But I do, anyway.'

She turned her face away, staring out to sea.

'Jo?'

'What?'

'Didn't you hear what I said? About running away with you?'

'I thought you were probably joking. It's not what people do, is it?' He didn't answer. '*Is* it?'

He said, 'It is where I come from.'

She moved closer, and he felt her shudder. 'In that case,' she said shakily, 'you'd better take me back to town so I can get on with giving George the heave-ho.'

* * *

He went for a long swim in the afternoon. Then he lay on the beach and slept.

He woke up disoriented.

Was Jo back? Across the road was a bar with a public telephone. The directory was an incomprehensible mass of Greek; he enlisted the help of the barman, who found the number. He asked to be put through to Jo's room.

The ringing tone went on for some time, then her voice said, 'Hello?'

'Hi,' he said, 'It's me.'

'Ben! Sorry, I was in the shower. I've been asleep.'

'Me too.'

'Where are you?'

'On the beach. Not your beach, another one.'

'Oh.'

There was a pause. Then he said, 'Can I see you?'

'Yes. George is taking people out to dinner — clients.'

'Right. The bar opposite your hotel, in an hour. Okay?'

'Yes.'

He rang off. He didn't like the idea that she was only able to see him because George was doing something else.

At the bar he bought a bottle of cold white wine, asking for two glasses. The barman provided bowls of olives and nuts, and Ben went out to a table on a wooden balcony overlooking the beach.

She arrived, cool in a loose white blouse and short black skirt. She looks so unapproachable, he thought, watching her before she had spotted him, I can't believe she kissed me like she did this morning.

Then she saw him, and the aloofness in her face disappeared. She hurried out to him. 'Hello,' she whispered.

'Are you okay?'

'I am now.'

'How was lunch?'

She made a face. 'Awful. Well, the food was nice, and the drink. That was too nice, George was walloping it back as if prohibition was looming. I told him I was going home on Thursday, and he said why, and I said something about money, and he said why didn't I move in with him, and I said no, and he got shirty.'

He said tonelessly, 'I didn't know you were going so soon.'

Her head shot up. 'Oh, Ben, I'm sorry — oh,

God, it's all so complicated.' She drank quite a lot of wine, then went on, 'I don't like the idea of being here with George, and neither do I like the idea of being here after I've told him to piss off.'

He looked at her. So much about her's unknown. But if she's going home in four days I don't have the luxury of finding it all out slowly.

He said, 'Do you like the idea of being here with me?'

She replied quietly, 'I like the idea of being anywhere with you.' She lifted her face and he kissed her.

He felt her draw in a deep breath. 'I think I'd like to go.'

'Okay.'

They went down the wooden steps onto the beach, walking slowly along the shoreline. When they had passed the last light they turned away from the sea and sat down on the sand. He lay on his back and put his arms round her, pulling her to him. He gathered her hair in his hands, twisting it around his wrist.

'Let's go to France,' he said suddenly.

She was silent for a while. Then she said, 'Is that possible?'

'It is for me.'

'But what about . . . oh, I don't know. Haven't you got a job, or a flat?'

He smiled. Maybe she hadn't had much to do with shiftless beach bums. 'I have a room which I rent by the week. My job ceases the moment I decide not to do it any more. But I accept it may be more complicated for you.'

She thought for a while. 'Not really. As you accurately surmised yesterday, I'm out of a job. If I go back to London on Thursday, it won't take me long to tie up the loose ends.'

She'll make a good beach bum, he thought. 'How long? A few days?'

'Mmm.'

She was silent for so long he thought she'd forgotten the question. 'Is that it?' he prompted.

'Mm? Oh, sorry, I was thinking about my mother.'

'Right.' Why not? 'So, a few days.'

'Yes. Then I'll meet you in . . . where? Nice?'

'Okay.'

'I know!' Her face lit up. 'I could send you a telegram when I've booked a flight.'

He looked at her resignedly. 'Now there's a good idea. Then I won't have to meet every plane from London till you finally get off one.'

'Don't mock. It's all right for you, I've never done anything like this before.'

He hugged her very tightly. 'I don't make a habit of it, either.'

He felt a tremor run through her. 'I must be mad,' she muttered.

He shifted his body against hers and began to kiss her, gently at first but with increasing persistence, waves of excitement running through him. And she responded, her lips and tongue moving to his rhythm, her body curving under his hand as he ran it down over her hips, across her stomach and into her waist. She moaned softly as he moved to her breast, gently cupping the round fullness, his fingers

107

reaching inside her blouse to touch bare flesh.

He made himself stop.

She whispered, 'What is it? What's wrong?'

He sat up, pulling her up beside him.

'Jo, nothing's wrong. But, not here. You know?'

She let out a great sigh. 'I suppose you're right. There's probably a by-law against it.' She drooped dejectedly. Then she twisted round, looking into his face. Her expression was a mixture of the mischievous and the seductive that almost changed his mind.

He stood up hurriedly. Shaking his head, he began to laugh. 'Come on.' He took her hand, dragging her to her feet. 'Race you back to the bar.'

★ ★ ★

'What about tomorrow?' he asked as they climbed back up onto the road.

'Oh, God! I forgot.'

'What?'

'George wants us to take a boat out tomorrow. He wants you to come so we can use your equipment.'

Bastard, Ben thought angrily. 'Too bad if I'm planning on doing something else,' he said sarcastically.

'Are you?' she asked in a small disappointed tone.

He hugged her. 'No. It's okay, I'm not sore at you. Sure, I'll come.'

★ ★ ★

He drove home. He didn't relish the idea of a day in George's company, even if — especially if — Jo was there too. Why couldn't she get rid of him? What was so hard about saying, get lost George, you bastard?

Then he felt sorry. Hell, she's not doing too bad, she's just said she'll come to France with me.

He didn't think he'd really taken it in till that moment.

France. With Jo.

He felt again the surge of desire he'd felt for her on the beach, the response in her that had nearly driven him on to take her there and then.

He reckoned he could be patient a while longer.

8

George telephoned in the morning, and Ben acted surprised but said he'd go with them. George asked him to collect 'me and my woman' — which made Ben wince — from his apartment. He tried not to react when he saw Jo with George. It was tough, especially when George said something about the breakfast he'd just made for her.

'I had an early call at my hotel,' she said in her clear voice. 'They seemed amazed at someone wanting to be woken up so early.'

'You could have had a lie-in if you'd been staying with me,' George said to her as they got into the car.

He didn't catch her reply, but it sounded like, 'Shut up, George.'

The exchange didn't bode well for the day ahead.

Ben drove out to a fishing village where he knew several of the fishermen. He spotted his friend Takis, sitting on the quayside smoking, apparently doing nothing at all. Takis was prepared to take them, and after an amicable haggle over the price, they went on board.

Ben realized straight away he should never have agreed to go. He stood with Takis as the sturdy little boat chugged away from the quay. George had moved to sit by Jo, and he put his hand on her shoulder, pushing back the sleeve of her T-shirt and caressing the bare skin, his dark head close to hers as he spoke urgently to her. I'll kill him. Jeez, I wanted her badly enough already.

You didn't have to do this, baby.

Ben only had two sets of scuba equipment, so he suggested coldly that Jo and George should dive first. As he tightened the straps on her air-tank her eyes caught his. He looked away.

She and George disappeared over the side.

After only a short time, a head broke surface a hundred yards towards the shore, followed by another. 'George has got a nosebleed,' Jo called out. 'Can you give me a hand?'

He swam to where they were bobbing on the gentle swell. George's nose was pouring blood.

'What happened?' Ben asked. Perhaps Jo had belted him.

George was wiping his face, staring aghast at his bloodied hand. 'I don't know! It just began pouring out.' He made a retching sound. 'I can't stand the sight of blood!'

'Particularly when it's your own,' Jo said.

'You might show some concern, darling,' George began, 'you — '

Ben said, 'Turn on your back, I'll tow you to the boat.'

It was difficult to keep George on his back; he seemed to find it hard to relax. Preoccupied, Ben was only vaguely aware of Jo swimming along behind. She was singing happily to herself. It didn't seem appropriate, and he wondered what George was thinking.

She waited in the water while Ben got the

equipment off George and sat him down, handing him a towel. Strapping on the air-tank, Ben said, 'Takis'll give you some wine, if you ask him nicely.'

George was staring at him accusingly. 'Are you just going to leave me?'

'Reckon so.' Ben tightened the waist strap.

George scowled over the side at Jo. 'And what about you?'

'I'm going diving with Ben.'

'See you, George,' Ben said, and flipped back into the water.

They swam underwater some way. She didn't seem to be taking much notice of the beauties of the seabed; she reached for his hand, and pointed upwards. He kicked out for the surface beside her, and as soon as she had removed her mouth-piece she said, 'I'm sorry, Ben, I really am sorry. I didn't think it'd be like this.'

'Like what? I'm having a great time. It's fun out here, just the three of us.'

'I said I was sorry.' She sounded near to tears.

He laughed shortly. 'Another mistake, huh?'

She nodded miserably. 'I didn't plan it — him being all over me.' She looked straight into his eyes. 'I saw you watching us. I wasn't doing it on purpose.'

'No, I know that. It's okay.' Suddenly he felt happier. 'Good about the nosebleed. I reckoned you'd socked him.'

'I might have, given a bit longer. Over breakfast he kept talking about these friends of his who made love under water.'

112

He felt sick. 'And he had it in mind for you to do the same?'

She lifted her chin. '*He* might have done. Fortunately it takes two.'

He felt suitably reprimanded. 'Right. Come on, let's swim.'

★ ★ ★

It was better, after that. They swam ashore to a deserted bay where they sat on a rock and amused themselves watching George beckoning to them. They pretended they thought he was waving, and waved cheerfully back.

Back at the boat, it was obvious he was restraining his annoyance with difficulty. 'You've been a hell of a time,' he grumbled as they climbed aboard. 'Didn't you see me telling you to come back?'

'Telling?' Ben said quietly.

'It was lovely,' Jo said. 'I could have stayed down all day.'

'I thought you were going to,' George said tartly.

'How's the nose?' Ben asked.

'All right.' George sniffed. 'Perhaps I won't sue you after all.'

'I'm not responsible for the state of your blood vessels.' Ben felt his anger rising.

'You're liable if I come to harm because you left me out here instead of getting me back for treatment. You — '

'You haven't come to harm,' Jo interrupted. 'Now for God's sake let's have some lunch.'

113

★ ★ ★

They lazed on board after lunch; Ben said they shouldn't dive again after drinking two and a half bottles of wine. George kept trying to talk to Jo, and she pretended to be asleep. Ben knew she was pretending because once she opened the eye nearer to him, winked, and closed it again. Eventually George gave up, turning away from her and lying down. Is he really asleep, or is he pretending too? Ben wondered. Still wondering, he closed his eyes and felt himself drift off. It's not surprising I'm tired, he thought drowsily, I didn't get too much sleep last night.

When he woke, clouds were building up; Takis announced that it was going to rain, then shambled into action and got the boat heading for home.

Ben thought they might make it ashore before the rain began. As they edged alongside the stone quay, black clouds were gathering right overhead, threatening down malevolently as the first resounding clap of thunder blasted out across the bay. Huge drops of rain began to fall, bouncing on the water like stones shied by children; the brooding gloom was fleetingly lit by flashes of lightning which cut through the clouds and stuck their jagged trident ends down deep into the sea.

Ben, sorting out a fold of notes for Takis, threw his car keys to George. 'Go open up the car,' he said.

Jo climbed onto the quay behind George, and they ran quickly up to the car. But after a moment

114

she came back. She jumped down into the boat, panting and flushed.

'I forgot to say thank you,' she gasped, holding out her hand to Takis.

'*Tipota*,' he said.

'Okay?' Ben asked her as they ran back to the car.

'No!' She sounded furious. 'I'm coming in the front with you. George just tried to get my clothes off on the pretext of rubbing me dry. He makes me *sick*.' She was red with anger. 'He's taking me out to dinner tomorrow, and that will be the last time I *ever* see him.'

'But why — '

She turned angrily to him. '*Not now*.'

Christ, he thought, I don't believe this. One minute he makes her sick, the next she's having dinner with him. He grabbed her arm. 'Tell him now,' he said urgently.

'Don't tell *me* what to do!' she hissed back. 'I just want to get back to my room.' She glared at him. '*On my own*.'

Terrific, he thought as she got into the front seat and slammed the door. So now what?

He drove them back into town in stony silence. At one point George told Jo she should go back with him to have a hot bath. She said icily, without turning round, 'I have a perfectly adequate bathroom in my hotel.'

'You could — ' George began.

'Oh, bugger off, George.'

Ben caught sight of George's face in the rear view mirror. One nostril wadded with stained cotton wool, his face pale, he didn't look too happy. Despite everything, Ben felt a stab of sympathy.

* * *

He left her alone the next day. It wasn't easy, and several times he almost picked up the phone to call her. But the continuing presence of George irritated him to the extent that it almost spilled over and made him cross with Jo as well. Until she'd got rid of George, he didn't want to know.

* * *

All through the long afternoon and into the evening, he waited. Why the hell couldn't the bastard have taken her to lunch instead of dinner? He needed to know what was going on. At eleven he tried calling her, but there was no reply. He tried again at midnight, and she still hadn't come back. Unable to remain where he was, he went to look for her.

The hotel was quiet. There was a light in the lobby and, watching from the darkness across the road, he saw the clerk sitting at the desk. After some time the man got up, yawning, and disappeared into the back of the hotel.

Ben ran quickly into the lobby and up the stairs.

Jo's door was locked, but the lock gave quite easily when he inserted a strip of stiff plastic into the door-jam and pressed back the latch. He went into the room, closing the door behind him. He sat down to wait.

Thunder was growling in the distance. After a while it began to rain heavily, and he got up to close the balcony doors.

★ ★ ★

It was after two in the morning when she came back. He had been through torments, imagining dreadful scenarios culminating in Jo deciding it was George she wanted after all and climbing into bed with him. Some dummy I'm going to look, he thought bitterly, waiting all night for a woman who's sleeping with someone else. But he couldn't leave.

He heard dragging footsteps, and the door opened.

He got up, staring at her as she came into the room.

She looked dreadful. She was soaked, her dress was torn and clinging to her, and the sandals she carried in her hand had a broken heel. Her face was streaked with mascara, and her eyes were red and swollen.

She stared at him. 'Ben,' she said. And fell forwards into his arms.

He held her tightly, feeling her body tremble. 'You're home now,' he said, rocking her gently and rubbing his face against her wet hair. She smelt very strongly of alcohol — brandy, he thought. 'You're all right now,' he went on soothingly, watching as rivulets of muddy water ran from her over the stone floor.

She went on clinging, not speaking. She felt very

cold. 'We could stand here for the rest of the night,' he said softly, 'which'd be fine by me. But you're very cold, and I reckon a hot, deep bath would be a good idea.'

'A hot bath,' she echoed. 'How lovely.'

'I'll run it for you,' — he hoped his confidence in a small Greek hotel's ability to produce hot water at two in the morning wasn't misplaced — 'and you can tell me what happened. If you want to?' He looked into her face. She was very pale, her eyes ringed with black. 'You look like a panda,' he added, 'a panda out on the razz.'

'Yes. No.'

'Right.' He decided she needed a bit of guidance. 'Sit down,' he pushed her into a chair, 'I'll tell you when your bath's ready.'

He put a lot of her bath foam into the water. He tried not to think about what could have led to her coming back so late and in such a state. 'It's ready,' he said, emerging into the bedroom, 'hot and steamy.'

Wordlessly she got up and went into the bathroom. He heard her clothes drop onto the floor, and water running as she cleaned her teeth. Then there was quite a lot of splashing, and he heard her go, 'Ooooooh.'

'What's up?'

'Hot water, finding all the bits that hurt.'

It sounded as if she was washing herself very thoroughly. He didn't want to think about that, either. She came back wearing a bath robe, her head wound up in a towel.

'I had to wash it,' she said, rubbing at her hair, 'it was full of brandy.'

'Right.' No doubt she'd explain in her own good time.

She came and sat limply beside him on the bed, and he took over rubbing her hair.

'What happened?' he asked.

She closed her eyes. 'I never want to see him again. And I should think he feels exactly the same about me.'

'Why?'

She looked at him sheepishly. 'I hit him on the head with a decanter.'

He couldn't help smiling. 'So that's why you came home reeking of brandy? From the decanter?'

She nodded. 'Yes. It went everywhere, all over him, and into my hair and my eyes.' She shuddered. 'He'd been drinking a lot all evening, first over dinner, then in this frightful night club. When we got back I still hadn't told him what I had to — I tried, really I did, but it was as if he knew and wasn't going to let me — and so I went up to his flat with him.'

'You're a dummy, Jo,' he said gently.

'I know.' She put her face down into her hands. There was a pause. 'I was so stupid, I thought I could handle it. I told him I didn't feel like that about him any more — you know — and he said he'd show me I did, he'd have me begging him for more, and then . . . then . . . oh, Ben, he pushed me down on the floor and tried to rape me.'

He put his head down on her shoulder and took a deep breath. He said, 'I didn't want you to go. I almost called you and asked you not to. We could have seen him together, told him together. Christ, I wish we had.'

'I know. I just felt . . . it seemed like something I had to do on my own, to get myself free. Before you — we . . .'

He took hold of her hands. He couldn't look at her. Gently he touched the bruises on her wrists, imagining George holding her down. He thought bitterly of all he had wanted to do with her, and how George had ruined everything. He said quietly, 'Did he hurt you?'

'Not really. I knelt on a bit of glass from the decanter.' She lifted her knee up to have a look.

'Do you have a Band Aid?' he asked. 'It's still bleeding.'

Silently she pointed, and he fetched a plaster and ointment from the dressing-table drawer. He felt her watching him as he mopped up the slow-welling blood. He couldn't speak.

Suddenly she said, 'He didn't do it, you know. He didn't rape me — he didn't even get near.'

He raised his eyes to look at her. The relief was huge, and he was honest enough to admit it was as much for his own sake as for hers. 'Oh, good,' he said inadequately.

Her green eyes studied him intently. Then slowly she smiled. He moved up closer to her, and she put her arms round him. 'I hit him when he — when it was just starting.' Her voice was low. 'He was lying on top of me and I couldn't push him off, and then I got hold of the decanter and broke it over his head. That stopped him.'

'Yes, I imagine it would have.'

'Do you think he'll be all right?'

'I don't honestly care. Probably.' He stared into her face, drawing his fingers down her cheek. 'How do you feel now?' he asked softly.

'Fine. I'm very resilient.'

'Great.'

'Why?'

He looked solemnly and steadily into her eyes. 'Because,' he broke off to kiss her, 'I love you, and if you feel the same about me, we might consider doing something about it.'

Her eyes blinked quickly a couple of times. '*Love*,' she whispered. Then: 'Yes, I do love you.'

He kissed her again, and her mouth was warm, soft and responsive. She tasted slightly of brandy overlaid with toothpaste. He pushed her back against the pillows, kicking off his shoes and swinging his legs up onto the bed.

He stroked her hair, reaching underneath it to curve his hand around her neck, and she sighed. He loosened the sash of her bath robe, and slipped his hand inside. She was naked, her body warm. She reached up to unbutton his shirt, and he took it off. He looked down at her, then opened her robe.

Revealed before him she was beautiful. His eyes ran over her, then focused on her breast.

The fierce pressure of George's fingers had made dark bruises. Three distinct black marks, two fainter ones.

He turned his head away. She must have realized what he had seen; she pulled him back, holding him very closely. 'Don't,' she whispered. 'Don't draw away.'

He buried his face in her damp hair.

'Don't let it spoil things,' she said urgently. 'Please.'

He raised his head and looked down at her. 'Okay.'

They kissed, hands running over each other setting them on fire. Their breath came fast, quickening together, their hunger for one another flaring till it was irresistible. She was reaching down, unzipping his jeans. Then he, too, was naked.

For a moment he held back. Then he kissed her again, feeling her body arch up towards him, knowing how much she wanted him. But he was hesitant still, haunted by what she had been through.

Something in him released its hold. Responding at last to the strength of her desire for him, his passion overwhelmed him. Holding her tightly, kissing her as though he would never stop, he began to make love to her.

9

Ben stood in the concourse of Nice airport, listening to the announcement informing him the flight from London Gatwick was an hour and a half late.

What do I do with an extra ninety minutes of waiting?

He looked around. There was a restaurant upstairs; he might as well go get some lunch.

It was less than a week since she'd gone, but it had been interminable. I miss her this much, he thought, because we spent every minute together, those two days before she went back to London. He smiled, remembering how they'd woken up in her hotel room that first morning and she'd immediately wanted to go out, in case George came after her with another decanter. They'd gone up to Bellapais, then found a remote beach.

He'd suggested taking her to stay with Michael, where there was no possibility of George finding her. She said, 'Why can't I stay with you, in your place?'

'It's too small. And it's crammed with my stuff, you'd have to stand up all the time.'

'Why wouldn't it be you standing up?'

'It's my room.'

★ ★ ★

123

He never told her, but after he'd deposited her safely with Michael he went to visit George.

'What do *you* want?' George said ungraciously, standing in his doorway in a black silk dressing-gown, white-faced and bloodshot-eyed.

'Not much.' Ben pushed past him into the apartment. The curtains were still drawn, and the disarrayed room stank of brandy and stale cigarette smoke.

'I suppose you want some money for yesterday,' George said. 'How much? Let's get it over with, I don't feel like company.'

'The hell with yesterday.' Ben looked at him coldly. 'I'm here to tell you if you can't make it with a girl except by force, you should leave it alone.'

George stared blankly at him. Hungover and heavy with sleep, he was slow to grasp the implications. 'She broke my sodding decanter!' he shouted suddenly. 'It was bloody Waterford, too!'

'You asked for it.'

'What the hell's it got to do with you — and how do you come to know about it, anyway?' George came closer.

'It has everything to do with me,' Ben said quietly. 'And I'm telling you, leave her alone.'

'So you fancy my woman, do you?' George said, an unpleasant smile on his face. 'At least it shows you've got taste.' Scathingly he looked Ben up and down. '*You* won't get anywhere with her.'

Ben took a deep breath. 'I wouldn't say any more, George.'

George sat down on the sofa, laughing unpleasantly.

'She used to be fun, terrific in the sack,' he taunted, 'but she's gone sophisticated. Not your type at all.'

'That's for us to decide.'

But George had shot up again. Judging by the fury suffusing his face, he'd just cottoned on. 'So that's it!' he said in total amazement. 'It was you buggered it up!'

Ben stood silent, his eyes cold and hostile.

'Fuck you, Ben!' George exploded. 'I introduced you!'

'You didn't.'

'You bastard! You've had her, haven't you? Last night, was it? After I'd got her roused for you?'

'Shut up,' Ben said warningly.

'I invite her out here, get her lined up nicely,' George went on, unheeding, 'and then you pinch her from me before I have a chance to get what I want! Can't you find your own bloody woman?'

Ben was breathing hard. 'I won't take this, George,' he began.

'All right then, damn you both! But just you listen to this!' George put his face close up to Ben, almost spitting with rage. 'If that little bitch can flit so quickly from my bed to yours, she'll be in just as much of a hurry to open her legs for the next man!'

Something flared up in Ben. White light flamed before his eyes and he watched as his fist slammed into George's face.

George sank onto the sofa, his hand to his bleeding lips, pain, shock and rage in his eyes. 'I'm calling the police,' he mumbled.

'Go right ahead. I guess they won't like attempted rape any more than I do.'

He slammed the door hard behind him and leapt off down the stairs, taking in great gulps of air. It was a while since he'd lost his temper — he'd been about eight and his sister had hidden his football — and already he felt ashamed.

He sat in the car for some time. Finally he reached down to start the ignition. As the car moved off, a slow smile spread over his sombre face.

He made a vulgar gesture in the direction of George's apartment and said aloud, 'Last time you kiss anyone for a while, pal.'

★ ★ ★

Dinner with Michael seemed civilized, by comparison. As they sat over coffee, Michael presented Jo with a jewellery box full of the most exquisite examples of his work.

'You have to choose something,' he said to Jo. 'I have Ben to thank for very many pieces of rock. He will not permit any other reimbursement, so only you can release me from my indebtedness.'

She was easily persuaded. She chose a heavy gold ring in the shape of two hearts joined at the top, with a diamond set in the middle. Without a word she handed it to Ben, who put it on the third finger of her left hand.

Then Michael opened champagne.

★ ★ ★

The last day had gone too quickly. When it was dark and quiet, Ben drove them out into the hills and they made love, lying afterwards looking up at the stars and listening to the racket of the cicadas.

'I wish they'd shut up,' he murmured drowsily.

'That one just there is Tithonus,' she said.

'Who?'

'Tithonus. He was a mortal who fell in love with Aurora, and he used to get up early every morning to watch her bringing the dawn. She asked Zeus to give him immortal life, but she forgot to ask if he'd give him eternal youth as well, so he grew older and older, and all dried up and wizened, so in the end she turned him into a grasshopper.'

He laughed quietly, and she said, 'What is it?'

'You put me in mind of a buddy of mine.'

She was thoughtful for a few moments. Then she said, 'Do you think I'd like your friends?'

'You'd like this one. He has his head in the clouds much of the time, too.'

'I do not have my head in the clouds!'

'Yes you do. You need someone like me, I have no idea how you've managed all these years.'

She put her arms round him.

'I haven't, either.'

★ ★ ★

His reverie was interrupted by another announcement: the London flight had landed. He paid his bill and ran downstairs.

She came at last, flying across the concourse

and flinging herself into his arms. They kissed for a good ten minutes, but this was France and everyone simply walked round them. He had found them a small hotel room for the night, and they went straight to it. Their passion for each other was too raw to wait, and they didn't emerge till morning.

'What shall we do now?' she asked as they sat over breakfast coffee and croissants.

'Finish our vacation.'

'Here?'

'No. I don't think I like Nice, it's too up-market for rucksacks.'

'All right. We could go west.'

'Okay.'

They spent the next two weeks meandering along the Riviera. They had whittled their possessions down to a few clothes, some cooking implements and two sleeping-bags. Jo said they were like the Wandering Hedgehog, whoever he was, with the whole wide world theirs to wander through.

They talked of going to Spain and then crossing into North Africa, or retracing their steps and going down through Yugoslavia into Greece. But apparently she found his way of thinking easy to catch, adopting his philosophy — this is lovely, why strive for anything more? — and they stayed where they were.

They spent a lot of time on beaches and in the sea, and he watched as she became as deeply tanned as he was. She attracted him fiercely, and he couldn't get enough of her; his thoughts were dominated by speculating where and when they'd next make love. Sometimes they would quietly disappear up into the hills in the evening to sleep beneath the stars, and sometimes they would stay in rooms, always the cheapest they could find. They spent so little time indoors that it didn't much matter what the accommodation was like; a clean bed was the major requirement.

They were together for almost every minute of the day. He had rarely spent so much concentrated time with another person, but such was her pull for him that he never found it too intense, never wanted the company of anyone else. They talked endlessly, telling of their pasts, their families, their schooldays, their loves and hates, and very soon he felt as if they had been together all their lives.

After some time they wanted a change. They had enjoyed the holiday mood long enough, and wanted to be somewhere quieter, somewhere they could slip in alongside people living their ordinary lives. They moved westwards until one evening, over a beer at a pavement café in St Raphael, they fell into conversation with a solitary English boy who had been working on a farm near Aix-en-Provence.

'It's hard work,' he said, and showed them his hands, the palms rough with callouses.

'Gosh,' Jo said. She caught Ben's eye, and he could see she was trying to keep her face serious.

'But they're friendly people,' the boy went on, 'typical of the peasantry round here, you know. And the food's great. *And* the wine, although newcomers have to take it easy at first.' He looked at Ben, smiling smugly.

'Right,' Ben said. 'I'll try to remember that.'

He heard Jo smother a laugh. 'What about the accommodation?' One-track mind, me, he thought.

'Oh, it's all right.' The boy seemed to have taken offence, and stood up to go.

'Would you give us the address?' Jo asked. She gave him an entrancing smile, and the young man blushed.

He sat down again. 'Of course I will.'

* * *

The farm was in a village to the east of Aix. 'Farm' was an inaccuracy, as far as Ben was concerned: they stood in the road looking at the hilly scrub rising up behind the farmhouse, and he said, 'Farms are meant to have cattle, and green rolling pastures with water-mills slowly turning.' He screwed his eyes up against the sun.

'And cowboys with guns.' Jo added, 'wearing chaps and stetsons.'

'No, that's ranches.'

'It's time you abandoned your stereotypes,' she said sternly.

She marched up the rutted track to the farmhouse. Oh, I like a determined woman, he thought, following her. She rapped on the door, and about a hundred dogs started barking. She looked at him. 'What do we say?'

He smiled. 'What's this 'we'? You're the one who speaks French.'

She coughed nervously. 'Oh.'

But he reckoned she did well. When the farmer came to the door, she launched instantly into

130

conversation with him. 'He doesn't want anyone on the land,' she said, turning to Ben, 'but he asks if we can do horses — he runs a livery stable. At least, I think that's what he's saying.'

'Can you do horses?' he asked, grinning.

'I'll manage. How about you?'

'Oh, sure.'

The farmer's formalities for the engaging of labour were sketchy. They could start in the morning, and he'd give them board and lodging plus pocket money. When he didn't want them any more he'd tell them.

Jo, her face tense with concentration as she tried to translate the farmer's rapid-fire Provencal French, said to Ben, 'What do you think?'

He thought the farmer was probably getting a good deal; he would be able to lay them off the moment their expense was no longer a sufficiently small percentage of what they earned for him. But it was an attractive place, and he didn't want to go any further.

'It's fine,' he said. 'Tell him we'll take it.'

⋆ ⋆ ⋆

They met the household over dinner. The farmer was a robust man on the verge of vigorous old age, and it was clear he forced a living from his truculent acres only by making his three sons, his wife, his daughter-in-law and his labourers work even harder than he did himself.

Later, the farmer showed them over the farm. Market garden produce was grown alongside the

131

slow river that curved close by the long wooden-shuttered farmhouse. In addition to the neat rows of vegetables — set out with slide-rule precision — there were apple and pear trees. Where the land began to struggle up towards the mountains, among the spicy aromatic herbs and the lavender bushes, the farmer's wife kept her bees.

They settled in very quickly. The farmer observed them closely for a day, less closely for a couple more, then apparently concluded that they knew what they were doing and left the running of the stables entirely in their hands. As long as one of them brought him the correct amount of money at the end of the day — and they always managed to — he was satisfied.

Jo and the cobbled courtyard behind the farmhouse became all the world to Ben that summer. Initially he slept with her in a small attic room, but it was hot up there so close under the roof, and he was very aware of the presence of the household close by. As he and Jo found their way around the stable block they discovered rooms above the tack room and feed store, reached by an external staircase. These upper rooms still contained furniture which, although dusty and cobwebby, was solid and serviceable.

'We could move in up there,' he said. 'It's dry, it only needs a clean.'

'Do you think he'd mind?'

'We can ask him.' She shot him a look. 'Okay, you can ask him.'

She spoke to the farmer over dinner, and he had no objection.

'*Mais il faut faire ce nettoyage le dimanche, eh?*' he said, fixing her with a glare.

'*Oui, bien sûr.*'

'What did he say?'

She smiled. 'Guess! He says we have to do it on a Sunday. He obviously doesn't want us sorting out our domestic arrangements in working hours.'

The next Sunday, they moved out the furniture and gave it a wash, then scrubbed the walls and floors and slapped on a couple of coats of whitewash. They cleaned the windows and the cupboards, then rearranged the furniture to make a bedroom and a kitchen/living room. The old iron bedstead was in reasonable condition, and, with the addition of the mattress and bedding from their attic, comfortable.

Hot, sweaty and dirty, they stood in the middle of their new kitchen, arms round each other, leaning together for support.

'We've cracked it, Dimitrios!' he said happily. 'Let's have a party, to celebrate.'

She laughed. 'It'll have to be a select gathering, we know so few people. There's the farmer, and Madame, but I don't really think . . . '

He silenced her with a kiss. 'I know you,' he said after some time. 'I wasn't reckoning on asking anyone else.'

10

Days on the farm began early. People liked to ride before it got too hot, and the horses had to be ready by eight o'clock. Paths led up into the herby hills behind the farmhouse, and rides had been marked out. Most people took a one or two-hour hack before ten or after four, although the afternoon riders often failed to turn up.

'Too much vino,' Ben remarked. 'Newcomers need to take it easy.'

They had lunch in the farmhouse with the family, always ravenously hungry after the long morning. Although the food was plain it came in vast quantities, and was washed down with a red wine so dark that it turned the teeth black. The family made it from their own grapes. Ben, overindulging one evening and waking up with an appalling headache, referred to it as Napoleon's Revenge.

Jo's rudimentary French flourished. Her confidence grew by the day, and he admired her for the way she was making herself at home in a strange environment.

'Why don't you try?' she asked him.

'Try what?'

'Speaking French.'

He only knew a few words. Whenever communication became difficult, he would shrug amiably and leave it to her. He hadn't realized she'd noticed. 'Not my strong point, languages,' he said airily.

'I could teach you, if you like.'

He thought of Hal, trying patiently to teach him basic Greek. Hal had got virtually nowhere; Ben's Greek began and ended with 'What time is it, please?' He didn't see why Jo should do any better.

'I'd sooner you didn't,' he said, planting a kiss on her cheek because she'd looked momentarily disappointed.

★ ★ ★

The whole farm took a siesta after lunch, two blessed hours when all activity ceased. Ben and Jo would return to their courtyard to go upstairs to bed. Often he'd be too tired, too full of food and wine, to want to make love, and he'd alarm himself with visions of losing the urge forever.

Shortly before four they'd get ready for the evening clients. The last of these had to be back by seven, and, after seeing to the horses and taking the farmer his money, that was it for the day. They'd have supper, then walk down to the village for a drink.

It was a pleasure to get back to the courtyard, where the peace of the hills fell on them like a soothing hand, where the strange foreign scents of herbs, lavender and citrus blew in through the open window. Then they would draw close, and the happy contented companionship of the long

135

day burst into passion. No need to have worried, he'd think.

One day during a short spell of cooler, rainy weather, they had no customers at all.

'Let's take off, before anyone turns up,' Jo suggested. 'We'll tell the farmer we've got to exercise the horses.'

'Okay,' he said. 'You go get us some food, and I'll round up a couple. Which one d'you want?'

'I don't mind, there's not much to choose between them. Get the two that are easiest to catch.'

She went over to the farmhouse to fetch food, water and a bottle of the fierce red wine, and he tacked up the horses and found a couple of sacks to keep the rain off.

By midday it was fine.

They followed the course of a wide, shallow river that curved slowly between banks of willow. They walked the horses along in the water, watching the enamelled colours of dragonflies hovering over the surface.

'Walking in water's good for horses,' she said, 'they do it with racehorses to strengthen their legs.'

He reflected on the efforts it took to coax this pair into anything more than a grudging trot. 'I think we're wasting our time.'

Rounding a bend, they came across a man and a woman standing in the water, hands outstretched, trying to attract the dragonflies. They were having some success until Jo and Ben splashed into sight and scared the insects away. 'Oh!' the woman exclaimed, 'they've gone!'

'Sorry,' Jo said, dismounting, 'we didn't mean to disturb the peace. Damn!' She had just discovered that the water was much deeper where she was, and she had wet her jeans up to the thigh.

'Thanks for the warning,' Ben said, and rode to the bank, where his horse squelched noisily out of the water. He glanced over his shoulder at the older couple. 'There won't be a dragonfly in miles, now.'

They got into conversation, knee-deep in the water while the horses stood tethered under the trees, tearing at the long grass with their tails lazily swishing the flies away. The man and woman were English, retired and taking a long holiday in a camper. They invited Jo and Ben to stay for a drink; they joined the older couple on the bank above the river.

Jo handed Ben a coarse doorstep. He looked dubiously at the hunk of French bread with its thick slice of ham. She must have seen, and he watched her face with amusement as she caught sight of the older woman deftly slicing all manner of vegetables into a pretty pattern on two plates, adding hard-boiled eggs and neat triangles of bread. The woman noticed too, and said kindly, 'I expect your young man appreciates something nice and solid.'

He dug his teeth into the doorstep. I'm not so sure, he thought, reckon I'd prefer what they're having.

'Have some more wine,' the older man offered. Another refill all round finished it off, and he remarked, 'Rotten little bottles, aren't they?' Ben

137

apologetically shared out the Napoleon's Revenge, which the man said admiringly was the roughest wine he'd ever tasted.

They finished the meal with coffee, made in the camper, then Ben and the older man went back to wade in the river, leaving Jo and the woman deep in conversation. When Ben and Jo finally decided they really had to go, they found themselves warmly shaken by the hand and hugged.

'Wasn't that nice?' she said as they rode away.

'Yeah. What were you talking about?'

'Marriage and morals. How about you?'

He smiled. 'Nothing so worthy.'

'What, then?'

'Fishing.'

Her laughter echoing on the water beneath the trees sounded to Ben like birdsong.

★ ★ ★

A week later, Jo slipped on the staircase leading up to their quarters and fell heavily on to her left shoulder.

Ben was down in the yard, and came running round to see what the racket was. He found her lying biting her lips, clasping her left arm where the blood was oozing out between her fingers. She had gone quite white.

He felt as if someone had just kicked him very hard in the stomach.

He knelt down beside her. 'You can go 'ouch' if you like,' he said, trying to make his voice normal. She emitted a noise between a sob and a giggle.

'Have you busted anything?'

'No, don't think so.'

He moved her arm up and down gently and made her wiggle her fingers. 'No, it's okay. It's just cut badly. Can you make it up the stairs?'

'Apparently not. But I'll have another go.'

He was worried at how pale she was. 'Did you bang your head?'

'Yes.' She took hold of his hand and guided it to a great lump coming up on her forehead.

He exclaimed sympathetically. 'Ah, poor baby. Real Tom and Jerry stuff, huh?'

'Yes. And you should see the stars I'm seeing.'

He waved his hand in front of her face. 'How many fingers am I holding up?'

She grinned weakly. 'Seven. No, it's all right, I'm joking. Two and a thumb.'

He helped her upstairs and put her to bed, washing the cut in her arm and bandaging it. Then she promptly went to sleep.

He went to try to explain to the farmer what had happened, miming that he thought Jo ought to stay in bed. The farmer agreed, and offered to send across one of his labourers to help while Jo was laid up. He sent her some brandy, which Ben thought was kind and made him regret they'd made unkind remarks about the farmer's avarice.

She felt much better the next day, and he put a chair out for her in the yard so that she could be with him. Her arm and shoulder remained too stiff for her to work, and she asked him to see if he could get her something to read. He went into the village, coming back with an English newspaper that was four days old and a paperback copy of 'Biggles Flies West', which she said she'd read. She finished both in a morning.

'Will you get me something else?' she pleaded. 'I can't just sit here watching you, it's too frustrating.'

'Tomorrow,' he said. 'I know all about concussion, I had it one time. I don't want you having a relapse.'

He realized, as he watched her sleep the afternoon away, just how much he didn't want her having a relapse.

The next day, unable to find any more suitable reading matter in the village, he brought her back a thick pad of paper and a biro.

'What's this?' she asked.

'Paper and a biro. No more books, they've sold out. You have to write your own.'

'Oh!'

'Now's your chance, baby.' He kissed the top of her head as she sat in the sunshine, the paper on her lap. 'You told me the day after I met you that you were going to write your own stories.'

She laughed. 'I'm sure I didn't!'

'Yes you did. I remember it clearly.'

She looked at the blank pages. Then she looked dubiously up at him.

'You can do it,' he said gently. 'A thousand words before lunch.'

She made a face. He smiled at her. 'You can stop if your bump starts to hurt.'

Several times during the morning he looked over to where she sat, her fair head bent over the pad, writing furiously. He had absolute faith that she could do it; he had come to realize that all sorts of things went on in her mind. The jumble of myths, tales and odd facts she came out with suggested she'd read a lot, and indicated a colourful imagination.

He found he was looking forward to lunchtime.

The last clients finally departed, and he went and stood quietly in front of her.

'Hang on,' she said, 'I've just got to get her away from the Chimaera.'

'Okay,' he said. 'Can I see?'

He took the sheaf of papers from under the stone she'd weighed them down with. There were eight pages, covered on thirteen of their sides with her close writing. The remaining three had detailed illustrations. He glanced at a sketch of a serpentine creature with three wildly different heads all glaring formidably at a diminutive figure with transparent wings, then began to read.

'In the topmost branches of an ancient oak was a house made of goose down and gipsywort. In this house lived a winged creature.'

His eyes still scanning the pages, he sank slowly to sit on the ground beside her.

So Jo's Elfie was born. Ben hadn't much use for fairy stories, but he could see that this one of Jo's had something. It was simple, but had a dream-like quality which appealed to the imagination. The illustrations were beautiful, which wasn't surprising since she'd spent years making her living doing drawings.

'What do you think?' she asked him sometime later.

141

He regretted that he hadn't made a comment straight away. She seemed on edge, as if it really mattered what he said, and he found it touching.

'I think it's great.' He grinned at her. 'And I'm a philistine, so if it appeals to me, it'll appeal to anyone.'

She looked back at him, her face serious. She said, 'I don't think you're a philistine.'

'Ah, but you're prejudiced.'

She shrugged. 'I expect so.' Then she said, very softly, 'I'm glad you liked it.'

★ ★ ★

The weeks passed, and, as September progressed, custom at the stables dwindled. It came as no surprise when, over lunch one day, the farmer informed them that he was dispensing with their services at the end of the week.

They went back to their room to review the situation. They had quite a lot of money, since they'd saved most of their pay. He watched her sitting on the floor counting the notes. He noticed that she was putting them all in one pile; he found it endearing that it clearly hadn't occurred to her to divide it in two.

What now? he wondered.

The long summer of living with her, working and relaxing side by side, had consolidated his strong initial desire for her into something much deeper. He couldn't imagine life without her now.

I reckon I really must love her, he thought.

'That's it,' she said, finishing her counting.

'There's nearly . . . Oh!' She stopped as she saw his expression. 'What is it?'

'Come here, it's not something I can say at a distance.'

She went and sat beside him on the bed, and he put his arms round her. 'Let's go home.'

She drew in her breath. 'We haven't got a home,' she whispered.

'I know. We'll make one.'

She turned towards him, he felt her shaking. He reckoned she was probably crying.

'I thought it was quite a nice idea,' he said mildly.

'Oh, so do I! So do I!' Her voice was quavery.

'We have to decide where to have this home,' he said, 'and we can either live in America or England.' She said nothing. He smiled; likely it was only a temporary reprieve. 'It's so long since I've lived at home,' he went on, 'that they've probably let my room and forgotten who I am, so we'd better go to England.'

There was a strangled sound, which he took for assent.

'In any case, we have to get a professional opinion on that heap of fairy stories of yours.' The first story had merely been the beginning; she had written ten more since. 'You can find someone to look at them in England?'

He felt her nod her head. 'Okay?' She nodded again.

He put his hand under her chin and lifted her face. Her eyes were swimming with tears, but he still thought she was beautiful.

During their last few days in Provence, he did a lot of thinking. He realized that, while it was okay to live for the day when it was just you, it wasn't such a good plan when someone else depended on you for their happiness.

And I guess I depend on her for mine, too. He remembered the cold blade of fear that had stabbed him when he'd found her at the foot of the staircase.

Beyond a vague idea that it'd happen one day, he had never thought much about marriage. Girls had come and girls had gone, and he'd said goodbye sometimes with pain and sometimes with relief. But there was no way he could imagine saying goodbye to Jo.

The logical next step was to make sure he didn't have to.

★ ★ ★

They were sitting on the 'up' platform of Lyons station waiting for the Paris train, which was twenty minutes late. Jo had just had a chocolate ice-cream, and she was wiping the remains of it off her chin with the back of her hand.

'I think,' Ben said, 'it'd be nice if we got married.'

She stopped in mid-wipe. Then she turned to look at him. She said, very softly, 'Oh, Ben.'

Then she was in his arms. She still smelled of chocolate, she must have missed a bit. She tasted of it, too, he thought as he kissed her. But he didn't care.

Interlude

Cornwall, Autumn 1973

Jo woke up just before seven on her wedding day.

She lay in bed wondering whether somebody would bring her a cup of tea, looking at her wedding dress hanging on the door. It was broderie anglaise; there was enough left of her French tan to make wearing white all right.

She thought about the day's arrangements.

Everything was ready for the reception later that day; her parents' house was full of autumn flowers, shining in the mellow October sunshine looking its gracious best.

Good old Mum. Jo smiled, thinking how her mother, faced with the prospect of organizing a wedding and a reception for forty people within a matter of weeks, had blanched. 'Why does it have to be so soon?' she had wailed, breaking off from muttering about guest lists and caterers.

'Because we want to be together!' Jo was quite incapable of putting into words her need to be united with Ben *now*.

Elowen Daniel regarded her worriedly. Then she shrugged. 'Very well.'

Jo thought, it was nice of her not to ask if I was pregnant.

She and Ben would have been happy with a modest register office ceremony, and she suspected her mother agreed. But Paul Daniel announced that he only had one daughter, and wanted to see her married in style.

'Then you can see to the invitations,' his wife said.

★ ★ ★

Jo had been so wrapped up in Ben that it hadn't occurred to her to warn her parents they were coming. Or that they were getting married. They arrived at the house late one evening, splashing out on a taxi from the station; they'd been travelling all day and were tired out.

They stood on the doorstep, brown and dusty, and Jo gave her father top marks for the aplomb with which he said, 'Jo! How nice. And I suppose you must be Ben. Come in and have a drink.'

It had been a surprise to find her father at home. Over the years, his work had taken him away for longer spells, to London first and then to Zurich, until now he only came to Cornwall for the occasional weekend. Jo thought little of it, although once she had asked her mother why she didn't live abroad too.

Elowen said something about having her heart too firmly in the South-West. 'I was born in this house. It was my parents', my grandparents' and my great-grandparents' before that. I love it.'

So Elowen stayed on in the elegant old house at the tip of Cornwall, pouring herself into her life there while first her husband, then her two sons, withdrew further into the enthralling world of

146

business. She referred to the house, or possibly to herself in it, as the 'family stronghold'; Jo thought they all felt better for having her there.

★ ★ ★

Now Elowen's stronghold was full again. She and Paul were in residence in the master bedroom, and their elder son Philip and his wife shared the best guest-room, which had its own bathroom. Jo and her other brother Geoffrey were back in the rooms they'd had as children.

'Typical bloody Jaqueline,' Jo grumbled to her mother. 'I'm the one getting married, yet she's managed to install herself and Phil in the luxury suite.'

Elowen said, 'I know, darling. But frankly I've got too much to think about to argue. I knew you wouldn't mind.'

Struck with a pang of guilt at all the worry and work her hasty marriage was giving her mother, Jo gave her a silent, intense hug.

★ ★ ★

It had taken Jo a while to wake up to the fact that her father might have reservations about Ben as a son-in-law. She found it difficult to see him through eyes other than her own, and she thought he was perfect. She sounded out her mother first. 'Mum, doesn't Dad like Ben?'

Elowen smiled. 'Darling, you can't *not* like Ben. Dad's as affected by his charm as the rest of us.

147

But fathers always worry about their daughters.'

'Do mothers?'

'Not as much.'

But then Ben wasn't a total surprise to her mother. Jo had told her about him when she'd come back to England in May, between Cyprus and France.

She had been amazed at Elowen's reaction. On being told that Jo was going to France to spend the summer with a man she'd known less than a week, Elowen said she was so relieved Jo wasn't going to marry George Fleming that *anything* else was preferable.

Her relief had taken a tangible form. As Jo saw her off at Paddington, Elowen pushed an envelope into her hand.

Jo opened it on the bus going back to her flat. Inside was a cheque for £250, and a note: 'Here's something for the rainy day I hope you never have. Good luck with your Ben. All love, Mum.'

Elowen had actually spoken to Ben. He phoned the flat, and Elowen had answered. She would never reveal what Ben said in the few moments it took Jo to get out of the bath and come to the phone, but Jo thought it must have been pretty impressive, because from then on her mother had a soft spot for Ben.

* * *

But her father wasn't given to soft spots. He remarked that Ben seemed to be something of a drifter. 'Does he propose to live solely on the earnings you may or may not receive from these fairy tales you've written?' he asked Jo.

'No!' She was indignant. 'He's got money saved which he's using now. Then he'll find work, he always does.'

'And where are you going to live? Has he thought about that?'

'*We*'ve thought about it. We do that sort of thing together nowadays, Dad, it's not just up to the man.' Paul made a sound like a snort, which she ignored. 'We've found a flat,' — hardly that, she thought ruefully — 'and Ben's going to move in and start getting it ready.'

It hadn't helped that Ben had needed to make two calls to America. He wanted someone called Hal to be his best man, but apparently had no idea where this Hal was. So he had to phone Hal's father in Chicago, and before he could do that he had to call his own parents so that they could look in his address book for the number.

Paul stood in the hall observing this transatlantic abuse of his telephone. He just happened to overhear Ben ask his father who was quarter-back for the 'Forty-Niners that season.

Jo caught her father's expression and gave Ben a nudge. 'Hurry up!' she hissed.

Later Ben went to find Paul. 'May I pay for the calls, sir?' he asked politely. 'I have the amounts.'

He had, too — he must have asked the operator. Paul looked slightly abashed. 'No, it's all right. Will your friend be able to come to the wedding?'

'I guess not.' Ben looked downcast. 'His father doesn't know where he is right now. The last

149

address he had for him is six weeks old, and he knows Hal's moved on. He's going to call back if he finds out.'

'Oh. Well, I hope he's in time.'

'Me too.'

The next day Ben bought Paul a bottle of whiskey, 'for the calls'. Paul, a gin man, didn't like scotch, but he appreciated the gesture.

★ ★ ★

Two weeks before the wedding, Sam Dillon phoned with the news that Hal had broken his ankle in Ithaca and was now lying in traction in a Messolonghi hospital. Ben returned from the hall and announced these tidings over dinner.

'What a frightful place to have one's leg in traction,' Paul remarked. 'Byron died there. I pity your friend, Ben.'

'Oh, Dad!' Jo could see how disappointed Ben was. It was hardly the time to talk about people dying. 'Did you get an address, Ben?'

Ben looked down at the piece of paper in his hand. 'Yeah.'

'Do you think he'll make it?'

'No, I don't imagine so.' She got up and went to hug him. With a visible effort Ben smiled and hugged her back. 'It's okay, I'll get my brother-in-law Steve to be best man instead.'

He went up another notch in Paul's esteem.

★ ★ ★

The person called Hal must have sent a telegram the moment he received Ben's letter; quite an effort, Jo thought, wondering how you'd go about it when lying in bed in a Greek hospital.

'*Sorry Ben no way I can make it STOP haven't even been up for a pee yet STOP wish you both all luck STOP writing Hal.*'

A few days later a bulky envelope arrived containing a formal negative reply to the wedding invitation, addressed to Elowen, and a letter for Ben. Jo watched his face as he read it. 'Poor guy stepped back and fell down some temple steps,' he said. 'He says he's getting our wedding present sent from the States, and that he knows it's something I've always wanted.'

Hal sent them an enormous, lavishly-illustrated book on the early history of the Americas. Ben, opening it, burst out laughing. Jo lost an entire morning to it when she should have been seeing the florist and the man about the cars.

★ ★ ★

Elowen did eventually bring Jo a cup of tea, and the news that she could have the bathroom in half an hour. The ceremony was at eleven; there was no more time for reverie.

The family assembled in the hall. Watching them depart, taking their places in the procession heading for the village church, Jo began to feel nervous, smitten with the seriousness of what she was about to undertake.

Ben set out from the flat, where he'd spent the

151

morning hoovering and arranging the presents and the cards. He and his brother-in-law, smart in US naval uniform, were almost the first to arrive at the church.

Ben's parents and two sisters walked the short distance from the inn in the village. Elowen had offered to put them up, but Mary MacAllister declined. 'You'll have more that enough without us,' she said. It was probably just as well, since Ben's married sister had an eleven-month old daughter who was teething and wanted the world to know it.

Relations and friends filled the little church, creating a soft noise of happiness and expectation. Elowen took her place, making her entrance on her younger son's arm, and then the stage belonged to Jo.

She took her father's arm, and they began the walk up the aisle. The ushers had done a good job of diverting many of the vast majority of 'bride' people to the MacAllister side, and at first she couldn't see Ben over all the heads. She spotted his father — no, Ben's not much like him — and the brother-in-law in uniform.

Then Ben stepped forward, turning round to smile at her.

She had never seen him look like that. He'd had a haircut, he was dressed in clothes his parents must have brought over — charcoal-grey suit, white shirt — and he had a white carnation in his buttonhole.

She thought, he's standing there waiting for me.

She began to tremble.

The scent of roses filled the air as they spoke the timeless words of commitment. She had chosen as her wedding ring the one Michael had given them; for the second time, Ben put it on her hand.

Church bells and organ music saw them jubilantly out into the sunshine. She wished afterwards that the euphoria hadn't affected her so strongly, because she found it hard to remember anything with any clarity after they left the church. It was all a confusion of loving good wishes, kisses, hats, flowers, speeches, laughter, cake and champagne.

But through it all was Ben, always Ben. She loved him so much she could hardly bear it.

Jo

Autumn 1973 – Summer 1980

11

Their wedding was the last that Jo and Ben saw of style and graciousness for some time. It was an abrupt step down to the austerity of their chilly little flat, but as the weeks went by they gradually made it more comfortable. Jo made curtains on her mother's sewing-machine, and Ben filled the cracks in the walls and painted everything light cream.

As their savings dwindled, Ben began to look determinedly for work. He was prepared to take on anything, but his talents lay in the outdoors; winter wasn't his time. Eventually he started labouring. His lean body grew stronger, but Jo silently lamented over the wreck of his finger-nails and the way the palms of his hands felt rough when he touched her. In the evenings he worked behind the bar in the local pub, which he claimed to enjoy even if some nights he looked dead on his feet by closing time. Jo, knowing he still had to wash up all the glasses before he could come home to bed, would viciously wish every last customer gone, quietly hating those who thought they'd just make room for another half and uncharitably hoping it'd choke them.

'I want to work in the pub, too,' she said.

'You've got your work already,' he replied.

She bought a second-hand typewriter, and a few days later Ben announced he had a surprise for her. 'Shut your eyes,' he said, taking her arm. He led her into the flat's living-room, placing her hands

157

on something that seemed to be made of wood. 'Okay, you can look now.'

He'd got her a beautiful old desk, with a raised section along the back full of little cupboards and shelves.

'Ben, it's wonderful! It must have cost the earth!'

'It didn't. It was in that old house we demolished. They were going to stick it in the auction, but I told them it had woodworm so they let me have it for £10.'

'Oh. Can we treat it with something?'

'I told *them* it has woodworm,' Ben said patiently.

She started to laugh. 'Ben, that's awful!'

'Sure, I know.'

★ ★ ★

All that hard winter she visualized Ben labouring while she sat typing in the warm. She knew how tough it was; he was often so worn out he'd fall asleep immediately after supper. Sometimes his nights were disturbed by nightmares.

She was desperately inspired to do her best. Eventually, her best was good enough; in May the following year, she had her first acceptance. By the time her stories had been edited, and her paintings reduced to child-sized pages, the small book of illustrated tales didn't seem a lot to show for all that hard work.

But success was infinitely sweet. With money in her hand again, she went out and bought three LPs, a thick navy pullover and a pair of jeans for Ben, a pad of expensive cartridge paper and fifteen pencils for herself, and champagne for the celebration.

Something about her Elfie caught on. Her agent sold the stories in America, and accompanying her first modest royalty cheque came a request for more. By autumn, another volume of tales was ready. Their fortunes had improved dramatically by then, for Ben had been working all summer for the local salvaging subsidiary of a multinational company, and they paid very well. He had also resurrected his teaching career, now including water-skiing and surfing.

He built up a good reputation. They like him, she thought, but it's more that that. It's as if he's lucky. Living in Cornwall most of her life, she knew the old superstitions of the sea were as strong as ever.

The time had come to buy a place of their own. In October, just after Jo's birthday and a week before their first wedding anniversary, they moved into a cottage on the Helford estuary, where the river met the sea.

★ ★ ★

Elowen was greatly relieved to see their life-style improving. She hadn't enjoyed their year in the flat, torn between a desire to help out and a determination not to hurt their feelings — especially Ben's — by appearing to have noticed they needed help. Sensibly, she'd let them be, although often when Jo went over to see her she'd send her back

159

with baskets of baking.

'I love cooking,' she'd say, 'and I always bake too much. It goes stale before I've got through it.'

Ben used to refer to it as the Marshall Plan. But the food was welcome, and Jo could see that he took it in the spirit in which it was sent. He would take Elowen things, too, usually something for her beloved garden; a cutting from a plant that had caught his eye, or a couple of bags of manure for her roses. Jo amused herself with the thought that not many men gave their mothers-in-law sacks of manure. He spent one weekend helping Elowen replace fifteen cracked slabs on her patio; Jo looked on with happiness as Elowen's soft spot for Ben grew to encompass most of her heart.

They waited till Jo's father was home to throw their first dinner party in the cottage. Elowen and Paul arrived bearing a house-warming present of a Persian rug, which looked as beautiful as Elowen had hoped in front of the wide fireplace in the beamed living-room. Paul also bought a bottle of gin and some tonics, in case Ben was still labouring under the delusion that he drank whisky.

'It's a nice place,' Paul said to Ben, who had been showing him around while Elowen and Jo chatted in the kitchen. 'Mind you,' he confided, 'can't see why you want to bury yourselves down here. Why don't you come out to Zurich, see what you make of life there?'

Ben smiled. Jo caught his eye; she had heard her father's words. 'Well, Jo seems to like it here, and to be honest, Zurich wouldn't be a whole lot of good to me. I find the sea a help in my line of work.'

Paul gave a bark of laughter. His son-in-law was turning out better than he'd thought.

★ ★ ★

Ben's parents came over for a month's holiday in the early spring of 1975. Jo wasn't writing, and Ben was waiting for the seasonal pick-up in work, so the four of them spent a lot of time together. Jo's parents-in-law were easy people; you could see why Ben was the man he was. Bernard and Mary MacAllister were so nice to each other, too; she loved the way they always said 'we' and 'us', as though neither could imagine doing things without the other.

'Come see us next,' Mary suggested when they said goodbye.

★ ★ ★

By the summer of 1976, she was beginning to feel broody. Ben is too, she thought, watching him lying on the grass with a friend's toddler climbing all over him. He was in his cricket whites, and the child had dribbled orange lolly down his trousers. Not that it mattered, since he was out. She loved watching him play, but he was better fielding than batting. He had only started playing that season, and still had a tendency in moments of excitement to fling his bat down and run off at rightangles to the crease.

'Baseball,' Jo had explained to amused spectators, 'he used to play for his college.' She had no idea if

161

he had, but it seemed likely.

In September she thought she might be pregnant. By October she was sure, and Ben got to work constructing a stair-gate. Then he made a toy garage.

'We won't need either of these for ages,' she protested, moving the stair-gate out of the way for the tenth time.

'I know. But I want to do something too.'

'I haven't done anything yet. I don't even know how to knit, except in straight lines.'

He looked up at her with a particularly sweet expression which she sometimes saw on his face. It was infinitely precious to her. 'You're growing a baby.'

Edmund Benjamin MacAllister was born the following May, an easy birth, an easy baby, and from the start the image of his father. Ben adapted to parenthood in the same way he took to everything; Jo thought they must have had Ben in mind when they coined the expression 'laid-back'. Her friends thought she was lucky to have a husband who would change nappies and who had even been known to get up in the night and bring Edmund to her to be fed.

'I'll teach him to swim,' Ben said, lying in the bath with Edmund splashing on his chest, 'and maybe we'll take up sailing.' Edmund threw the soap at him. 'You don't want to sail, huh? Okay, we'll get a boat with an outboard.'

★ ★ ★

We'll have been married five years in October, she thought, making a cake for Edmund on the eve of his first birthday, and it's gone by in a flash. She glanced up at Ben, out in the garden digging a sandpit as a surprise birthday present for his son. He looked no different from the moment she'd first seen him, when she'd thought he was awful George coming to look for her. She laughed suddenly — she'd heard that George got married to a rich Italian widow who had an enormous house on Lake Garda. Probably she'd have bought him a new decanter.

She watched the muscles across Ben's shoulders as he threw shovelfuls of sand into the pit. Five years, and she still wanted him every bit as much. Maybe not quite so often, she thought with a smile, but oh, God, as love and companionship grew, desire didn't wane.

The cake was in the oven, and she set the automatic timer in case she forgot about it. She had a bath, then went outside into the twilight, two gin and tonics in her hands. She crouched beside him.

'Have you nearly finished?' she asked.

He looked up. She was wearing her frilly dressing-gown. He smiled. 'Almost.' He leaned over and kissed her, then took his gin. 'You smell nice. Did you finish the cake?'

'Yes. I've just had a bath.'

He kissed her more thoroughly. 'I'm sweaty,' he said. 'Give me five minutes to shower, then I'm all yours.'

She stood up with him, putting her arm round his

waist as they walked together towards the cottage.
'I know.'

★ ★ ★

Summer came, and Ben was offered more work
than he wanted. Much of it he turned down; he
had a boat now, and often spent the day taking
out water-skiers. But he felt obliged to accept some
work with the salvage company, in case they found
someone else.

A coaster went down off Manacle Point, and
a hotly-disputed insurance claim was lodged. 'It's
local,' Ben said, having agreed to lead the salvage
team.

She didn't like the name Manacle Point. It made
her think of despair. She wondered why it only
struck her like that now, when she had known it
all her life.

He sensed she was disturbed. 'The money'll
be nice,' he said cheerfully. 'We'll put it in our
vacation fund.'

They were going to San Francisco in September,
taking Edmund to meet his other grandparents. Jo
perked up; she was looking forward to the trip,
and she knew Ben was too: 'Hal's home,' he'd said
happily when they first discussed going, 'we'll see
him — it's been years.'

★ ★ ★

Right from the start it was a pig of a job. The
coaster had gone down in a place where conflicting

164

currents made access difficult, and the barge Ben and his team were working off bobbed about like a cork. Some of the team suffered from seasickness; all of them got frustrated. Ben would come home frowning, and it seemed to take an effort to throw off the tension. A violent thunderstorm brought on one of his nightmares.

But after a week he was more cheerful. 'We're nearly there,' he said over supper. 'There's a beam lying crossways, and it's been tricky getting a lifting rope attached. The visibility's bad, we're working half under a shelf of rock where the tide pushed her.'

'How much longer will it take?'

'Tomorrow, maybe. Not much more.'

She didn't know why she felt so hugely relieved.

★ ★ ★

Ben went back out to the wreck in the morning, but unexpectedly came home at midday, carrying a bottle of wine. 'That's it,' he said, flinging himself down on the grass. 'It'll be straightforward now.'

'Are you going back?' She thought not; it was unusual for him to drink at lunchtime if he had to work later.

'No. It'll need two or three to guide the beam up, but I'm not reckoning on being one of them.' He smiled up at her.

They had lunch in the garden, then she went inside to wash up. When she came out again, Ben was asleep. She fetched a cushion and gently put it under his head. He smiled slightly, but didn't wake up.

She made a pot of tea later. The telephone rang inside the house.

'Hell.' He went to answer it. When he came back he was frowning.

'What is it?'

'The goddam beam's stuck one end. And the weather's worsening.' He stood gazing into the distance. 'Shit, if they leave it overnight and there's bad weather, it'll undo all we've done so far.' He turned to her. 'I'll have to go back, baby. I don't want to, but I'd like to see it finished.' He bent to kiss her. 'I won't be long — I hope!'

She heard the car drive off.

She wandered into the house with the tea things. Then she noticed that Edmund was looking a bit flushed from running around in the heat, so she put him up into his cool bedroom for a nap. It was nearly three o'clock. She felt very restless.

An hour later, the front doorbell rang. On the step stood a man in a dark suit. Behind him was a man in T-shirt and shorts. He had wet hair. They had a policeman with them.

She felt terribly sick.

'Mrs MacAllister?' the man in the suit said.

'Yes.' Her mouth was dry. She knew the man in shorts: Dave somebody. He worked with Ben. 'Dave, what is it?'

'There's been an accident.' The suit man had a twang to his voice. 'I'm very sorry, I don't know how to . . .'

The policeman was past middle age. He had grey

hair and a nice face. She turned to him. 'He's dead, isn't he?'

Slowly he nodded. 'Yes, my lovely, I'm afraid he is.'

She shook her head, but not in denial, for in her heart she knew. She was trying to shake away the tears that were blinding her. The warm voice of the policeman spoke. 'Come along in, now. Come and be quiet in here.'

She found herself sitting on the sofa. The man in the suit and the other man — Dave — were talking quietly.

'Go and make some tea,' the policeman told them. They handed Jo hers in Ben's Yogi Bear mug. He'd been using it, a little over an hour ago.

'Ben,' she cried, 'oh, Ben, Ben!'

She was shaken by the awful sound of her own sobbing. The policeman held her hand very tightly. She heard him mutter, 'I'm gettin' too old for this job.'

'Shall I phone your mother?' Dave was asking. She couldn't speak, couldn't even think.

'Yes,' the policeman said. 'And a doctor.'

★ ★ ★

In a dream she saw people come and go. A doctor whom she didn't know injected something into her arm, and she felt sleepy. The policeman, still holding her hand, laid her down on the sofa and put a blanket over her. She wondered suddenly where Edmund was, then she saw Elowen standing with him in her arms. Edmund had his thumb in his mouth and his hair was sticking up at the back. Elowen's face was crumpled with tears.

★ ★ ★

She didn't know where she was when she woke up. Slowly she let her eyes wander round the room. She recognized it, but it wasn't hers and Ben's. Yet it made her think of him. Yes! It was her mother's best guest room, where Jo had thought she should have slept before the wedding.

Then it all came flooding back. She turned her face into the pillow and wept.

★ ★ ★

It was evening when she woke again. She no longer felt as if she was perceiving things through a wad of cotton wool. She felt alive all over, and every single bit of her was wracked with the agony of knowing Ben was dead.

She got out of bed and went slowly downstairs. She stood in the open doorway of the living-room. Elowen sat on the sofa with the nice plump woman who was her dearest friend. They were holding hands. They looked up as they heard Jo; they were pale and red-eyed.

Jo said, 'Oh, Mummy!'

Elowen stood up, her face anguished. Jo went to her, and her mother wrapped her in her arms, rocking her. After a while Elowen said, her voice shaking, 'It's because he was so very special, my darling. That's all it can be — because the gods loved him too.'

She asked Jo if she wanted some tablets. The doctor had left some. 'No, thank you.'

She went and sat in the hall. She could hear Elowen and her friend talking. She just wanted to sit there.

★ ★ ★

She sat there for hours in the course of the next night and day. Elowen tried to get her to speak, to eat, to do something for Edmund. But she just went on sitting there.

Suddenly her father was beside her.

She found out afterwards that, in response to the frantic telephone call from Elowen, he had literally dropped everything and flown straight home from Zurich, something unprecedented and unrepeated in all his long life.

She thought, hell, things must be bad, if Dad's come back.

She took the first step back towards the rest of humanity. She said, 'Hello, Dad. Whatever are you doing here?'

★ ★ ★

Elowen's friend took Edmund off with her. Then the three of them, parents and daughter, spent a week in the quiet house. Somehow it was a comfort to be inside those old walls, for the house had witnessed human grief before. Nothing was new, so many other people had broken their hearts crying for the dead. It helped, a bit.

Paul decided it was up to him to see to the practical things. Jo didn't object when he asked her permission to go through her papers, so he took her door key and drove over to the cottage. He found the relevant documents in a case under the stairs. He turned over passports, marriage certificate, birth certificates, insurance policies. Separating the policies from the rest, he put the suitcase back and went home.

After an hour alone in the dining-room and a couple of phone calls, he went to sit by Jo in the hall. 'At least you won't have any worries over money,' he told her gently.

She turned to him blank-faced.

'Ben had a very valuable life insurance policy.' Paul had been surprised at just how valuable; perhaps Ben had arranged it in some sort of apologetic recognition of the perils of his profession. 'It'll pay off the mortgage,' he went on, not sure if Jo was taking it in, 'and also provide you with a considerable lump-sum payment.'

She tried to concentrate on what he was saying. She was pleased because it was nice having her father approve of something Ben had done.

But then her devastated brain said to her, Ben did this, Ben loved you so much that, full of life, he made sure of all this wealth for you if he died.

Then she couldn't take in any more.

★ ★ ★

170

The next day she said to Paul, 'I can't go back to the cottage.' The cottage was Ben, Ben and herself, and every inch of it screamed of him.

'No, Jo,' Paul agreed. 'I understand.'

'Where do you want to go, darling?' Elowen asked. 'Will you stay here?'

She closed her eyes. Here wasn't a lot better. 'No, Mum. Thank you. I'll go right away.'

'Abroad?' Paul asked.

'No. West Kent. I used to go down there from the flat. When I was in London. Remember? I like Kent.'

Paul took her out to lunch, to an expensive, discreet restaurant that imposed self-control.

His cool manner boosted her courage; it was as if he was saying, I know you won't break down and make a spectacle of us. And she didn't.

Arrangements were put in hand for the sale of the cottage; Paul would invest the proceeds for her till she was ready to move. He contacted estate agents in west Kent, and they sent her some details. One day, she thought, looking blankly at them, I'll be interested. I'll go and find my house.

★ ★ ★

But before that, there were two more things she had to do.

★ ★ ★

At the inquest, a verdict of accidental death was brought in. A lot of mud was slung at the salvage company, and she listened in a daze as they went on about liability and responsibility. A letter arrived for her shortly afterwards, in which condolences were offered in discreet terms that didn't actually say anything about anyone being to blame.

But Paul, to whom she'd passed the letter, stared at a figure mentioned in the second paragraph. Wordlessly he pointed; the enormous sum was the amount of compensation the company was offering to Ben's widow.

★ ★ ★

'Dad, I have to take him home,' she said.

'Ben,' Paul said, after a moment.

She nodded. 'There's no point in him staying here if I'm leaving. It's best if he's near his parents.'

'Very well.'

'Will you come with me?'

'Wouldn't you rather have your mother?' He glanced at Elowen.

'In a way, yes. But I think Mum's better at looking after Edmund, if she will. I shan't take him.'

'Of course,' Elowen said quickly.

'Will you phone them?' Jo asked.

'I will.'

It had been Elowen who had broken the news to Ben's parents. This call of Paul's was, by comparison, relatively easy.

* * *

She could remember hardly anything of that trip.
Other than the broadest outlines and the most
piercing moments, it was all obliterated in the
tumult of grief that followed.

12

Jo stood at the open window, watching Edmund as he pedalled his tricycle round the lawn.

Her mind was far away from the peaceful scene in her Kentish garden: she was thinking about going to America.

★ ★ ★

It was almost two years since Ben had died. Acceptance of a sort had grown; days, even weeks, passed without her sinking into the misery that had beset her for so long. Now it was rare for her to wake with the hopeless feeling that it didn't matter what she did or how hard she strived, she'd never be free from grief for the man she'd adored.

She had never returned to the cottage. She went to Kent as soon as she could, staying with her mother and Edmund in a hotel while they looked at houses. She liked the countryside of west Kent; its gently beauty gave her a measure of peace. But house-hunting and being homeless were tiring; she bought a small seventeenth-century farmhouse near Hawkhurst. Set in a narrow winding lane among fields, woods and low hills, it was miles away from the savage, unforgiving sea that had robbed her of Ben.

Elowen stayed with her for a month, and they exhausted themselves scrubbing and painting. Jo found a local firm to do some alterations; there was a quiet pleasure in watching Copse Hill House blossom.

The desire grew to try life alone. But it was hard to know how to say so, without sounding ungrateful for all that Elowen had done. 'Mum,' she began tentatively, 'I've been thinking.'

Her mother watched her. 'And you think you can manage now?'

'Mm.' She couldn't meet her mother's eyes.

'Yes. I think you can, too.'

'You do?'

Elowen laughed briefly. 'Darling, I think you must.'

Jo swallowed the lump in her throat. 'I couldn't be saying that — couldn't have got to here — without you. You do know that, don't you?'

Elowen nodded, momentarily unable to speak. Then she got up and went out to the kitchen. 'I'll make some tea.'

★ ★ ★

Jo had never lived on her own before. She found she liked it. Edmund imposed a structure her life might otherwise have lacked; for his sake, there had to be three meals a day, a reasonably clean house and freshly-laundered clothes. For his sake, there had to be contact with other people; she registered with a GP, joined the library and went to meet the woman who ran the playschool.

It all helped. Other things did, too, such as her discovery of the pleasure of music. Ben had always liked music around him, happy, easy sounds. But she had packed all his records away in the attic. Then she thought, Ben, I'll never be able to play them again. She gave the lot to the Boy Scouts for their jumble sale.

Now she listened to classical music. She knew nothing about it, but loved the emotional appeal; there was solace in thinking, other human beings have reached the depths and the heights, and some of them managed to express it in music. She was often moved to tears, but felt oddly comforted, as if a hand touched her shoulder and a kind voice said, I know, I've been there.

She'd been to the depths, so overwhelmed by grief that she'd thought she'd never be happy again. But she had an optimistic nature, and deep within her must have lain the unconscious knowledge that she'd rediscover the heights. Slowly the sadness was overcome; one night, she managed to look at Ben's photograph without her heart twisting.

'I'm getting there, Ben,' she said softly. 'Don't worry, I'm not so sad any more.'

Edmund was three, a loving child whose resemblance to his father increased as he grew out of babyhood. It was a consolation: she had lost Ben, but his essence remained with her in his son.

His relationship with Elowen, who regularly came to stay, was all that either could ask of it. But Jo was aware of the two other grandparents, patient and contained in their grief for their son, who waited for the day she'd feel strong enough to bring their grandson to meet them.

She pulled herself away from the window and re-read Bernard's letter.

'Jo my dear, we do not want to cause you distress, and it may be still too soon for what we propose. But we would very much like to welcome you here on a visit this summer. We should surely love to see you and Edmund, and would all do our best to make your vacation a happy one.'

She imagined how difficult it must have been to write to her. Imagined him trying to find the right words so as not to hurt her.

Imagined — knew — just how much the visit meant to them.

She wanted to go: it felt right. Pictures of Ben flooded her mind — were never far out of it — but the background was most often Cornwall. She didn't think she could have gone to Cornwall. But San Francisco was different. She'd never set foot in America apart from taking Ben home, and she couldn't remember that.

She wrote a short reply, simply saying she'd love to go and would telephone when she'd booked a flight. Having committed herself, she became swept up in the momentum of the trip.

As departure loomed, Jo found herself re-checking the arrangements with a distinct lack of confidence that she'd never known before. She told herself sternly that it was high time she did something like this.

Elowen went with them to Victoria and saw them on to the Gatwick train. Kissing her goodbye, for a moment Jo's nerve failed. Elowen understood; she pushed her onto the train, lifting Edmund to join her. 'Get a seat and settle down,' she said firmly, 'I'm off to the shops. Goodbye, Edmund — here's a little present to open when the train starts. No sooner!'

Jo looked longingly at her mother. Then she followed Edmund into the carriage.

'Will the train start soon, Mummy?' Edmund was picking at the very corner of the wrapping paper.

'Yes, I expect so,' she said absently. She looked at her son. He seemed so small, sitting there on the seat with his legs dangling high above the floor. Her heart turned over. Oh, God, more emotion. 'I know,' she said brightly, 'let's listen for the guard's whistle, because that'll tell the driver he can go. Then you can open your parcel.'

As they began to discuss the likelihood of Edmund becoming an engine-driver when he grew up, the picture of Elowen walking away receded and she began to feel better.

At Gatwick, they checked in and she waved a relieved goodbye to the two big cases as they trundled off down the conveyor belt.

The flight was called. She felt Edmund's hand fumble for hers. His blue eyes looked solemnly up at her. 'I think my rabbit's a bit frightened,' he confided.

Suddenly he was just a small scared three-year-old; his dependence made her feel strong. She picked up him and his old rabbit, hugging them close.

'Tell Rabbit there's nothing to be frightened

about,' she said reassuringly. 'Come on — there's a new country waiting for us!'

★ ★ ★

Her overriding first impression of San Francisco was that it was very small. She'd expected a sprawling, teeming city, and she was totally taken aback by the clean streets and the elegance. It reminded her a little of Brighton, which was surprising and possibly due to jet lag.

The city was white, tidy, and well cared for; she fell immediately under its spell.

Meeting Bernard at the airport was hard, going home to Mary was worse. When Bernard showed her into the house, Mary was waiting. Suddenly her eager face was superimposed by a parallel apparition. But in this one, Mary was dressed in black and her eyes were swollen.

For a moment the sick confusion of that earlier time pressed down hard upon Jo. Then she felt a small hand tugging at her arm, and the vision faded.

Edmund was trying to hide behind her, overcome with the strangeness of it all. 'Mummy, I have to do a wee!' he said, his voice made too loud by nervousness.

'All right, darling,' She tried to disguise her reluctance to enter the house, forcing a smile. I've *got* to! I can't keep the poor child waiting, he'll do it where he stands.

She fielded all her courage and went in.

Mary had arranged for Edmund, not Jo, to sleep in the room that had been Ben's. Jo was shown to a pleasantly impersonal spare room, for which she was profoundly grateful.

But had Jo's visit required justification, it came very quickly, when she watched Mary's face as she sat on the floor with Edmund, playing with the same toys with which she'd once amused her own son.

★ ★ ★

On the Friday morning after her arrival, Jo sat at the breakfast bar drinking coffee. Ben's younger sister Emily was due home that evening, and Mary was busy. She seemed on edge. As soon as Edmund was out of earshot, Mary came to sit on an adjoining stool.

'Jo dear, I was thinking. Before Emily arrives, maybe you and I could take a walk to the cemetery?'

She spoke tentatively; Jo sensed that she was nervous. I want to see Ben's grave, Jo thought, and it's a good idea to go just with Mary, the first time. 'Yes.' She couldn't look at Mary.

'We don't have to stay long,' Mary said. 'I'll just show you how to get there, then another time you can go on your own.'

It all feels so strange, she thought frantically, running upstairs to fetch her sandals, being here in a country with people I've scarcely met. But they're not strangers, we're bound by a tie of blood, my son's their grandson. She's still a stranger, though, no matter how kind she is, and any minute now I've got to . . .

Don't think about that.

Oh, God, what am I doing?

Mary was waiting for her in the hall, holding a bunch of garden flowers. She gave them to Jo.

They walked down quiet residential streets. Crossed a square. Went through a high-gated entrance between clipped yew hedges. The wide green lawns, the marble and the tidy flower-beds took Jo out of herself and into the realm of dreams. She experienced again knowing she'd been here before but being unable to remember.

Mary walked quietly by her side, pointing the way. Elaborate statues, ornate headstones and huge mausoleums crowded round, and she began to panic that she would find Ben lying beneath something nightmarish that she would hate. Mary took her under an arch into a quiet area bounded by hedges of cypress.

'Over there, she said, 'at the end of that row.'

Jo walked on alone.

Ben's grave was marked out in stone with a plain tablet at its head. The turf was well-tended, and there was a pot for flowers. She stood in silence, looking down.

She thought desolately of his body lying there, so far beyond her reach. Tears streamed down her face and she ached for him, picturing him so vividly that she could feel his presence. Yes, I know I've been here before, I can remember Dad's hand on my arm, the priest's robe with splashes of mud on the hem. Trying so hard not to think about Ben being left here all by himself.

She bent down and put her hand on the smooth clipped grass. The earth felt solid and firm. She laid down the flowers and looked up at the headstone.

She knew the words by heart, but it gave her comfort to see them now here in the place they were meant for.

BENJAMIN CHARLES MACALLISTER

3 June 1948 – 5 August 1978.

Beloved son, husband and father.
'Many waters cannot quench love,
Neither can the floods drown it.'

The visit had a beneficial effect, although it was some time before Jo appreciated it. All she knew, as she and Mary walked home arm-in-arm, was that she felt better. Lighter.

She wondered if her peculiar mental state at the funeral had meant she hadn't really accepted his death. Now, although it gave her enormous sorrow to look down on where her dead husband lay, her mind no longer refused to admit reality.

★ ★ ★

She knew from Ben that he and Emily had been close. At the wedding Emily had been a leggy sixteen-year-old, her eyes shining with love as she

182

looked at her brother. It's hard enough, Jo thought, for a sister who loves her brother to get used to him having a wife. God knows how she feels now that she's lost Ben and there's only me.

Emily took her sightseeing, and did a comprehensive job of introducing her to the city. They took a cable-car ride to the waterfront, then climbed Telegraph Hill. They took the elevator ride ('*Lift*,' Jo said firmly) up the Coit Tower, then bought food and ate it in a grassy square in the midst of tall houses, following with their eyes the progress of a solitary female jogger.

'D'you run, Jo?' Emily asked.

'No,' she replied firmly. 'What about you?'

'Sure. I jog, swim, play tennis, sail . . . ' She stopped abruptly.

'Like Ben,' Jo said. 'He used to talk about the things you did together.' She glanced at Emily. 'He was really proud of you. He said you were the easiest kid in the world to teach.'

'Did he?' She looked pleased. 'He was a great teacher. I worked like crazy to please him. I'd have done anything for him.' Then she suddenly burst out, 'How can you *bear* it?'

Jo thought, it's not only me. 'Because I have to,' she said bleakly. 'My life didn't end when his did, although at the time I couldn't see why. And then, when I . . . when a bit of time had passed and I started to think again, there was Edmund.'

'I shouldn't have mentioned him,' Emily muttered.

'Yes you should. You won't upset me by talking about him, it'd upset me far more if we didn't. Wouldn't it you?'

Emily stared at her, for the first time looking her straight in the eyes. Then she nodded.

* * *

The next week Emily had to go into the university about a job. She suggested to Jo that they meet for lunch afterwards, and Bernard said he'd drive her in.

'Here we are.' Bernard pulled into the side of the road. 'I'll wait with you till Em comes along.'

After a few minutes Emily appeared, in conversation with a tall man wearing glasses and carrying a stack of books.

'There she is,' Jo said. 'Bye, Bernard — thanks for the lift.'

She stood for a moment waving goodbye to him, then walked towards Emily.

'Hi, Jo,' Emily called.

'Hello! How was it?'

'It was okay!' Emily sounded enthusiastic. 'I reckon I got it.' She hesitated. 'Jo, this is a friend, a family friend — I just ran into him.' She seemed very awkward. 'This is Hal Dillon.' She turned to the tall man by her side, who was leaning forwards slightly to get down to her height, 'Hal, this is Jo, Ben's wife . . . widow . . . oh, hell, I'm sorry!'

'It's all right.' Jo held out her hand. 'How do you do?'

'Hi,' Hal said, and took her hand.

'We've known Hal for years,' Emily was saying, still uneasy but becoming less pink. 'He . . . We . . . '

'I knew Ben very well,' Hal said, forestalling her.

'Yes, I know,' Jo said. Recognition had dawned. 'You were Ben's first choice for best man. You sent us that beautiful book.'

Hal smiled suddenly. She noticed how it lightened his serious face. 'You remember.'

'Of course. It was the most unusual present we had.'

'I'll bet you never got Ben to look at it,' Hal remarked. 'I don't recall him ever opening a book just for the hell of it.'

She hesitated, good manners preparing a white lie. But she realized it wasn't necessary. 'No,' she agreed, 'but then I expect he already knew all he wanted to about early American history.' Hal's smile deepened. 'I made up for him,' she added, encouraged.

'Glad you liked it.' He continued to look at her, studying her face. Then he went on, 'Emily said you and your son are over for the summer?'

'Yes.' She glanced at Emily, who still seemed uneasy; she smiled at her, and Emily relaxed a little. 'The family are making me so welcome.'

'How old is your boy?' Hal asked. 'Two? Three?'

'He was three in May.'

Hal was still staring at her. She sensed he was about to say something else, but Emily got in first. 'I'm hungry, let's go eat. Come with us, Hal?'

'I'd like to, Em, but I have to meet someone.'

'Drop by soon,' Emily said. 'Come over Friday, Mom's doing a barbeque, Annie and the girls are coming.'

'Friday?' He hesitated, then said, 'Sure. So long, Jo. Bye, Em.' He waved a hand at them both and disappeared back inside the building.

Jo noticed Emily gazing after him.

'I love being with Hal,' she said dreamily. 'He makes me think of Ben. We used to see a lot of Hal, when . . . ' She broke off, then said quietly, 'When Ben was alive.'

'Come on.' Jo took her arm, feeling momentarily very close. 'Let's find some lunch.'

13

Jo wasn't sure how she felt about the barbeque. Enjoying being with the MacAllisters was one thing; meeting a whole lot of strangers was something else. I'll offer to lend a hand with the preparations, she thought, it'll give me something to do. Put me in the party mood. But with mistaken kindness Mary said, 'No, you're the guest of honour, you go put your feet up. The girls and I'll manage.'

She wandered off upstairs. She could hear Emily laughing with Ben's other sister Annie, who had arrived that afternoon. Edmund was playing with Annie's two daughters.

For a moment she felt very low. Stop being stupid, she told herself. Go and have a bath, make an attempt to smarten up. She slipped back downstairs and helped herself to a stiff scotch. She didn't think they'd mind.

★ ★ ★

She could hear cars outside, laughter from the patio. She stood on the landing taking deep breaths, then set off down the stairs. Bernard took her arm and walked round with her, introducing her. She warmed to the kind good manners of people who had known Ben well, yet managed not to make her feel she was interesting only because she'd been his wife.

187

The smell of grilling meat drew the guests out to the barbeque. Jo took her heaped plate and sat down on a low wall beside Emily and a young man called Dean. The three of them were well into their supper when a voice said, 'May I join you?'

'Hal!' Emily exclaimed. 'Sure, move up, Dean.'

Hal sat down by Jo, deftly managing to eat one-handed from a plate balanced on top of a glass of beer.

'You've done this before,' she said, watching him.

He looked up at her. 'Enjoying the party?'

'Yes. You couldn't not, everyone's so friendly.'

'Want some more, Jo?' Emily had an empty plate.

'No thanks. But you could get me another drink, please.'

Jo let her eyes wander over the scene, very aware of Hal beside her. I ought to say something, she thought, I'm out of practice at socializing. But Hal said, 'Emily got her job in the library, I heard.'

'Yes, she's very pleased.' She was grateful to him. 'Do you work there too?' Ben had said Hal was something to do with the university.

'Not exactly. I lecture in ancient history.'

The words 'ancient history' aroused her interest; her imagination was setting off down fascinating paths when she heard him laugh. Turning to him, again she watched as a sudden brightness lightened his face.

'Gets people every time,' he said. 'How the hell do you reply?'

'I can't speak for people,' she said. 'But I should

imagine that to lecture in ancient history must be absolutely fascinating.'

'You should?' He seemed to be mocking her gently.

'I should. Ancient history of what?'

He finished his supper, getting up to put his plate on a table. She noticed he wasn't wearing his glasses, and took a good half-dozen years off the 'forty-fiveish' she'd provisionally ascribed to him.

'Are you interested?' he asked abruptly.

'Yes.'

'Only it bores the pants off most people.'

'But not me.'

'Okay.' He sat staring at her for a moment, frowing slightly. Then, as if shifting into another gear, he leapt into a succinct account of possible prehistoric links between the new world and the old. He spoke fluently; she was able to follow him with ease.

'But what . . . ' she began, to be interrupted by Emily with the drinks.

'Sorry I took so long.' She handed Jo a full glass. 'Come meet Dean's pop. He's been to London.'

She took her drink and stood up. Hal was watching her. He held her eyes for a long moment, then grinned. 'Another time.'

Once or twice over the evening she looked out for him; he was tall enough to stand above most people. He seemed at home in the MacAllister household.

Ben's friend, she thought.

★ ★ ★

189

July moved into August. The barbeque sparked off return invitations; Jo enjoyed rediscovering a social life. People who'd been fond of Ben gradually felt able to talk about him, which gave her an odd emotional feeling: painful, but also strangely a pleasure.

Hal often attended the same functions, and she looked forward to seeing him. She was eager to talk about his work, but when there were other people around he never mentioned it. Remembering his remark about boring people, she was reluctant to ask; she found him slightly daunting, especially when he wasn't smiling.

But once she found herself alone with him, and plucked up her courage to raise a point that had stayed in her mind from their previous conversation. He looked slightly surprised, but then responded.

He was telling her about the Atlantis legend when suddenly she thought of Desdemona, falling in love with Othello because of the potency of his storytelling. Not Hal's own dangers he has passed, she conceded, but then I dare say Othello wasn't above a bit of plagiarism.

Then surprise and shock hit her, that she had thought of this in the context of Hal.

She spent a couple of sleepless hours that night wondering at the deviousness of her own mind. Where's the grieving widow now? she demanded. She was embarrassed at the audacity of her thoughts. God, whatever would Hal think? But she had to face the fact that only part of her still saw Hal as she'd originally seen him, a friend of Ben's whose company she enjoyed merely because he and Ben had been close.

Now she had to accept that part of her didn't seem to see him like that at all.

But the next day her worries seemed fanciful, and when Hal called by in the afternoon she managed to say hello in what sounded like her usual voice. Mary brought cold drinks out to the yard, and they watched Edmund playing in a large paddling pool.

'Is this the first time you've met our grandson, Hal?' Bernard asked.

'I saw you at the top of the stairs one night, didn't I?' Hal said, poking a finger at Edmund's bare tummy.

Edmund filled up his watering can and demonstrated, all over Hal's feet, how well it poured. 'You can do that,' he said shyly.

Hal refilled the can, then poured water down the little boy's back, making him shriek excitedly. Mary, laughing, went to get a towel, and Bernard fetched the hose to fill up the pool.

'He's like Ben,' Hal said quietly.

'Even more like Ben was at that age. Mary showed me some photographs.'

'Must be specially nice for them.' He nodded towards where Mary and Bernard were playing with Edmund beside the pool.

'They love him,' she said. 'It's good, isn't it?'

'Sure. Your visit's making them happy.'

He looked at her intently. She thought he was going to say something, but apparently he changed his mind. He turned back to watch Edmund pretending to wash his grandfather's hair.

She went into the kitchen to pour Edmund a drink. Hal followed her into the house. 'I'm going.'

'Oh. Goodbye.'

He made no move but stood watching her. Suddenly he said, 'I'm invited to a party Saturday.'

'Oh.'

'It's one of my students,' he said casually, 'twenty-first do, at a beach house north of here.' He glanced up at her. 'D'you want to come?'

Yes, yes, yes, she cried silently.

But she was ashamed of herself for wanting so much to go. What will I say to Bernard and Mary? Whatever will they think? I've only been here five minutes and here I am gallivanting off with the best friend.

She looked reluctantly up at him. He was watching her, with an unusually gentle expression that suggested he knew very well the line of her thoughts. 'Yes,' she said finally, 'I'd love to.'

'Eight-thirty Saturday. I'll pick you up.'

As he walked out he turned to grin at her. For a moment, she almost thought he'd given her a wink.

★ ★ ★

She became increasingly nervous as Saturday came closer, the relatively minor worry about what Bernard and Mary might think paling into nothing beside her alarm at the prospect of being alone with Hal all evening.

She didn't sleep much on Friday night. Saturday went quickly; too soon it was evening. She said goodnight to Edmund and went downstairs to wait. She sat looking at a magazine. Bernard gave her a gin and tonic.

A car went by, and she felt her palms go sweaty. I hope he won't want to hold my hand! Hell, I'm thirty-one, not seventeen. The clock in the hall struck the half-hour; just as she was beginning to wonder if she'd be glad if he didn't turn up, she heard a car stop outside.

She shot to her feet, reaching for her handbag.

'Have fun!' Mary called from the kitchen.

'Cheerio!' she called, running to the front door. Bernard was already opening it.

Hal stood there looking down at her. 'Hi. Ready, Jo?'

'Yes. Goodnight, Bernard.'

'Night, honey, see you in the morning. Bye, Hal.'

She and Hal got into his car. As he started the engine the car's cassette player came to life with what he had just been listening to: it was Bruch's violin concerto. He reached to turn it off.

'Oh, no, please don't!' she said impulsively. 'I love this.' And the music obviated the need for conversation.

'You like that sort of music?' he asked when the work came to an end.

'Yes, very much. That's one of my favourites. Do You?' Of course he does, dummy, or he wouldn't have it playing in his car.

'Yeah. My father plays the cello, so I grew up with classical music.'

They were almost out of the city, heading northwards. They followed the coast highway for some miles, then he turned off into a small beachside community with expensive-looking properties on the shore. He pulled up behind a line of cars already taking up most of the street.

She felt very nervous. They went up timber steps into a loud, friendly crowd; the noise was deafening. Hal shouldered a way through the crush and out onto a big wood-railed verandah. He introduced her to a few people, but it was difficult to make out what was said. The music got louder; guests were spilling down the verandah steps on to a paved area below, where there was a huge sound system.

'Want to go down on the shore?' Hal said in her ear.

She nodded. He collected a bottle of white wine and a couple of glasses, then led the way down the steps and out onto the firm sand.

'Oh, that's better!' she exclaimed as they walked away from the noise.

Soon they had left the group of houses behind. They came to an outcrop of rocks, and sat down. He poured out the wine. The night was warm and the air moved gently as though in time to the swell of the Pacific stretching vastly away before them.

'Do you like the ocean?' he asked.

'I used to.' Her eyes were on a distant light far out on the horizon. 'We lived by the water, Ben and me — we had a cottage on a river estuary.

But I moved away, afterwards. I didn't like the sound of the waves. It's insistent, the bloody sea,' she said with sudden bitterness.

'Does this upset you?' He indicated the great spread of ocean.

'No. It's different.'

There was a sense of anticipation between them. Then he said, 'I never heard exactly how Ben died. Can you tell me?'

She'd known all along it was coming. The feeling of being on the brink had been steadily growing. The tension increased. 'Yes,' she said eventually. 'He's on my mind all the time. Especially tonight, with you.' She turned and looked into his eyes. 'I'll tell you.'

He waited in silence.

'They were salvaging a coaster off the Manacles,' she began. The name wouldn't mean anything to him, but to her it was death. And the memory was vivid; she was reliving things she hadn't thought about for a very long time, wrenching them up from where they lay buried painfully deep.

Briefly she told him about that last day with Ben. How he had come home for lunch and then gone out again. How he'd said, 'I won't be long'.

But it was hard, so hard, to think of that moment. The last time she had seen Ben alive. She wiped her hand across her wet eyes. 'They came to tell me,' she whispered. 'But you know. There's something in people's faces. I said, he's dead, isn't he? and they said, yes, he is.'

She choked. 'They said . . . they said there was no need for me to see him. Identify him. But I had to, I couldn't not. He didn't look dead, just so pale, so still. And his face was too smooth, sort of expressionless — all the fun had gone. The doctor — at the inquest — said he'd died instantly. It wasn't terrible for him.'

'What happened?' Hal asked quietly.

She'd almost forgotten he was there. She became aware of him, realized that, caring for Ben too, this was as painful for him to hear as it was for her to relate. And he didn't know until now, she thought, nobody told him.

'It was the winch. It got stuck. They'd attached a rope to a beam they had to lift, but it wasn't lifting. They thought it must be caught on some snag they couldn't see — they were working half under a shelf of rock and the visibility was poor. Ben was underneath the beam, feeling for the obstruction. But the winch had only stopped because it was jammed. When they started pulling again they increased the power too much. The winch's wire broke and the beam fell on top of him. He didn't drown — it broke his neck.'

He muttered, 'What a waste.'

'I know.' She was weeping, couldn't stop. 'They went on endlessly about whose fault it was, but it couldn't make any difference. There's no consolation, nothing that means anything, because in the end he was just Ben, and I loved him so much, and he's gone.'

She buried her face in her folded arms. After a moment he reached out and took her hand. It felt enormously comforting. Gradually her crying stopped.

They sat for some time, not speaking. She guessed they were probably thinking the same thing, sharing a grief that couldn't be put into words. After a while she heard him take a breath and cough quietly. Her heart lurched at the depth of emotion she felt in him.

He drained his glass and poured them both more. 'You came back here with his body.'

'Yes, though the memory's been erased.'

'I remember standing at the graveside thinking I wouldn't have recognized you from the MacAllisters' photographs.'

'You were there? I don't think I saw you.'

He smiled slightly. 'I guess not.'

She turned to look at him. Without knowing why, she said, 'I'm glad you were.'

'The bottle's empty.' He got up. 'We'll go back.'

She reached for her bag. 'I'm not sure I'm ready for company.'

'I didn't mean back to the party,' he said gently. 'I meant home. I guess they won't miss a couple of glasses.'

'Oh. Okay.' She shivered violently. Noticing, he took off his jacket and put it round her.

They walked back along the shore to the car, and he set off for the city. The clock on the panel said 11.30 p.m. She looked out at the ocean away to her right and felt a weird sense of displacement. In that moment, Hal seemed the only certain thing, the still centre of a whirling Catherine wheel of emotion and memory.

He stopped at a waterfront bar. 'What'll it be?'

'Oh — brandy, if they've got it.'

He grinned at her briefly. 'They will have.'

'It hasn't been a great evening for you,' he said abruptly as they sat over coffee and shots of brandy 'I'm sorry I took you through it.'

'Don't be.' She thought briefly. 'It had to happen. It was the first time I've talked about it.'

He digested that. Then he said, 'Maybe it'll help some. They say it's therapy, but I guess it's natural, part of human grieving.'

'You sound as though you've had a wealth of experience.'

'Some.' He didn't elaborate.

They finished their drinks, then he drove her home. He stopped a few yards up from the house, then turned to her. 'Will you risk another evening with me if I promise not to make you cry?'

She wanted to see him again: something about the deep emotional experience they'd just shared made her want to be sure he didn't revert to merely a casual friend.

'Yes.' She added, 'It's all right, with you.'

He nodded. 'Okay.' He hesitated, then said, 'Tonight wasn't just so I could ask you about Ben.' The thought hadn't occurred to her. 'I'll call you.' Gently he brushed the back of his hand across her cheek.

He walked with her to the house, turning to go as she let herself in. She heard him say quietly, 'Goodnight, Jo.'

The house seemed to welcome her. A night-light burned in Edmund's room. Ben's room. She went in to kiss her son.

Then she said under her breath, 'Ben, darling Ben. I do like your friend.'

14

They let Jo sleep on in the morning. She went downstairs to find Mary alone in the kitchen; Bernard and Emily had taken Edmund to the park.

'They'll be back soon,' Mary said, pouring her some coffee.

'Thank you for the lie-in.'

'Sure, that's okay. Did you have a good party?'

'Yes, it was lovely. We . . . Hal and I went down on the beach — it was a bit noisy in the house.'

'I'll bet!'

'I told him about Ben, how he died,' Jo said in a rush. 'He said he didn't know how it happened exactly, and I thought, with them having been friends . . . '

'Oh, Jo,' Mary said. 'Oh, my.'

Jo tried to smile at her. 'It wasn't too bad.' She wished her voice sounded less shaky. 'He said . . . Hal said it helps, sometimes.'

Mary came over to Jo and put her arms round her. 'They told me that, too,' she whispered. Jo leaned against her briefly. 'He's had his share of sorrows.' Mary broke away from the dangerous ground of her own son. 'He ought to know what helps folks get over things.'

'Yes, he seemed to be saying that last night.' Jo felt disloyal to Hal. 'What did he mean?'

Mary sat down beside her at the breakfast bar

and poured herself some coffee. 'Well, he lost his mother when he was little,' she began, 'he'd have been about five, I guess. She had pneumonia — she'd never been too strong, apparently. Then there was a girl who died — I don't know too much about it. Hal had been living in Mexico. He was here with Ben one day. Oh, he looked so bad — thin, tired and unshaven, and his eyes gone deep.' She put a hand up to her face, her eyes troubled. 'Ben just said he'd wanted to marry a girl, and that she'd died. We never did get to hear any more. They went on a trip together, and when they got back, Hal was all right again. My, that was 1969, all of eleven years ago!'

Jo watched her kind face, full of distress at the memory. I know what it's like, Hal. And you could have said the same thing to me, last night. Reliving the moment when he'd taken her hand she thought, perhaps you did.

★ ★ ★

The days went on, and she decided she should set a date for her return. But she didn't want the MacAllisters to think she was bored with them. They won't, she thought, of course they won't — they'll probably be relieved I'm finally going.

On impulse she asked Bernard and Mary if they'd spend Christmas with her. She was very happy when, clearly touched by her invitation, they said yes, we'd love to.

A few days before her departure, Hal invited Jo, Emily and Dean to supper. His apartment was in a big old house in a quiet back street; they went into the lobby, and Emily pressed a button on the intercom.

He was waiting on the landing to usher them inside. She looked around; they were in a big living-room, with a dining alcove at one end and a wide sofa at the other.

Jo wandered round Hal's bookshelves. I wouldn't mind being snowed up here for a month, she thought, then felt herself blushing. She picked up a volume of dramatic photographs of Machu Picchu while she regained her composure. What the hell's the matter with me? she wondered wildly.

'No pretty sunset tonight,' Emily said. Jo joined her at the window. The evening was muggy, the sky darkening as clouds gathered. 'There's going to be a storm,' Emily went on, 'a bad one.'

Hal went through to fetch supper, and Emily went to help. 'You didn't cook all this!' she said accusingly as they brought in plate after plate of Chinese food.

'No, I didn't,' he agreed calmly, 'I'm way too busy.'

The food was good. Having a take-away, Jo thought, is a sensible way to entertain if you're pressed for time. Even if you're not. I'm glad he hasn't been slaving away all afternoon just for us. She looked across to where Hal sat back, his long legs stretched out, a hand on his wineglass.

'You were right about the storm, Em,' he said, glancing out of the window. 'There's lightning over the ocean.'

He brought across a branched candelabra and lit the candles. The soft light was warm and mellow, and with the night shut out, the room was cosy.

But outside the storm was gathering momentum; the rumble of thunder was an insistent obbligato to their conversation. Emily glanced across at Jo, who hadn't spoken for a while, but Jo was watching the candle flames.

Suddenly the storm was right overhead, full-blown and fierce. Emily, startled by a particularly loud crack, caught sight of Jo. Horrified, she stared at her. She was sitting absolutely still, eyes wide and fixed; tears were rolling down her face.

Emily nudged Hal ferociously, knocking his elbow off the table. '*Look*,' she hissed. 'What's the matter with her?'

He got up and led Jo out. He said to Emily and Dean, 'Stay here.'

Jo moved like a sleepwalker, unaware of him. He took her across the hall into his bedroom, closing the door behind him. The room was unlit except for the glow of streetlights and the irregular flashes of lightning.

He put his arm across her shoulders. 'What's up?' he asked softly.

She reached up to clutch his hand. 'It's storms. He . . . he didn't like storms. He used to have nightmares sometimes — he had them if it wasn't thundering too. He'd wake up, only he wasn't awake, not really, he'd be sweating and yelling and it was as if he could hear something else, something horrible, and was getting it confused with the thunder. He used to shout, 'Put it out, *put it out!*'

Tell me about it, Hal thought. He was remembering a night in the Rockies, reliving his fuddled terror when the joint cacophony of Ben's screaming and a violent storm had rocketed him awake.

He was remembering further back, too. He knew exactly when Ben's nightmares had started — and why — although he doubted if Jo did.

Christ, he thought, I hope not.

'Then . . . then he'd tremble and mutter,' she was sobbing, 'and he'd shout someone's name, and he'd swear, and, oh, Hal!' She began to cry harder now, tears streaming down her face.

She swallowed hard and tried to go on. 'He used to *cry*, and I couldn't bear it, he was so scared, so hurting, and I'd take him in my arms to try to soothe him, and I couldn't, Hal, I couldn't make him stop, and oh, I can't bear it, *any* of it!'

She was crying so hard that he could hardly make out the words. He turned her gently round towards him and tentatively put his arms round her. He was quite prepared for her to push him away, but she didn't. She threw herself against him and wrapped her arms tightly round his waist, and he let her abandon herself to her grief for Ben.

He began stroking her hair. 'Something had to snap, kid,' he said quietly, 'ain't nobody can carry it round for ever.' But he didn't think she heard.

Gradually she grew calmer. As she regained

control, she straightened up and disentangled herself from him. He felt vaguely disappointed.

She turned away, hands covering her face. 'I'm very sorry. I'm not quite sure what happened there.'

'It's okay. But you shook me some.'

'I shook me some, too.' He detected the slightest smile in her voice. She took her hands away from her face and looked at them, wet with tears. 'Could you fetch my bag?'

'Sure.' He left the bedroom door open. Jo heard Emily say, 'What is it? Is she ill?', and Hal reply, 'No, just upset. Tired out, I guess.'

Soon he was back, her handbag in one hand and a bottle of brandy and a glass in the other. 'I'll put your purse on the bed. I got you some brandy.' She stood with her back to him. 'D'you want me to put the light on? I'm still not looking,' he added.

'Please.'

'Emily and Dean have gone.' He moved towards the door, turning on the light as he left. 'I'll be through there when you're ready for company.'

He closed the door. Picking up her bag, she went to look at herself in the mirror on the chest of drawers. Oh, God. She drank the brandy down in a gulp. Reaching for tissues, she managed to scrub off the smudges of mascara. She wondered why she was bothering.

Then she picked up her empty glass and went to join Hal.

He was sitting on the sofa. He got up and took the glass from her, silently pouring her some more. 'Here.' He handed her the brandy.

'Thanks. Thunderstorms, tears and brandy,' she muttered.

'How's that?'

'All the dramas of my life seem to revolve around thunderstorms, tears and brandy,' she said wearily, 'though not necessarily in that order.'

She leaned back against the cushions, feeling disorientated and very tired. Elements of this evening — thunder, being upset, being comforted in warm arms — were playing great chords of memory in her strained mind, bringing back so vividly that long-gone night with Ben, who was long-gone too.

She drank some more brandy. It was making her feel warm and it was blurring her thoughts, reasons enough to go on drinking it. She felt Hal get up from the sofa, and watched as he moved out from the circle of light.

Presently music came softly into the room.

'I should know what this is,' she said, humming.

There was silence for quite a long time.

'Don't worry about it,' he said kindly. 'It's Brahms, the violin concerto.'

In the break before the final movement she sat up suddenly and looked at him. 'Thank you.'

'You're welcome.'

She settled back again, her eyelids slowly drooping. He took the glass out of her hand; she'd managed to drain it again. She put her head down and closed her eyes.

When the concerto came to an end, he got up to turn off the cassette player. He came back and stood looking down at her. She was curled up like an exhausted child.

'Are you okay, kid?' he said quietly.

She didn't answer. He went into his bedroom, returning with a pillow and duvet. Then he went to take her shoes off, but she'd already done so. He covered her with the duvet.

'Goodnight, Jo,' he said. 'Sweet dreams.'

He blew out the candles, and walked in the darkness out to the telephone. He looked at his watch in the hall light, then picked up the receiver and dialled the MacAllisters' number.

'Hi, Bernard,' he said, 'I'm sorry to call so late. Hope I didn't wake you.'

'No, Hal. Emily told us about Jo — how is she?'

'Okay, I guess. She's gone to sleep.'

'Will you bring her back?'

'No. She's flat out on the sofa. I reckon she'll sleep till morning.' Especially after all that brandy, he thought, but he didn't say so to Bernard.

'Fine, Hal,' Bernard said. 'What was it, d'you think? Emily said she just started crying.'

If Ben's father hadn't known about his son's particular response to thunder, there was no point telling him now. 'I guess it was the storm. She said something about thunder being upsetting.'

'Poor kid. We'll see you tomorrow then, Hal — tell her not to worry about Edmund, we'll look after him.'

'Right. Goodnight, Bernard.'

Leaving the hall light on and the living-room door ajar, he fetched himself a glass of water and went to bed.

15

Jo woke to the smell of coffee. Someone was moving about in the kitchen, Hal presumably. There were sounds of washing-up, and music was playing quietly. After some time, she recognized the Saint-Saëns organ symphony. She shut her eyes to enjoy it.

'Are you awake?' Hal asked. Her eyes shot open. He was padding barefoot across the room carrying two cups of coffee.

'Yes.' Oh, God, what must he be thinking of me? 'I've been listening to Mr Saint-Saëns,' she said brightly.

'Monsieur. Or De Heer. He was Belgian.'

'Oh.'

'He composed music as easily as an apple tree produces apples.'

'Is that what they said about him?'

'No, that's what *he* said about him.'

She began to feel easier. 'I recognized it, eventually.'

'Something of a give-away, when the organ comes in.'

She propped herself up, and he handed her the coffee. 'How d'you feel?'

'Fine. I'm sorry I ruined the evening.' She was pleased they were talking about it straight away; he was easier than she'd imagined. 'Should I ring the MacAllisters?'

'I called them last night. It's okay,' — he glanced at her — 'I told them you were sleeping on the sofa.'

She blushed. 'Oh, dear!'

He stood up, taking her cup from her.

'That's it, I don't do breakfast in bed. You getting up?'

'Yes.' She threw back the duvet and looked down at herself. 'May I have a shower?'

'Help yourself.'

She went through to the bathroom and had a very hot shower. The steam made most of the creases drop out of her clothes. She put toothpaste on her finger and scrubbed her teeth, then combed her wet hair and put on some make-up. Okay, world, I'm ready for you.

She went across into the kitchen. Hal was lying on his back on the floor, his head and shoulders inside the cupboard under the sink.

'I dropped a chopstick down the garbage disposal,' came his muffled voice. 'Come hold the torch.'

She crawled in beside him and took the torch from his hand. 'Isn't this cosy?' she said conversationally.

'I still can't see,' he complained. 'Go fetch my glasses, will you? From beside my bed.'

She got up and went into his bedroom. It gave her a strange feeling to stand by his bed. Hurriedly she picked up his glasses and went back to the kitchen.

'I hope you weren't cold in the night.'

He took his glasses and handed her back the

torch. 'No, wasn't nothing I couldn't handle.'

He turned his attention from the u-bend and briefly looked at her, then resumed his efforts. 'Ah! That's it!' he said with satisfaction. He extricated his long form from beneath the sink and straightened up, putting the spanner away in the cutlery drawer. 'D'you want breakfast?'

'I wouldn't mind, if it doesn't mean retrieving anything else from under there.'

'We'll eat with our fingers. It'll only be toast.'

'Perhaps I should phone the MacAllisters.'

'Go right ahead.'

She spoke to Mary, told her she was fine, and was reassured that Edmund was quite happy. Mary called him to the phone, and Jo got the distinct impression he found it a bit of a nuisance having to interrupt playing with his grandfather to talk to her.

'I've been given the day off,' she said, returning to the kitchen.

'Right.' He jingled his car keys. 'Then we'll go out.'

In the car, he asked if she'd been to Muir Woods. She hadn't. Redwoods, she thought. Muir Woods is where the redwoods are. After a while Hal started humming something, then pushed a tape into the cassette. She wondered if he was ever without music for long.

Muir Woods was perfect for her mood. Paved trails wound beneath the shade of the enormous trees; the silence had the overawing quality of a great Gothic cathedral.

They found a wooden seat in a clearing and sat

down. 'Do you live near London?' he asked.

She jumped. Her thoughts had been far away. 'Fairly. Why?'

'I'm going to be in London next year.'

'Oh! Are you?'

'Yep.' She was very surprised. Then her heart leapt for joy. 'You do seem glad,' he said wryly.

'Oh, I am!' Not glad! 'It — you just took me aback. You hadn't mentioned it before.'

'I'm mentioning it now. Can we see each other?'

'Yes, I'd like that.' Some understatement. 'What will you be doing in London?'

'Giving a course of lectures.'

'Where?'

'All over.'

'How long for?'

'Six months.'

Why is this making me so happy? 'You must be quite clever,' she said cheekily. 'Fancy them paying you for that.'

'Not only do they pay me, they also provide me with an apartment — in Bloomsbury.' He pronounced it 'berry' at the end.

'Move over, Virginia Woolf.'

'Not my sort of writer, sweetheart.'

Sweetheart. She couldn't think how long it was since she'd been called that. Even in fun.

★ ★ ★

They walked back to the car and drove along the coast, then inland through the hills. As the afternoon wore on she said eventually that she ought to be getting back.

He stopped outside the house. She looked quickly across at him, and he said, 'I'll come in with you.'

She felt grateful. She'd been feeling increasingly embarrassed about facing them, after last night.

★ ★ ★

But the family were tactful. Mary whispered, 'Okay now?' but otherwise nobody referred to her outburst. Jo was deeply relieved. They had supper, then eventually Hal got up to go.

She went out to his car with him. 'Thank you for a lovely day.'

He looked down into her eyes. 'You're welcome. When is it you go?'

'Wednesday, morning flight.'

'See you Tuesday?'

'Yes.'

To her complete surprise, since nothing in his behaviour had led her to expect it, he took her face in his hands and kissed her full on the mouth. She responded eagerly, a surge of sexual desire flooding powerfully through her.

'Oh!' she exclaimed when eventually he released her.

'Thought I'd give you something to think about,' he observed. 'But don't worry, I won't do it again.'

He got into the car. 'Till Tuesday.' Then he drove off.

She leaned against the house, shaking all over.

'Oh, God,' she whispered. 'Oh, *God*!'

In the morning she was fiercely determined to stay busy; she didn't dare think about Hal. She fussed at anything that would keep her occupied, keep out of her mind the amazingly erotic dreams she'd been having all night. She felt slightly ashamed of herself. But it's well over two years since I did anything more sexy than kiss people on the cheek — it's hardly surprising!

Her pottering got in Mary's way; she accepted Jo's offer of help and gave her a stack of ironing to do. It's no favour to her, Jo thought, ironing a T-shirt with the sort of intense concentration usually reserved for something more precious, most of it's ours. 'I'm so glad you're coming at Christmas,' she said suddenly.

'Me too.' Mary looked up from her baking and smiled.

Jo hesitated, then said, with an attempt at casualness, 'Did you know Hal was coming to London next year?'

'Sure, he mentioned it a while back.' Mary didn't sound as if she found it all that earth-shattering. 'Will you see him, d'you think?'

'Oh, I don't know.' She sounded unconvincing, even to herself. She looked up from her ironing and saw that Mary was watching her. Hastily she dropped her eyes. 'Yes,' she said quietly. 'I hope so.'

★ ★ ★

On Tuesday her nervousness reached an all-time high, and she couldn't eat. Mary and Bernard charitably accepted her explanation that it was excitement at the prospect of her journey next day. She began to worry in case they'd guess that it was Hal who was disturbing her so much; it became a strain to try to act normally.

'Is it okay if I go and have a long soak in the bath?' she asked Mary in the evening.

'Sure,' Mary said. 'I'll see Edmund to bed.'

She'd like that, Jo thought with a pang, on our last night. So would he. Pity I didn't think of it. I'm too selfish, by far.

She soaked for half an hour, then wondered how she was going to make the prunish wrinkles disappear before Hal arrived. Her cheeks, pink enough before the bath, were now on fire. Her body felt hot and glowing but her hands and feet were icy. She felt queasy.

She heard Mary put Edmund to bed, and went to kiss him. Then she followed Mary downstairs and sat down to wait for Hal. In no time she was up again, going across to the window to look out. 'He's here!' she said sharply, making them jump.

'Night, honey,' Mary said calmly. Bernard barely looked up from his paper.

She ran out to meet Hal. He got out of the car and opened the door for her. 'Hi. How are you?'

'Fine.' She sat looking straight ahead, too discomfited for speech. She felt as if he'd witnessed her entire mental processes since Sunday evening. She bit at her fingernail. Then, since he had neither spoken nor made a move to go, she glanced quickly sideways at him.

He burst out laughing. 'You're great, kid.' he said. Still chuckling, he set the car in motion. 'We'll go eat at Fisherman's Wharf.'

As they sat down at a table in a waterfront restaurant, he took hold of her hand. 'You'd better let me have your address and your phone number.'

She wrote them out for him. He looked at what she'd written, then folded the paper and put it away in his wallet. He gave her his card.

'What does 'S' stand for?'

'Samuel.'

'And the 'H' — Hal — is that short for Harold?'

'No. Henry.'

As the waiter left with their order, she tried to think of something sensible to say. 'What can I give to Bernard and Mary?' she asked. 'They've been so kind, I'd like to get them a present.'

'You've left it a bit late,' he observed.

'I meant I'd send something from home.'

He glanced at her, amused. 'I ain't too familiar with English shops,' he remarked.

'No, I suppose not.' Damn.

'Why don't you send them a guide to your part of the country?' He knew about the MacAllisters' proposed trip to see her at Christmas.

'Maybe they'll let me borrow it,' he said.

★ ★ ★

'Summer's nearly over,' he said as they left the restaurant and walked off along the waterfront. 'Pity you're not staying. We could have gone up to Yosemite. It's real beautiful in the fall. Chestnut coloured trees under a clear blue sky, and the mountain tops brilliant with the first snows. Big log fires in the hotels.'

'Yes, I love the autumn,' she agreed hastily. She didn't want to think about log fires and hotels and being alone with him in romantic places. 'It's my favourite season in England,' she hurried on, 'because it never lets you down.'

'Is that right?'

'Yes. Have you ever been to England?'

'Nope.'

'Well, the climate's very unpredictable. Spring tends to be a let-down, which is a shame for May Day celebrations. Children round the maypole in pretty new dresses, with garlands of flowers in their hair,' she explained.

Noticing the way he was looking at her, she stopped. 'But you won't want to hear about that,' she muttered.

He put his hand under her chin and lifted her face, making her look at him. 'Jo?' he said quietly.

'Yes?'

'Shut up.'

She stared up into his eyes. 'I'm so confused!' she burst out.

'Me too.'

'Are you?' She'd been so busy with her own emotions that she hadn't spared a thought for his.

216

'Oh sure.' He said ironically, 'There's something stops you making a pass at your buddy's wife, even if he is dead.'

He was looking away from her, distant suddenly.

'I see,' she said in a small voice.

He put his arm round her shoulders and they walked on. 'Don't worry,' he said after a while.

'No.' Then she asked doubtfully, 'Shall we write to each other?' Courage born of desperation, she thought.

He said calmly, 'Sure. If you like.' Then: 'I'll take you home. You have to be up early in the morning.'

★ ★ ★

In the car, he pushed a tape into the cassette player. 'Oh, sod you!' she exclaimed, recognizing it.

He grinned. 'Thought you'd remember. I'll bet you still have no idea what it is.'

After a moment she said, 'I wish you'd play something else.'

He glanced at her quickly. 'Oh, hell, you're not going to start crying again, are you? Come here.' He pulled her towards him.

'You're not doing my delicate emotional state any good at all,' she murmured.

'Nor you mine,' he said equably.

He stopped the car up the street from the MacAllister house. Then he put his arms round her and kissed her.

The feel of his mouth was wonderful. He bent her back, pressing her into the gap between the front seats, and she wound her arms tightly around his neck, thrusting her body against him. He was setting her on fire; she felt as though she were melting into him.

Then abruptly he broke away.

'You said you weren't going to do that again,' she said shakily.

'So I'm a liar.' He leaned back, his eyes shut. He looked severe, and she didn't know what to say.

After a moment he opened his eyes. 'You take care, now.' He managed something approaching a smile, 'Watch out for that little Teddy of yours.'

The moment had come. She didn't want to think about the half-world which was shortly to separate them.

He drove the quarter-mile to the MacAllisters' house.

'So long,' he said. He made no move to touch her.

'Goodnight.' She couldn't bring herself to say goodbye either.

She stood watching in the doorway as he drove away.

★ ★ ★

Stop thinking, brain, she told herself as she lay awake far into the night. At last she fell asleep, only to dream evocatively of Ben kissing her on the forehead and saying sonorously, 'It's the beginning of the end.'

PART TWO

16

Jo returned to a late summer ripening into autumn.

She came home with an intense desire to be on her own, and for a week she didn't tell anyone she was back. The brief period of solitude came to an end when Edmund's playschool term started; she invited Elowen to stay, and, realizing that the holiday would be the major topic of conversation, made an effort to pull her thoughts into some kind of order.

Elowen had been with her a couple of days before Jo could bring herself to mention Hal. Her feelings about him were in chaos; she tried not to think about him but couldn't stop herself.

Jo brought up the subject of Christmas one afternoon when they were out for a walk.

'I won't come, darling, if you're having the MacAllisters,' Elowen said. 'You'll have more than enough to do.'

'No. You must. But I don't mind if you insist on doing some of the cooking,' she added with a smile. 'What about Dad?'

Elowen hesitated. It suited her and Paul to spend Christmas apart, but she felt defensive when her children suggested they spend it together. 'Dad's going to be in England before Christmas. Perhaps he'll see you then.'

September came to an end, and Elowen felt the pull of home. For the first time since Jo had moved to Kent, Elowen didn't feel bad about leaving her.

'So you're glad you went?' she said on their last evening, watching as Jo poured coffee for them both.

'Oh, yes.'

'And it wasn't too sad, living in Ben's house? Meeting his friends?' Jo looked up, then returned to the coffee. 'Visiting his grave?'

'It was sad. But I had to do it.'

Elowen didn't like to push, but this was important. 'And it's helped?' she prompted.

'Yes. I don't think I'd accepted his death, not deep down. But after — ' She stopped.

Elowen waited. Then: 'After what?'

Jo shook her head. 'Nothing.' If I tell Mum about sitting on the shore and talking, at last, of Ben's death, I'll have to say it was Hal who brought it about. And I'm not ready for that. 'After being there a while, it was better,' she finished lamely.

Elowen watched her. Whatever had happened in San Francisco that Jo wasn't prepared to talk about, she thought it must have been good.

★ ★ ★

Jo was becoming friends with her neighbour, who had a three-year old daughter at Edmund's playschool. Jenny knew why Jo was on her own; it's small-community living, Jo thought, I expect everyone's aware of all the gory details. It was another hurdle to clear, coping with people being sympathetic. But to Jo's relief, Jenny said nothing

222

beyond a brief expression of regret.

The friendship deepened when Jenny was ill one morning. Jo had an early call from her husband, asking if Jo would take over Jenny's turn on the playschool run. Jo found the child by herself downstairs.

'Mummy's in bed,' Laura said. Jo went to look, and found Jenny sleeping deeply. When she brought the children home at the end of the morning, Jenny was up but looking so awful that Jo took Laura away again.

'She can have lunch with us,' she said. 'Give me a ring when you're feeling better, and I'll bring her home. What is it, a tummy upset?'

'No, a sodding migraine,' Jenny said weakly.

'Oh, poor you. See if you can sleep again. Laura'll be quite happy with us, I'll take them for a walk later.'

Jenny telephoned in the late afternoon, and when Jo arrived with the children she was making a cup of tea.

'You look better,' Jo said. 'How's your head?'

'All right now. I've been asleep for hours. I've just had a bath.'

'Do you want me to do anything? What about the evening meal?'

'No thanks. Tom's going to be late, and I shan't bother.'

'Well, sit down and I'll give the children some tea.'

'It's nice of you to help,' Jenny said, watching as Jo made herself at home in the kitchen.

'Don't give it a thought,' Jo said. Hal flashed

into her mind: she found herself using his turns of phrase as if, despite her efforts not to think about him, part of her mind was determined she should. 'I know how awful it is having to cook when you're ill,' she hurried on. 'Food's so revolting when you've just thrown up.'

★ ★ ★

One afternoon she thought about the book for Mary and Bernard. She'd written to thank them for their hospitality, but repressed thoughts of the book — it made her think of Hal suggesting it.

She informed Edmund that they were going to his favourite bookshop in Tunbridge Wells. While he sat on the floor looking at children's books, she browsed among the travel guides and the tourist books until she found what she wanted; she felt sure the MacAllisters would like it. She suppressed the companion thought that Hal would, too: 'Maybe they'll let me borrow it.'

She thought exclusively about Hal for the rest of the day. It was now four weeks since she'd left America; why hasn't he written? Why haven't I written to him? Is he going to? Is he waiting for me to write first? Has he forgotten all about me? Did he mean what he said? What *did* he say, for God's sake? What did one kiss — all right, two kisses — mean, anyway?

And why am I so bothered? She gave Edmund his tea and put him to bed in a lip-biting fervour of anxiety, feeling guilty and going back to kiss him again to make up for having been so distant. In the peace of the still house she agonized endlessly until, for sheer self-preservation, she eventually made herself act.

She searched through the old briefcase where she kept maps and guides, and found what she was looking for: the handbook she'd bought at the British Museum. Well, he definitely said he was going to lecture there, she told herself, so wouldn't he like an idea of what to look at in his lunch-hour? Now, unless I'm going to send it anonymously, I have to write him a note.

She poured herself a brandy. It's important, she told herself, that I don't develop an unbreakable link between brandy and crying, with or without the thunder. I don't want to end up like Pavlov's dogs.

She stood thinking, swirling the brandy around in the glass. Then, inhibition eased by the application of neat spirits, she wrote, 'You'd better go and see the Elgin Marbles first, in case they send them back to Greece. Love, Jo.'

Light-hearted, she finished her brandy and went to bed.

★ ★ ★

The next couple of weeks were an exercise in not watching for the postman and in thinking up a hundred reasons why people failed to reply to letters. Her birthday fell two weeks into October. Thank God Hal doesn't know, she thought; it would have been devastating if she'd known he'd known and he'd failed to send her a card.

She was woken up on her birthday morning by Edmund clumping up the stairs with the post, singing his own version of 'Postman Pat'. She dropped him and Laura at playschool and then wrote to Elowen. In the middle of the morning the parcel post delivered three parcels; Elowen had sent her a Liberty scarf wrapped round a box of chocolates, her father had sent her a book on Chagall, and to her surprise Mary and Bernard had sent her a scarlet sweatshirt that said *San Francisco*; she'd forgotten they knew it was her birthday.

Jenny brought the children home, and she and Laura stayed for lunch. Jo had put a bottle of white wine in the fridge and prepared a salad. Jenny gave her a kiss and a bar of '*L'Air du Temps*' soap.

'It's not very original,' she said, 'but I saw the perfume in your bathroom and thought you'd like the soap.'

'I do,' Jo said. 'It's sweet of you, thank you.'

They took the children for a walk in the afternoon. I love my birthday, she thought, I'm glad it's in the autumn. Perhaps that's why I like the autumn — it's my season. Suddenly she was walking hand in hand with Hal on Fisherman's Wharf.

They ran home across the fields. Jo went to put the kettle on, looking out some candles for the cake, while Jenny got the children's boots off and took them to wash their hands.

There was a ring at the doorbell. She put down the candles and went into the hall. Her neighbour from the other side stood on the doorstep. 'You and Jenny must have been out when they called,' she said with a smile, 'so I took these in. Aren't they glorious?'

She held out her arms. Across them lay an enormous bouquet of autumn flowers in shades of dark brown, bronze, russet, orange, soft yellow-blonde and pale cream.

'Is it your birthday, dear?' the neighbour asked.

Jo, standing slack-jawed, eyes fixed on the flowers, pulled herself together. 'Oh — yes, it is.'

'Someone must be thinking of you! Happy birthday!'

She closed the door and carried the flowers into the living-room.

'Hey, aren't they fabulous?' Jenny cried, coming in behind her. 'Who are they from?'

'I don't know.'

'Isn't there a card?' Jenny peered over her shoulder. 'Yes, look, here!' She reached to pull it off, then, glancing at Jo's face, stopped. 'You'd rather open it yourself, I expect,' she said tactfully. 'Have you got something to cut the ribbon with?' Jo pointed at her sewing basket, and Jenny fetched the scissors. 'Come on, get on with it!'

Jo opened the envelope and took out the card.

'*Floribunda International*, for your greetings anywhere in the world.'

She looked at the writing underneath, and burst into tears. It said: 'Happy Birthday, love from Hal.'

'What's the matter, Mummy?' Edmund came running in, flinging his arms round her; Jenny swiftly swept the bouquet off her lap. 'Why are you crying?'

'Hay fever,' Jo said, sniffing. 'It's the pollen,

making my eyes water.' Jenny shot her a look. 'I'm fine, darling.'

Jenny took the card out of her hand and looked at it. 'Hal who?'

'Hal Dillon,' Jo said automatically.

'Come on, kids,' Jenny said, 'let's make the tea. You go and wipe your eyes,' she added to Jo, 'then you can tell me why this Hal Dillon bloke sending you a hugely extravagant bunch of flowers — in exactly your colours, I might add — is making you cry like a baby!'

Jo went to dry her face. Idiot, she said to herself in the mirror, fancy *crying*, damn it. Stupid, over-emotional bloody woman.

She joined the others in the kitchen. 'Can you take the cake in, Jen?' she said. This is me being sensible, she thought. In control. 'I'll just get some vases.'

When the candles had been blown out and relit seven times and the children had at last tired of 'Happy Birthday to You' and gone off to watch television, Jo and Jenny sat over a last cup of tea in the kitchen.

'Who is he, then?' Jenny asked.

'He was a friend of Ben's,' Jo said. 'The family introduced us. I saw a bit of him while I was in San Francisco. Well, I saw lots of people. Hal was one of them.'

'I could have worked that much out for myself,' Jenny remarked. 'Nice of him to send flowers.'

'I expect it's because I'm Ben's wife.'

Jenny eyed her disbelievingly. 'I wonder why you reacted like that?'

228

'Well, it was a surprise,' Jo hedged. 'I didn't think he knew it was my birthday.'

'Your in-laws sent you something, you said, so they must have known. Perhaps he found out from them.'

'Yes, I expect that was it,' Jo agreed. Then, quickly: 'Let's have a drink before you go. Sherry? Gin?'

'No thanks. I've got Tom's supper to cook yet.'

She called to Laura, and Jo saw them to the door.

'Enjoy the rest of your birthday,' Jenny called over her shoulder. Then she added, mimicking Jo's voice, 'I saw a bit of him while I was in San Francisco.' She raised her eyes heavenwards and disappeared into her own garden. 'Come on, Laura, the woman's deluded!'

After Edmund was asleep, Jo put on her recently-acquired recording of the Bruch violin concerto and sat down to write to Hal.

She covered several pages, telling him about her birthday and going on to describe the beauties of the autumn landscape. Do you remember us talking about the autumn? she asked him silently. Perhaps I'll show you an English autumn. One day.

I'll send him a book, she thought, going to look along the shelves. Something that gives the flavour of this part of the country . . . Her eyes fell on 'Puck of Pook's Hill,' and she took it down with a smile of pleasure.

'I'm sending you some more reading matter,' she wrote. 'When you get here you'll have to get used to everything being steeped ages deep in history.'

When you get here. The thought sparked off visions in her head. I'll take him to all sorts of places, and we'll . . .

No. He's not here yet. Anything could happen.

And I don't really know what it is I want. Do I?

Her thoughts were beginning to disturb her. She finished the letter, then sealed it up before she could change her mind.

She had a last look at Hal's flowers. Autumn colours. It was tempting to think he'd chosen them all individually, but he probably hadn't.

She didn't care.

17

Jo's birthday happiness stayed with her. One morning she woke at dawn with a profound sense of joy. She'd been dreaming of Ben. She closed her eyes and tried to make the dream come back. The picture was vivid still: he was all in white, and appeared to be an angel. A sun-tanned angel, she thought drowsily, with blue eyes and such a smile . . .

The image of Ben remained with her. In the evening she got out her sketch pad and pencils, wondering whether she could record it.

Edmund came to see what she was doing.

'That's your Daddy,' she said gently.

'I know.' Edmund's attention was fixed on the drawing. 'He's in heaven.'

'Mm. Shall we give him some wings?' He nodded, and she drew a luxurious pair of wings like Pegasus's, smooth and thickly-feathered.

Edmund ran his finger delicately around the curve of a wing. 'Angels stop you falling over, don't they, Mummy?'

'Yes, amongst other things.' She knew what was in his mind: at playschool there was a picture of two children walking perilously close to the edge of a cliff, with a guardian angel dressed similarly to this Ben of her drawing stretching out a protective hand to keep them safe.

'Is Daddy my angel?'

'Yes, my love, I'm sure he is.' She leaned over to kiss him. The beginning of a story was forming in her mind.

★ ★ ★

In the peace of the night, she began to write a simple tale about a boy who lost his father. The boy was like Edmund, only a couple of years older; the father was Ben, returned to earth to be his son's guardian angel. The text would be illustrated by a series of drawings.

She found it heartening that she wanted to write again, for the first time since Ben had died. She'd always known that, if she did get back to it, it would have to be something new. There could never be any more Elfie stories; Elfie belonged to the Ben days, to the warm midsummer magic of a dusty French courtyard where Jo sat writing while Ben worked for both of them. Elfie was as dead as Ben; she couldn't bring either of them back.

★ ★ ★

The autumn days grew shorter, and November came. One morning a bulky letter arrived bearing American stamps. It wasn't Bernard's writing; it was a confident, stylish hand. She knew straight away it was Hal's.

It was a strange sensation, to hold something he had touched. When her thumping heartbeat had slowed down a little, she opened the letter and started to read.

Hal was spending a few days with his father, who lived to the south of San Francisco in a place called Morro Bay. This little oceanside town was remarkable, he said, by virtue of having an enormous plug of volcanic rock standing in the bay, giving you the illusion there was a dip in the ocean floor just there and a monstrous camel was walking in it with only its hump showing. He went on to say he'd found out about her birthday from Mary, he was glad she'd liked the flowers, and he and his dad were both avidly reading Puck, sneaking the book away when the other wasn't looking.

'The house is full of the sounds of the cello,' he wrote. 'Right now I'm listening to a tape of the Elgar concerto; earlier Dad was playing the melody from the first movement. He says his joints have gotten too stiff to play, but I reckon his fingers are so familiar with these works he loves that they'll play them for him till the day he dies.

We've been thinking what to send you in return for Puck. We chose this book that's enclosed. We hope you like it. Read 'Springtime à la Carte' first — it makes me think of you.'

She looked down at the book he'd sent; it was a collection of stories by O. Henry. She opened it and read on the flyleaf, in an unformed but fairly dashing hand, 'H. S. Dillon, September 1953.' A photograph fell out; a boy sitting on the deck of a yacht, smiling at the camera. It was obviously Hal. 'Dad insisted I send you this,' he'd written on the back. 'Punchy little bastard, wasn't I?'

The letter went on to say he was going to Mexico in November to finish preparations for his lectures in England. He thanked her for the British Museum guide; having studied the plan in the middle, he now felt confident he could find his way to the lecture theatre.

> 'Give that little Teddy of yours a kiss from me, and I guess you'd better have one too. I picture you sometimes in Muir Woods. It was real nice to see you laughing.
>
> See you soon, love Hal.'

See you soon, she thought, folding the letter and absently pushing it back in the envelope. I wonder when?

★ ★ ★

After playschool half term, the children began to rehearse their Nativity Play. Christmas excitement started to tingle in the air; Jo put up an Advent Calendar, and Edmund ceremoniously opened the first door. He was going to be the innkeeper in the play; a small but crucial role, Jo thought, listening as he repeated his two lines. Laura was to be the Angel Gabriel.

'Starring role,' Jo observed to Jenny. 'I hope you're not going to turn into a showbiz mother.'

'Not likely,' Jenny replied.

'No tap-dancing lessons? Auditions for the Pears Soap child?'

'No. Tom's got her a football for Christmas.'

'She'll make a lovely angel,' Jo said. 'You must be a bit pleased?'

Jenny sniffed. 'Any pleasure I might have had evaporated the moment I discovered I have to make the sodding costume.'

'You shouldn't swear in the context of nativity play costumes,' Jo said piously.

'It's all right for you, all an innkeeper needs is an old shirt and a bit of rope for a belt.'

'I'll help. If you like.'

'Will you?' Jenny looked doubtful. 'It's got to have wings.'

'Nothing I can't handle.'

They settled down to costume-making one afternoon in Jenny's living room. Jenny found one of Tom's shirts for Edmund — 'He doesn't wear it, honestly, he hates it — my mother gave it to him' — and tied a tea towel round his head.

By evening they'd finished, and had to get the children out of their new costumes before they damaged them.

★ ★ ★

When Jo and Edmund arrived home, the phone was ringing; it was her father. 'I'll be in London next week,' he said. 'I'd like to see you.'

'How nice, Dad.' It was like a royal progression; when her father announced a pending visit, nobody ever said no.

'Next Wednesday. I'll go on to Gatwick on Thursday morning.'

'Okay. Bye, Dad.'

* * *

He arrived at half-past three, pulling up outside the house with a soft scrunch of gravel and the subtle whisper of a powerful engine. She went out to greet him.

'Would you like some tea? Edmund's next door with my neighbour.'

'Tea would be nice.'

She went into the kitchen, loading a tray with cups and saucers and a cake. 'How's Mum?' she asked.

'Very well. Looking forward to Christmas with you and your parents-in-law.'

'It's a pity you can't be here as well, Dad.'

'Thank you. I have to be back in Zurich before Christmas.'

There was no need to press the matter. She'd made the offer, he'd declined; that was that.

They made fairly stilted conversation till Jenny brought Edmund home. Jenny accepted a cup of tea, and Jo watched her trying to work out what to make of Paul Daniel. Quite soon she made her excuses and left; 'He's a dish,' she hissed to Jo in the hall. 'But does he *have* a sense of humour?'

Amused, Jo went back into the living-room. Edmund was sitting on the sofa beside Paul; overawed by his grandfather, he ate his tea quietly and carefully. Washing up out in the kitchen, she

236

heard them talking; she looked through the open door and saw that her father had abandoned her copy of *The Times* and was watching Bugs Bunny with his grandson.

'Granfa' said he'll read me a story,' Edmund told her when she put him into his pyjamas.

'Did he?' She was surprised. 'Let's choose one that's not too long,' she searched among Edmund's books for a modest-length Beatrix Potter, 'because I don't think Grandfather's very used to reading aloud.'

★ ★ ★

When Edmund had been put to bed, she got drinks for her father and herself. 'Dinner's in half an hour,' she said.

He nodded. There was silence for some time, then Paul said, 'Your mother says you enjoyed your trip to America. I admire the way you've got on with your life. I was inclined to query the wisdom of your visit — I thought it might interfere with your progress.'

She wasn't sure what he meant. 'You thought seeing Ben's family would put me back?'

'I wondered, yes.'

'It hasn't. I feel much better now.' I really do! she thought, faintly surprised. 'I suppose it's accepting that a phase of my life is finished.'

'Good.'

Did he intend to prod me into realizing that? she wondered. Clever of him.

But he was already forging on. 'Have you

given any thought to the future? What about your writing?'

She hesitated. She had completed the first draft of the new story, and was working on a set of ten water-colour illustrations. She was pleased with it, but it was secret; the tender theme and the fact that it was the first thing she'd produced for so long made her protective. 'I've started something new.'

'Hmm. Your visit did do you good. Will it lead to a resurgence of your lucrative writing career?'

Typical Dad, she thought. Nine out of ten people would have said, oh really, what's it about? but not him, he goes straight for the throat and asks about the money. She wanted to smile. 'I don't know, Dad. It's just one idea. But it may lead to more.'

She got up to refill their glasses. His face thoughtful, he said, 'Bright boy, your Edmund. Astonishing vocabulary.' She hoped fervently Edmund hadn't tried out 'poo-poo-willy-shit' to see if it had the same effect on his grandfather as it'd had on his mother. 'You obviously read to him a great deal.'

'Yes.' Apparently he hadn't.

Her father smiled. 'I'm pleased with my first grandson.'

'I'm glad. Do you anticipate more?'

He sighed deeply. 'Who can say?' Then abruptly: 'When is supper ready?'

'Now, if you like.' She got up. 'Will you open the wine?'

★ ★ ★

Over the meal he answered her questions about her mother and happenings at home. While she cleared away he disappeared up to his room, returning with a bottle of brandy. 'You make coffee, and I'll pour us some of this. Where are the glasses?'

'Rémy! Thanks, Dad.'

He was standing in the doorway, watching her. She was almost certain there was something he wanted to say. She led the way back to the living-room and, when they were settled, looked at him and grinned. 'What is it, then?'

He smiled briefly back. Then: 'Would you consider coming to Zurich to work for me?'

'Dad!' She was amazed. 'But I'm the arty one, remember?' He had said that somewhat disparagingly when she'd insisted on going to art college instead of taking up the place he'd got her at a first-class school of business studies. 'I'd be useless!'

'No you wouldn't.' He spoke forcefully. Good grief, she thought, he means it. 'You're intelligent, you learn quickly, and you've proved how adaptable you are. Look at the way you manage here,' he waved an arm around him, 'your life is secure, solid and sensible.'

Oh, hell, is it? It doesn't sound a lot of fun. 'But you already have the boys working for you,' she protested. 'Why do you want me?'

He looked at her. 'Partly because you're the one with a son.'

'What's that got to do with it?'

'Oh, I don't know.' He seemed slightly embarrassed. 'Family continuity, someone to leave

239

things to . . . ' He trailed off. No wonder he seems awkward, she thought, he's getting dangerously close to being emotional.

'But surely Phil and Jaqueline will have children?' she said. 'They've only been married . . . how long?'

'Eight years. And with every year that ridiculous woman becomes more self-centred, and less likely to give up her fatuous high life in favour of motherhood.'

'Oh,' she said lamely, surprised by his sudden vindictiveness. 'I didn't realize.'

'No, of course not. You don't live in Zurich and have to endure the spectacle of your son being led by the nose by someone with a tenth of his intelligence but so much bombast and misplaced self-confidence that she can't even see herself how appallingly stupid she is, let alone admit it to anyone else.'

He sat back angrily, taking a mouthful of brandy. She didn't know what to say. 'Can't you talk to Philip?'

'No. He closes up, won't confide in me. I think she may be persuading him away.'

'Oh, Dad.' She realized just how little she knew of the doings of her family, other than Elowen; it was ages since she'd taken much notice of them. Paul could have been speaking of strangers. 'What about Geoff?'

Her father snorted. 'He has a lot of growing-up to do. He's still acting the silly ass, enjoying his affluence but not prepared to throw himself into earning it.'

'Well, he's only thirty-four,' she said protectively.

'He's two years older than you,' Paul retorted, 'and I can't see him coping with the tragedy you've had.'

'Maybe he'd be more mature if he'd had to, but that's no reason to wish it on him.'

'No. I'm sorry,' he said, more gently.

They sat in silence. Then he said, 'Will you come to Zurich?'

She looked up at him. 'No, Dad.'

'Can you say why not?'

'Because I like my life here.'

'I see.'

'And also, — I should have put this first — if I worked full-time, for you or anyone, I'd have to employ someone else to bring up Edmund.'

'And you couldn't have that,' he concluded for her. 'Not for Ben's boy.'

She was surprised he'd said that, surprised even that he'd thought it. She made herself think about her brothers. 'Surely the situation can't be that bad. They can't both be useless, unless you're asking the impossible of them.' 'You're probably right. I know how things must be done, though. Neither of them puts enough into the job to have a worthwhile opinion.'

'Do you ever ask for their opinions?'

'No.'

'That,' she said triumphantly, 'is a circular argument. If you never listen to what they say, how can you possibly know it's no good?'

Paul gave a sudden bark of laughter. 'Do you play chess?'

'No.'

'Pity.'

They were quiet for some time. She got up to put on some music. It was Mozart, a piano concerto. 'You ought to listen to some decent music, you know, Dad.'

'Send me some. On tape, then I can listen in the car.'

Yes, she thought fondly, when you're a captive audience. Because even you can't do much other than listen while you're driving.

* * *

In the morning Paul prepared to leave. She went out to the car with him. I wonder what happens to it at Gatwick? she wondered idly. Does one of his minions pick it up? Nice for them, to drive back to town in a Roller.

Paul was reaching into the boot. 'Is Edmund looking?' he asked. 'I've got some Christmas presents here.'

'Thanks, Dad! No, he's still in the house. But be quick, he'll be out as soon as he's got his wellies on.'

Paul gave her a big bag of wrapped presents, and she hid them in the back of the garage. 'I'll send you some tapes for Christmas,' she promised.

He stood with his hand on her shoulder for a moment. 'If you ever change your mind, the offer will remain open. You don't know how you'll feel when Edmund's older.'

'I won't change my mind.' She spoke with

conviction. 'But it means a lot, that you asked me.'

He bent down to say goodbye to Edmund, who had just emerged from the house with his boots on the wrong feet. She stood waving as the Rolls glided away, then, with a slight feeling of release, took Edmund inside and closed the door.

18

'I hope you'll venture out for a Christmas Day drink with us,' Jo said to Jenny one morning while the children were at playschool. 'Oh, why did I have to buy Edmund a wheelbarrow? I can't even make two bits of paper go round it.'

'Here,' Jenny said, cutting off strips of sellotape to attach a third sheet. 'Yes, we'd like that. Did I tell you it's just going to be the three of us?'

'Repeatedly. I thought I'd ask Mrs Thing, too, from next door. What *is* her name?'

'Watson.'

'And is there a Mr Thing? Come on, Jen, you've lived here two years longer than me, you're meant to know these things.'

'I do. Mr Thing goes up to town each day, and he binds books in his spare time, so nobody, including his wife, sees much of him.'

'Well, I'm going to ask them anyway,' Jo said decisively.

★ ★ ★

Cards began to arrive, and every morning Edmund sat in silent excitement right behind the letter-box. She let him open them, even though they often emerged bent. One came from Hal, postmarked Mexico City. It was a tender study of the Madonna and Child; she gave it pride of place on the mantleshelf.

Hal wrote that he'd been taking pictures of some stelae, which were particularly interesting since they showed how Mayan astronomers predicted eclipses with such precision. The trouble with knowing someone as intellectual as Hal, she thought ruefully as she thumbed through the dictionary, is that he makes you realize your ignorance. I don't suppose he imagined for a moment I wouldn't know what stelae were.

He still didn't say when he was coming to England.

★ ★ ★

The MacAllisters arrived on the Saturday before Christmas. Jo and Edmund went to meet them, driving to Gatwick on roads bordered with white-frosted hedgerows.

They said stoutly that they weren't tired, but when Jo suggested a rest in their room after lunch, they thought that'd be nice. Although Edmund protested he was tired too and ought to lie down with them, she made him go for a walk with her instead.

'*Why* can't I?' he grumbled as they climbed the style.

'Because you're a noisy little boy who can't keep quiet for five minutes.'

'I can!'

She looked at her watch. 'Bet you can't.'

He folded his lips firmly together, frowning with

245

the effort. Two and a half minutes later a pheasant shot up out of the hedge and he said, 'Mummy, peasant! Look!'

She smiled smugly and refused to accept that there were mitigating circumstances; walks were more fun when they were chatting.

* * *

When they got back Mary was in the kitchen making a pot of tea.

'Oh, good,' Jo said, 'I'm glad you're making yourself at home.'

'Well, you won't want to be making every drink, snack and meal throughout our vacation,' Mary said sensibly, 'I reckoned I'd start as I mean to go on.'

Over dinner Jo caught up on people she'd met in the summer. Emily had settled well in her new job; she and Dean were going to Annie and Steve for Christmas.

'We haven't seen anything of Hal,' Bernard said. 'He went down to stay with his father, then he was going on to Mexico.'

'Yes, I know. He wrote to me from Morro Bay, and we had a card from Mexico City. Er — do you know when he gets to England?'

'No, honey,' Mary said, 'he just told us next year.'

That could be April, or August, or October, Jo thought.

Elowen arrived after lunch the next day. Bernard and Mary tactfully went up soon after dinner, saying they'd catch up on some sleep. Elowen and Jo settled down companionably in front of the fire.

'How was Dad's visit?' Elowen asked when Jo had finished telling her about Edmund's stage debut as the innkeeper.

'I enjoyed it. Did you know he was going to ask me about Zurich?'

'Yes. I said I didn't think you'd go.'

'No. But it felt good to be asked. Are things better now?'

'I believe so. He was very down at the beginning of November, he came to you in sheer desperation.'

'Thanks, Mum.'

Elowen laughed. 'That's not to say he didn't mean it. He's looked at you with new eyes, darling, because of the way you've picked yourself up and reorganized your life.' Jo felt pleased.

They sat for a little longer, watching the fire die down, then reluctantly got up and went to bed.

★ ★ ★

Christmas Eve was busy with baking, and they listened to the service of lessons and carols from King's College Chapel with aromas of spice floating through the house. In the evening, parcels began to appear under the tree, and Jo fetched the little presents she'd bought for Edmund's stocking, stuffing them down into one of a pair of thick socks that Ben used to wear under his wellies for gardening.

The house fell quiet, and she put on some soft

music. She sat relaxed on the sofa, gazing absently at the Christmas tree. The past few weeks had been so busy that she'd had little time for reflection, and, as she now thought back over the year since the previous Christmas, she realized how much things had changed.

For a moment, she couldn't picture Ben. She leapt up, fetching the photograph albums from her desk. She turned the pages, looking at the Ben and Jo that once had been. Then came Edmund, first as a bump in his mother's tummy, then a bundle in a blanket, then a real baby, sitting up and glaring at the camera.

We've all changed, she thought. Edmund's no longer a baby, I'm no longer that young wife, and Ben, oh Ben, you're no longer here at all. She sat with tears in her eyes, but it wasn't simply at the sorrow of losing him. This year, the year she'd pulled herself up and got on with living, she had finally begun to leave Ben behind.

It was stark and it hurt. But I can never leave you entirely, Ben, she thought, her eyes fixed on the very last photograph of him. We belonged only to each other. But you're not here now, and I still am.

What shall I do, my love? she asked him. But there was no answer.

★ ★ ★

Christmas Day began with Edmund climbing into bed with her in the darkness. 'Mummy, do you think he's been?' he whispered.

She opened her eyes and peered at the red figures on the digital clock: 4.48. 'He may not have quite been yet,' she whispered back. 'Let's see if we can sleep a bit more, just in case.'

Next time he woke her it was 7.30, which was a reasonable time to start the day. They crept downstairs into the living-room, where the curtains were still drawn from last night. She switched on the tree lights, then turned to look at her son's face. His eyes were round and shining and glued to the stack of presents under the tree.

'Oh, Mummy,' he said reverently, 'he *has* been.'

Breakfast was informal, eaten in their dressing-gowns. We're a family, Jo thought, and the closeness deepened as her parents-in-law threw themselves wholeheartedly into the day. They spent the next hour kneeling amid presents and discarded wrapping paper, then Jo brought in a bottle of champagne.

Jenny and Tom arrived, with Laura clutching an enormous doll. There was a less flamboyant ring at the door, and Jo went to greet Mr and Mrs Watson. She wondered if they felt the cold; although they'd only come from next door and the weather wasn't all that wintry, they seemed to be wearing an inordinate amount of clothing. Jo introduced them to her mother and parents-in-law; she was finding everything slightly funny, and wished she'd gone easier on the champagne.

But no one seemed to notice; everyone's the same, she realized with relief. Mrs Watson's modest glass of sherry seemed to affect her disproportionately strongly, and presently she began to struggle out of her thick fluffy cardigan. Mr Watson put down his glass and rushed to help her; 'Mother gets a little overheated,' he remarked to Tom. Jo caught Jenny's eye but hastily looked away.

'Oh, look,' Jo said to Bernard later as they cleared away the glasses, 'Mother's left her cardigan behind!'

It's been a good day, Jo thought as they sat sleepily together in the firelight, best Christmas I've had for a long time.

★ ★ ★

On Boxing Day she took them walking, over footpaths to Bodiam Castle, dramatic amidst frost-covered fields under a clear blue sky. On Saturday, ordinary life began again: Jo and Mary went out to buy some bread. They had a late lunch, after which Jo offered to take them out for a drive. Her guests all looked guiltily at one another and said they'd really rather stay where they were.

Jo let them off. 'But we're going out tomorrow,' she said firmly, 'or we'll all seize up.'

After tea, they were startled to hear the doorbell ring.

'I expect it'll be Mrs Watson, come for her cardigan,' Jo said, getting up.

She went to open the front door. Bernard, peering through the curtains, said, 'I don't reckon it is, unless Mrs Watson got herself a black BMW for Christmas.'

'Who does she know with a black BMW?' Mary asked Elowen, who shrugged.

Jo opened the door.

To her total amazement, Hal stood on the step. He had a stuffed zebra under his arm.

She was so surprised she couldn't think of anything sensible to say.

'I thought you were Mrs Watson, come for her cardigan!' she cried.

'Nope. May I come in, all the same?'

'Oh! Oh, yes, of course!'

In total confusion, she stood aside to let him in. She had forgotten how tall he was; he looked huge in her low-ceilinged old house.

'Look!' She stood in the living-room doorway, arm flung out with the air of Michaelangelo unveiling David.

'Hal! Well, hi!'

'What are *you* doing here?'

Mary and Bernard got up to greet him. Jo went over to Elowen, taking her hand and drawing her forwards. 'Mum, this is Hal Dillon. Hal, this is my mother, Elowen Daniel.'

They shook hands.

'We thought you were in Mexico!' Mary said.

'I got back a week before Christmas,' Hal replied. 'The London apartment was ready, and as my dad had already gone away for the vacation I reckoned I'd come on over.'

'When did you get here?' Jo asked.

'Couple of days before Christmas Eve.'

'Oh, Hal!' She was dismayed. 'You spent Christmas all by yourself in a strange city! Why didn't you let us know? You could have come here!'

'You have a house full.'

'Not that full.' She looked at him, preoccupied at first with feeling sorry that he'd been alone on Christmas Day. Then, his well-remembered grin spreading slowly over his face as he stared back at her, she began to feel embarrassed. And very happy.

'We can make space for one more, can't we, Jo?' Mary asked.

'Yes, of course. You can't go back, Hal, now you're here. How did you find us? It's not all that easy.'

'I bought a map.'

'Oh.'

She thought she heard him laugh. Then he said, 'Hey, Teddy, take a look in the hall, there's an animal there who needs someone to love.'

Edmund ran into the hall and returned with the zebra.

'Take him out of the bag,' Hal suggested. Edmund did so. Then he got up beside Hal and whispered in his ear. Hal laughed. 'Okay. If you think you can love him back, he's yours.'

Jo watched Edmund's face as he stroked the stripy fur of his new toy. Mary asked Hal where he got it, and he said Mexico. Jo felt absurdly pleased that, deeply involved with Mayan stelae and astronomical calculations, he'd bothered to go out and buy a present for her son. Not only buy it but cart it all the way from Mexico to San Francisco, and then to London.

She found she was smiling at him.

'It sat on my lap on the airplane,' he said, watching her. 'I'd gotten quite attached to it.'

She felt herself blush, and quickly turned away in confusion.

'Jo, I'll go back to London,' he said to her later.

'Oh, don't! You can have my bed, I'll sleep on the sofa.'

'No. I'll come back another time, when you're quieter.'

'Please don't go, Hal.' She looked steadily up at him.

'Okay.' He grinned suddenly. 'But *I'll* sleep on the sofa.'

'Don't be daft!' It was a relief to giggle. 'Just you go and try!'

He stretched out along the sofa. It was fine, provided he didn't expect to get his head and his feet on at the same time. 'What's wrong with that?' he asked.

She laughed. 'I'll go and get my room ready for you. You'll have to have Teddy in with you; he's in a folding bed on the floor.'

'I don't mind if he doesn't. D'you mind, Teddy?'

'I don't mind.' Edmund had hardly taken his eyes off Hal.

'You have to watch him in the mornings,' Jo said, 'he throws Star Wars toys on the bed and they're awfully sharp.'

'Ain't nothing I can't handle.' He smiled up at her, still lying on the sofa. 'Hey, Teddy, I'll read you a story.'

Edmund ran to get a book and clambered up on to Hal's stomach. 'This one, please,' he said. He pushed the book at Hal.

'Okay, but you're sitting on my glasses — hold on.' He shifted the child's weight while he reached inside his jacket for his glasses. Edmund, not accustomed to people wearing spectacles, wanted to inspect them; Jo could see even from where she stood that he'd put at least two sticky finger marks on the lenses.

Edmund's at home with Hal, straight away, she thought. And Hal with him. The child, still fascinated, kept putting his thumb on Hal's glasses.

' . . . and she lived with her father and her two THUMB elder sisters in a big house THUMB in the country,' Hal said. Edmund started giggling.

'I think I'll leave you to it.' Reluctantly Jo got up. 'I know how it ends anyway.'

Hal looked up briefly. 'Don't tell us.'

'I won't.'

She went upstairs to get her room ready for him. She could hardly believe that he was here, that he'd come to find her.

But there was something in the air, something exciting that had arrived with him and was already weaving itself into the atmosphere.

I'd better start believing it.

19

Hal had arrived in England just before everything shut down for Christmas. Gatwick was packed, the hurrying thousands adding to his confusion at being dumped apparently in the middle of the country. His luggage labels all said LONDON GATWICK, yet as the airplane circled in its descent there had been no sign of any sizeable city.

He got a train from Gatwick and a cab from Victoria, too tired to notice much as London whizzed by the window and glad when he was dropped off in Bloomsbury.

'This is it, mate,' the cabbie said, sitting tight and making no move to help him get his luggage out, just as earlier he hadn't helped him put it in.

'Thanks, pal,' Hal said, and didn't give him a tip.

He stood on the pavement looking at his new abode. The apartment was in a terraced house, elegant with white paint and black wrought iron railings. Three other terraces formed a square, and in the middle was a railed-off park.

He went into the vestibule and located the caretaker's flat. He was given his keys, which he had to sign for. The caretaker said he had a bad leg, which Hal took to mean he wasn't about to help with the luggage either.

He liked the apartment straight away. The living-room was austere, with a leather-topped desk beneath the window. Wing chairs and a chesterfield stood in front of the fireplace. The bookshelves were full of bound volumes of magazines and articles. The colours were so muted as to be indistinguishable, and the place smelt very slightly of pipe tobacco.

There was a compact kitchen and two sparsely-furnished bedrooms. In the larger one, the double bed was made up with blankets, counterpane and eiderdown. He felt the daunting weight of bedclothes and sighed.

He unpacked, making a list of things he had to buy. Then he went out, walking till he found a road busy enough to have taxis cruising.

'Can you take me to the department stores?' he asked a taxi driver.

'Oxford Street do yer?'

He got in. But soon the traffic become so thick that further forward progress seemed unlikely. 'Reckon I'll walk,' Hal said.

'Righto, mate. Follow the crowds, you'll find yer way.'

★ ★ ★

He crawled under his new duvet and had a long sleep in the afternoon, worn out by travelling, luggage-humping and shopping with a million other people. Then he took a shower and went out to eat. He found a pub with space at the bar, and contemplated the long row of beer pumps, all of which produced a much darker beer than he was used to.

He enjoyed his solitude. He stocked up with food, and spent pleasurable hours cooking. He'd bought a new cassette player, and listened with quiet pleasure to his great collection of tapes. He had no work to do; there were notes and papers to finish before he began his lectures in the New Year, but he was going to have a break first. Reckon I've earned it, he thought.

He spent an afternoon in the British Museum, and suddenly felt at home. He contemplated sending Jo a postcard to tell her he'd been using her museum guide. He'd been thinking about her continuously since he'd arrived. He'd been totally mixed up in the summer. He found her very attractive, and, had she been anyone other than who she was, he'd have gone after her a lot harder. But she was Ben's wife, and it made her special. It made him feel he couldn't make a move till he'd sorted out his own feelings. Which, he thought, I stirred into a whirlwind by kissing her. Now I have no idea where physical desire ends and real liking begins.

He missed her after she'd gone home; when she wasn't there any more he appreciated just how much he'd enjoyed being with her. He'd wanted to write, but was reluctant to push it if she'd decided not to.

His trip to Mexico had been unavoidable; there had been material he'd needed for his lectures. But he hadn't had to go to Mexico City.

It had been a test. And it hurt, it still hurt. The memories were vivid, sharp. But, enduring them, he held on to a mental picture of Jo, and it helped.

Thanks, sweetheart, he said to her. He chose her

a special Christmas card, in mute gratitude for her unwitting presence.

★ ★ ★

On the morning of Christmas Eve he picked up his new car and nearly scared himself to death driving it round Hyde Park Corner. What I need, he thought as he stopped with some relief outside his apartment, is a gentle drive out into the country.

In the afternoon he joined the last-minute shoppers and bought a map. 'God-awful time to be buying maps,' he said apologetically to a man whose foot he'd just trodden on.

'God-awful time to be buying anything,' the man replied lugubriously.

He worked out the impossible journey to Hawkhurst. I can't go right now, he thought, she'll be way too busy. On Christmas Day and Boxing Day he thought the same. Then on Saturday he decided he couldn't leave his new car standing expectantly outside any longer. He packed a bag, picked up his map and the stuffed zebra he'd bought for Edmund, and set out before he could change his mind.

It took him a long time to get out of London. But after a while he got used to the car, and to driving on the left, and to having to look out for signs saying A21 in a bewildering variety of size, colour and shape. Eventually he got onto a stretch of dual carriageway, and put his foot down.

Then the road changed character yet again. Jeez,

he thought, traffic racing past as he pulled into a lay-by to put on his glasses and consult the map for the eighth time, how the hell do they all do it?

The road leading to Jo's house was so narrow that he was sure he was going up a private drive. And the signposts had given out, too; he had to ask somebody for directions. He began to think Copse Hill House was a figment of his — her — imagination.

But he found her in the end. And her only comment on that goddam lousy journey was, 'It's not all that easy.'

British understatement. And it came so naturally to her.

★ ★ ★

He woke up in her bed, and found that someone had left him a cup of tea. He sat up to drink it. There were quite a few toys on the bed, although the child had gone. Nice kid. Jo must have taken him off with her when she brought the tea. He took a shower, then went downstairs.

He watched Jo moving about the kitchen, busy making coffee and toast for them all. She put a rack of toast on the table with a determined thump. 'We're going out today,' she announced. The MacAllisters and Elowen looked up politely. 'We're going to Rye, and I shall show you lots of interesting things.'

There were various murmurs of assent. She turned to him. 'We'll have to take two cars. Can

Mum and Mary go with you?'

'Sure. Is it far?'

'Oh, no. Ten, twelve miles. And they're quiet roads.'

'Maybe, but they're so damned narrow.'

'Oh!' Her face fell a little. I have to stop teasing her, he thought. 'It's okay.' He gave her his reassuring smile. 'I'll manage.'

★ ★ ★

She set off in a mud-splattered Range Rover, her face serious with responsibility. She's different here, he thought, pulling out into the lane behind her. It's like she feels it's down to her to make us all happy. He noticed how frequently she looked in the rearview mirror. Okay, sweetheart, I'm right here. Her brake lights flashed on suddenly: she'd slowed down to drive very carefully past a flock of sheep.

'Not exactly Jehu, are you?' he remarked to her as they bought 'Pay and Display' tickets. 'I could have gotten here in half the time if I hadn't been stuck behind you.'

'No you couldn't, you didn't know the way.'

'And sheep, for God's sake, in the middle of the road.'

'Yes, we're so quaint in our ways, aren't we?'

She took them all around Rye, pointing out its interesting features — there were many — and fielding most of their questions. As they came out of St Mary's Church, he gave her a pound.

She looked up at him. 'What's that for?'

'Always tip the guide, when she's doing a good job.'

They had lunch in a wine bar that didn't object to small children, then went down to the Ypres Tower and stood on the parapet looking out across the misty flats.

'I thought you said Rye was a port, a Cinque Port?' Mary said. 'The sea's right over there.'

'It used to have one of the best harbours of all the south coast ports,' Jo said, proceeding to bemuse her mother-in-law with an involved history of the decline of medieval Rye.

Hal looked on with amusement. Mary said, 'Thanks, honey,' then quickly changed the subject. He reached in his pocket and quietly handed Jo another pound.

Back home, he came into the house to hear her talking with her mother in the hall. 'Mary and Bernard and I think we'll have a quiet evening's TV tonight, darling,' Elowen was saying, 'so why don't you and Hal go out?'

She looked furtively over her shoulder at him, then turned back to her mother. 'Wouldn't you mind?'

'No. We want to watch the film.'

'Oh. What do you think, Hal?'

'What's the film?' he asked. He looked down at Jo, trying not to smile. He couldn't resist teasing her. Elowen told him. 'I've seen it, it's good.' He grinned at Jo. 'But I'll skip it. Sure, we'll go out.'

★ ★ ★

'D'you want to drive or shall I?' he asked her as they left the house later.

'We could walk. There's a nice pub about a mile away.'

They set off up the lane, the ground hard and cold beneath their feet. He was very aware of her beside him in the silent darkness. He said, 'Give me your hand. I can't see where I'm going.'

She put her hand in his. Even through the thickness of two gloves, it felt small and delicate. He heard her draw in her breath.

They walked on in silence for a while. Then Jo said, 'I loved your O. Henry.'

'Good. Dad and I loved your Puck. I guess it was written near here — I keep seeing place names I recognize.'

'Yes. Kipling lived in Burwash. We could go there,' she added in a sudden rush of confidence, 'his house is open to the public. The grounds are lovely — you can see the places where Dan and Una played, and where they met Puck.'

He laughed quietly.

'What are you laughing at?'

'You.' Then he said, 'It's a long mile to this pub of yours.'

'It may be a little over the mile. But it's downhill going home.'

The pub was low-ceilinged, warm and welcoming. He thought now might be the time to get used to English beer.

'What do you think?' she asked.

'Hmm. I reckon you have to treat it as a different drink altogether. If I don't expect it to taste like what I understand by beer, it's okay. In fact,' he finished his pint, 'it's good. What's that you've got?'

'Guinness.' She pushed her glass across to him.

He tasted it. 'Now that's different again. Kinda thick.'

'It's good for the blood. Full of iron, you know. Guinness is good for nursing mothers, I used to drink a bottle a day when I was feeding Edmund. Teddy,' she added.

'Get him to take his toys off my bed, will you? Yes, I know, you did warn me.'

They talked on easily. He told her some more about his father, and she said shyly that she'd bought some of the music he'd mentioned listening to in his father's house.

'Is that it?' he asked as the barman clanged a bell behind the bar.

'Yes. Sunday hours, half-past ten closing. Let's go and have a brandy at home.'

They left the pub, and turned off back down the lane. He put his arm round her shoulders, pulling her close to him.

They walked in silence, speaking only rarely. When they turned into her lane, he stopped under the single street-lamp. 'I won't surprise you this time.' He drew her to the side of the road. 'I want to kiss you.'

She put her arms round him and held her face up. He kissed her very gently, then leaned back to look into her eyes. 'It's good to see you,' he said. 'You've been on my mind.'

'And you on mine.'

'I'm pleased we're going to be closer to each other.'

She was silent for a moment. Then she said, 'In what way?'

'Geographically.'

'Oh.'

He'd never known anybody who could put such a variety of meaning into 'oh'. He wondered why she suddenly sounded desolate. Maybe he had answered wrongly. It was the first thing that had come into his head. She took a breath and laid her head against his chest. He felt her shiver.

'What is it?' He turned her face up. 'God, I never knew such an unpredictable woman. One minute you're skipping along by my side, the next you're trembling and trying to get inside my coat. What's up?'

'It's just — I was just thinking — where do we go from here?'

He sighed. Her eyes staring up into his looked stricken. He said, very quietly, 'I know exactly what I want us to do now.' He stared gravely at her, wanting to make sure she understood what he was saying. 'It's just I'm not sure you're ready too.'

He watched her expression change. She mayn't say much, he thought, but she doesn't need to, it's all in her face. Suddenly she was smiling, but there were tears in her eyes.

'Jeez, you're not crying! What the hell for?'

She laughed slightly hysterically. 'I'm not! I can't explain, it's just — oh, I've gone through rather a lot of mood changes over the last few minutes.'

He hugged her and they stood close. He wanted

very much to get through to her. 'There's a kind of innocence about you,' he began, 'like you're only just waking up. Those times I kissed you, back in the summer, I felt like I could have gone right ahead and made love to you, and you wouldn't have stopped me. But somehow it felt like I'd have been taking advantage of you, so I didn't.'

'Oh.'

'That's what I like about you, kid, you're so communicative.'

'I'm sorry. I don't know what to say. I'd hardly thought of myself as virginal.'

'I don't mean that, you know I don't,' he said impatiently. 'I guess it's because you lost Ben. It put your clock back to zero, and now you're starting again. But it makes me feel I want to be very careful with you.'

He was finding it difficult to say what he wanted to. She seemed to understand, though; she pressed against him, and something about the compliance of her body made him think she knew exactly what he meant.

'I hadn't thought about it like that,' she said. 'But I know I've felt different, this past couple of years. It *has* been a bit like being asleep, or at least not fully awake. Time I woke up.'

She reached up to touch his face, gently running her fingers over his jaw, into his hair. He bent to kiss her forehead.

'So,' she said, 'what *do* we do now?'

'We go on being together, and you tell me when you're ready.'

'Oh!'

'Goddammit, there you go again! Shit, you tell me so much!'

She shook her head mutely. She seemed to be temporarily beyond speech. He could feel her body trembling. Going back swiftly over what they'd just been saying, he realized that maybe this wasn't the time to get impatient with her. 'I'm sorry, kid.'

She shook her head again. 'No,' she muttered.

'No what?'

'No, you don't have to apologize, and no, I'm not ready. You're right,' she said.

'Okay. But . . . '

'Yes?'

'When you are — ready, you make sure you tell me, huh, not anyone else?'

'Oh, Hal! You and nobody else among these hordes of men hanging round? Oh, I will, I will!'

She reached up to kiss him on the cheek, the corners of his mouth, full on the lips. He groaned. 'I ain't made of stone! We'd better go find that brandy.'

He swung her around and pulled her on down the lane, gulping in deep breaths of the cold night air. Good thing it's winter, and there's frost on the ground, he thought; he'd been sorely tempted to go on kissing her, and God only knew what that would have led to.

'Do you think they'll still be up?' she asked as they walked up the drive, trotting to keep up with his long strides.

'No. They're all way too diplomatic.'

She giggled breathlessly. 'Isn't it nice? The opposite of being teenagers.'

'Did your pa wait up for you with a shotgun?'

'They both did — oh, not with shotguns! My parents' house is out in the country, and the last bus didn't go all the way, so before I got on to boyfriends with cars they often had to turn out to meet me.'

'That was nice. Real caring.'

'I know.'

The porch light had been left on for them, but the others had gone to bed. She went into the kitchen and called. 'Oh, look.' Her mother had left a tray laid for them with mugs, spoons, a tin of drinking chocolate and a saucepan of milk. She had written on a piece of paper, 'I hope Hal likes drinking chocolate.'

'Do you?'

'Sure, why not? So long as it's not instead of brandy.'

'No, it's as well as. My father gave me a bottle of Rémy.'

'Nice dad.'

She heated the milk. 'Would you like a piece of Christmas cake?'

'No thanks, sweetheart, not on top of beer.'

She had been moving towards the cake tin with a plate in her hand, but apparently changed her mind. They went through to the living-room.

'Where's all this music you've been buying?' he asked.

'In there.' She pointed beneath the shelves that held the stereo. He sat down on the floor, then picked out a tape.

'Makes me think of my dad,' he said, putting it

on. 'He'd be glad to know you have it.'

He'd selected the Elgar cello concerto. He listened, thinking he liked it even better now he was in England. He went to sit beside her on the sofa and took her hand, and they sat together till the music finished.

'I'm going to bed now,' he said, leaning over to kiss her briefly. 'My self-control has been tested enough for one night.'

'All right.' She bent to put the cups on the tray, and he couldn't see her face. 'See you tomorrow.'

She took the tray out to the kitchen.

He wanted to stay with her, wanted to kiss her again. The sofa where they'd been sitting was soft and inviting, her duvet rolled up right there beside it. The pictures he was seeing in his mind were all but irresistible.

Taking the stairs two at a time, he went up to bed.

20

The next day Hal announced over breakfast that he was going back to London to prepare for his lectures. Jo's face fell. 'Maybe Bernard and Mary'd like to come up with me for a couple of days? Then we could all return here New Year's Eve.'

Mary looked across at Jo. 'Would you mind, honey?'

'No, of course not.'

'It'll give you and your mom some time alone before she goes back.' Mary gave Jo a smile.

He spread his map out, trying to retrace the outward journey. He wasn't any too keen at the prospect of struggling back into London.

Jo sat down beside him. 'Would you like me to come with you? I wouldn't stay, I'd just show you the way.'

'D'you think I'd get lost?' he asked, grinning.

'Undoubtedly. London will be much busier than when you left. And getting out is relatively easy — getting back to where you started is a different matter.'

'Good God. Okay. Sure you don't mind?'

'Quite sure.'

'Kind little thing, aren't you?'

She smiled suddenly, shaking her head. 'I'm five foot six,' she said, standing up. 'I don't think I've ever felt little, till you.' Then she went pink and hurried away.

She drove her own car to the local station, so that she'd be able to drive home later. He waited with the engine running, watching her run towards him. You don't have to rush, sweetheart, I ain't about to go without you.

She got into the car. Bernard and Mary were in the back, studying the book she'd given them; it was open at the Tower. She directed Hal through the narrow local roads, and presently they came to traffic lights and turned right onto the A21.

'Straight on to London,' she remarked.

'Oh yeah?' he said disbelievingly.

'I've got a London street plan here,' she went on, ignoring him. 'Where exactly are we going?'

He told her the address. She sat frowning, muttering street names under her breath. He thought it sounded alarmingly complicated. He glanced across at her. She was outlining the route lightly in pencil.

They got onto the dual carriageway he recalled from his journey down, and he pulled into a lay-by. 'You can drive now,' he said. 'Get the feel of the car before we encounter all this heavy traffic you've been telling me about.'

'Me? But I thought I was just going to direct you?'

'No, you can drive,' he repeated. He got out and went round to open her door.

He heard her say, 'Oh, Lord!', and she shot a glance at Mary.

'Go on, honey, you can do it!' Mary said reassuringly.

Jo got into the driver's seat. She looked nervously

at him, then back at the array of dials and switches on the panel. He knew what she was thinking; he hadn't yet worked out what they were all for either.

She moved up through the gears without any difficulty. He didn't say anything; he didn't want to interrupt her concentration. He looked out to the left, where the slope of the North Downs fell away to the wide valley of the Weald. Nice part of the country. The car was responding eagerly and Jo moved out into the fast lane, overtaking a long line of lorries and cars before signalling and pulling back to the left.

He glanced over her shoulder at the speedometer. 'Shouldn't think that's necessary,' he remarked. 'Nothing much wants to pass when you're doing 115.'

'What!' She sounded horrified. 'Oh, hell's teeth!' She eased up her right foot. 'I didn't realize how fast it pulled away.'

He smiled, thinking of his similar experience going round Hyde Park Corner. 'Don't worry about it,' he said easily. She looked pleased.

Soon they were in the snarl of London. As she drove she pointed out landmarks. 'This is Whitehall . . . and that's the Cenotaph, it means 'empty tomb' — oh, I expect you know that.' She glanced quickly at Hal. 'This is Trafalgar Square . . . that's the Mall,' she jerked a thumb back over her shoulder, 'Buckingham Palace is at the far end . . . this is the Strand . . . we go left here . . . '

'That's the house,' he said when they got to

Bloomsbury and she was edging into the square. 'You can park there.'

He got out, opening the back doors for Mary and Bernard. Jo handed him the keys. She kissed her parents-in-law, and Mary said, 'You did okay! Much better that I could've done.' Much better than I could've, too, Hal thought.

'D'you want to come in?' he asked her, jingling the keys.

She looked at her watch. 'No, I won't. There's a train in three-quarters of an hour — I can catch it if I go now.'

'Okay.' He leaned forward and kissed her forehead. 'Thanks for the ride, kid — see you Wednesday.'

★ ★ ★

He was glad Bernard and Mary were with him. They made themselves at home, and their presence added a warmth to the apartment.

In the evening they went to the pub he'd been to the day he arrived in England. The large brunette behind the bar greeted him with a friendly wave. When he went up to buy a second round of drinks, she leaned her generous bosom on top of the bar and said, 'Tell yer Mum 'er 'andbag's open. She don't want nobody to go nickin' nothin', does she?'

He glanced over to where Mary was sitting, talking animatedly to Bernard. 'Sure, I'll tell her,' he said.

Your Mum. He wondered fleetingly just how far

a man could go in replacing his friend in the hearts of those who had loved him.

★ ★ ★

In the morning he woke full of the desire to work. Mary and Bernard said tactfully that they were going out and would see him for dinner. 'Right,' he said. 'D'you want to eat here?'

'Maybe,' Mary said. 'But don't you worry, we'll see to it.'

She kissed the top of his head as she stood pouring him more coffee. 'Why don't you go get started? We'll see to the dishes.'

He got up and stretched, grinning at her. 'Okay. Thanks.'

He worked for half an hour, oblivious to Mary and Bernard in the kitchen, gradually realizing with annoyance that he was going to have to change his typewriter ribbon. When he was in the middle of doing that, the telephone rang.

'I'll get it,' he called. 'Hello?'

'Hello.'

He remembered that voice over the phone, from the times he'd called her at the MacAllisters in the summer. 'Hi, kid. How're you?'

She said nervously, 'Sorry I'm disturbing you, but Jenny — that's my neighbour — has invited us to a party tomorrow night, and I wanted to ask you three if you'd like to go.'

'Wait, I'll go check.' He put the receiver down and went into the kitchen. 'Sure, they'd like that fine,' he reported back to Jo. 'They send their love and Bernard says is it a costume party?'

'I don't know. Hang on.' He heard her talking to someone, and a more distant voice answering. 'She says you can dress as fancy as you like, but just hats will do. Is that all right?' She sounded anxious.

'Sure, don't worry about it. See you tomorrow.'

Soon afterwards Bernard and Mary went out. The apartment was silent, Hal was alone, and he had mastered the typewriter ribbon; there was nothing to stop him forging ahead. Ruthlessly he put Jo's soft voice out of his mind and made himself go back to Ancient Mexico.

★ ★ ★

He'd finished all he wanted to do by mid-afternoon the following day. Bernard and Mary had bought hats: Mary had a cream wool beret she'd found in the Scotch House, and Bernard had a bowler.

'He's always wanted one,' Mary said fondly. 'I guess he'll never get a chance like this again.'

'What'll you wear, Hal?' Bernard asked, trying on his bowler at various angles.

'I'll get out my pinstripe and do the Al Capone bit,' he said. 'I reckon I'll need a fedora.'

Setting out in the evening for Hawkhurst, they made an incongruous trio. The trip was easier this second time, and it helped having two more pairs of eyes to read the map and look out for signs. They reached Jo's house soon after eight-thirty, and were met at the door by Elowen.

Hal wondered where Jo was. He heard a door

274

close, and looked up to see her coming down the stairs. She wore a black velvet dress, low-necked and full-skirted, a frill of white petticoat at the hem. Her hat was a cartwheel of black and white.

He moved to the foot of the stairs to meet her. She looked down at him, tilting her head to see him beneath her brim.

'You look beautiful,' he said softly. 'Happy New Year.'

'And to you.' She was smiling. 'You don't look so bad yourself — those vertical stripes make you look about nine feet tall.'

They could hear cars arriving next door. Jo greeted her parents-in-law, then said, 'Shall we go? Teddy's there already, he's in with Laura tonight. Although whether either of them gets any sleep remains to be seen.'

They joined a short queue outside the house next door. Hal could see a woman in a long red dress standing in the doorway, accompanied by what appeared to be a bearded nun, welcoming people inside.

'That's Tom,' Jo said, pointing at the nun. 'He's Jenny's husband — he likes dressing up.'

'Apparently.'

'And that's Jenny,' — she was laughing — 'in the Tudor gear.'

'So this is Hal,' Jenny said as Jo introduced him. She looked him up and down. 'You didn't say he was on the wanted list, Jo. I hope we won't get busted by Elliot Ness.'

The house was full of music and light. People were dancing in the lounge, and there was a table loaded with food in the dining-room. Tom was handing out mulled wine smelling strongly of spirits. Hal decided he'd stick to beer — it would likely be a long evening — and Tom showed him where the cans were and told him to help himself.

He decided quite soon it had been a wise decision; Tom's mulled wine began to take effect. He and Tom stood together in the hall — Hal noticed Tom was also drinking beer, which was revealing — and listened to two of Jenny's friends giggle and shriek their way through an account of somebody's brother's skiing accident. Watching the two women stumble off to tell their tale elsewhere, Hal observed laconically, 'Strikes me the dark one ain't got both oars in the water.'

'She hasn't,' Tom agreed. 'She's a neurotic cow.'

'Charitable of you,' Hal remarked.

'Steer clear,' Tom warned. 'She took her former husband to the cleaners, poor bugger.'

'I will.'

'Another beer?' Tom drained his can and held out a hand.

'Why not?'

'I refuse to be beaten by prohibition!' Tom said cheerfully, and muscled away to the kitchen.

Hal looked for Jo, and saw her standing by the buffet table talking to a short woman wearing a turban with an enormous feather in the front. Somebody moved between them, then Tom came back and told him a joke that was unsuitable for anyone dressed as a nun. It reminded Hal of a similar one, which Tom hadn't heard.

When he could see Jo again, she was being led off to dance by a man in an Afro wig. I'm watching you, pal, he thought. I think I'll dance with her later.

He saw Mary come in, and went to talk to her. Jenny told them to help themselves to supper, and came to eat with them. 'Your husband's a great dancer,' she said to Mary. 'All the girls want to waltz with him, they say he's the only man here who knows how.'

Mary smiled. 'I'll never get him home,' she said.

Jo came to join them. 'Have you eaten?' she asked. 'Oh, you are.'

'Have some,' Jenny said, waving a chicken leg towards the buffet. 'They're not exactly falling on it like vultures.'

She picked up a stick of celery. 'Actually I'm not all that hungry.'

'Either you eat it now or you take it home in doggy bags,' Jenny said firmly.

'I haven't got a dog,' Jo said straight-faced. Hal laughed quietly. She turned to him, and smiled bewitchingly. She leaned towards him, her soft hair brushing his face. 'I want to dance with you,' she whispered.

He suspected she was slightly tight: it was making her bolder than usual. He smoothed the hair away from her cheek. 'Just what I had in mind,' he whispered back.

'See you in the hall, on the last stroke of midnight.'

He watched her walk across the room and help herself to some bread and cheese. Then a sheik asked her to dance and, still chewing, she went off with him. I'm watching you, too, pal, Hal thought.

★ ★ ★

He had been up to the bathroom. Temporarily unable to get back through a press of people in the hall, he sat down on the stairs. A hand appeared through the stair rail, holding a can. 'Have another beer, Hal,' Tom said.

'Cheers, Tom.' He opened it and drank, eyeing the people in the hall. He caught sight of Elowen, and watched as she made her way to the stairs.

'May I sit by you?'

'Sure.' He moved along and made room for her.

'I've been dancing with Bernard,' she said, 'he's wonderful.'

'Yeah, I heard. The waltz king, huh?'

He was sure she hadn't sought him out merely to make small talk. After a moment's pause she said, 'Were you coming to England anyway?'

The directness of her approach took him by surprise. 'Before I met Jo in the summer, you mean?'

'Yes.' She met his stare unflinchingly. Her eyes were dark blue, quite unlike Jo's. In fact Jo's not much like her at all, he thought, except for maybe something about the mouth.

'It was on the cards,' he said, repaying honesty

with honesty. 'Meeting Jo clinched it.'

Elowen smiled. 'I'm sorry,' she said, 'I have no business to be talking to you like this. Jo would hate it if she knew.'

He grinned back at her. 'I won't tell her, if you won't.'

'I won't.'

'She's pretty terrifying,' he said ironically.

'Don't be taken in by that amiable exterior,' Elowen replied, 'she can be fierce enough when necessary.'

He said, 'I'm not taken in by any of her exteriors.'

'Good.' She looked down at her hands. 'She can take care of herself, really,' she said. 'I'm probably over-protective. After Ben, you know.'

'Sure,' he said quietly.

She looked up again. 'You and he were close friends, weren't you?'

Hal nodded. 'You must have missed him badly when he died.'

'I still do. You don't get more than one buddy like Ben in a lifetime.'

'No.' She was thoughtful. Then she went on, 'I find it surprising that you were such friends.'

'Appeal of opposites,' he said tritely.

'More than that, I think.' She was looking at him searchingly. He thought, what the hell.

'Something happened at college,' he said. 'Ben and I were both involved. A kid committed suicide, and we should have seen it coming.'

'Oh, how dreadful!' She looked shocked.

I'll spare her the details, he thought. 'We got

each other over it. You rely on a guy when you've been through that with him.'

'Yes, I can see how you would.' She was quiet for some minutes. Then she smiled, very sweetly. Now she looked like Jo. 'He was the first man she ever loved. She'd had dozens of boyfriends, but when she turned up on the doorstep with Ben she looked like a different girl. He was the one, you could tell that.'

He said nothing. She turned to look at him, her expression oddly sympathetic. 'He even won over Jo's father, and he'd quite made up his mind Ben was a useless drifter.'

'He probably was,' Hal said.

Elowen patted his leg. 'He'll be a hard act to follow.'

He sighed. 'Sure.'

They were quiet for a while, and two or three people stepped over them.

'Oh, there you are,' Jo said, appearing at the foot of the stairs.

'Go away, darling, we're talking,' Elowen said.

'I came to see if you're all right.'

'I'm fine. Go and talk to that nun.'

Hal smiled at Jo. She looked slightly dishevelled, and her cheeks were pink. 'See you, kid,' he said dismissively.

She shrugged and turned away. 'I shall just have to find someone else to dance with,' they heard her grumble as she walked off.

'Shouldn't be a problem,' he remarked.

★ ★ ★

They were still there nearly an hour later, when, just before midnight, Tom rounded up the guests. He turned off the music and switched the radio on. 'Costumes straight, hats on, please!' he shouted.

Hal and Elowen stood together, then Jo came and squeezed in between them. Her sheik was with her, but there wasn't room for him and Hal wasn't about to move up.

Jo clasped her hand round Hal's. He raised her brim. 'Just checking,' he said. 'I don't want to hold anyone else's hand. Tom said there's a woman here who takes men to the cleaners.'

She nodded sagely. 'There is. It's all right, she's upstairs throwing a wobbler.'

'Shouldn't someone — '

'Hush! Shut up!' Tom shouted as the chimes of Big Ben led up to the hour. ' . . . nine, ten, eleven, *twelve!*' people yelled. 'Happy New Year!'

Hal removed his fedora and bent right down to get under Jo's hat. He kissed her. Then they were separated by people shaking hands, kissing, swaying unsteadily into the ritual of Auld Lang Syne.

The older guests began to leave, Bernard, Mary and Elowen among them. They came over to where Jo and Hal stood, still hand-in-hand, to say goodnight.

'You don't mind if we stay?' Jo asked.

'No, you enjoy yourselves. It would be a pity to leave yet,' Elowen said.

'In any case,' Hal said quietly to Jo when the older people had gone, 'we haven't had our dance yet.'

'No, we haven't.' Suddenly she knelt down on the floor.

'What are you doing?'

She took off her hat and flung it on a chair. 'I've lost my shoes.'

'I won't tread on your toes.'

'Okay.'

She stood barefoot beside him. Her feet were small, and she had a bruise on the arch of the right one. He wanted to stroke it. He took her in his arms and she leaned against him, her face pressed to his chest.

The music was slow and undemanding; they moved in among the other barely-moving couples.

'Are you enjoying the party?' she asked.

He gave her a squeeze. 'Now I am.' She was singing quietly. 'I reckon you're tight,' he observed.

'Of course I am!'

He rested his head on top of hers, stroking her hair with one hand. The music changed; Roberta Flack started to sing, 'Let it be me'.

He said, 'How appropriate,' then put his hand under her chin and turned her face upwards to kiss her. He didn't want to stop.

When the track ended, she sat down abruptly on the sofa. She was looking up at him out of huge eyes, her mouth slightly open. He went to crouch in front of her. 'What is it?' he asked.

She stared at him, then slowly shook her head. 'Nothing.'

He took hold of her hand. 'Home?'

'Home.'

He went to collect their hats, and found her shoes in the hall. She got up unsteadily.

'Loved your hat,' he said, plonking it on her head. 'Real Ascot.'

'Loved yours, too. Real . . . '

'Chicago,' he supplied. He stood looking at her in the dim light of the empty hall.

She pulled herself upright. They let themselves out and walked slowly home, the night air cold and damp after the heat of the party.

'You won't have Teddy playing in your bedroom in the morning,' she said suddenly.

'No.' I would like to have you. 'I'm used to sleeping on my own.'

'Me too.'

She opened her front door, and he closed it behind them. When he turned round she was standing quite still in the middle of the hall, watching him. He was not sure he could read her expression. Her eyes closed for a moment.

'Goodnight,' she said, in a very low voice.

He put his hands on her shoulders and bent to kiss her forehead. Then he let her go.

'Goodnight, kid.'

21

New Year's Day marked the end of the holiday. Elowen went home, leaving Bernard and Mary to enjoy their last few days with Jo. In the evening Hal went back to London.

His lecture tour began. He soon got used to travelling around England, and became familiar with the road network, pleased he'd treated himself to a high-performance car roomy enough for a man of six foot three to drive comfortably all day. He would listen to music, part of his mind going over the next lecture, part always with Jo. He phoned her sometimes, usually on impulse and far too late: standing in the bar at night he'd think, I'll call her, without bothering to look at his watch.

One night when she was almost incoherent with yawns he said, 'I didn't wake you, did I?'

'Yes. It's nearly midnight.'

'Hey, I'm sorry, kid.'

'It's okay, it's nice to talk to you.'

And it was nice to talk to her. But he resolved to call earlier; she wasn't at her most scintillating when she'd just been woken up.

He went to Scotland, and sent her a postcard of Edinburgh Castle. He sent her lots of postcards, often continuing the message over two or three sent on consecutive days. She would be puzzled sometimes to receive a card beginning in mid-sentence.

He came racing back from Scotland full of the desire to see her. It was a month since New Year; he needed to be with her. He picked up the phone as he came into his apartment, dropping his bag at his feet.

'I want to come down Saturday,' he announced, not even waiting to say hello.

'Hello, Hal. Yes, that would be lovely.'

'Great. Bye, sweetheart.'

That week he gave the first of his lectures in London. He looked with pleasure at his name in *The Times*; I've cracked it, he thought. 'Mayan Trade Routes', it said in the 'Talks, Lectures, Films' column next to the crossword, 'Illustrated talk by H. S. Dillon, British Museum, 11.30 a.m'.

He wondered if Jo would spot it: he knew she took *The Times*, she'd got him hooked on the crossword over Christmas. He almost invited her up to hear him, but it seemed like a smart-ass thing to do.

★ ★ ★

He watched as the small audience filed in. Someone came up to ask a question, and he put on his glasses to consult his notes. The auditorium retreated into a coloured blur.

He enjoyed giving the talk. The audience was well-informed, and asked a lot of questions. Someone from the back asked about human sacrifice — someone always did — and he took off his glasses to focus on the questioner. He saw a very familiar figure slip out through the rear

285

doors. With an effort, he brought his mind back to the Mayans. As soon as he could, he ran out to find her.

'Did you see a fair-haired woman in a black leather coat?' he asked the man on the door.

'No, mate. Have you lost one?'

He sat down on one of the benches in the entrance hall, absurdly pleased that she'd come. He wished she'd stayed around to say hi.

* * *

He set out early on Saturday and was in Hawkhurst by ten. Jo and Edmund were waiting for him, and they went down to Romney Marsh. He was tempted to ask her how she'd liked the lecture, but then decided against it; he was trying to remember not to tease her. Instead he pushed a tape into the cassette player and said, 'Remember this?' The look she shot him as the Bruch violin concerto rang through the car made him think maybe he should have asked about the talk after all.

They walked by the Royal Military Canal, and she pointed to the bank where she'd seen two kingfishers one summer day. Edmund showed him where he'd found a dead mole.

'To the little gentleman in black velvet,' Jo remarked.

'How's that?'

'The Jacobite toast.' He was none the wiser. 'You know, the supporters of the Stuarts, who wanted James II back on the throne.'

He nodded tentatively. He was a total novice

when it came to the long, intricately-woven tapestry of the British Monarchy.

'Well, they say that William III — that was William of Orange, the Protestant Dutchman who replaced James on the throne?' He nodded again. 'He died after a hunting accident — his horse put its foot down a mole-hole. So the Jacobites toasted the mole. Drank its health, I mean.'

'Right. I wasn't thinking they cooked it.' He glanced sideways at her. 'I don't know, though.'

They walked hand-in-hand with Edmund in the middle, providing a continuous background chatter. At one point he said, 'I want to do a wee-wee.' Disengaging his hands from Jo and Hal, he turned to face the canal, then said over his shoulder to Hal in a spirit of masculine camaraderie, 'Make sure nobody sees my bottom.'

Hal obligingly went and stood behind him. 'Hope no one'll think it's me,' he remarked to Jo, grinning.

She glanced across at them. 'They won't. Wrong trajectory.'

Edmund turned round at Hal's laughter, and Hal ruffled his hair. Cashing in on the attention, Edmund said he thought he was a bit tired, so Hal put him up on his shoulders and carried him back to the car.

★ ★ ★

'Are you staying tonight?' Jo asked. He glanced quickly across at her. She was relaxed, and he judged that the question didn't carry any more than its surface meaning. He was beginning to know her; it was unlikely that, if and when the time came when she did mean more, she'd be open about it. And it wouldn't be in front of Edmund.

'Yes please,' he replied easily.

In the evening he read the paper while she prepared supper. They both went up to kiss Edmund goodnight, and Hal wondered if she was enjoying it as much as he was. They sat together on the sofa; she had been quiet for some time, trying to finish the crossword. Suddenly she said, 'How did you become interested in your subject?'

He was half asleep. 'How's that?'

'Ancient history. What interested you in it?'

He roused himself, stretching. 'My dad, I guess. He took me to museums when I was a kid.' He could picture Sam, pointing and explaining, never noticing how other people would stop to listen. 'I remember one day we looked at the mummy case of an infant, and he told me how the child's mother had eased her grief by observing the burial customs, how it had helped her, knowing she'd done all she could for her child in the next life.'

'It's a pity everyone doesn't have someone like your dad to teach them history.'

'Maybe. He was — is — a born storyteller. He made sure I heard all the tales from my mother's side of the family, too.'

'What sort of tales?'

'My mother's mother was a Hungarian Jew, she married my grandfather when she came to America. She kept the folk tales alive, passed them on to her children. But my Mom died when I was five, so it was left to Dad to pass them on to me.'

'Do you remember your mother?'

'Sure. She was small, and when I hugged her I could feel her little light bones, like a bird's under its feathers. I used to think I shouldn't hug her too hard because I'd heard my grandmother say she was delicate, and I thought she meant delicate like china.'

'What did she look like?'

'She had dark hair, smooth and long, and dark brown eyes. She had a soft expression, as if half her mind was thinking about something else. She and Dad were so happy together — they'd take me on walks and entertain each other telling stories. They started my interest in the past, then in high school my history grades were always my highest, so I guess I just went on doing what I was best at.'

'You did your degree in history?'

'Right. Then a year's postgrad in Mexico. Got my first article published there.'

'No wonder it stayed important to you. Mexico, I mean, and the Mayans and things.'

He sighed, looking down into the fire. 'There was another reason.' She gasped, and he looked at her. 'What?'

'You don't have to,' she muttered.

'I don't have to what?'

'Mary told me you'd lost someone, a girl. I'd forgotten it was in Mexico. I wasn't trying to get the story out of you, though it must look like it. But honestly I wasn't, I wouldn't be devious like that.'

She said it all in a rush then stopped, biting at

her lip. He took hold of her hand. Devious? Jeez, if she was devious then the rest of the world was cunning beyond redemption. She hadn't even got to first base.

'I never had you down as devious. I was going to tell you anyway. I reckon it's time you knew something of my past. I know most of yours.'

'Oh.'

He shot her a smile. Then he returned to gazing into the depths of the fire. 'There was a girl,' he began, 'and yes, she did die.'

I'm conjuring up Magdalena for her, he thought; I guess this is significant. As he spoke he put his arm round her; her closeness eased that old, deep pain, just as thinking of her had helped in Mexico City.

When he told her about returning to discover that Magdalena was dead, she said very softly, 'Oh, Hal. And you were all on your own.'

That was it, kid, he thought. That was the killer. 'Right.'

'What did you do?'

He told her how he'd come home, how he and Ben had gone off for the summer. 'After a while he made me think I'd be okay,' he concluded. 'Good buddy, Ben.'

Presently he disengaged himself. 'Think I'll go to bed now. D'you mind?'

'No. Will you sleep?'

'Eventually.'

He lay awake for a long time. He wanted very much to go to her, to take her in his arms just for the comfort of having her close. But he knew it wouldn't end there; he didn't think she'd turn him away. And the time wasn't right. Not tonight.

★ ★ ★

February came, bringing snow, sleet and blizzards. Hal's schedule was tight; occasionally he was in London overnight, but rarely for longer. On the phone one evening she told him an editor was interested in a story she'd written.

He found a copy waiting on the mat the next time he returned to his apartment. He put it in his bag to look at when he had a moment, then set off on a three-week trip to Manchester.

He lectured in venues throughout the area, constantly busy, entertained to dinner by several universities. He finally got to read Jo's story half-way through the tour; firmly closing his door one evening, he took the phone off the hook and poured himself a large bourbon.

It was the first time he'd read anything she'd written. It didn't take long to recognize it for what it was: a tribute of love to Ben. Despite the wings and the guardian angel robes, the illustrations had caught Ben's likeness with the fidelity of adoration.

He read straight through fifty pages while his coffee grew cold beside him. Then he put the manuscript back in its envelope, wishing he didn't feel so depressed. He'd planned to call her, but now he didn't want to. What was suddenly so forcefully on his mind wasn't something he could discuss over the phone.

* * *

His days were full, with little time for private thoughts. In the evenings he kept forgetting to phone until it was too late; when he finally got through she had a cold and sounded awful.

'I'd better let you get back to bed,' he said reluctantly, after a short and, on her part, unenthusiastic exchange.

'Yes. I feel rotten. And Edmund's got a cough.'

'Okay, kid. Take it easy, now.'

He stood in the hotel doorway. Outside the rain had turned to sleet, and a strong wind was blowing the icy droplets horizontally. The deserted streets were shining with a black, inhospitable gleam. He returned disgruntled to the bar. He thought morosely, Manchester in February sucks.

* * *

He set off with relief for London. The sleet had become snow, falling with soft insistence until everything lost its identity under a smoothing of white. He struggled down the M6 in a single-file convoy in the wake of a snow-plough, and, although conditions improved on the M1, he ran into a tail-back and sat almost stationary for an hour.

By the time he reached London it was after ten o'clock. He was too tired to be hungry and the apartment was freezing, so he went straight to bed. With an effort, he closed his eyes on after-images of a thousand pairs of rear-lights and a million blobs of snow, hypnotically and endlessly coming towards

292

him down the beam of his headlights.

He was dreaming, an anxious dream in which someone was rudely poking a finger in his chest and making a bell ring. Then the ringing resolved itself into the telephone.

'Oh, God,' he moaned, falling out of bed in a tangle of duvet. It was quite dark. Dazed with sleep he couldn't remember where he was; he stubbed his toe on a chair he'd forgotten about. 'Hello,' he said huskily.

'Hal? Is that you?' She sounded frantic.

'Yeah, kid.'

'Oh, thank goodness! I thought you weren't there.'

'I am. I was asleep. What's up?'

'Oh, Hal, Teddy's got croup, he's been coughing all night and he won't stop. He looks awful, and I'm so worried!'

'Are you at home?' His brain had begun to function; her anxiety had acted like a slap across the face.

'No, we're in hospital, they let me stay with him but I had to sleep on the floor.'

God. 'Which hospital?' She told him, giving the name of the ward. 'What did you say he has?' He frowned, trying to write without his glasses.

'Croup.'

'Okay.' He wasn't sure what croup was. 'I'll be right there.'

'Thank you,' she whispered. And rang off.

He looked at his watch: 7.35. The roads would be quiet — it was Sunday. He took a shower, made coffee and drank it as he dressed. He was on the road fifteen minutes after putting the phone down. Responding to her need, he was full of urgency; he kept the car around fifty till he got on to the Orpington by-pass, then opened up and let it fly.

It didn't take long to reach the hospital. He found the ward, and went into the sister's office.

'Mrs MacAllister,' he said.

The sister looked up in surprise. 'Are you Hal?' He nodded. 'You've come from London, since Mrs MacAllister phoned?'

'I have,' he said patiently.

'That was quick!'

'I didn't hang around.'

She showed him where to go.

Edmund lay asleep, arms flung out and mouth open, in a bed enclosed in a clear plastic tent into which steam was being pumped. His zebra was on the pillow. Jo sat beside him, bolt upright on a hard chair, her eyes closed.

He crossed the room, bending down to put his arms round her. 'Hi.'

Her eyes opened. She looks like she did that night of the storm, he thought, when she cried for Ben.

She stood up and tightened her arms round him, pulling him close. She rubbed her face against his. 'Thank you for coming,' she whispered.

'Sure. I may be a bit rough,' — he put a hand to his face — 'I didn't stop for a shave.'

'I don't care.'

'How is he?' He remembered with an effort what he was doing there.

'He's fast asleep.' She looked lovingly down at

the child. 'He's still coughing, but not as much. He's worn out.'

'Poor little kid. What is croup, anyway?'

'Inflammation of the windpipe. It makes it constrict, so that you cough all the time and can't get your breath. We had to make the kitchen all steamy, but it wasn't enough so the doctor sent us in here.'

He wondered how many nights of lonely anxiety she'd had. Several, by the look of her. 'You look awful,' he said kindly. 'Why don't you go home and have a sleep?'

'What about Teddy?'

'I'll stay with him. I'll charm that sister into feeding me.'

She smiled, immediately looking more like herself. 'I don't think you will. But there's a snack bar place. I'll make sure I'm back before the night lot come on duty — there's this harpy of a staff nurse, she'll probably ban you.'

He kissed the top of her head. 'Let her try. Okay, I'll see you this afternoon.' She still looked doubtful. 'Go on!'

'All right. Give him my love when he wakes up.'

'I will. Don't worry, I'll look after him.'

'See you later.' She turned to look at him as she left.

★ ★ ★

Edmund slept for four hours. Hal sat by the bed, and people tended to assume he was Edmund's father. He found he liked it.

He watched the sleeping child. Ben's son. He was thinking, very hard.

★ ★ ★

When Jo came back he was drawing animals with Edmund. He watched her as she approached. She looked brighter. Her face lit up as Edmund called out to her. 'He's better!' she said joyfully. Edmund held up his arms for a hug. 'How are you, darling?' She was talking to Edmund, but the look she shot at Hal made his heart thump.

'I came out of my tent, Mummy, and we had jelly for lunch, and Hal did me a yellow dinosaur called Andrew.'

'Andrew. Lovely!'

'And we sat in an armchair with a blanket and Hal read me a story, but I coughed a bit so we went back in the tent, and Hal said we could pretend we were people up a mountain having to shelter because it was snowing a lot.'

She looked at Hal, her eyes full of gratitude. 'Thank you,' she said quietly.

'You're welcome.' He smiled at her. She mattered very much to him. 'You look better, too.'

'Amazing what sleep can do,' she said lightly, her eyes leaving his. She seemed embarrassed. 'Let's draw some more animals.'

They invented increasingly fantastic animals, then Hal looked at his watch and said he had to go. He kissed Edmund, promising next time he'd draw him a capybara, a capercaillie and a caravanserai.

She walked with him out into the corridor. 'A caravanserai isn't an animal,' she protested, 'it's a . . . well, it must have something to do with caravans.'

'Right,' he agreed, 'but Teddy doesn't know that. It can be a three-humped Persian camel till he finds out. Will you be okay?'

He stood looking down at her. Her eyes seemed enormous, ringed underneath with grey circles.

'Yes. I'm not worried any more.'

She made no move to go.

'You'll sleep better tonight,' he said. 'I got that sister to arrange a proper bed for you.'

'You miracle worker,' she whispered.

'Call me tomorrow?' He tried to speak normally.

She nodded.

He turned to go. She called out, 'Hal.'

He swung round. For a moment she didn't speak. Then, across two yards of hospital corridor separating them, she said quietly, 'Hal, I love you.'

He looked at her intently. He realized he was holding his breath, and let it out with a smile. 'I guess that's just relief and gratitude talking.' He hadn't intended the slight note of query in his voice.

She shook her head. 'No, it isn't. I do love you.'

He took a rapid step towards her, taking her in his arms and pulling her head down on to his chest. 'Sweetheart, I love you too.'

He felt her trembling. A tear fell with a splash onto his shirt, already damp from sitting in the steam tent. He stroked her hair. 'I might have known,' he said softly. 'Anything more likely to make you cry, I can't think of.'

She smiled up at him, tears making her eyes even bigger.

' 'She would have made a splendid wife',' he said solemnly, ' 'for crying only made her eyes more bright.' '

She looked startled. '*What* did you say?'

'Just quoting, kid. Your pal O. Henry again.'

She stood on tiptoe and kissed his lips. He held her face in his hands, brushing away the tears with his thumbs.

Then he turned and left her.

All the way home he could hear in his head the echo of her voice.

★ ★ ★

He had appointments in London all next day. He went out for lunch with a colleague, but had little appetite for food, drink or conversation. He'd intended to work in the afternoon, but he sat at his desk and did virtually nothing.

The phone rang in the evening.

'Hello, Hal,' she said. Her voice was warm, very soft.

'Hi. How's Teddy?'

'Much better. We're home, and he's fast asleep.'

He didn't know what to say. He thought for a moment. 'I'm going to Cambridge Thursday. I'll be away a week, but then I could come down.'

He heard her draw in her breath. 'I have another suggestion.'

There was a silence. Then he said quietly, 'Oh, yeah?'

'If Teddy's all right, I thought perhaps I'd leave him with Jenny and come up to London for a couple of days.'

He closed his eyes. He'd known this was coming, known since she'd phoned yesterday morning. He said, 'You could.'

'You're with me, then?' She sounded anxious.

'Sweetheart, I'm way ahead of you.'

'Oh. Oh, good.'

'Will you drive up?' he asked, in something more like his usual voice.

'No. I'll come by train.'

'Tell me the day and the time.'

'Friday morning — Friday week, that is. Ten-thirty.'

She had it all worked out. 'I'll be there.'

'Send me a card from Cambridge?'

'I will.'

★ ★ ★

The sun came out as he got to Cambridge. On a free afternoon he walked out to Grantchester and stood leaning on a gate, looking across the meadows sloping gently down to the river. Ben was on his mind.

Sometimes he found it hard to remember Ben was dead: he seemed merely far away, in another country. An image of Ben lived on in his memory and it showed no hostile face, no resentment that Hal and Jo had come to love each other. Not in your character, buddy, jealousy. Was it? I hope you know about this, Ben, I reckon it'd make you glad.

He went to King's, sitting quietly in the Chapel close to the altar while something of its exhalting, eternal beauty seeped down into his soul. He didn't think Jo had ever been to Cambridge; maybe they'd go together. He bought her a postcard of the Adoration of the Magi: 'I just spent an hour in here. It got dark outside, and someone was playing the organ. It was peaceful, and I thought of you. See you at the station Friday. Hal.'

★ ★ ★

He went back to London, and spent a day cleaning and tidying the apartment. His mind was too full to rest, and in the evening he went out for a long walk. He called in at the pub on his way home.

'Nearly the weekend,' the barmaid remarked. Her brown hair was backcombed into a huge halo, and she had sparkling ear-rings like forks of lightning.

'Right,' Hal said. He grinned at her.

'Got something nice planned?' She raised a pencilled eyebrow at him.

He started to laugh. 'Reckon I have.'

She leaned across the bar a little closer to him. 'Good for you. Pretty, is she?'

'She sure is.'

She looked as if she might be about to say something coarsely funny, but she stopped. She patted his hand. 'Lucky girl,' she whispered, and moved away to serve another customer.

'Lucky man,' Hal said quietly.

22

Jo woke in the cold pre-dawn. She got up quietly and had a shower, feeling surprisingly calm. She packed an overnight bag, then prepared breakfast. Edmund joined her, excited about going next door to stay.

'Good luck,' Jenny said, seeing her off. 'You look lovely. And you *smell* lovely.'

'Thanks. It's very kind of you to have Teddy, I'll do the same for you one day.'

'That'd be nice. But I'll have to find a lover first.'

'Mr Watson? Still waters run deep.'

'Yes, but they're probably stagnant. I think I'd rather go with Tom. Have fun!'

'We will. See you on Sunday.'

She got on the train. No one knows where I'm going, nobody knows what I'm going to do. I wonder if any of them are going to have a day like mine? And a night like mine? I wonder if that man is — maybe he has a beautiful quadroon mistress in St John's Wood, and tonight she'll feed him ripe muscatel grapes and caress his legs with her naked dusky thighs. She turned hastily away as the subject of her contemplation, unaware of the erotic sensual orgy she was planning for him, looked up and caught her eye. Quickly she turned to the crossword.

There, I've done three clues, she thought as the

train flashed through Orpington. Oh, no! Not long now! She bit at her thumbnail. The train rocked through London Bridge flat out then slowed to a dead crawl all the way to Waterloo. I'm going to be sick.

When at last they moved off she pushed her way through the carriage and stood by an open window. She looked down at the greenish water as the train went over the Thames . . . now it's only *seconds*. Oh, supposing he's not there? He will be, he said he would.

She could feel the rapid thumping of her heart, and wondered why she should feel so awful when she was about to do something she wanted so very much.

He was standing by the barrier, leaning against the ticket collector's booth. He put out his arm like a digger's scoop and separated her from the throng of people as she was swept by.

'Hi,' he said. 'You're not meaty enough for this.'

'Hello.'

They stood smiling at each other, then he put his arms round her and hugged her. 'D'you want to stand here all day?' he asked presently.

'Not necessarily. Had you thought of anything else we might do?'

'A whole heap of things,' he said very quietly into her ear, 'but we could go to the Museum,' he added, more loudly and not in her ear.

'Oh, yes! I haven't been there for — oh, well, for some time.'

He seemed to find that amusing. 'Okay. We'll

drop your bag at my place first.'

It was raining slightly, and he hailed a cab to take them to Bloomsbury. She waited in the lobby while he took her bag upstairs. She watched him as he came towards her: he was wearing a thick brown roll-necked pullover that made his eyes look very dark.

He took her hand to walk the short distance to the British Museum. 'Where first?' he asked as they went up the steps and into the front hall. The uniformed attendant on the door said, 'Good morning, Dr Dillon,' and Hal said, 'Morning, Arthur.'

I didn't know he was a Doctor, she thought reverently.

'Shall we give the Greeks a bash?' she suggested.

In the Room of the Harpy Tomb a dark young man approached her and asked haltingly where the Parthenon Marbles were. She showed him, and he thanked her and said he was from Athens. She said she was sorry he'd had to come all this way to see them, but she didn't think he understood.

She felt lightheaded. She was so aware of Hal that her skin felt sensitive. What are we doing here? She wanted to laugh: I couldn't have arrived and got straight into bed with him, it wouldn't have done. We had to do something else first. Then she felt the hot blood rush to her face, and peered into a display case before he noticed.

They stood in front of statues of Athena and Poseidon fighting for possession of Attica. Hal put his arm round her, and her heart beat faster. 'The people said they'd name their capital city after whichever of the two gods gave them the most valuable present,' he said. 'Poseidon gave them the horse and reckoned he'd won hands down, no contest. Athena came up with a scrubby little olive tree, and Poseidon told her to chuck it back where she'd found it. But the people planted it and nurtured it, and before long built up a hugely prosperous industry based on it, so they said, thanks very much, we'll call our city Athens.'

They went upstairs to the Daily Life room, then retraced their steps to the Egyptian mummies. But a party of Japanese tourists had taken over, intent on having their photographs taken in front of a mummy.

'Oh, God!' he groaned. 'C'mon, we'll try again another day when they've all gone back to Tokyo.'

They walked out into the quiet empty space at the top of the stairs.

'Have you had enough?' he asked, grinning at her. 'Your eyes have glazed over.'

His smile was melting her. 'It's not my eyes so much, it's my feet.' She tried to speak casually.

He put his arm round her as they headed for the staircase. The mosaic representations of hunting Carthaginians gazed impassively down on them.

Rounding the first bend, he stopped and looked down into her eyes. He stroked her cheek with his fingers, taking hold of her jaw to turn her face up to his. He bent to kiss her, lightly at first. But her lips met his with all the passion she'd been holding in, and her mouth opening under his made him press her tightly to him, kissing her as urgently as she was kissing him, bending her body over with the force of his own.

She heard footsteps coming down the stairs. A prim female voice said, 'Well, really!'

She opened her eyes to see a couple of middle-aged women. Hal said, 'Afternoon!'

Two tweed backs continued frostily down the stairs. There was a disapproving sniff. She dropped her face against him.

'You didn't know them, did you?' he asked.

'No!' She smothered her laughter. Then she raised her head and they stood solemnly looking at each other.

'I guess we'd better not do that again till we're alone, huh?'

She whispered, 'Okay.'

He took her hand and they walked outside, joining the crowds on the busy street. It was beginning to get dark.

'Are you hungry?' he asked.

'Not at all.'

'Are you thirsty?'

'No, not very.'

He squeezed her hand. 'What do you want to do?'

She paused for a moment. There was only one honest answer. She said, 'I want you to make love to me.'

She watched as the familiar half-smile spread over his face. 'Then we'd better go home.'

They went back to his flat, up the wide flight of stairs to the first floor. She went in and he followed, kicking the door shut behind him. He walked across to draw the curtains, then knelt down on the hearth, putting a match to the fire.

She perched on the end of a leather chesterfield and gazed around. The austere setting was softened by big bright cushions on the floor, splashes of colour on top of the dull carpet. It's the sort of room Sherlock Holmes's brother would have had, in his old Diogenes Club, she thought abstractedly. What was his name? Mycock? No, Mycroft. I don't suppose he'd have gone overboard on the floor cushions, though — he'd have sat upright in a wing chair, in his wing collar.

She shot a nervous glance at Hal. Her breathing quickened.

He came to stand over her. 'Come here,' he said.

He pulled her to him, his lips on hers, and instantly the passion came racing back. He ran his hands over her body and her skin began to tingle. He moved his hands to her breasts, and she swayed against him.

He led her over to the fireplace, and they lay down on the cushions. The flames were lighting up the planes of his face as he settled beside her. Then he kissed her again. She ran her hands up beneath his sweater, feeling his skin smooth and warm. He eased off her clothes, bending to kiss her neck, her shoulders, her breasts, caressing her, evoking in her a symphony of sensation, overwhelming her in the very essence of him. She pulled up his sweater and he took it off. She heard him breathe deeply as he smoothed his cheek over the skin of her shoulder. He said quietly, 'Much more of this, sweetheart, and there ain't going to be no stopping.'

She moved her head sensuously against his face as he nestled into her neck. 'So who wants to stop?'

She could sense he was smiling. He let out a low, throaty laugh as he reached down to unzip her skirt.

He sat back on his heels and stared down at her as she lay naked in the firelight. 'Will you look at that,' he said softly.

He stood up to finish undressing then lay beside her, his long body warming the length of hers, squeezing her legs between his own. He cradled her head on one arm as he kissed her, running his hand down over her hips and thighs and across her stomach.

Eventually, as if he knew she couldn't bear to wait another moment, he shifted over to lie on top of her. She moved her legs beneath him and he came into her, slowly and with infinite patience, taking her with him into a steadily-mounting swell of ecstacy that ended at last in tumultuous, heart rending fulfilment.

★ ★ ★

Some time later he got up. She watched him, unable to take her eyes off his body. She felt cold and vulnerable all down the side where he'd been lying, and wanted him to return.

He wasn't gone long. He returned wearing a thick cream towelling robe, carrying a sweatshirt that said '49ers', two cans of beer and two glasses.

308

'Here,' he said, and handed her the sweatshirt.

She sat up and put it on. He leaned down and kissed her, more leisurely now. He poured them both a beer.

'Now I'm hungry,' she said, leaning against him.

'So'm I. I have eggs, and bread. Or I can go get us a takeaway.'

'No!' She didn't want him getting dressed and going out. 'Let's have scrambled eggs. I'll do them, I'm good at eggs.'

★ ★ ★

They went back to the fireside with coffee and brandy, sitting down side by side on the chesterfield. She hastily got up again.

He looked up at her, amused. 'What's up?'

'Leather,' she said shortly, embarrassed. He started to laugh. 'It's cold, on my — on my skin.'

'Sit on me.'

He felt strong and firm beneath her and, so close to him, she could smell his skin, smell again the scent of him that was now irrevocably linked in her mind with their lovemaking. We're talking, we're drinking our coffee, she thought, but his hand is running up beneath this shirt he's lent me, and resting against my stomach as if he's done it a thousand times, and I don't want to talk, I want to . . .

His hand had dropped to her thigh. She closed her eyes, and a low wail escaped her because he could make her feel these things, he could touch her like this and make her lose herself.

She felt his lips on her cheek. He said, so quietly that she barely heard, 'It's all right.'

Then he stood up and carried her into his bedroom.

Now, there was all the time in the world. He made love to her with great tenderness, moving her to tears whose cause she scarcely knew. And, her cheek against his, she transmitted her emotion to him. His hands, his mouth, his body overcame her, driving out all but him and what he was making her feel, lengthening the unbelievable crescendo, steadily increasing the pace until a great shattering cry broke out and she knew with amazement that it was hers.

A little later he said, 'It's been a long time, huh?'

A long time. Oh, yes, such a long time. 'Two and a half years.'

'Maybe I shouldn't have asked you?'

She thought, you could ask me anything. 'I don't mind.'

He was silent for some time. Then he said, 'Ben's been on my mind this week. Because of you.'

'And mine.'

'I want to talk about him. Is it going to bother you?'

'No.' It was inevitable. She waited, but he didn't speak. So she said, 'Emily told me she liked being with you because you made her think of Ben. I didn't understand what she meant, then. Now I think I do. You sort of feel like him. Oh, I can't explain it,' she was interrupted by his brief laugh, 'just knowing about you and him makes you special.'

'You too, kid.'

The quiet reply took her by surprise.

★ ★ ★

Making love had taken away the last of her reticence; it seemed to have done the same for him, and they talked long into the night.

'I feel so bad for him,' he said. 'He had it all, and he died smack in the middle of it. And now — '

'What?'

He pulled away from her slightly. 'Nothing.'

She let it go. Then: 'When was the last time you saw him?' It was something she'd long wanted to ask.

'The summer he went to Cyprus. Year before he met you.' He paused, then said, 'I knew after that an era had come to an end.'

She said, very softly, 'I'm sorry.'

'It's not something to be sorry about. He was made for marriage. I just hoped you'd make him happy.'

She was crying again. He stroked her cheeks with his hand, brushing away the tears. 'You did,' he said quietly, 'you know you did.'

★ ★ ★

They slept for a few hours, and she woke up to full daylight. Hal was still asleep, and she lay watching him. His face in repose was stern; she felt he was distant from her. She thought of a cryptic comment in one of Elowen's recent letters: 'Don't dilly-dally too much making up your mind about Hal because he is a different sort of man from Ben, and won't have Ben's tolerance.'

Yes. There was a toughness in Hal, a self-sufficiency that made him content with his own company so that he wouldn't work overly hard at a relationship that was unsatisfactory.

But it wasn't unsatisfactory. Well, it certainly wasn't in one important way. She moved her legs under the duvet, stretching in sheer animal pleasure, rolling against Hal. She began to kiss his shoulder and his neck, moving over to lie on top of him. Slowly he opened his eyes, his arms going round her.

'Who are you?' he asked croakily.

'You devil! Don't say you've forgotten already!' She bit gently at his ear.

He closed his eyes. Slightly disappointed, she sighed and put her head down on his chest. After a few moments he said sleepily, 'Go get the orange juice. Sometimes it wakes me up.'

'Worth a try,' she said, disentangling herself. She got out of bed and put on his towelling robe. It smelt of him. She wandered over to the window to part the curtains, and a small shaft of sunlight came in. She looked at her watch: 8.35 a.m.

'It's probably because you haven't got any children,' she remarked magnanimously, 'if you had, you wouldn't expect to be still fast asleep at half-past eight.'

He opened his eyes and glared at her. 'The reason I'm still asleep,' he said sternly, 'is because I've been making love to you half the night and talking to you the other half, and I ain't twenty-one any more.'

A feeling of enormous tenderness welled up in her. She said, smiling involuntarily, 'Oh, Hal, I infinitely prefer older men.'

He grinned back at her. 'Bring me my walking frame.'

Suddenly the air between them was warm with affection. 'Do you know,' he said thoughtfully, sitting up, 'you're the first woman I've made love to in this bed.'

'But I thought . . . ' she began, turning round. Then she saw that he was smiling.

★ ★ ★

It was mid-morning before they were ready to go out. The weather was fine, and they set off arm in arm with no firm idea of where to go.

'Let's take the tube down to Hyde Park,' she said as they approached Russell Square Underground. 'This station's on the blue line — that's the Piccadilly Line, I think. It goes to Hyde Park Corner.' He looked at her doubtfully. 'You ought to get to know the Underground,' she told him, 'it's much better than taking taxis everywhere.'

'That is a matter of opinion. Okay, we'll give it a try.'

'Not that bad, is it?' she said later as they sat side by side in an almost empty compartment bowling down to Hyde Park Corner.

'No, I guess not,' he said cautiously. 'There's less graffiti than in the New York subway, and what there is, is more intellectual.'

She giggled. 'Except that bit.' She pointed out through the window. On the end wall of a station someone had scrawled, 'Arsenal are wankers.'

'All of them?' he said, grinning. 'Difficult to see how they can play football.'

'Someone obviously thinks they can't.'

He put his arm round her, pulling her towards him, and bent to kiss her gently on the lips. She smiled up at him, feeling happiness bursting out of her. 'We're lovers,' she announced.

'We sure are. Bet those folks over there are glad to know that.' He nodded towards an elderly couple sitting a few seats away.

'Oh, they didn't hear, did they?'

'What the hell? Come here, I want to kiss you again.'

They got out at Hyde Park Corner. Before going into the park, she took him along the road to point out Apsley House.

'That's Number One, London,' she said, 'Wellington used to live there.'

'Is that Wellington?' He pointed across to the statue standing with its naked back towards Park Lane. 'I never knew he had such a cute ass.'

They had a beer and a sandwich in a pub off

Oxford Street. Hal said he fancied cooking Chinese food for supper, and bought the ingredients on the way home.

She wanted to buy him a present. She left him debating with himself about noodles and sesame oil, and hurried through the shop to the glassware section. I'll buy champagne, she thought, and a couple of glasses.

He was laden with three carrier bags and announced there was no way they were going to punch home on the Underground. To her relief he hailed a cab; she'd been wondering how she was going to protect her fragile purchases in the Saturday afternoon roughhouse on the tube.

★ ★ ★

She gave him the heavy cut-glass flutes and the champagne, feeling awkward. 'It's a house-warming present,' she explained. 'I'm sorry it's a bit late.'

He smiled at her. 'Well, I guess the apartment didn't warm up till you got here, so that's okay.' He took her in his arms and kissed her, still holding the glasses and bottle. The combination of his unusually sweet remark and the way he was arousing her made her want him there and then. But he disengaged himself and went into the kitchen. 'I'll put this on ice. Now I have to cook.'

She wandered round the room. There wasn't anything to interest her on the bookshelves, and she went to sit down at the desk. Hal's typewriter stood in the middle with its cover on, and a thick stack of papers lay on top in a clear plastic folder. She smiled — obviously he hadn't been expecting to do any work this weekend. She turned her head sideways to read the title page through the plastic: '*The Minoans and Egypt: trade links and cultural influences.*'

'Hal?'

'Yeah?'

'May I read about the Minoans and Egypt?'

'Help yourself.'

Some time later he emerged from the kitchen. She'd been vaguely aware of him, listening to a Brahms symphony and singing along above the clatter of his cooking, but otherwise she'd been absorbed in his writing. Much of the text was outside her field of knowledge — honestly, she thought, I've only just finished ploughing through that great library book on the Mayans and got to grips with them, and now he's gone and moved on to the Bronze Age Mediterranean. The piece was incomplete; there were big gaps in the typewritten paragraphs where pencilled notes listed references or said things like 'KNOSSOS' or '?Cairo museum.'

'Time for a drink,' he said, opening the champagne.

'Oh, good. I'll be with you in a minute — I just want to finish reading what this Dillon bloke thinks about the end of the Minoans.'

'This Dillon bloke hasn't made his mind up. He'll have to go to Crete sometime.' He brought her over a glass of champagne. 'You can come with me,' he added.

She was joyful suddenly. I don't know what's ahead, she thought, but it'll be all right. I know it will.

Hal's meal was delicious. When they'd cleared up they went to sit by the fire with coffee.

'I can't believe we've only been here twenty-four hours,' she said, curling up on the cushions and leaning back against his legs as he sat above her on the chesterfield.

'I've been here much longer than that,' he observed.

'Together, I meant.'

'Sure. I know. Neither can I.' He bent over and nuzzled his face into her hair. 'I'm taking refuge in being flippant.'

'Yes. I know.'

He put his arms round her and began to kiss her, pulling her up on to the sofa beside him. She felt as if her body had been patiently waiting for this moment all day, and it seemed it was the same for him. He's so intuitive, she thought, it's as if he knows without me saying exactly where I want his touch.

But she was being distracted, her attention, her energy demanded by her hungry body; with a release that sent her soaring, she gave her entire being to him.

★ ★ ★

They had a quiet Sunday, sharing Hal's *Sunday Times*, and after lunch he drove her back to Hawkhurst. He left soon after six; he was going to Bristol the next day. She went outside to the car with him.

They stood close together, arms around each other.

'See you soon,' he said.

'Yes. Take care.'

'I will. I'll call you.'

She watched as he got into the car. He switched on the ignition, looking at the fuel gauge. 'Damn, I have to get some gas. And I don't have my credit card.'

He opened his wallet. It was full of notes.

'You don't have to pay me,' she said flippantly.

He looked up at her. 'I don't have enough,' he said simply.

She watched the car's lights disappear from sight. She knew she had a time of quiet reflection ahead, knew she needed to allow her heart and mind to catch up, to expand and encompass all that had happened.

When the lane was once again quite dark and silent, she went back into the house and closed the door.

23

She spent an introspective week. The fact of Hal lay deep within her; he was constantly on her mind.

He was more mature than any man she'd been close to before. He'd made his solitary way in the world and was intensely involved in his work, which he clearly loved. But so what? she thought. It's perfectly possible to love someone very much while keeping back part of you for yourself — I'm doing the same. I'm not going to throw all of me into him. I gave all of me to Ben and I nearly didn't recover when he died.

He's my lover, she'd think, and a startling stab of recollected pleasure would shoot up through her. And it's not just because of the long lay-off that it's so nice now — nice! How inadequate. There's more to it than that.

She let her mind go back to the past. To Ben. We were explosive together — we didn't even think about it, we were young and fiercely attracted to each other, deeply involved almost before we knew it. She smiled, remembering. But sometimes I felt I was being tested, measured up against some universal norm to which lovers had to aspire. It wasn't Ben, it was me. And my own judgement on myself was 'could do better'.

Perhaps I've improved, she thought. It occurred to her that it could have something to do with Hal, but she didn't want to dwell on that; it felt like dangerous ground. It's being more confident, she thought instead. I know I can cope, now, that I can manage life on my own if I have to. I value myself more. I'm not turning blindly to Hal because I need someone to prop me up. I'm turning to him because he's him.

And because he makes me laugh! The serious mood dissolved as she recalled a moment on Sunday morning when she cuddled up to him and said whimsically, 'Let's be small furry animals — what shall we be?'

His mind on making love to her again, he rolled over on top of her and replied, 'Rabbits.'

★ ★ ★

He phoned her one evening to announce he was going to Canterbury the following Saturday, and did she want to come?

'Yes. Why are you going to Canterbury?'

He sighed. 'I believe there's a cathedral there. D'you think Teddy would mind not coming if we take him somewhere else on another weekend?'

'No — he'd rather be here with Laura. He's making a takeover bid for her Christmas Lego.'

'Okay. Can you be ready by nine?'

'Oh, yes,' she said confidently.

'See you Saturday.'

The weather had been drizzly all week but Saturday showed optimistic patches of blue sky. She had delivered Edmund next door but was still drying her hair when Hal arrived.

'Would you like some coffee?' she yelled down

the stairs over the noise of the hairdryer.

'No need to shout,' he said, appearing in the bedroom doorway. He took the hairdryer out of her hand and began to kiss her, holding her tightly in his arms. 'Oh, I can be ready by nine,' he said in her ear.

'I thought we were going to Canterbury,' she said some time later.

'We are.' He kissed her lightly on the forehead and broke away. 'Soon as you've dried your hair.' He looked at her partially-clad body and smiled. 'And I guess you'd better put some more clothes on.'

It was an easy run to Canterbury, apart from getting round Ashford, which was choked with Saturday traffic. She'd been day-dreaming for the last few miles; staring out of the window, her eyes suddenly focused and she said, 'Oh, look! What's that big church ahead?'

Hal glanced at her pityingly. 'I imagine it's Canterbury Cathedral.'

They parked by the West Gate and set off towards the cathedral, walking down the pedestrian precinct and under an ancient archway into the cathedral grounds.

'Now I'm going to make like a tourist,' he said, going to buy a guidebook. She watched as he put on his glasses and began to read.

'You've got your concentrating face on,' she observed. 'Why don't we go round independently? I'll meet you out here if I finish before you.'

He looked up at her, his face intent. He smiled briefly. 'Okay.'

She wandered off on her own. She wasn't in the right frame of mind to concentrate on the glories all around. She'd visited the cathedral with Elowen the previous summer, and she reminded herself reassuringly that she'd managed to pay it proper attention then. I'm not, she thought, always the lowbrow I seem to be today.

She made a full circuit of the cathedral. She could see Hal, still at the top of the nave; she reckoned he'd be another half-hour at least. She bought herself an ice-cream and sat down on a bench in the sun to wait for him.

He emerged in just under the half-hour. He opened his arms as he approached and she leapt up, running to hug him.

'I'm through with culture, let's go eat,' he said.

'Did you like it?'

He thought for a while, then said, 'It's too immense to say you like or dislike it. It's full of humanity, centuries of people's desperate prayers, of their celebrations. It's all there, it's seeped into the stonework. Know what I liked best?' He looked down at her. 'The steps, the way they all have a dip in the middle from all the feet. So many feet, to wear away stone.'

'And knees.' She caught his meaning. 'People used to come on their knees, if they were very penitent.' She found it hard to think of anyone coming all the way from Southwark on their knees — it would hurt so.

They went to a pub that served home-made food, and had beer and a pie each. Hal had been going to try a steak and kidney pudding until, watching another customer dig his fork into one, she remarked that they were known in some parts of Britain as baby's heads.

'Oh, God,' he said in disgust. 'Hey, barman, make that two pies, will you?'

★ ★ ★

'Let's go back a different way,' she suggested. 'If we go south from here, we can look at a bit more of your Puck's Romney Marsh.'

'Okay. We'll send my dad a postcard. Do we go anywhere near Dymchurch?'

'Dymchurch-under-the-Wall,' she said thoughtfully. 'We can, but it's not what you're thinking, it's all chalets and bungalows and caravan sites, and bucket-and-spade shops and fat lady postcards.'

'Dad wouldn't appreciate a fat lady. Poor old Puck.'

They drove off from Canterbury in strengthening sunshine. The warmth flooding the car gave a feeling of intimacy and somnolence. Or perhaps that's the pint and a half of lager, she thought, her eyes closing.

Some time later she felt Hal's hand on her thigh. 'You've been asleep,' he said accusingly.

'Mmm. Have you been talking to me?'

He smiled. 'Not after the first fifteen minutes.'

She felt warm, well-fed, utterly content and, as his hand up under her skirt began to stroke her leg, decidedly aroused. 'Why don't we find a quiet side road and stop for a while?' she suggested shyly.

'Just what I am doing.' Then, a few minutes

later, 'What about that?'

He turned into a narrow lane, and an ungated entrance led to a patch of sparse woodland where tree-felling operations had been going on.

She could feel a rich feeling of happiness and desire between them. You get to know the feel of someone so soon, she thought vaguely, his kissing beginning to distract her, you know just what feels best. Her thoughts petered out as physical pleasure took over.

Some time later she moved back into her own seat, tucking in her shirt and reaching for her handbag. Hal watched, grinning, as she combed her hair.

'That's it, then, is it?' he said.

She flashed him a glance. 'We'd probably get arrested if we went any further. I'm sure it must be against the by-laws — affront to public decency, or something.'

'We'll go take a walk by the sea,' — he started the car — 'and hope there'll be a cold wind blowing.'

As they drove down to the coast she realized she hadn't yet thought about the evening and the night. Hal hasn't said if he intends to stay, she mused, but if he does, where is he going to sleep? Teddy always comes into my room in the morning, and he mustn't come across us in bed together. Perhaps it'd be all right if Hal disappears into the spare room before morning?

No. It wouldn't be all right at all. If I sleep with him and then pretend I haven't, it'll paint the whole thing with a furtive tinge of guilt that just isn't there. There wasn't any guilt in London, and that still holds true. No guilt now, either.

'Are you asleep again?' His voice broke in on her thoughts.

'No, just thinking.'

'Right. Anything I should know about?'

'I was just wondering about tonight. Are you going to stay?'

'Do you want me to?'

'Oh, yes, I want you to. But . . . '

'Yeah, I had a feeling there was a but.' His voice was slightly sarcastic. 'Shoot.'

She took a deep breath. 'I was thinking about Teddy.'

'And you want to tell me you can't be the you that you were last weekend, alone with me in London.'

'Yes.'

'Go on.'

She glanced across at his profile. She couldn't tell how he was feeling, what he was thinking. It felt horrible; she realized she'd been taking for granted their usual high level of unspoken communication.

'I don't honestly see how we can sleep together with Teddy there,' she began, more forcefully than she'd intended, 'because he might wake up and come to find me. Us.'

'And that wouldn't do.' It was a statement, very flat.

'Well, not really, would it?'

He was silent for a long time. She began to feel an awful foreboding. 'Hal? she said eventually. 'Are you cross with me?'

He smiled briefly. 'No. But if that's the way of it, don't kiss me with all that promise again.'

They had driven through Dymchurch without even noticing. Jo, turning away and looking out of the window at the restless sea, wondered what she'd done.

★ ★ ★

When they got home they were once again talking amicably, but she knew something had shifted out of gear. They had supper with Edmund, and later she put him to bed.

She went reluctantly downstairs. I don't know what happens next, she thought, I don't know what to do. He's so — unapproachable. He can still seem like a stone wall, even now. Now that we're lovers.

'Would you like a drink?' she asked him.

He was reading the paper. He put it down and took off his glasses.

'Come here, kid,' he said. She went to sit beside him. 'I understand what you're telling me,' he went on, 'and although I don't agree with your all-or-nothing approach, I'll go along with you.'

She relaxed against him in relief.

'But I don't think I'll stay tonight.'

Her head shot up and she stared at him. A month ago, a week ago, she thought wildly, I'd have burst into tears. But it won't help, not over this. Not with him.

She sat up straight, moving away from him.

'So, what now?' she asked quietly.

'You'd better come up to London again, soon as you can.'

★ ★ ★

When he had gone she gave herself up to the tears she'd held back, putting her head down on her arms and crying with frustration. When the crying was over she tried to stop acting like a spoilt child and think it through rationally. I couldn't have acted other than I did. Really I couldn't. Oh, God, I'm not ready for this. I don't know where I am, and it's making him miserable too.

She went to bed, taking a novel with her in the hope that immersing herself in fictional loves and disappointments would help her forget about her own. She'd been in bed about an hour when the telephone rang.

She went down to answer it.

'I'm sorry,' Hal's voice said. 'I've stopped sulking now.'

Thank God. 'I'm sorry, too, Hal.'

'Are you okay, kid?'

'I am now.'

'Come up tomorrow — bring Teddy, we'll take him to the zoo.'

'Are you sure?'

'Yes. I want to be with you.'

'All right. See you in the morning.'

'Right. Night, Jo.'

'Goodnight, Hal.'

★ ★ ★

The upheaval of that weekend set the pattern for their life together. It was a double life, she was well aware; the mood when they were alone was subtly different from when they were in Copse Hill House and Edmund was with them. The fact that it was the sexual element making the difference threw it into sharp relief; it seemed like a detachable part of their relationship instead of the integral thing it was.

And it's all my fault, she thought, but I don't know how to alter things. I wish I could talk to him, but I'm afraid to. He's exercising all his tolerance in not trying to make me change my mind. I haven't got the courage to risk upsetting things. To risk losing him.

For the first time, she came face to face with what a terrifying thought that was.

She realized that it wasn't Edmund's discovery of herself and Hal in bed together, even making love, that was bothering her. It was what that would mean. Hypocrite! she silently accused herself, you won't admit it! Because if Teddy were to know, if Hal and I were to come out in the open and act all the time like the lovers we are in secret, then I should have to admit to all the world that I am in love, that there is a new man in my life.

That Ben has been replaced.

When finally she admitted the truth, she was ashamed of her double standards and very sad at what she was doing to Hal. It *is* me, it's all my fault. I shouldn't have got so deeply involved with Hal while I still cling so tenaciously to being Ben's. I can't have it both ways.

But why, how, was I able to give myself so totally to Hal? I didn't manage to muster a single atom of resistance when he finally made love to me — good grief, quite the contrary.

She was distressed, scatter-brained and nervy, and succeeded in making her own life miserable as well as everyone else's. But how can I help it, the whining little devil of self-pity inside her head would howl, when it's all so difficult?

She got up one morning after a wretched night, determined to do something. Shall I go down to Cornwall and see Mum? No, Dad's there — I'm too bloody selfish even to think of that and be pleased for them.

She gave Edmund his breakfast, paying scant attention to his chatter. Then she pushed him out to play in the garden, and soon he was joined by Laura; Jo had forgotten she was to look after her while Jenny went shopping.

'Are you all right?' Jenny asked as she left. 'You look awful.'

'I didn't sleep very well.'

'Do you want to talk?' Jenny's voice was kind.

'Oh — perhaps, yes. Thanks, Jen — the trouble is, I know what's the matter, but I don't know how to put it right.'

'I'll bring us something nice home for lunch,' Jenny said cheerfully. 'Hang on in there, kid!'

Kid, Jo thought. That's what Hal calls me. Oh. Hal.

★ ★ ★

She organized an impromptu picnic in the living-room for the children so that she and Jenny could have lunch on their own.

'Go on, then,' Jenny said, 'why are you so miserable?'

Jo was opening a bottle of wine. 'It's stupid,' she said, 'I had everything to be happy about, but I wasn't because something didn't feel right, and now that I've finally winkled out what it is I wish I hadn't.' Don't *cry*, for God's sake.

'Let's look at it logically,' Jenny said practically. 'Concentrate on what this awful discovery is.'

Jo blew her nose and drank half a glass of wine. She looked at Jenny solemnly. 'I seem to have fallen in love with Hal. I want us — I want to be with him. But that means Ben's now in the past. I don't think I can live with that.'

'What's so unexpected about that?' Jenny demanded. 'I should have thought that's how anyone would feel if they'd lost a partner they loved and were about to make a go of it with someone else.'

'Maybe. But it's more complicated than that. I've lost my way.'

'How do you mean?'

'I feel — sort of nervous, as though I'm on the brink of great huge changes and I'm going to leave somewhere safe and secure to venture out into the unknown.'

'That's because you are, you nit,' Jenny said heatedly. 'But surely you never meant your nice secure haven to be permanent? I can't imagine that — not for you.'

330

'I've got used to it.'

'I expect a person in chains in a dungeon gets *used* to it, but it doesn't mean he likes it, and it doesn't mean he wouldn't give his eye-teeth to get out of it.'

'No.'

'You, my girl, have a great deal too much time to think.' Jenny topped up their glasses and banged the bottle down on the table. 'You analyse things so finely that they become meaningless. No wonder you don't know where the hell you are.'

'I've done nothing but think, recently,' Jo said mournfully. 'Hasn't got me anywhere.'

'No, nor Hal. You're not being at all fair on him, you know.' Jenny frowned at her. 'Poor bugger can't know whether he's coming or going, with all your airy-fairy changes of heart. You can't expect him to wait around while you think things out to the millionth degree and then still don't decide what you want.'

'That's more or less what my mother said.' Jo thought with a smile that Elowen had expressed herself marginally less emphatically.

Jenny leaned her elbows on the table and fixed Jo with a stare. 'What you and Hal need is a holiday,' she said decisively. 'Time by yourselves might make you feel more like a couple and less like a pair of occasional players.'

Jo burst out laughing. Jenny smiled reluctantly with her.

'Would you be prepared to have Teddy?' Jo asked.

'Yes. I wouldn't have suggested it otherwise,

idiot. But *use* the time with him. Don't come back still sitting on your ruddy fence, or you might just find it'll stop supporting your weight.'

* * *

Later she sat down to write to him. She'd tried to phone him, but without success. She was quite pleased that he wasn't there — it was easier to write what was in her mind than say it. She wrote that she felt they needed time together, hoping fervently he'd think so too.

She had to wait nearly a week for her answer. He was often out of touch for that long, and usually it didn't bother her. But this time it was different. Jenny had been absolutely right in saying she had too much time to think, and during that week her tormented thoughts kept her miserably awake. She'd convince herself in the dark hours that he was doing it on purpose, that he didn't care at all about her and had probably decided to call the whole thing off. In the unreasoning mood of the night she forgot all the ways he showed her she mattered to him.

Then one evening he telephoned. His voice was just the same as usual, and he spoke to her with the same warm endearments. As half of her mind listened with huge relief to him saying he'd got back from Leeds that moment and only just found her letter, the other half was telling her firmly, remember this, and don't be so daft again.

'Where do you want to go on this vacation?' he said.

'France? Somewhere not too far away, if we're only going for a week.'

'Okay. I have three weeks free after Easter. How about then?'

'All right. What . . . '

'Look, kid,' he said decisively, 'I'll come down tomorrow evening.'

'Oh, yes, okay.' Tomorrow!

'About eight,' he said, and rang off.

★ ★ ★

They spent a business like hour planning the trip. When they'd covered everything she got up to fetch them a drink, and, coming back, found he'd moved from the table and was stretched out on the sofa.

'Come over here,' he ordered.

She went to sit beside him, and he put his arms round her.

'I find the prospect of a week in France with you quite exciting,' he said, kissing the top of her head.

'Oh good. And the food and drink aren't bad, either.'

'Right. Hey,' he was suddenly impatient, 'turn round, will you, I can't kiss you properly from this angle.'

She turned obligingly, looking solemnly into his brown eyes. He stared intently back, but there was a hint of a smile about his mouth. 'I can read your thoughts, kid,' he said quietly.

'Oh. Oh, Hal.'

She bent her head down to him, and as they

began to kiss his arms closed around her and he pulled her down beside him. Quite soon she was able to distinguish two contrary orders issuing from mission control in her brain: the sensible part, which had once set down rules of behaviour here in this house, with her son asleep upstairs, was commanding *stop*. But there was mutiny in the ranks, and a wild, blood-pounding part that didn't give a toss for rules or for sense was gaining the ascendant and ordering *go on*.

He was lying on top of her, and she became aware in an almost detached way of her eager body responding to him, matching him in mounting excitement. In a dream, here eyes half closed, she felt him begin to undress her.

She felt him pull away a little, and opened her eyes to look at him. He was propped on one elbow, grinning down at her.

'I don't intend to stop,' he said.

'No. I know you don't.' She reached up to unbutton his shirt

Later she lay with her head on his chest, listening to his strong steady heartbeat gradually returning to normal. She felt strange and disorientated, aware that something had been acknowledged between them.

'So why was tonight different?' he asked presently.

'I don't know. I've decided I think too much, so I'm not going to work out an answer.'

He smiled. 'Okay. We'll just say it's because we haven't made love in a fortnight.'

'Is it that long?' She reached down to run her hands over his body. 'I hadn't realized.'

★ ★ ★

When they finally went up to bed, he stopped on the landing to kiss her goodnight.

'I'm not going to push my luck,' he said. 'In any case, I'm bushed. I'll see you in the morning.'

She couldn't prevent herself wondering why it had been all right — far more than all right, I'd have made the first move if he didn't — to make love here tonight. It was more than just absence from each other.

She had a feeling the French holiday was going to make some changes. They might even be positive ones. She drifted towards sleep feeling more then slightly optimistic.

24

They went to France on a cold, bright April morning. Setting out from Calais on a straight road with little traffic, Hal remarked that France appeared to be empty and put his foot down.

She liked driving fast with him. She loved listening to his music, not minding the occasional embarrassing moment such as driving through a small town with the car windows open and *Le Corsair* overture belting out at full volume. He pointed out it was written by a Frenchman, they damned well ought to appreciate it. France seemed to put him in a Berlioz frame of mind; he played the *Symphonie Fantastique*, telling her the tale of the young man's doomed love. She thought, it'll always make me think of this moment of happiness, speeding down a dead straight, tree-lined French road with Hal beside me.

They concentrated on Normandy, which was new to both of them. It was redolent with names that made her think of history lessons, and her memory was stimulated into action, rooting out stray facts and half-remembered tales. She found it very satisfying to tell Hal things he didn't already know.

They went to Bayeux and spent a long afternoon looking at the tapestry, full of life and colour even after nine hundred years. Then they shot forward to the present century and went to Arromanches to see the D-Day Museum and the remains of the Mulberry Harbour. They stayed the night in Avranches, where they came across Patton Square.

'Hey, old Blood and Guts!' Hal said, pulling Jo across the road to look at Patton's memorial standing in the square, a stark monolith in a semicircle of trees.

'They're American trees,' she said, reading from an explanatory notice, 'and they're planted in American soil. Like in Rupert Brooke,' she added, 'a bit of Normandy that's forever America.'

'There's enough Americans buried round here for it to be a sizeable bit,' Hal said. 'Especially round Caen. My dad's brother Peter was killed there.'

'Was he? This mentions Caen.' She was still reading from the plaque. 'It says General Patton had his headquarters here during the recapture of Normandy, in the push for Caen.'

They went to Falaise, and walked round the ruins of the castle where William of Normandy was born.

'Bet you didn't know William the Conqueror was the bastard son of the Duke of Normandy and Arlette the tanner's daughter,' Hal said, relieving her of her guidebook.

'William the Bastard, they called him,' she said thoughtfully. 'I expect that's why he felt he had to conquer England, so that he could change his name.'

In one village they walked round a war cemetery, uniform rows of white headstones tucked into a corner of the graveyard. All those young lives, she thought, standing sorrowfully in front of an inscription that read, 'I waited and waited for my boy but he did not come, and now I shall never see him again.'

They spent the last night in a picturesque town on the Seine, to the north of Paris. The river was wide there, moving with a powerful current between dramatic limestone cliffs on one side and a panorama of grass and fields on the other. The cliffs were clad in beech forests, brilliant green with spring growth. High above the little town stood a castle that had been built by Richard the Lionheart.

★ ★ ★

The end of the holiday, she thought miserably in the morning. After all their happiness, the prospect of not being with him hurt. Especially after the passion of the night before. She thought, he was affected by it too, by that depressing knowledge that it was the last time, that we have to go back to all the complications we've escaped from. He had held her in a desperate closeness, and, deep inside her still, said quietly, 'It's like being one person.'

He didn't say things like that very often. She remembered them all clearly, stringing them on a strand of memory like precious jewels on a necklace, to be turned over and treasured in times when he was far away.

★ ★ ★

They drove in silence. Towards lunchtime, he slid a hand across to rest it on her thigh and said, 'Cheer up.'

She put on her sun-glasses. Her eyes kept filling with tears.

He stopped the car in the next town and marched her into a restaurant. He got them a drink, found a menu, and while she was vaguely wondering whether or not she felt like eating, told her a barrage of increasingly funny jokes until the ache in her stomach made her beg him to stop.

' . . . and the hooker said, man, I ain't gettin' amorous, I'm trying on the sneakers!' he finished triumphantly, and her shout of laughter caused a newly-arrived party to vacate the table they'd just selected in favour of one further away.

'*Ivrognée!*' a woman hissed, glaring at her.

'Now are you hungry?' he asked. 'Or do I have to tell you another?'

'Please don't.' She began to laugh again. 'I used to get like this at school — the funny things keep coming back into your head, and you just can't be serious.'

He grinned smugly. 'That was the idea.' He pushed the menu at her.

He devotes the same attention to cheering you up as he does to everything else, she thought later; she'd been weak with laughter when they left the restaurant. It wasn't far to Calais, and they boarded a ferry within half an hour. The Channel was much rougher than on the outward crossing, and, after a woman sitting beside them in the lounge had unexpectedly and colourfully been sick all over her tray of food, they'd decided to go up on deck.

They found a spot on the leeward side and stood close together under the overhang of the deck above, sheltered from the heavy spray and the waves. They watched the south coast getting nearer, and as the ship finally entered the calmer waters of Dover Harbour, he bent down to speak into her ear.

'Thanks, kid,' he said. 'Can't recall when I've enjoyed a vacation more.'

He smiled at her. Her heart was so full that she couldn't think how to reply. Not with words, she thought, laying her head against his chest. He stroked her hair, hugging her close and sheltering her with his body, and they stood quietly until they were summoned down to the car deck.

★ ★ ★

As the memory of the holiday receded, Jo wondered what it had achieved; there was still no clear way ahead. But she was happy with the present, and whenever she worried about where it was all leading, she would simply say to herself, it'll come right.

She rarely went to London now; they had come to an unspoken agreement to stick to the pattern set the night Hal came down to discuss the holiday. He took up occupation of the spare room, and their intimacy was reserved for the late evening, before they went their separate ways to bed. Sometimes, turning to him suddenly, she would catch on his face the tail end of a look that she couldn't identify. It was new, and it seemed to affect her deeply; she wanted to hold him, to offer him love and security. But he gave her no opening.

May lengthened into June and the Kent countryside was impatient with life. Hal was busier than ever as the end of the academic year approached; when he did manage to come down, he spent a lot of the time asleep. Watching him in the garden one afternoon, stretched out in the shade, she noticed how strained he was looking, shadows beneath his eyes and a slight frown even in his sleep. He's going grey, she thought, surprised by the great surge of tenderness that swept through her. She almost reached out to touch him, then thought, he needs the sleep, and made herself get up and leave him alone.

★ ★ ★

One midweek evening he telephoned. 'What are you doing Friday?'

'Not a lot — I might wash my hair, start a new library book, dead-head the roses . . . '

'Be ready at eight. I'm taking you out.'

'Oh, lovely! Where?'

'I'm not saying.'

'What sort of 'out', though? Tell me a bit more, or I won't know what to wear.'

'Something pretty. See you Friday.'

★ ★ ★

Friday was hot. Edmund was despatched to Jenny at teatime, and later Jo sat at her open bedroom window day-dreaming. She wondered where Hal was taking her.

She went outside to wait for him, drinking in the warm, moist-green smell that the grass and earth were exuding at the end of the hot day. She stood spinning slowly on one foot, feeling the full skirt of her new dress flare out round her bare legs, remembering girlhood party frocks.

When she was in mid-twirl, Mrs Watson called out over the fence, 'Good evening, dear.'

'Hello!' she called back. Oh, Lord, I'm sure she thinks I'm nutty — she always seems to catch me when I'm thinking about something else, like when she brought Hal's flowers and at Jenny's party.

She saw Hal's car pull into the drive, and ran to get in. He was wearing his Al Capone suit. He leaned across and kissed her. 'You look great. Hope you're hungry.'

'Very.'

She smiled to herself. He reached out to hold her hand.

After some miles he slowed, then made a right turn and a left into the car-park of a small and very expensive restaurant.

'I hope you know what you're doing,' she said, awed. 'They have menus the size of hoardings here, it's frightfully expensive.'

'Sure, I know.' He grinned at her. 'Ain't nothing I can't handle.'

The restaurant was like a dignified private house. The hall was cool, decorated with vast bowls of flowers whose scent mingled with a faint smell of beeswax polish. In the bar, French windows opened onto a terrace.

'Would you like to order?' a waiter asked quietly, appearing beside them as they began their second drinks. He returned a little later to escort them through to the dining-room, moving so smoothly and silently that Jo said he must be on castors. Hal smiled, but didn't flash back a response. He seems preoccupied, she thought. He's been overworking.

It was late when they left. The night was clear and starry, and as they walked in the moonlight to the car, he put his arm round her and kissed the top of her head. 'Let's go on somewhere,' he said, opening the door for her. 'I want to talk to you.'

Her heart sank suddenly. 'We could drive over to Bodiam.'

'Okay.'

As they drove slowly through the lanes, he took her hand and put it on his thigh. The gesture reassured her, but she was still uneasy. Oh, God, I don't like it when people say they want to talk.

The moon was shining out over the valley when they got to Bodiam. They left the car by the road and climbed over the gate, walking up the path towards the castle. The sheen of moonlight on the moat made the strong old walls appear starkly black; it was hauntingly beautiful.

They sat down on a seat. He put his arm round her, and gazed down across the valley.

'If you don't say something soon,' she said eventually, 'I shall run screaming down that slope and throw myself in the river.'

'I'm sorry. I was thinking.'

'I know. What are you thinking about?'

He didn't answer.

'Hal, I feel . . . sort of ominous.' Please, please talk to me.

'It's okay,' he said quickly. He turned her face up to kiss her.

He lapsed into silence again. But then he straightened up; he seemed to be preparing himself. He said, 'I've finished my lectures. I'm going back to the States.'

It was her turn to be silent. Her brain was perversely letting her down, going into hiding and refusing to come out and meet this attack that had just been launched at her.

She made a huge effort. 'I didn't realize the time was up.' He said nothing. 'When — when do you leave?'

'I don't know.' He sighed deeply.

She felt sick. She was cold and trembling. Everything seemed to hang suspended, as if the valley below and all the lands beyond balanced on the edge of a precipice.

'Please, Hal,' she said very quietly, 'what about us?'

'Sweetheart, I don't know that, either.' He took his arm from her shoulders and buried his face in his hands.

She was shaking violently. '*What* don't you know?' she asked desperately.

'Ah, don't cry, please don't.' He turned to look at her, his face taut.

'I thought you loved me!' she cried angrily.

'I do love you.' He spoke quietly but with a force that stopped her dead. 'The whole purpose of this evening, the meal, coming here, wanting to talk to you, is because I want to ask you to marry me, but I'm scared to because I think you'll say no.'

She pulled away. Feeling had returned; her mind was no longer dead but racing. Oh, God, Hal, she cried silently, how can I tell you what I'm thinking at this moment? She wiped at her face with her hand. There was no way she could tell him, no way on earth that she could make herself confess the thought that had leapt into her head.

I'm already married.

There was an unbearable tension between them.

'I'll take you home,' he said starkly.

They walked in silence to the car. He reached to start the engine, but the sight of his set profile was too much for her to bear.

'Hal,' she said, leaning towards him, 'oh, Hal, please . . . '

Immediately he took her in his arms. 'It's okay, kid,' he said gently, stroking her hair. 'It's okay, don't cry.'

'Can we talk about it?' she whispered.

'Oh, sure. Talk, think, find a way. But not tonight.'

They drove home. She was half-way between dream and nightmare, and in the empty house there was no question of their sleeping apart. He treated her like a child, undressing her, washing her face and putting her to bed. Then he climbed in beside her and took her in his arms.

In the morning he told her he wanted them to get married and return to San Francisco to live.

She almost agreed.

But something stood in the way. Something wasn't right.

Until she could isolate it and deal with it, she couldn't make any undertaking about the future; she looked at him, at his face pale with strain, and said silently, I love you far too much to make promises I mightn't be able to keep.

She asked him simply for time. With a long last look at her, he nodded briefly and left.

★ ★ ★

The week that followed exhausted her. I want to go to him, she mourned silently, but I can't till I've come to a decision. Oh, God, whoever really makes a decision? Surely most of us just go for whichever alternative is less unsuitable, less painful? Or the alternative that presents itself more imperatively? You couldn't call that *making* a decision.

On that basis, I have to select the option of marrying him. He's being imperative, and he's nothing if not suitable. I love him, he loves me. He's formed a wonderful relationship with Teddy, who'll miss him terribly if he disappears.

And they'll all tell me I'm crazy not to marry him. I can already hear the family and friends chorusing, 'it's what Ben would have wanted.'

But is it what I want?

I don't know. Something's holding me back.

Until that moment she had failed to see what it was.

As enlightenment came she thought, but it's so simple! Each step that takes me closer to Hal severs another link with Ben. Ben's no longer the last man who held my hand, kissed me, made love to me, held me tight in his arms through long nights of passion.

There's only one thing Ben was that Hal isn't.

My husband.

Even Teddy looks on Hal as a father — he's superseding Ben for Teddy, too. Oh, Ben, darling Ben, poor Ben, you were only a father for a little over a year.

That's it. That's why I'm holding out. I don't want to sever the last link. I'm still called by Ben's name, I'm still his wife.

I've made up my mind, then.

But then the vibrant green of her new love shot up in protest. How on earth can it be right to accept everything Hal offers except marriage? What an impossible, rotten position I've put him in. Yes, Hal, I'll sleep with you, go away with you, accept you as everything except my husband. You can't be that, can't come and share our home as husband and father, because that's Ben's place.

She experienced an instant of clarity, seeing it all through Hal's eyes. She wept for the pain she was causing him.

★ ★ ★

At the end of the week she caught a train up to London. She didn't know what she intended to do; some time during the endless days the combination of indecision and lack of sleep had shifted her mind's balance, and she was acting without reason or logic; instinct told her to go to Hal, but it didn't tell her what to do when she got there.

The pain in his face lashed out and hit her. In panic, she leapt to the conclusion that she couldn't drag out the uncertainty any longer; any decision must be better than none.

He sat down opposite to her. 'Well?'

'I don't think I can marry you,' she heard herself say. Who is this person saying this? She looked at his haggard face and ached to hug him, to do somehing to wipe away that awful look of suffering.

'I don't have to ask why,' he said.

She forced a smile. 'Couldn't we go to America anyway, and carry on as we are?' This woman doing the talking was quite good. Very calm.

He looked at her wearily. 'No,' he said. 'That's the whole point.'

'I don't see why.'

'I don't believe this!' he said harshly. 'Goddam it, Jo, I've wanted to marry you for months. Can't you see? I haven't pushed you, but it's enough, for Christ's sake. I don't want to wait any more. I'm sick of uncertainty.'

She shook her head. 'There isn't any uncertainty about loving you. But you see, I'm already married.'

'You're *what*?' He leapt up, striding across to her. 'You're crazy!' he shouted, his face close to hers.

'Your husband's dead, Jo, he died three years ago, and there ain't no resurrections outside the Bible!'

She shrank from him. 'I know, Hal.' Her mind reeled with misery. 'Perhaps it's the only thing I do know.'

I have to get out of here. I can't bear it. There, over there, is the fireplace and the stack of cushions where we first made love.

It was intolerable to be in that room, at the end of everything.

She got up and walked towards the door. He came rapidly after her, grasping her shoulders and turning her round to face him, holding her very tightly with hands that hurt.

'I won't hang around, Jo,' he shouted. 'I'm going home, either with you or without you.'

He stared down at her, the eyes that she loved so much, knew in so many moods, full of anger that made him a stranger. She tried to move out of his grip, out of the sight of him, but he was too strong for her.

'What can I do, Hal?'

'Come with me, marry me,' he stormed, as if trying by sheer force to make her do what he wanted.

She cried out, '*I can't!*'

Abruptly his hands fell from her and he turned away. 'Then you'd better go.'

★ ★ ★

She left the flat, closing the door behind her. She thought, I'll go to Tottenham Court Road. Get the

349

tube to Charing Cross.

She caught a train from the main line station. Her mind registered nothing; only habit got her home. At the local station she had to walk. It was a long way. I must have walked this morning, too, she realized; her car wasn't in the car-park. She let herself into the house, went upstairs and quietly got into bed.

Later, she became aware of ringing and banging. She went down to the front door. It was Jenny.

'Oh, Jo,' she said, taking one look at Jo's face. 'Oh, love, what's happened?'

What *had* happened? She frowned. Then she knew.

'He's gone. He's going back to America and I'm not going with him. I'll never be with him again.'

A pain swept through her, so agonizing that it took her breath away. She broke out into loud, rasping sobs. Jenny pushed her into the house and slammed the front door, running to the kitchen to pour a large shot of brandy.

'Stop it,' she ordered. '*Jo!*' she bawled, shaking her by the shoulders. Jo sank to her knees howling at the top of her voice, and Jenny swung her hand back and slapped her hard across the face, forehand and backhand. Jo's eyes shot open, and the dreadful noise stopped.

Jenny thrust the brandy at her, and she gulped it down. Then she collapsed on the floor. She looked up at Jenny.

'Oh, God,' she moaned, 'what have I done?'

Jenny stayed with her until late into the night, holding her hand while she wept. At last Jo got exhaustedly to her feet and went to make them a cup of tea.

She regarded Jenny out of painfully pink eyes. 'I'm okay now,' she said quietly. 'Thank you for staying with me.'

Jenny looked doubtful. 'Are you sure? I could sleep here. Or you could come over to us.'

'No. It's kind of you, but I want to be on my own.' Jenny still looked dubious. 'It's all right, I haven't got a shotgun, the carving knife's as blunt as old boots, and there are only three aspirins in the first aid box.'

'Well, if you're sure. Come over in the morning, though.'

'Okay.'

★ ★ ★

The night closed in silently. Jo was past hysteria, past anything except an agony so great she had no idea how to manage it. This is the me who could cope with anything, she thought, this is the woman who was always going to keep a bit of herself safe, never to be given away.

Hal, oh, Hal, why did I give all of myself to you? Could I only cope because you were there? And how did it happen? I didn't intend it to end like this — I don't remember what was in my mind when I went to find you, but it certainly wasn't finishing with you.

Did I think we'd work out a pleasing compromise? But he didn't agree to any compromise, he didn't let me influence him, and now I've lost him.

The consequences of her own actions flooded into her mind and she wept with pain.

As dawn came it occurred to her, this hurts as much as losing Ben. She wondered whether she was capable of sustaining such pain a second time. Do I love Hal as much as I loved Ben, then?

In the still, dew-heavy desolation of the early morning, she heard quite clearly her own inner voice say, you idiot, you love him more.

After that there was no more to think about. She stood at her bedroom window looking out at the sleeping countryside. I can't go on living. I can't, not now I've lost Hal. She stood there for a long time, quite incapable of coming to terms with life as it now would be, without him. Then abruptly she flung herself across the bed and slept.

Later she went next door and was ushered in by Jenny and Tom, gently and carefully as though she had been very ill. Tom whispered something to Jenny and disappeared.

'Poor Tom,' Jo said with the smallest of smiles. 'How awkward for him. I'm sorry, Jenny.'

'Are you up to seeing the kids?' Jenny asked as they sat down in the living-room. 'It might help.'

Jo didn't think anything would help. 'Okay.'

'Stay to lunch,' Jenny urged, 'I don't think you should be alone.'

The day was endured, somehow. It was a relief to them all when evening came and Jo got up to go home.

'We're here, if you get desperate,' Jenny said.

'It's okay. I've imposed on you long enough. Thanks, Jenny.'

'What will you do?'

'God knows.'

★ ★ ★

The days passed. Jo could neither eat nor sleep, and the effort to appear normal for Edmund's sake was almost more than she could manage. By the end of the week she couldn't endure the four walls of her house any longer, and asked Jenny if she'd have Edmund for a couple of nights.

'It's the last time, I promise,' she said tensely. 'I shall make a decision — I've got to. Perhaps I'll go to Cornwall, or out to Zurich to see my brothers — I don't know. But I can't *think*, here.' Tears sprang into her eyes.

'Yes, I know, love. I'll have Edmund, it's okay. Where will you go?'

'Rye. Do you think they'd have a room at the Smugglers' Inn?'

'They might have a single. People usually go there in pairs, what with those low ceilings and oak panels and four-posters, so maybe you'll . . . ' Jenny stopped abruptly. This wasn't the most tactful thing to say to Jo at the moment.

But Jo wasn't listening. 'See you next week,' she said distantly.

'Yes. Look after yourself.'

Jenny watched her walk off. Then she went inside and closed the door.

25

Late the next night the rural peace was shattered by a car screaming down the lane to Copse Hill House.

It skidded to a halt and was left, engine running and headlights blazing on full beam, while Hal threw himself out and raced up to Jo's front door. His ringing and thunderous knocking brought no response from the dark house.

He ran up Jenny and Tom's drive, thumping on the door with both fists, oblivious to the disturbance.

'Where is she?' he demanded, pushing past Tom into the house. 'Is she here? She is, isn't she?' His face was very white, with deep lines incised from his nose to the corners of his mouth.

'No, she isn't,' Tom replied mildly. 'Er — I take it you mean Jo?'

Hal scowled at him. 'Of course I mean Jo,' he said impatiently.

'She's — er, I think she's gone away for a few days,' Tom said.

'I can see that,' Hal snapped. 'Where the hell to? She's not at home, you say she's not here, she's not with her mother — I've called Elowen four times. You have to know where she is.' He rounded on Tom, grasping his arm. 'Where's Jenny?' He looked around him wildly.

'I'm here.' Jenny came into the hall from the living room.

'Will you tell me where Jo is?' Hal demanded. 'This dumb sucker of a husband of yours ain't giving.'

'Keep your voice down, Hal,' Tom said reprovingly, 'you'll wake the children.'

'Shut up!' Hal barked.

'Don't you *dare* talk to Tom like that — ' Jenny began, but Hal interrupted.

'Children! You said children!' he shouted triumphantly. 'You have Teddy here.' He lunged towards the stairs, pushing Tom violently aside.

'Stop it!' Jenny's voice rang out sharply as she ran to block Hal's path at the foot of the stairs. 'How dare you push your way in here, shoving Tom aside, insulting him, disturbing the entire household? Just be quiet, and for God's sake *calm down*, then perhaps we can talk!'

She stood in front of Hal, fists raised aggressively, quivering with anger and indignation.

Hal's fire abated. He sank down onto the stairs and buried his face in his hands. 'I'm sorry,' he said, his voice muffled. 'Jenny, Tom, I'm sorry.' He looked up, his face defeated and suddenly very old. 'I'm way out of line.' He held out his hand to Jenny, and she took it. Tom came cautiously back from his path of retreat towards the kitchen.

'Christ, Hal, I thought you were going to hit me!' he said sheepishly.

Hal managed a weak grin. 'Sorry,' he said again. 'I'll behave, I promise.' He looked from one to the other. 'Where is she?'

Tom and Jenny exchanged glances.

'Oh, god, you have to tell me!' Hal implored.

'I don't know what I'm doing any more, I can't even — ' He broke off.

Jenny said hesitantly, 'Teddy is here, yes. Jo's gone away.'

'Where?'

Jenny looked steadily into his eyes, her chin stuck out stubbornly. 'Look, Hal,' she said, with a firmness she was far from feeling, 'Jo didn't want anyone to know where she was. So if you want me to tell you, you'll have to give me a very good reason.'

'Okay, I will.' He looked like a man who had lost all hope. 'I don't know how much she told you, but she thinks I've left for the States without her. But I haven't, and I won't be going anywhere till she and Teddy come with me.'

Jenny watched him intently. Then: 'She's gone down to Rye. She was hoping she'd get a room at the Smugglers' Inn.'

Hal looked surprised. 'Why?'

Jenny's eyes flashed and she said spiritedly, 'Because she couldn't stand going slowly mad inside that house!'

Hal leapt up and clutched her to him in a bear hug. Before she could break away he kissed her full on the lips. 'You're great, kid!'

He rushed out, slamming the door. His footsteps pounded away down the drive, and briefly the car's engine revved ferociously. Then there was a sudden silence.

A few moments later, there was an apologetic ring on the bell. Jenny wrenched the front door open again. 'Great merciful heavens, Hal, what is it now?'

He said awkwardly, 'I can't remember how to get to Rye.'

★ ★ ★

He drove to Rye with a total disregard for his paintwork and the highway code. The car responded eagerly to his haste and he shot through the deserted roads as if he were on a racetrack. Scorching down the hill through Playden he realized he was doing over ninety, and slowed down.

He parked in the old town, more confident of locating the Smugglers' Inn on foot; he could double back if he missed the way. But he didn't need to: he walked straight to it.

The receptionist looked up as Hal appeared before him and a look of apprehension came into his face. Hal was desperate to get to Jo, determined not to let anything stand in his way. He leaned on the desk, and the receptionist shrank back.

'I'm looking for Mrs MacAllister,' Hal said quietly. 'What room is she in?'

The receptionist coughed nervously. 'I — er — is she expecting you?'

'No.'

'It's rather late for visitors,' he glanced at his watch, 'goodness, yes, it's nearly midnight.'

Hal looked at him steadily. 'Mrs MacAllister's room number, please,' he repeated.

The receptionist, five foot four to Hal's six

foot three, bravely stood his ground. 'Perhaps, Mr . . . ?'

'Dillon.'

'Perhaps, Mr Dillon, you would care to leave a message, and I will undertake to give it to Mrs MacAllister in the morning?'

Hal reached out and firmly removed the receptionist's hands from the hotel register. He turned it round and glanced down the list of entries till he saw Jo's handwriting, then he swung the book back in front of the receptionist. He grinned suddenly. 'It's okay, buddy. I'm going to marry her in the morning.'

He disappeared up the stairs.

He found the room, and then came to a halt outside.

This was the moment he had been working towards since very shortly after Jo had walked out of his apartment. But reaching the decision to go after her, and then doing so, had become ends in themselves.

And now I've found her. I've done what I set out to do. What next?

Of all things, the image that came into his mind was of Jo standing in the market place of a French town, watching three enormously fat people getting out of a three-wheeler. She'd turned to him, her face full of worried amusement, and said, 'They probably choose to come here instead of their nearest town. It wouldn't be worth all that effort and discomfort, would it, to drive just down the road?'

I don't know anyone else with a mind that works

like hers, he thought. Added to which she has guts, she's loyal and she's loving.

That's why I'm here. I don't want to be without her.

He shook his head, smiling, and tapped on the door.

Her voice said quietly, 'Who is it?'

He said, 'Me.'

He opened the door and went in. The room was almost in darkness, lit only by a candle. As his eyes adjusted he made out Jo, sitting in a chair by the open window.

He moved closer. Her face was white and blotched and her swollen eyes were circled by deep black lines. His heart turned over.

She was watching him warily. 'I thought you'd gone home.' Her voice was husky, as if she had a cold.

He went and sat on the bed. 'No, I haven't gone home.'

She continued to watch him. The silence extended. Then she asked, 'Why not?'

'I can't go without you.' She said nothing, just went on looking at him and biting at the inside of her lip. 'Jo?'

'Is this another ultimatum?' she asked suddenly. 'I thought it was marriage or nothing.'

He sighed. 'Well, it ain't.'

She stared at him, not responding.

'Goddam it, Jo, I don't want to go and live half a world away from you!'

Her face twitched. 'So what's new? Why are you here?' Her voice was barely audible.

'Hell, I don't know!' he said in exasperation. 'It's all gotten too complicated for me. I just want to be with you, and I guess it no longer matters on whose terms. These last few days when I've been without you, thinking I was always going to be without you, were — well, I couldn't take it. I lost one woman I loved, I'm not going to lose the other. So if being with you has to be the way you say, then I'll have to learn to live with it.'

He surprised himself. It doesn't come easy, he thought, baring your soul.

She said nothing. Her face was averted, turned towards the open window and the night sky.

Suddenly he was angry. He felt vulnerable, with his emotions exposed and hers still locked up inside her.

'Goddam you, Jo, can't you contribute anything to this?'

'I — I don't know what I can say.' Her voice trembled and he knew she was crying.

It was too much. Kid, I can't see you hurting any more.

He got up and knelt beside her, putting his arms round her. 'Sweetheart, don't,' he said gently, 'don't cry.'

She reached out blindly for him. She was muttering something, but he couldn't make it out — it sounded like, 'I can't believe you're here.'

'Oh, I'm here,' he said softly. 'And I'm staying.'

He held her closer, horrified at how cold she was. He wondered how long she'd been sitting there, and whether she knew there was rain on her hair. After a while he picked her up in his arms and laid her gently down in the bed. It wasn't a big bed, but he didn't think it would matter. He didn't intend to let go of her all night anyway.

★ ★ ★

It was late in the morning when they woke. He'd been holding her against him as he slept, and when he opened his eyes she was looking at him fixedly.

He smiled sleepily at her. 'Hi,' he said.

'Oh, Hal, yes, yes, yes, I will!'

'Great. You will what?'

'Marry you, you cretin, if you still want to.'

'I still want to.'

She laid her head on his chest. They both had most of their clothes on — it had been a strange night.

Presently he said, 'How d'you feel?'

'Wonderful — I think.'

'I could use a shower.' He stretched, yawning mightily. 'Care to join me?'

'There isn't a shower. But there's a bathroom down the corridor.'

An elderly man in a plaid dressing-gown emerged from the bathroom, courteously wishing them good morning. There was a smell of eau-de-cologne on the air. Hal closed and locked the door, and Jo went to turn on the taps.

'Do you think he used the bath?' she asked, rinsing it round carefully. 'I don't really like sharing it with other people.'

'Well, you don't have to share with him, he's finished.'

She looked up at him and laughed.

It was a long time since he'd heard her laughter; life just hadn't been the same without it.

They took it in turns in the bath. Looking at her face in the morning light, he thought she looked exhausted.

'Shall we stay here tonight?' she was asking.

He smiled lazily at her. 'Sure, if you want.'

'You don't sound very keen.'

'Sweetheart, I don't give a damn what we do, as long as we do it together.'

★ ★ ★

'Are you hungry?' she asked him as they got dry.

He thought how long it was since he'd eaten. Two days? Yes, he'd been eating a hamburger the third time he'd phoned Elowen. He hadn't finished it, it must still be on the table by the phone.

'Did you call your mother?' She'll be worried sick, he thought.

She seemed unperturbed by the apparent *non sequitur.* 'Yes.'

He was relieved. 'I'm hungry,' he said.

'Me too. Let's go and have an early lunch.'

★ ★ ★

They had lunch in a pub. Communication between them was physical rather than verbal; he held her hand constantly. The week of being amputated from her had affected him deeply and he felt shell-shocked; it shook him to discover how much she meant to him.

They walked round Rye after lunch, and he began to feel exhausted, wanting to lean on her but sensing that she was just as spent. She happened to look up at him as he was suppressing a yawn, and said, 'Shall we go back for a sleep before tea?'

'Practising for our old age?' he said, smiling. It seemed like a great idea.

★ ★ ★

A burst of laughter from the courtyard below finally wakened him. It was dark; looks like we missed tea, he thought. Jo was still asleep, lying across him with her head on his chest.

He gently stroked her hair, and she woke up. 'Are you still going to marry me?'

'Yes.'

He tutted. 'I sure hope you know what you're doing.'

'I don't. I'm just very brave.'

You sure are, kid. 'Then we have to celebrate.'

They had several drinks in the bar, then went in to dinner. Hal thought he should legalize his resident status, and went to see the receptionist. It was the same man he'd seen the previous night.

He was smiling when he returned to Jo.

'What's amusing you?'

'The desk clerk. He refers to you as Mrs Dillon.'

'Oh! A little premature.'

'Last night I told him I was marrying you this

morning. I didn't reckon he was too happy about letting me in.'

Her face was suddenly serious. He understood; he didn't want to think about last night, either.

They went out into the evening air, and drove to Camber Sands, walking for some time along the flat shore, watching the sky darkening. His mind shot back to another shore; her silence suggested she was seeing the same memory.

So this is how it ends. This is what it's all been leading to.

★ ★ ★

'Go on up,' he said, parking the car. 'I'll be right with you.'

'All right.'

She'd got as far as washing her face and taking her shoes off when he came into the room. 'What's that?' she asked, trying to see what he was holding behind his back.

'I'm not through celebrating yet.' He swung a bottle of champagne up onto the bedside table.

'Lovely! But isn't everything closed downstairs?'

'I got my pal in reception to get it for me.'

She started to laugh. 'He'll be glad to see the back of you!'

He moved across to her and wrapped his arms round her, looking down into her happy face. 'Kiss me,' he ordered, and she did.

Then at last on that peculiar day desire came back, and a passionate need for her flooded him. Making love to her, he thought, I nearly lost you, kid, we almost chucked this away. His face pressed to hers, he could feel the wetness of tears on her cheek and had no idea whether they were hers or his own.

★ ★ ★

They checked out in the morning, and drove back to her house. She dumped her bag in the hall, then they went to fetch Edmund from Jenny. Walking up the drive, Jo took his hand and confessed she felt slightly awkward.

He grinned. '*You* feel awkward. Last time I was here I almost broke their door down.'

'Oh dear! Did you?'

'Tom thought I was going to hit him.'

Jenny was baking, with the washing-machine churning in the background. The children were watching television, and didn't notice them come in. Jenny made them coffee, regarding them balefully as the kettle came to the boil.

'I must say I'm relieved you're together again,' she said. Then, shooting Hal a wicked look, 'I expect Tom will be, too. I hope this means we can all sink back into our bucolic stupor?'

'I reckon so.' Hal smiled. He hadn't expected to get away without at least one reference to his behaviour the other night. 'We're going to get married. Aren't we, kid?' He gave Jo a nudge.

'Yes!'

'Thank God for that.' Jenny hugged them both. 'Mind you, it's about bloody time — I can't think why you didn't do it months ago.'

366

'Me neither,' Hal agreed. 'It would have saved us all some trouble.' He caught Jenny's eye.

She smiled. 'Never mind,' she said kindly. 'It came out right in the end.'

★ ★ ★

They took Edmund home. Over lunch Jo explained to him that she was going to marry Hal, and that they'd all live together, just like other families.

Hal watched the two faces, Jo's with a smile that didn't disguise her anxiety, Edmund's so faithfully like Ben's. What d'you reckon, Ben? he asked silently.

Edmund pushed his sausage into a pool of ketchup. 'Will Hal be my daddy?' His blue eyes were intent on Jo.

'He'll be your second daddy, darling. Not your real daddy, but he's going to take Daddy's place, because Daddy can't be here any more.'

Edmund said nothing. Hal wondered what Jo was thinking. She glanced at him and he winked at her. Her expression immediately lightened.

Then Edmund said, 'Can I choose what yoghurt I have? I don't want that strawberry one, it's smelly.'

When he had gone to collect his zebra to get ready for watching 'See-Saw' Hal said quietly, 'What d'you reckon?'

She was looking relieved. 'Isn't it always the way? You expect your revelations to be accompanied by wailings and gnashings of teeth, then people react as if they've known all along. Teddy responded like a four-year old Jenny — he wasn't surprised at all.'

He glanced at her. 'Just why should telling people you're going to marry me make them gnash their teeth?'

'Pity. They're imagining how frightful my life with you will be.'

'I'll make you chuck out your smelly yoghurts.'

'See what I mean? Bullying me already.'

★ ★ ★

In the evening, Hal got them a drink and said they had to talk about the future. 'When does Teddy have to start school?' he asked, amused at her expression; she seemed to be trying to work out the relevance of Edmund's schooling.

'A year next September.' She abandoned the attempt. 'Why?'

'Then it doesn't matter if we're not in England for a year.'

'No, I suppose not. Would we live in America?'

'No.'

'Where, then?'

He watched her for a moment. Then he said, 'I'm thinking of taking a sabbatical. We'd go off to Europe, the three of us — Rhodes, Crete. Then Egypt, maybe.'

She was silent. Then: 'What for?'

'To look at things, talk to people, find out facts. Then I write it all up, and there's my next series of articles done, and the wolf is kept from our door for a further indefinite period.'

'So you'd be working?'

He grinned at her. 'I'd be working. Does that make it okay, in your puritanical little heart?'

'Yes.'

He hugged her, and she leaned against him. 'It'd be great,' he said. 'Wouldn't it?'

'Yes.' Maybe she was seeing the possibilities. 'It would give us all a chance to get used to being together. In neutral territory.'

'Right.'

'We could let this house,' — she was suddenly enthusiastic — 'my father says you should always make your assets work for you.'

He laughed. 'Sure, if you want. Though I don't reckon we have to worry too much about finance.' He put his hand under her chin and lifted her face. 'You may not have noticed, because I'm very modest, but I do have a few bucks to my name.'

'Oh, good. I'm glad I'm not marrying a pauper. But then, so do I.'

'Great. I like rich dames, they smell good.'

Later he said, 'So when do we get hitched?'

'As soon as you like.'

'Don't you want a big affair? Church, party, hundreds of folks in hats?'

'No. Do you?'

'No.'

'I'd just like you and my parents. And Teddy.'

'Okay. I'd like my dad, too.'

'Then we could all go for a sumptuous lunch somewhere nice, and — '

'And then,' he finished for her, 'I shall take you away for several days and nights till I reckon you've gotten used to being married to me.'

She didn't reply. She leaned over to kiss him. After some time, he panted, 'We'll fix the rest tomorrow. Let's go to bed.'

★ ★ ★

In the morning he took his second cup of coffee and settled on the stairs with the telephone and the local directory. He spent a fruitful quarter of an hour in conversation with a helpful woman in the Register Office, asking questions and making notes.

'Surprisingly simple, getting married,' he remarked, coming back and bending to kiss her.

She smiled lovingly at him. 'I can still hardly believe it. Can we set the date right now then? Today?'

'We can. Except we have to go to London to fill in some forms, I'm not resident in this area, then we'll have to go to the Register Office in Tunbridge Wells.'

'Can we do that today, too?'

He smiled. He didn't entirely share her sense of urgency, but he was willing to go along with it. 'Sure. And I'll buy you a diamond, then you'll know I mean it.'

'I know that already.'

It was an unusual day. They let Edmund miss playschool and come with them, and he picked up their happiness. They went first to the Register Office in Tunbridge Wells. It occurred to Hal, as he and Jo sat filling in forms, that the presence of a four-year old child might suggest the wedding was coming somewhat late in the day. But he didn't say so to Jo; she was maintaining an expression of such exemplary gravity that it would have been mean to make her laugh.

Then they went up to London; in less than a morning they'd accomplished all that was required to make them man and wife in fourteen days' time.

In a small jeweller's shop in the City they found Jo a simple solitaire diamond and a plain wedding band. She bought him a heavy gold signet ring.

He'd never worn jewellery in his life before.

I've never been married before either, he thought, observing the happiness in her face as she put his signet ring carefully away in her handbag. If I can make the big change, I guess I can make a few small ones as well.

After lunch they went home to make some telephone calls.

'You first,' he said, and handed her the phone.

She started to dial her parents' number.

He watched as she told Elowen all in a rush that she was getting married, to Hal, and that it was in two weeks' time, and that Hal was going to phone his dad in a minute, and could she go down and stay for a few days, with Edmund, oh, and with Hal?

He laughed quietly, and she glared at him.

'All right?' he asked, when after a few more exchanges she put down the receiver.

'Yes.' She had tears in her eyes.

He started to laugh again.

'*What?*'

He put his arms round her. 'Sorry, kid. I'm not laughing at you. I'm just wondering how in hell I'm going to get you through a wedding ceremony when the very thought has you doing this.'

She sniffed. 'I'll manage,' she said with dignity. 'Come on, it's your turn.'

He dialled the long list of digits to get through to the West Coast, frowning slightly. Jo, watching him, started to move away, but he grabbed her skirt and pulled her back, sitting her down between his thighs and squeezing so she couldn't get up again.

'Where did you think you were going?'

'Oh — I thought perhaps you'd want to talk to your father in private.'

'This ain't private, sweetheart. Not from you.'

The endless series of clicks and whirrs settled down into the ringing-out tone. 'It's ringing,' he said superfluously. Then: 'Hi, Dad.'

Sam greeted him as if he were calling from just down the road, and seemed all set to tell him about painting his boat. Hal interrupted. 'Dad, Jo and I are fixing to get married. Will you come over?'

'That's great news, son. Sure I'll come. Tell me when.'

Hal told him, and Sam said he'd send details of his flight as soon as he'd booked it.

'Was your dad surprised?' she asked when he was through, looking happily as if she expected him to have been.

'No.'

'Oh.'

'My dad hasn't been surprised at anything since

372

Pearl Harbor, and even then he probably said, saw it coming a mile off.'

She laughed. 'Will he make it?'

'You bet. Give me Bernard and Mary's number.'

He watched her face for signs of distress — it had to be something, having your dead husband's parents informed you were marrying someone else — but it was okay. She still looked one hundred per cent happy.

More than anything, that gave him confidence: I did right, he thought. *We* did right.

★ ★ ★

She was asleep before him that night, and he lay for some time listening to her peaceful breathing. Now he had caught her urgency; it felt to him like he was already married to her, and he was impatient for it to become a fact. Maybe I'm a little old to be giving up my single way of life, he thought. But I don't reckon it'd be the same, now.

I'd miss her.

26

Jo and Edmund went down to Cornwall at the end of the week. Jo gave in to Edmund's pleas to go on the train; it made sense anyway, since Hal was going to join them at the weeked and would drive them home.

The prospect of some quiet time with her parents before this next major step in her life was very appealing. But something else was calling her to Cornwall, urging her to revisit the places where she'd been so happy with Ben. Perhaps it's a final test, she thought, to prove that the past is over. Perhaps it's simply for a valediction.

Her parents were glad about her forthcoming marriage. Elowen told her so on the way home from the station; Jo thought how nice it was to have a mother who, once she realized your mind was made up, backed all your decisions so wholeheartedly.

The lazy days with Elowen and Paul, reminding her of secure, undemanding childhood times, were just what she wanted.

Late on Sunday afternoon she asked her parents if they'd mind if she went out for a while. The day was still warm, and the clear sky promised a spectacular sunset. Paul lent her his car, and she drove through the well-remembered lanes towards the Helford River. She stopped several times: at a stile that led to a favourite walk; by a pub with a pretty garden where a baby could crawl in safety; by a quay with steps leading down to a mooring for small boats.

Eventually she arrived at the little cottage that had been hers and Ben's. She could see inside the house; the front door stood open into the white-painted hall, and beams of late sunshine fell across the tiles.

For a few precious moments Ben was with her. She could hear his voice, visualize his cheerful presence, and a thousand happy memories flew to mind. She said softly to his benevolent spirit, 'It *was* good, wasn't it, Ben?'

Then a man appeared round the side of the house pushing a little girl on a tricycle, laughing with her, enjoying their life in their home.

Not ours any more, Ben.

★ ★ ★

There was one more place she had to go. She drove south, turning inland away from the estuary and then coming to the open sea.

She parked, then set out across the short grass, stopping in a sheltered hollow. There, with the fast-setting sun lighting the great expanse of water to brilliant orange, she sat gazing out over the spot where Ben died.

The pain was still there, would always be there. But it was bearable, now.

She said quietly into the still evening air, 'Goodbye, Ben. Darling Ben.'

The great swell of the sea continued indifferent.

She knew that the past was gone. But here, in the place where she had lost Ben, she could at last encapsulate him in a portion of her heart, a special space that would always be his, where she would keep him with her for ever.

The rest of her heart, the rest of her life, were Hal's.

★ ★ ★

Eventually, long after the sun had set, she got up to go.

She stood in the twilight, reluctant to leave the spot where one part of her life had, at long last, finally come to an end. But it was right to go; she turned her back on the sea and the huge sky, glowing now with the remembrance of the sunset and the first faint stars.

She walked slowly back to where she had left the Rolls. There was another car beside it now.

He was leaning against it, hands in his pockets, half smiling. She ran across the grass towards him and he opened his arms in welcome, enfolding her as she laid her head against him.

'How did you know where to come?'

'Your mother suggested a few places. It wasn't hard reckoning where you'd end up.'

She lifted her face to look at him. 'I'm ready now,' she said. 'We can go home.'

He looked into her eyes for a long moment, his face serious. Then he smiled.

The wedding was barely mentioned over dinner. Instead the four of them talked enthusiastically about a dozen different topics; it was, Jo decided, a question of putting your hand up to get a word in. Hal and Dad might have appreciated each other anyway, she thought, listening to them discussing the Italian car industry — how does Hal know about that, for God's sake? — even if they weren't being thrown into proximity because of me.

The talk ranged to Greece. Paul went silent suddenly, frowning at Hal in intense concentration, his mouth half open. Then he said, 'Good Lord! You're the man who fell off the temple in Ithaca and broke his ankle!'

'I sure am,' Hal said. 'I still have the lump to prove it.'

'Didn't you realize?' Jo said, amazed.

Elowen smiled. 'No, he didn't. I'd quite begun to think the penny was never going to drop.'

★ ★ ★

Back in Hawkhurst, their wedding day approached fast. Sam telephoned to say he'd be arriving on Saturday; Jo wanted to go with Hal to collect him from the airport, but she'd done nothing at all in the way of preparations.

'What do you have to do?' Hal asked.

'Oh! I don't know . . . ' When it came to it, she couldn't actually think of anything. She frowned. Then: 'Yes I do.' She began to laugh. 'I've got to buy a wedding dress.'

'Can't argue with that,' he remarked. 'You can take my Al Capone suit to be dry-cleaned.' He looked up and caught her eye, and it seemed to her that the enormity of what they were doing hit him in the same moment it hit her.

He grinned. 'Okay, kid, no need to hit the panic button.'

'I wasn't going to!'

'I know.'

'We ought to book a table somewhere for this feast we're having afterwards,' she hurried on, before she was distracted by the way he was looking at her. 'And I've been thinking, let's ask Jenny, Tom and Laura to join us.'

'Okay. They've earned a place at the finish, huh?'

★ ★ ★

He announced he was taking Teddy with him to meet Sam. She wondered if it was such a good idea. She noticed he was watching her, the familiar half-smile on his face. 'There has to be a first time, kid.'

'Yes, I know. But what if he's sick?'

'Then I'll clear it up. There has to be a first time for that, too.' Then he added, 'Don't give him much breakfast.'

In three days we'll be married, she thought in the peace of the empty house. I wonder if he'll still call me kid when I'm his wife? It'll make me sound like a child-wife, like what's-her-name Copperfield.

Suddenly she thought, I'm going to buy my wedding dress this morning! and elation hit her. Not even the queue for the car park or the hot impatience of the Saturday crowds could dampen her enthusiasm; she knew she was going to find exactly what she wanted.

She ordered buttonholes, bought a new shirt and shorts for Edmund, and collected Hal's suit from the cleaners. Money was running away from her rapidly, so she called it a day and went home.

Hal's car was in the drive. She felt nervous; it mattered very much what Sam thought of her. She went upstairs to hang up Hal's suit and spread out her dress on the bed, then went down into the kitchen. Hal was making a pot of tea.

'How did you get on?' he asked.

'Fine! Oh — don't go in the bedroom, there's something there you're not allowed to see and I haven't put it away yet.'

'Okay. My dad and your son are in the garden.'

'Is he all right?'

'Who, Dad or Teddy?'

'Your dad — was his flight okay? Is he tired? Does he want anything to eat?'

'Go ask him.' He pushed her gently towards the door.

She went out onto the terrace. Edmund and Sam were at the end of the garden; they were hand in hand, peering out through the hedge to look at the cows in the field beyond.

She walked down the lawn towards them. 'Hello, Sam,' she said quietly, 'welcome to England.'

Sam straightened up and turned to face her. He was tall, almost as tall as Hal, and the lines of his face were similar only more deeply etched. His eyes were brown like Hal's, but kinder. More tolerant.

'Well, hello, Jo,' he said. Then, as though

there were nothing to add, he kissed her on the forehead.

She felt a surge of happiness. 'Come and have tea.' She took his hand. 'On the lawn under the chestnut tree, in proper English fashion.'

★ ★ ★

They talked easily over tea and on into the evening. Sam decided he'd like to catch up on some sleep, and Jo went with him to the foot of the stairs to say goodnight.

He regarded her solemnly, his head on one side. 'There's a deal I have to say to you,' he said with a gentle grin.

'And I to you.' She smiled back at him.

Hal looked up as she rejoined him in the living room. 'What were you whispering to Dad about?'

'Oh, nothing. I think we're going to like each other.'

'Obviously,' he said nonchalantly. 'You're bound to, since you have a common interest in me.'

'Arrogant pig.'

He pulled her to him to kiss her, and the kiss lasted quite a long time. Later, lying in each other's arms, he said, 'I'll go back to London tomorrow, then you and Dad can have an evening together. I have to see someone about the apartment, so I'll stay over. When did you say your folks are coming? Monday?'

'Yes.'

'Then I'll stay Monday night too, and see you Tuesday.'

'At the Register Office?'

'Yeah.'

'The day we're getting married.'

★ ★ ★

It felt strange to watch him drive off on Sunday afternoon, knowing that the next time she'd see him would be to marry him. She stood absently in the lane for some time after he'd gone, shaken out of her trance by Mr Watson gently bipping the horn; she was standing in the middle of the lane and he couldn't get by unless he ran her over. Oh, hell, she thought, standing aside with an apologetic wave, something else to add to Mrs Watson's file on the loopy woman next door.

She wandered round to the back garden to rejoin Sam and Teddy. She sat down beside Sam, and they talked about music. He asked what works she liked and why, and under the stimulus of his remarks she found herself looking at the subject with more objectivity. I'm learning, she thought, laughing as Sam digressed to relate an anecdote from his days as a professional musician.

As evening came on, they moved inside and played some of the works they'd been discussing; she put Edmund to bed with the haunting melodies of the Sibelius violin concerto soaring through the house.

Later they sat by the open windows looking out at the night. They were listening to the Elgar cello concerto, and Jo was thinking about Hal. She thought probably Sam was, too, as he'd just remarked that the work had always been one of Hal's favourites.

As the last movement finished, he put out a hand. 'Don't put anything else on, Jo — I'd like to talk to you, and I don't care to have music playing that's not being listened to.'

'All right.'

'I'm real happy about you and Hal,' he said after some minutes.

'I'm glad. It's all happened rather quickly, but we want to be together.'

'Best reason I know for getting married,' he said stoutly. He sat in thought for some time, humming, his fingers dancing an accompaniment on the arms of his chair. 'In any case, it came as no surprise to me when Hal said you were marrying.'

'Really? It surprised me.'

Sam shot her a glance. 'I know Hal,' he said simply. 'I reckoned he wasn't about to let you go.'

She bit at her thumbnail, gazing down the garden into the night-quiet fields. 'You can't always tell what Hal's thinking.'

'You will in time,' he said calmly.

'How did you know? That he . . . well, how he felt?'

'The way he spoke about you, when he came to stay with me last fall. He said he wanted you to be happy.' Oh, Hal, she thought, as long ago as that. 'He's known a lot of nice, pretty women,' Sam went on, 'but I don't reckon any of them touched his heart except Magdalena. Till you.'

She couldn't speak. It moved her deeply that

Sam took it for granted Hal had told her about Magdalena. She cleared her throat, aware that she should say something. 'I want to make him happy, too.'

'You do. Right from the start you made a difference. He'd been on his own too long — it was time he put out some emotion again.'

'That's a strange way of putting it.'

He hesitated. Then abruptly he said, 'He blamed himself for Magdalena's death. That put the brakes on getting involved again.'

'Oh, no.' Oh, Hal, bad enough that you lost her, without that. 'Why? What could he have done?'

'He thought he should have pressed her harder, made the decision for her. Then he'd have taken care of her and her death wouldn't have happened.'

She was silent for a long time, thinking. 'No,' she said finally. 'We can't ultimately be responsible for other people, no matter how much we love them.'

Sam made no reply but sat quietly, waiting for her to continue.

'In the end, you have to abide by your own decisions.' She was speaking more confidently now. 'If you allow others to decide for you, you've lost control and you become no more than their puppet. Supposing it hadn't worked out between her and Hal? It would have been an awful responsibility for him, taking her away from all that she knew, making her an outcast from her own people, then having to make sure she stayed happy for evermore.'

Sam sighed. 'I know. But because she was so

young, he did feel responsible for her, anyway.'

'It'd have hurt him terribly, if she'd ended up blaming him.'

'She might have blamed herself,' he said gently, 'for having gotten herself involved with him when she knew there wasn't any future in it.'

'Yes.' Suddenly she felt less than totally sorry for Magdalena. 'After all, it was her decision. She could have chucked in everything else and gone with Hal, couldn't she? Only she found that other things mattered more.'

Sam looked at her with a smile of approval. 'Right. But it sure was impossible to tell Hal that.'

They were quiet. Then Jo said softly, 'You go into hell, don't you, when you lose somebody?'

'Yes.'

'But I don't think you have to stay there. It isn't fair to the one that's gone, to hold them responsible for you not being able to go on without them. It's not their fault, is it? I mean, not many people choose to die.'

Sam said, 'I reckon you're lucky, you and Hal.'

She turned to look at him. 'Oh, so do I!' she said fervently.

He grinned at her, Hal's expression in an older face. 'It's time you got some sleep,' he said kindly. 'You have to be a bride, day after tomorrow.'

★ ★ ★

Elowen and Paul weren't expected till late afternoon the next day, and in the morning Sam said he wanted to buy her a wedding present. She protested there was no need, she and Hal already had two households of things, but he said he didn't have in mind anything like that, he was going to buy her some music.

'Thank you, Sam,' she said on the way home. 'I shall think of you when I play these works.'

'You're welcome. Don't you have to go to the beauty parlour or anything?'

'I expect I should, but I'm not. I might have a shower in the morning and stick on a bit of make-up.'

'Well if you're proposing to tramp all round Europe for a year, I guess Hal'll have to get used to you looking the way nature made you.'

'Poor old Hal.'

He glanced at her. 'He ain't doing so bad.'

★ ★ ★

Paul brought champagne so that the celebrating could start straight away. Elowen bore cards and presents from family and friends. One of Jo's brothers had written in his card, 'What have you got against Englishmen?'

'I hope Geoff and Phil don't mind not coming to the wedding,' Jo said to Elowen, watching her unpack.

'I don't think so.' Elowen was putting a very smart black and white dress in the cupboard. 'It was rather short notice, and it's not as though you're having a big do.'

'No.'

Elowen paused to look at her daughter. 'It couldn't be more different, could it?'

Piercingly Jo remembered her parents' house the day she and Ben had got married. 'No,' she said.

Elowen returned to her unpacking. Jo knew no more would be said to compare her second wedding day with her first.

She excused herself after dinner, leaving her parents and Sam deep in conversation; they were trying to do *The Times* crossword, but kept getting sidetracked onto interesting things to talk about.

There was an atmosphere of happiness in the house. She packed her case, relieved to be on her own. From downstairs she could hear the steady murmur of voices and the occasional burst of laughter; she was glad the evening was being fun, that coming here for her and Hal hadn't condemned their three parents to a boring evening of stiff politeness.

She went across to lean her elbows on the window-sill, looking out over the peaceful countryside. Eventually she got into bed. Just before she turned out the light she looked at the photograph of Ben that stood on the bedside table.

Tomorrow she was going to put it in Edmund's room.

★ ★ ★

Paul brought her a cup of tea in the morning, the first time that she could ever remember him doing such a thing. There was wry amusement in his face, as though he too thought it slightly unusual.

'It's a lovely morning,' he observed, standing at the window, 'clear blue sky, and already getting hot.'

'Oh, good.' She sat up in bed to drink her tea. 'Did I tell you I've ordered you a carnation? I hope white will go with your ensemble.'

'I had a red one when I married your mother,' he mused. 'She had freesias, and they scented the church.' He noticed Jo looking at him, and smiled briefly as he left the room.

Later Sam came in carrying a tray with a bowl of cereal and two poached eggs on toast. 'Your mother says you're to have this,' he said, putting the tray down on her lap. Then his voice dropped conspiratorially. 'Want me to help out?'

She laughed. 'No, it's all right! I'm hungry.'

He caught sight of the photograph of Hal as a boy, stuck in the corner of her dressing-table mirror. 'It's the only photo I've got of him,' she said softly. 'It's still jolly like him, isn't it?'

'It sure is.'

'What do you suppose he's doing at this moment?'

'He's probably having his breakfast and reading the paper.'

'Do you think he's feeling nervous?'

Sam looked at her, his expression full of affection and kindness. 'No, Jo, he won't be feeling nervous at all.'

Oh, thank you, Sam! She smiled up at him and he grinned back.

'See you later,' he said, and left her to her eggs.

Elowen came in and briskly stacked the plates and cup on the tray.

'Thank you for the breakfast, Mum.'

'I'm glad to see you've eaten everything. Perhaps you should think about getting up now.'

'Yes, in a minute. I'm enjoying being waited on — it'll be the last time for a while, Hal doesn't do breakfast in bed.'

Elowen bent to kiss her, and Jo hugged her in return. 'Dear little Mum. Isn't this the moment when you say some well-chosen words about the ways of men?'

Elowen snorted. 'I hardly think so. I imagine you know a great deal more about that than I do.'

An hour later Jo stood in front of her mirror, reaching to do up the zip on her wedding dress. It was cream, lace over heavy satin, and she was even more pleased with it this morning than she had been in the shop.

She stared intently at herself for an instant, then said aloud, 'Get on with it,' and went downstairs.

The wedding party set out for Tunbridge Wells in the middle of the morning, sweeping elegantly into the Register Office car-park in perfect time. Jo's sense of unreality had increased greatly. Sounds and voices seemed to come from a long way off; she felt she'd been programmed and was moving through the morning automatically. She noticed her mother's concerned eyes on her, and managed a quick smile.

A moment later Hal drove in behind them.

He'd needed to hurry to be there on time. He'd got up early and spent a relaxed morning, but five minutes before he was due to leave he'd suddenly decided he had to listen to the Bruch violin concerto on the way to Tunbridge Wells. It had taken him half an hour to find it because he'd put it away in the wrong box.

He got out of the car. Jo was standing with her parents, Sam and Edmund, and she started to walk towards him.

'Hi,' he said.

'Hello.' She stood staring up at him, smiling.

'Is that for me?' She had a white carnation in her hand.

'Oh! Yes, here.' She arranged it in his buttonhole.

He watched her intent face, taking in every detail of her. When she had finished she stood quite still, looking at him as if waiting for further instructions.

He said gently, 'I reckon we'd better go in. They don't marry people in the parking lot.'

The party walked together to the glass doors and through into the waiting-room. He was aware of her holding his hand very tightly. I didn't realize what a grip she has, he thought, amused.

As they were settling themselves, the door opened to admit a tall, elderly woman with short grey hair curling round the brim of a smart navy hat. Noticing her, Jo said politely, 'I think you've come into the wrong room. Can we help?'

Hal, striding across the floor to greet her, said

to Helen, 'You made it!' She returned his hug then, holding him at arm's length, whispered, 'I knew you'd look better without the beard.'

He turned to Jo, whose expression was a picture. Trying not to laugh, he said, 'Jo, this is Helen Arnold. We met in Peru.' Her puzzled face suggested it fell short of an adequate explanation. 'Helen, come meet the others.'

A door opened. 'Dr Dillon and Mrs MacAllister?' a calm voice enquired.

They were ushered into the marriage-room. There was a table decorated with a display of cream and yellow flowers, and facing it were rows of gilt chairs upholstered in red velvet. Elowen and Edmund sat down hand in hand in the middle of the first row, with Helen beside Elowen and Paul and Sam on either side. The hand-holding seemed to be catching; the five of them were linked like a row of cut-out paper dolls. He nudged Jo and nodded towards them, and she smiled.

The registrar began to speak. I feel calm, Hal thought, absolutely calm. He looked down at Jo; she was still clinging tightly to his hand. He listened to the quiet voice reciting the marriage vows, heard his own voice and Jo's repeating the words.

She seemed to be finding it hard to speak, and he began to smile, reaching into his pocket for a handkerchief. 'Hold it a minute, please sir,' he said to the registrar. 'I knew this'd happen.'

He mopped at her cheeks, catching the tears neatly off her eyelashes. Then he bent to kiss her. 'I should have put money on it,' he said quietly. 'Okay, kid?' She nodded. 'Right,' he turned back to the registrar, 'you can go on now.'

Then it was done. He put the ring on her hand, and they signed the register, Sam and Elowen acting as witnesses. The registrar shook them warmly by the hand, waving away Jo's apology for her tears.

'Poor kid, she's only been married to me five minutes and she's crying already,' Hal said.

'Never mind, it can only get better.' The registrar handed him the marriage certificate, with his best wishes, and then they were off, out through the doors into the sunshine, walking up the road and through a swing gate into a calm old park full of stately trees and spreading rhododendron bushes, where in front of a copse of silver birches they took the photographs.

They went off to lunch, joined by Jenny, Tom and Laura, whose vivacious presence added a new dimension; they all became very noisy and slightly high. Helen entertained them with the story of how a bearded stranger had stolen her bath-water, making it far more amusing than he recalled. At the end of the meal a waiter appeared with a wedding cake, decorated with icing flowers.

'I didn't know we were having cake!' Jo said. She looked across at her mother.

'You must have a cake,' Elowen said, 'it's lucky.'

Hal and Jo stood up together to cut it, and slices were handed round with champagne. He gave his glass to Jo.

'Don't you like champagne, all of a sudden?' she asked, drinking it.

'You know better than that,' he replied. 'But I have to drive.' He looked at her very seriously. He was about to say something more, but he realized she was already thinking it.

There was a quality in her expression that he'd never seen before. He felt a lurch of excitement. 'Don't smile at me like that,' he whispered in her ear, 'or we ain't going to get further than the foyer.'

* * *

They went off to change, giving their wedding clothes to Elowen; she and Paul were taking Edmund back to Copse Hill House, where they'd look after him till Jo and Hal returned.

Sam turned to Hal. 'You've done okay, son,' he said.

Hal grinned. 'Great, Dad. Just so long as you approve.'

'I do. There's much to her that I haven't even begun to touch on.'

'Me neither.'

Sam smiled at his son affectionately. 'That I don't believe.'

Hal shrugged. 'Doesn't do to be complacent. She's a surprising woman.'

Jo came over to them. 'Goodbye, Sam,' she said warmly, kissing him, 'come again, won't you?'

'I sure will.'

Helen was standing talking to Elowen. 'You come see us, too,' Hal said.

She gave him a considering look. 'I'd love to. I've

often wondered what became of you.' She glanced at Jo, who was hugging Paul. 'You've done far better than I would have imagined.' What's with them all? he wondered. 'Be kind to her,' Helen murmured.

'Sure.' Time to be gone, he thought, before anyone else falls over themselves telling me how lucky I am. He called to Jo, who instantly turned to him a face so full of love and joy that he reckoned maybe they'd be right. He grabbed her by the hand and pushed her firmly into the car.

She turned round to wave until the wedding party were out of sight, then settled back into her seat with a sigh.

'You have confetti in your hair,' he observed.

She brushed at it. 'What a give-away.'

He reached out for her hand, putting it on his thigh and covering it with his own. He could feel the unfamiliar heaviness of his new signet ring; it clunked solidly against the ring that Ben had given her, now on her right hand.

'Okay, kid?'

'Oh, yes.'

They drove on through the afternoon, speeding westwards into the sun, squinting and screwing up their eyes as it got lower in the sky and finally defeated even sunglasses and sun visors.

'Hell, we'll stop and have a beer till it's set,' he said eventually. 'I don't want to have a headache tonight.' He glanced across at her. Goddam it, there was that look again. He felt a shiver of anticipation.

They found a pub with a garden, and sat outside

with a couple of drinks and some sandwiches. Then as twilight darkened gently into evening, they returned to the car.

She had been looking at signposts. 'I think,' she said after some time, 'we're going to Wales.'

'Brilliant.'

He heard her laugh softly.

The road was beginning to climb and mountains were appearing ahead, silent and black against the glowing western sky. They arrived in a small village, and he drove into the courtyard of an old stone inn. They were welcomed by a smart young woman seated behind a desk. He signed the register, and she handed him a key.

It was very quiet; voices came from some way off, presumably from a bar or restaurant. The receptionist showed them to their room, then discreetly disappeared.

★ ★ ★

He closed the door. She stood in the middle of the room, looking around. He went over to her and took her in his arms, kissing her at length.

'Are you hungry?' he asked after a while.

'Not at all.'

'Thirsty?'

'No, not very.'

He smiled, remembering. He sought the exact words. 'What *do* you want to do?'

'I want you to make love to me.'

And he did.

THE GREENWAY
Jane Adams

When Cassie and her twelve-year-old cousin Suzie had taken a short cut through an ancient Norfolk pathway, Suzie had simply vanished . . . Twenty years on, Cassie is still tormented by nightmares. She returns to Norfolk, determined to solve the mystery.

FORTY YEARS
ON THE WILD FRONTIER
Carl Breihan & W. Montgomery

Noted Western historian Carl Breihan has culled from the handwritten diaries of John Montgomery, grandfather of co-author Wayne Montgomery, new facts about Wyatt Earp, Doc Holliday, Bat Masterson and other famous and infamous men and women who gained notoriety when the Western Frontier was opened up.

TAKE NOW, PAY LATER
Joanna Dessau

This fiction based on fact is the love-turning-to-hate story of Robert Carr, Earl of Somerset, and his wife, Frances.

McLEAN AT THE GOLDEN OWL
George Goodchild

Inspector McLean has resigned from Scotland Yard's CID and has opened an office in Wimpole Street. With the help of his able assistant, Tiny, he solves many crimes, including those of kidnapping, murder and poisoning.

KATE WEATHERBY
Anne Goring

Derbyshire, 1849: The Hunter family are the arrogant, powerful masters of Clough Grange. Their feuds are sparked by a generation of guilt, despair and ill-fortune. But their passions are awakened by the arrival of nineteen-year-old Kate Weatherby.

A VENETIAN RECKONING
Donna Leon

When the body of a prominent international lawyer is found in the carriage of an intercity train, Commissario Guido Brunetti begins to dig deeper into the secret lives of the once great and good.

A TASTE FOR DEATH
Peter O'Donnell

Modesty Blaise and Willie Garvin take on impossible odds in the shape of Simon Delicata, the man with a taste for death, and Swordmaster, Wenczel, in a terrifying duel. Finally, in the Sahara desert, the intrepid pair must summon every killing skill to survive.

SEVEN DAYS FROM MIDNIGHT
Rona Randall

In the Comet Theatre, London, seven people have good reason for wanting beautiful Maxine Culver out of the way. Each one has reason to fear her blackmail. But whose shadow is it that lurks in the wings, waiting to silence her once and for all?

QUEEN OF THE ELEPHANTS
Mark Shand

Mark Shand knows about the ways of elephants, but he is no match for the tiny Parbati Barua, the daughter of India's greatest expert on the Asian elephant, the late Prince of Gauripur, who taught her everything. Shand sought out Parbati to take part in a film about the plight of the wild herds today in north-east India.

THE DARKENING LEAF
Caroline Stickland

On storm-tossed Chesil Bank in 1847, the young lovers, Philobeth and Frederick, prevent wreckers mutilating the apparent corpse of a young woman. Discovering she is still alive, Frederick takes her to his grandmother's home. But the rescue is to have violent and far-reaching effects . . .

A WOMAN'S TOUCH
Emma Stirling

When Fenn went to stay on her uncle's farm in Africa, the lovely Helena Starr seemed to resent her — especially when Dr Jason Kemp agreed to Fenn helping in his bush hospital. Though it seemed Jason saw Fenn as little more than a child, her feelings for him were those of a woman.

A DEAD GIVEAWAY
Various Authors

This book offers the perfect opportunity to sample the skills of five of the finest writers of crime fiction — Clare Curzon, Gillian Linscott, Peter Lovesey, Dorothy Simpson and Margaret Yorke.

DOUBLE INDEMNITY — MURDER FOR INSURANCE
Jad Adams

This is a collection of true cases of murderers who insured their victims then killed them — or attempted to. Each tense, compelling account tells a story of cold-blooded plotting and elaborate deception.

THE PEARLS OF COROMANDEL
By Keron Bhattacharya

John Sugden, an ambitious young Oxford graduate, joins the Indian Civil Service in the early 1920s and goes to uphold the British Raj. But he falls in love with a young Hindu girl and finds his loyalties tragically divided.

WHITE HARVEST
Louis Charbonneau

Kathy McNeely, a marine biologist, sets out for Alaska to carry out important research. But when she stumbles upon an illegal ivory poaching operation that is threatening the world's walrus population, she soon realises that she will have to survive more than the harsh elements . . .

TO THE GARDEN ALONE
Eve Ebbett
Widow Frances Morley's short, happy marriage was childless, and in a succession of borders she attempts to build a substitute relationship for the husband and family she does not have. Over all hovers the shadow of the man who terrorized her childhood.

CONTRASTS
Rowan Edwards
Julia had her life beautifully planned — she was building a thriving pottery business as well as sharing her home with her friend Pippa, and having fun owning a goat. But the goat's problems brought the new local vet, Sebastian Trent, into their lives.

MY OLD MAN AND THE SEA
David and Daniel Hays
Some fathers and sons go fishing together. David and Daniel Hays decided to sail a tiny boat seventeen thousand miles to the bottom of the world and back. Together, they weave a story of travel, adventure, and difficult, sometimes terrifying, sailing.

SQUEAKY CLEAN
James Pattinson

An important attribute of a prospective candidate for the United States presidency is not to have any dirt in your background which an eager muckraker can dig up. Senator William S. Gallicauder appeared to fit the bill perfectly. But then a skeleton came rattling out of an English cupboard.

NIGHT MOVES
Alan Scholefield

It was the first case that Macrae and Silver had worked on together. Malcolm Underdown had brutally stabbed to death Edward Craig and had attempted to murder Craig's fiancée, Jane Harrison. He swore he would be back for her. Now, four years later, he has simply walked from the mental hospital. Macrae and Silver must get to him — before he gets to Jane.

GREATEST CAT STORIES
Various Authors

Each story in this collection is chosen to show the cat at its best. James Herriot relates a tale about two of his cats. Stella Whitelaw has written a very funny story about a lion. Other stories provide examples of courageous, clever and lucky cats.

THE HAND OF DEATH
Margaret Yorke

The woman had been raped and murdered. As the police pursue their relentless inquiries, decent, gentle George Fortescue, the typical man-next-door, finds himself accused. While the real killer serenely selects his third victim — and then his fourth . . .

VOW OF FIDELITY
Veronica Black

Sister Joan of the Daughters of Compassion is shocked to discover that three of her former fellow art college students have recently died violently. When another death occurs, Sister Joan realizes that she must pit her wits against a cunning and ruthless killer.

MARY'S CHILD
Irene Carr

Penniless and desperate, Chrissie struggles to support herself as the Victorian years give way to the First World War. Her childhood friends, Ted and Frank, fall hopelessly in love with her. But there is only one man Chrissie loves, and fate and one man bent on revenge are determined to prevent the match . . .

THE SWIFTEST EAGLE
Alice Dwyer-Joyce

This book moves from Scotland to Malaya — before British Raj and now — and then to war-torn Vietnam and Cambodia ... Virginia meets Gareth casually in the Western Isles, with no inkling of the sacrifice he must make for her.

VICTORIA & ALBERT
Richard Hough

Victoria and Albert had nine children and the family became the archetype of the nineteenth century. But the relationship between the Queen and her Prince Consort was passionate and turbulent; thunderous rows threatened to tear them apart, but always reconciliation and love broke through.

BREEZE: WAIF OF THE WILD
Marie Kelly

Bernard and Marie Kelly swapped their lives in London for a remote farmhouse in Cumbria. But they were to undergo an even more drastic upheaval when a two-day-old fragile roe deer fawn arrived on their doorstep. The knowledge of how to care for her was learned through sleepless nights and anxiety-filled days.

DEAR LAURA
Jean Stubbs

In Victorian London, Mr Theodore Crozier, of Crozier's Toys, succumbed to three grains of morphine. Wimbledon hoped it was suicide — but murder was whispered. Out of the neat cupboards of the Croziers' respectable home tumbled skeleton after skeleton.

MOTHER LOVE
Judith Henry Wall

Karen Billingsly begins to suspect that her son, Chad, has done something unthinkable — something beyond her wildest fears or imaginings. Gradually the terrible truth unfolds, and Karen must decide just how far she should go to protect her son from justice.

JOURNEY TO GUYANA
Margaret Bacon

In celebration of the anniversary of the emancipation of the African slaves in Guyana, the author published an account of her two-year stay there in the 1960s, revealing some fascinating insights into the multi-racial society.

WEDDING NIGHT
Gary Devon

Young actress Callie McKenna believes that Malcolm Rhodes is the man of her dreams. But a dark secret long buried in Malcolm's past is about to turn Callie's passion into terror.

RALPH EDWARDS
OF LONESOME LAKE
Ed Gould

Best known for his almost single-handed rescue of the trumpeter swans from extinction in North America, Ralph Edwards relates other aspects of his long, varied life, including experiences with his missionary parents in India, as a telegraph operator in World War I, and his eventual return to Lonesome Lake.

NEVER FAR FROM NOWHERE
Andrea Levy

Olive and Vivien were born in London to Jamaican parents. Vivien's life becomes a chaotic mix of friendships, youth clubs, skinhead violence, discos and college. But Olive, three years older and her skin a shade darker, has a very different tale to tell . . .

THE UNICORN SUMMER
Rhona Martin

When Joanna Pengerran was a child, she escaped from her murderous stepfather and took refuge among the tinkers. Across her path blunders Angel, a fugitive from prejudice and superstition. It is a meeting destined to disrupt both their lives.

FAMILY REUNIONS
Connie Monk

Claudia and Teddy's three children are now married, and it is a time to draw closer together again, man and wife rather than mother and father. But then their daughter introduces Adrian into the family circle. Young and attractive, Adrian arouses excitement and passion in Claudia that she had never expected to feel again.

SHADOW OF THE MARY CELESTE
Richard Rees

In 1872, the sailing ship *Mary Celeste* left New York. Exactly one month later, she was found abandoned — but completely seaworthy — six hundred miles off the coast of Spain, with no sign of captain or crew. After years of exhaustive research Richard Rees has unravelled the mystery.

PINKMOUNT DRIVE
Jan Webster

Twelve years ago, moving into the splendid new houses of Pinkmount Drive, they had thought the good times would go on forever. Then came the recession that would take its toll on all their lives.

EMMA WATSON
Joan Aiken

It has always been a source of great frustration to Janeites that Jane Austen abandoned THE WATSONS after only seventeen and a half thousand words. Here, Joan Aitken has used Austen's characters, but has made them her own.

THE MAKING OF MOLLY MARCH
Juliet Dymoke

Life is never easy for a workhouse girl, and Molly's is no exception. Yet fate has wider horizons in store for her. Molly finds herself following the drum in the Crimea, where her indomitable courage wins the reluctant admiration of Captain Matthew Hamilton.

WITH MY SOUL AMONGST LIONS
Gareth Patterson

When George Adamson was murdered, Gareth Patterson vowed to continue his work. He successfully cared for and restored George's lion cubs, who were once again orphaned, into the wild. Batian, Furaha and Rafiki became his life's work and he became one of their pride.

FIELDS OF LIGHT
Jim Rickards

In 1931, Brian Grover sought fortune and adventure in Stalin's murderously dangerous Soviet Union. In Moscow, he met beautiful Ileana Petrovna, and they began an extraordinary love affair that was to enchant the world. This is the true story of Brian Grover's courage, bravery and unswerving determination to be with the woman he loved.

THE LAST TIME I SAW MOTHER
Arlene J. Chai

Caridad is a wife and mother, a native of the Philippines living in Australia. Out of the blue, Caridad's mother summons her home to reveal a secret that has been weighing heavily upon her for years. So begins Caridad's journey of discovery as she is given the gift of her past.